# SONG OF RESURGENCE

## BALLADS OF MAE
### BOOK TWO

Salem Cross
www.Salemcrossauthor.com
Copyright © 2020 Salem Cross
All Rights Reserved
ISBN 978 – 1 – 7353482 – 2 – 3

# SONG OF RESURGENCE

## BALLADS OF MAE
### BOOK TWO

## SALEM CROSS

Dear Readers,

If you enjoy the Ballads of Mae series I highly encourage you to sign up for my monthly newsletter. Here you will find an exclusive short story from Rylan's point of view just before he meets Mae for the very first time. Also, you will be privy to exclusive sneak peeks at future books and series, hear about discounts, and learn about other authors in this same genre who have some amazing books they want to share with the world. Go online to www.salemcrossauthor.com to sign up for the newsletter today.

I hope you enjoy Song of Resurgence!

*Salem Cross*

# CHAPTER ONE



*RYLAN*

Distressed moans broke the silence of the room. I'd been expecting them. It had been two hours since Mae had fallen asleep which meant that any moment, she would be waking again. Her body tensed in my arms as she began to shake. I pulled her tight against my chest. A blazing heat flared through my veins and the darkness in our bedroom turned red.

I wanted the blood of the witch and god who had done this to my mate. While I had no idea how to kill her father, the god Zyroe, I certainly had a few ideas of how to rid this world of Autumn, Mae's mother and the witch who had made a deal with the enemy. It would be a joy to watch the life drain from Autumn's eyes after I ripped her head off with my bare hands. Or I could use my fangs to behead the witch… It would be a clean cut that way. There was also the option to rip each limb from her body. If I did that, it would prolong her death. I could almost hear her screams of agony as I removed each appendage. A cruel smile tugged the corner of my lips as I thought about those agonized screams.

Mae's screams broke the silence and paused my murderous thoughts. The red in the room vanished as my heart twisted in agony at my mate's distress.

"Shh, you are safe," I whispered into her wild curls. I could hear her heartbeat drumming rapidly in her chest.

"Rylan." My name on her lips sounded reverent. The half of my soul I carried reached out for her. I closed my eyes and breathed the sweet scent of her hair: a mix of vanilla and honey.

"I am here, Mae." My lips pressed against her forehead. *I will always be here for you.*

The power coursing just underneath her skin surged forward, and her veins began to light up. Her power flashed like lightning across her arms, legs, and chest. I ran my hand over her arm trying to soothe her. I waited for her power to leak. Before her trip to the Pocket, her power would have come crashing out. I braced myself, ready to capture it, take it within me, and pull more away from her. It needed to happen; it would give her some peace before it began to build again.

But the leak did not happen.

She had not expelled any power since her return two days ago. Instead, it festered within her. That power inside of her was building in strength as it drew energy from her body and slowly killed her. My mate thought she was sparing me by not telling me about her pain. As if I would not notice the way she looked away with her brows drawn together, her hard swallows, or the way she absentmindedly felt over the thick scars around her wrists with her thumbs where cursed bracelets had once sat. How could she believe I would not notice how her breathing had become shallower or her ever-increasing, erratic heart rate?

In my arms, Mae relaxed and let out a long sigh. Her hand slid down my chest slowly before stopping right below my navel. Her fingers teased the trail of hair there. Instantly, my dick stiffened. While we had made love three times that night my desire to bury myself in my mate again was overpowering. My arousal was so intense I almost rolled Mae onto her back and devoured her.

But that was not what she needed right now.

She needed restful sleep. More importantly she needed to let some of this energy go. Hopefully, we would be able to do that later today when we reached our destination. Her health and well-being were my utmost concern. My carnal needs could be put on the backburner.

Mae's breathing slowed. Her hand went limp on my stomach as she drifted back to sleep. I took her hand and held it. Her heartbeat never returned to its normal rhythm. Instead, it continued to flutter too fast in her chest. Fear that it would give out before we had a chance to truly be together caused my own heart to squeeze painfully in my chest. My throat tightened as did my grip on Mae's hand. She shifted uncomfortably in her sleep. Immediately, I relaxed my hold on her, afraid she would awaken.

I squeezed my eyes shut as I agonized over how to help her. I wanted to whisk Mae from here and hide her from everyone. I could easily buy a private island where it would only be the two of us and the sun. If I could, I would rip that power out of her, stripping her down until she was only a half-witch. I would satisfy her every need and want while keeping her all to myself and safe. I couldn't lose her.

Rage. Desire. Fear.

Each emotion was so new, so raw... They consumed me, twisting my thoughts and making them irrational. Before Mae, I had no emotions. Every thought I had was logical, precise. The only reason I would ever second-guess myself would be if a better idea surfaced. Now, I questioned every move I made.

We were on our way to a small, remote area just north of Jasper National Park in Alberta, Canada. There we would station ourselves for the next two weeks while Arthur, Jasmine, and I patrolled the south end of the park. That was the location Zyroe and Autumn had shown Mae, where the gates that would allow the demi-gods to return to this realm would open. The place we were staying was far enough away to keep Mae from any danger that could be present in the south end of the park. She would be safe.

Well... relatively safe.

If there was someone out here trying to open the gates to bring the gods back, they would not be alone. They would have minions to help them. We could be outnumbered and easily defeated should our foe find out that we were here to thwart their plan. There could be traps set all around to make sure no one got close to their lair. If this person was twisted enough to bring the gods back, it could also be assumed they might tamper with dark magic, which was unpredictable and deadly. Worst case scenario, our foe could find out about Mae and her connection to the gods, which would make her a target.

It was a risk bringing Mae here. I knew it, Arthur and Jasmine knew it, and deep down, despite her protests, Mae knew this, too. But what was the alternative? I could not leave her behind. With her growing power, she was a beacon for spider demons, which had already risked attacking her twice while in my care. Other supernatural creatures were bound to find her eventually, and it would pull her into a spotlight none of us wanted for her. Worse yet, another Guardian could stumble upon Mae. The thought sent a chill of fear down my spine.

More selfishly, I could not be apart from my mate. She was the air I breathed and the reason my heart kept beating. She was the only reason I cared what happened to the world. If she ceased to exist, then the world could burn. In any case, knowing how stubborn Mae was, she would find a way to make it here herself. Mae's experience with Autumn and Zyroe had shaken her enough that she wanted to confirm for herself that nothing was going on here.

I hated putting her safety at risk. If we stumbled upon any evidence that Autumn and Zyroe were right about their prediction, we would have to call in other Guardians. More Guardians meant there would be more wings in the air to help find our culprit, but it also meant we would be placing Mae in even more danger. They would see her as a child of a god, one of our mortal enemies. They might try to kill her. Or worse, they might covet her. With her ability to temporarily lift our curse, some of them would see her as the ultimate prize. Some would try to take her from me. Rage caused my gut to tighten at the thought.

I took a deep breath and stared up at the ceiling. Emotions… They made things much more complicated. For the rest of the night, I stared up at the ceiling, adrift in the waves of these new feelings inside of me.

Hours later, sunrays from the early morning light broke through the curtains just as Mae's screams started up again. I held her as her fear subsided. Instead of falling back to sleep, she sat up. Her curly hair tumbled around her face and down past her shoulders as she turned her violet gaze upon me. Before her kidnapping, her power only lit up under her skin and in her eyes when it slipped out. But for the past two days now, the glow remained. She hated and feared it. Violet light streaked through her face, down her neck, and throughout her body. She thought she was a monster. I did not think anyone could be more wrong about themselves.

I had lived thousands of lives, seen hundreds upon thousands of women across the world. I had seen the richest of women in the finest of clothes. I had witnessed the poorest of women in rags covered in filth. There had been thick, thin, fragile, old, and young women in my life. I had met what most had called beautiful, and maybe they had been. But none compared to the woman sitting next to me. Even tired and underweight, she was gorgeous.

"I'm sorry, I probably kept you up all night," she said softly with a frown.

I sighed. Of course she was upset that she thought she had disturbed me. Her well-being was never her first thought. She did not know that I could go weeks without sleep.

"You should have let me help you."

Mae's frown deepened. She clearly hated the idea. The Guardians' ability to compel someone seemed to unnerve her.

Mae had allowed me to compel her to sleep when she had returned from the Pocket, but that had only been on the condition that I fed. Now, she wanted to overcome the nightmares on her own.

Suddenly, Mae's frown flipped upwards. Her salacious smile and bright violet eyes made my body hardened. My erection came to stand at attention and Mae noticed.

"How about I make it up to you?" she offered.

Mae reached down and tugged my borrowed shirt over her head. She was a petite woman; her frame was too thin from not being able to eat often but even underweight she maintained full breasts and fantastic buttocks. Her flawless skin was naturally sun-kissed and soft, and her lips…They were perfect, just like the rest of her.

I was a lucky Guardian.

When her hands came down onto my chest, I could feel our souls reach out, craving the connection they needed. Her touch sent electrical pulses of pleasure throughout my body, and I closed my eyes to savor the feeling. How could something so simple, like the touch of one's mate, feel so incredible?

By the time Mae had finished with her sensual apology for keeping me awake all night, we were both quivering as we basked in our releases. Mae rolled onto her side and her lips skimmed across my jaw. The contact was delightful. I turned my head so mine pressed against hers. Her moan sent my body on fire all over again. She pulled away first. Her eyes scanned my body hungrily. By the time her eyes returned to my face, I was ready for another round. But then I noted the worry in her gaze.

"How are you feeling?" she asked.

Whenever Mae found her release, her power erupted from her, and I absorbed it. The first time it had happened the scorching energy had stunned me. Now, whenever she came, and her power rushed into me, I felt invigorated and alive. It lingered in my veins even hours after we made love. I became faster, stronger, and my abilities increased tenfold. Her worry was unnecessary.

"Desperate for my mate again," I told her, giving her a wide smile.

Her husky laugh caused my heart to soar. "You're insatiable."

"It is because you are addictive."

Mae rolled her eyes, still smiling. "Are you hungry?" She lifted her wrist and pretended to sniff it. "Breakfast smells amazing."

I laughed. Ah, amusement, the feeling caused me to feel so light and carefree. I loved how she evoked the feeling in me. I rolled myself on top of her, my hands braced on either side of her face.

"Not now, my Mayflower."

"Mayflower?" She giggled. "Where'd that come from? Because you docked your colonial ship in my port?"

I threw my head back and laughed. I shook my head. "No. It is because you are as beautiful as a flower that blooms in May." She laughed and pushed at my chest. I rolled off her and climbed out of bed. "We need to leave soon. Can you be ready to go in an hour?"

She nodded. With that I turned and headed into the bathroom to get ready for the day. By the time I walked into the kitchen I found Mae was just finishing up breakfast. Though she tried to hide it behind a smile, her evident pain was worrisome. Concerned, I walked over to her and put my hand on her shoulder. Before I could say anything, she cut me off, "Good, you're out of the shower. Now it's my turn."

She jumped up and disappeared down the hallway. I stared after her. Mae was hurting, and I could do nothing to help her. My hands curled into fists at my sides. This afternoon when we had the space and privacy, I hoped we could find a way to force that power out of her system. Angry that I could do nothing for her for the time being, I snatched my phone from off the counter.

Several messages flashed on the screen from Arthur House. The area around our lodging was secure, the preparations for my surprise for Mae tonight were made, and there was no more news from Gabriel about Zein's murder. My jaw clenched as anguish washed over me. Zein had been a good man, and to be murdered in such a horrific manner… Whoever was behind it was going to pay.

***

It was not long until we were on the road. Mae sat in the passenger seat, staring out the window admiring the scenery. It was beautiful in Alberta, Canada. The air was cleaner here, and nature seemed greener. I wished there was a different reason we were here. If we had been here on vacation, I would have taken Mae hiking to explore our surroundings. But we weren't here for pleasure. Autumn and Zyroe's warning echoed in my mind and chilled the blood that ran through my veins.

I had a feeling that Zyroe would not have stepped in to help a witch if there was no merit to her story. His concerns about his fellow gods left a bitter taste in my mouth. What made the situation worse was, according to Mae's biological parents, if their warning was true, she was the only person who could stop the end of the world.

Why would anyone want the gods to return? Their anger and vengeance would destroy the world leaving nothing in their wake. There had to be some ulterior motive. Autumn and Zyroe seemed certain that the gates would open within two months. Would we be able to figure out who was scheming to bring back the gods in time?

Would Mae's body last long enough to stop whatever sinister plot was afoot?

I reached over and took her hand in mine. I welcomed the contact. A glance in her direction told me she enjoyed it too. A smile played around the corner of her lips.

Mae turned her whole body in her seat to face me, her expression thoughtful, and asked, "Did Arthur and Jazz go out last night to check out the area? Did they find anything suspicious?"

I shook my head. "They only secured the property. They marked the territory and contacted the Alpha of the nearby wolf pack to let them know about our presence. They will go out today and do some scouting before we arrive."

Mae's eyes widened, "Wait… Alpha of a wolf pack? Are you talking about… *werewolves?*"

I frowned and said, "No, the pack in Jasper National Park are shifters, not werewolves. They were born able to shift into their wolf form. Shifters come in all shapes and sizes… and species. Werewolves are humans that were bitten by sick shifter wolves. They are considered dangerous mutants. Those bitten don't realize they turn into crazed beasts during every full moon."

Thank goodness werewolves did not run in packs. The havoc they would cause in their wake would be devastating.

Mae fell silent as she processed this information. "So… Is the Alpha okay with us hanging out here for a while?"

"We are Guardians. Should we wish to take up residence within a pack's territory, we will do so. Arthur and Jasmine let them know we arrived out of respect."

"That doesn't, you know, piss shifters off?" she asked, confused.

I tried to follow her train of thought. Why would shifters be annoyed at our presence? Did she think we were overstepping some type of boundary?

"The respect and power that we have gained comes from trust. Everyone knows that a Guardian's role is to be a moderator, a peacekeeper, and a protector not a ruler. Our word is regarded highly, and should our advice be needed, it is taken. Because there is trust, we are given more freedom than most species. As long as we do not disrupt their way of life, the pack does not mind our presence."

"Hmm… Guardians certainly think highly of themselves," she muttered playfully and rolled her eyes.

I could feel my frown deepen. From the stories I had heard, Guardians had much to atone for. This was the least that we could do for everyone in this world,

"After the pain we put everyone through, it is only fair to try to keep everyone safe from each other and the rest of the world. We take that responsibility seriously, and our honor has allowed us to maintain a neutral position in most situations."

We had been used as slaves and warriors for the demi-gods who had once walked this earth. Soulless and almost unstoppable, we terrorized, destroyed, and killed those who did not worship our gods. Of course, that was when we were not fighting amongst ourselves for those same gods. We had been true monsters back then. It would take forever to make amends to everyone.

"So, all Guardians are on the same page when it comes to being the world's protectors? There aren't any that think it's too much work or it's not in their best interests?" she asked.

"It is a great honor to help others. No Guardian would think of it as a waste of their time."

Mae nodded thoughtfully and turned to sit straight ahead again. The rest of the drive was relatively quiet. Occasionally, we passed abandoned towns. Mae asked about them, curious about the old buildings.

"This used to be a thriving coal mining area. As the world shifted to different power sources, the coal industry became almost non-existent," I told her.

The empty run-down shops and houses were an eerie sight. This was what the world could look like if what Autumn and Zyroe said was true and we failed to stop whoever was behind opening the gates between the realms.

Eventually, we turned off the major highway. We bumped along some unkept roads before they turned into gravel paths, which turned into dirt roads. Just as I turned the corner and the house we were staying at came into view, Mae gasped. She was out of the SUV before I could throw the vehicle into park.

# Chapter Two



"No way! Are you serious? This is where we're staying?" I couldn't contain my excitement as I hurried towards the log mansion before us. Was this for real? The place was magnificent!

The first floor, where the five-car garage was situated, was made up of pale tan stone. From there, the following three floors of the house were made up of thick wooden logs stacked on top of one another. Everything not made of wood was glass; massive windows adorned the structure, offering spectacular views of the area.

I skidded to a stop halfway to the door and impatiently waited for Rylan to follow. His expression was torn between confused and amused. Could he not see how magical the log mansion was before us? I shifted my weight from one foot to another impatiently as he walked over. When he paused to stand next to me, I took his hand and attempted to drag him to the front door.

"I did not realize how much you fancied such… rustic living quarters," he mused, not moving despite my best efforts to tug on his arm.

"Um, nothing about this place screams rustic. This is the most magical log cabin I have ever seen, and I never want to leave," I said breathlessly. "I thought I had an idea of what I wanted mine to look like one day but this… This _mansion_ is far nicer than what I had in my head!"

I tried to tug him towards the house again. I growled with frustration when he did not move. Rylan chuckled, "Then I will buy you one once this is all over."

I gaped at him before beaming up at him. "Usually I'm all about being an independent woman and buying my own stuff but I'll never be able to afford something like this on my own so I'm totally going to hold you to that."

Rylan laughed. I tugged on his hand and tried to pull him in the direction of the house once more. With a sigh Rylan's amusement faded.

"Before we head inside, come with me," he told me.

He tugged my hand gently in the direction of the woods that surrounded the cabin.

"But—," I stared at him then back at the house.

"Do you remember the first night in Salisbury?" he reminded me gently as he pulled me towards the trees.

Of course I remembered that night. My power had forced its way out of me in the most painful fashion yet. There had been nothing I could do to stop it once it started. That night had been a nightmare.

"Yeah, but—,"

"I do not want you to suffer any longer. We need to figure out how to release all that pent up power before it becomes too much." He said as he frowned. I opened my mouth to protest but he cut me off. "I promise the house will still be standing when we return."

My shoulders slumped in defeat. It wasn't like Rylan was wrong. I really did need to let this power out. The pressure building up under my skin was on the verge of unbearable. At any moment, I was sure my skin would split apart and all of this power would destroy everything around me. My skull felt like it would implode at any minute. For the entire car ride it had taken a conscious effort to take a slow steady breath in and then to let it out slowly without Rylan noticing how much I struggled. The excitement at seeing the log cabin, or mansion, had momentarily distracted me from the pain but now, forced to acknowledge and deal with it, the pain came back with a vengeance.

I nodded to let Rylan know I would follow him. Hand in hand, we walked several hundred feet from the house into the woods. As we walked I tried to think of anything but the pain building up in me. While impossible to ignore completely, I was able to distract myself by naming the types of trees we passed. It was something I had once done to pass the time when I had walked the Appalachian Trail. Rylan stopped abruptly and turned to place his hands on my shoulders. I lifted my gaze to meet his.

The encouragement I saw there caused my heart to swell.

"Rylan, I don't know how to use my power. It's different now," I admitted to him in a soft voice.

"Take a moment to get reacquainted with it, Mae. Close your eyes and listen to how it moves through you. I know you will figure it out."

I squared my shoulders and turned away from Rylan. I looked down at my hands, staring at the violet glow rushing through my veins, before balling them into fists. I took a deep breath and closed my eyes. I searched for some connection to the power I possessed.

Before I had met Rylan, I had managed to erect a mental barrier and shove the chaos behind it. Once the barrier was up, I figured out how to let it down when I needed to let some of my power out. It wasn't a perfect method. Shortly afterwards, I had spellbound myself. At the time, though, that mental barrier had been life altering. Somehow, I had gained a frame of reference of where my power was located inside me and how to tap into it. That had assured me that control was possible.

Now, it was like starting all over again. I could feel the power under my skin, humming with life, but I had no way to connect with it. With a hard mental shove, I tried to force it out. Nothing happened. The ground beneath me didn't tremble, and the trees didn't quake. I tried again, but still, I came up empty-handed. With my third attempt I chanted softly,

*"You are the Spirit within me, you are the Wind in my hair, you are the Earth beneath my feet, you are the Water that flows through me, and you are the Fire that drives me."*

Again there was nothing. I huffed in frustration and opened my eyes. A quick glance at the back of my hands told me that the pentagram had not appeared as it usually did when I used my power or chanted. Instead of dwelling on its absence, I focused on a tree just a few feet ahead of me. With all the mental force I could muster, I tried to push the energy in my body forwards, directly at it. The tree stayed perfectly still.

"You are overthinking this, Mae. Steady your mind."

Rylan's patience irked me. It was easy for him to say. He'd been alive for almost two thousand years. He had a fairly good hold on what he could and could not do. Me? Not so much. What little I had thought I knew about myself had been blown completely out of the water this past week. I felt unbalanced, and I hated the lack of control I had over anything that was going on in my life.

Channeling all the patience I could muster, I forced myself to focus on the task at hand. I started by listening to my own heartbeat. I did not let my thoughts wander as I listened to the irregular and rapid beating. As time slipped by, I began to realize the beating wasn't erratic. There was a tempo I had not noticed. The rhythm of my heart was harmonizing with the pulsing of my power. Like a drum keeping beat while the guitar did a wild performance. The beating of my heart and the power coursing through me were creating a seamless and endless loop of energy. My heart fed the power, allowing it to gather and grow within me.

I focused on the partnership. As I did, I began to visualize it in my mind. I could see my heart pounding, and I could see violet rushing through each vein, touching every blood cell, twisting around every organ. The moment I visualized it, I felt something click into place. The pressure in my skull eased and moved downwards, like sand from an hourglass tumbling through the small tunnel to the other side. As the pressure eased down into my shoulders, through my arms, and into my hands I opened my eyes. The pressure built in my palms, causing them to throb. But before it got too painful, I felt my power exit my body.

It oozed from my palms and slid down my fingers where it dripped from each digit onto the ground. The ground pulsed softly once, then twice, and then a third time. Then, as if the drips of power from my fingertips had beaten a trail, the rest of my power followed suit. The eruption of chaos around me was different than before. While it seeped out of me with alarming force, the wind didn't pick up, the ground beneath me didn't explode, and the shrubbery stayed put.

Instead, the ground shifted beneath my feet like water coming to a simmer. Around us, trees began to catch fire from the inside out. Violet flames burned their way through the trunks and engulfed the rest of the tree. I could hear crackling and snaps of electricity. Before I could figure out where the noise was coming from, thick bolts of violet lightning rose from the ground, arching wildly in every direction.

A lightning bolt struck a bush and disintegrated it. Another rippled up from the root of a small sapling and the plant exploded. This was a new level of terrifying. I wanted to scream, but the power coursing through my veins, running down my arms into my hands and out of my fingertips, was so strong that it was paralyzing. My heartbeat fed into the expelling power, almost egging it on. I stood there with my arms stretched out before me, unable to stop the rising chaos. I tried to picture the power rushing through me again, but I was so afraid of getting hit by the wild electrical current erupting from the ground I couldn't concentrate.

I should have known better than to panic.

Just as I thought the entire forest would go up in flames, the fire began to die down. Somewhere inside of me, I felt a familiar tugging sensation. The electrical display came to a halt and the ground stopped moving. Without the wild, deadly chaos crackling around the two of us, I was able to focus again. I concentrated on the pulsing power in my body and my heartbeat, visualizing the two of them again.

Now that I knew what I was looking for and what to visualize, I found it was easy to turn my power off. It was as simple as a flick of a light switch. Immediately I felt the difference in my body. The pressure under my skin and in my head was almost nonexistent. While I could still feel the pulsing of my power, it was so minimal, I hardly noticed it. All my veins had stopped glowing and even my heart rate had slowed back down to a normal rhythm.

The instant relief made me gasp and stumble forward. I caught myself before I fell and turned towards Rylan, close to tears and ready to celebrate my success. But my relief vanished as I stared at Rylan. His whole body had seized up as my power stormed inside of him. The veins in his arms and face were bulging, and his face was red. Sweat beaded his brow, and his body trembled as he stood there unmoving.

I screamed Rylan's name as I rushed towards him. I lunged to grab him, hoping that somehow I would be able to take it all back within me. Rylan moved then, snapping out of his paralysis to step out of the way. With what seemed like a great struggle, he turned his head to look down at me. His jaw was clenched tight, his nostrils flared wide. Then, he looked away from me, towards the charred, hollow trees I had destroyed. Suddenly, the trees went up in flames again, fast and without warning. Instantly they turned to ash, and the fire went out. Three thick bolts of violet lightning spewed out of the ground and into the air. The energy dispersed and disappeared into the sky.

The violet glowing in Rylan's body vanished, and his body relaxed. He fell to one knee; his breathing came in deep gasps. I quickly closed the distance between us and dropped to my knees in front of him. I took his face in my hands and forced him to look at me. His gaze was unfocused.

"Rylan talk to me. Can I help you? Can I— can I take it back somehow?"

Tears streamed down my face. It was just like the first time we had made love. The intensity of my power was too much for him. He was in pain because of me. I sobbed as I held his face and whispered his name repeatedly. Finally, Rylan blinked several times before his handsome teal eyes finally came back into focus. He took a deep breath as he reached up and grabbed my hands clasping the sides of his face. He brought them down and held them as he glared at me.

"What was that, Mae?" he snapped.

I bowed my head in shame. I didn't blame him for being mad. Rylan had just taken everything that I had expelled within himself in an attempt to minimize the damage around us. In doing so, he had to endure what I had been experiencing the last few days and I knew how agonizing it must have felt.

"I'm sorry, Rylan. I really am." Guilt sat like a heavy stone in my gut.

"I am not mad at you Mae," Rylan said with exasperation. His expression twisted with worry. He took my hand and rose to his feet, pulling me with him. "I am upset with myself. All that power was eating you alive. I wish you would have told me so we could have dealt with this sooner. You need to let me help you. You are no longer alone when it comes with dealing with your power."

I shook my head before he stopped talking.

"You're right. I probably should have said something. I just didn't want you to worry anymore about me than you already do. Next time, I'll let you know when I need to blow off some steam." I wiped a tear that had slid down my cheek and was trickling down my neck. "How are you feeling?"

"How am *I* feeling?" Rylan repeated incredulously. He took my chin in his hand while his brows furrowed together in concern, "Mae, how are *you* feeling?"

"Better. Just a little tired," I assured him.

Rylan sighed. Slowly, he leaned down and kissed me softly. I wrapped my arms around his neck and deepened the kiss, relieved that he was okay.

As if he understood the desperation behind the kiss, Rylan pulled away and said with a sigh, "Mae, I am alright. You have nothing to worry about."

"You're fine now. What about next time? Trying to absorb my power could kill you. What if it's too much for your heart? What if it gave you an aneurysm? Apparently now I can burn shit up; what if I accidently burned you from the inside out like the trees around us? This isn't safe for you," I told him bitterly.

I stepped away from him and looked around at the destruction.

"That will not happen," Rylan said dismissively.

"You don't know that," I told him. With a sigh, I let it go for now. "It was different this time. Calling for it, the destruction it caused… My power is different now. How is that possible? I've never started a fire before and the lightning… What was that about?"

Now that the pressure under my skin was gone and my heart rate had calmed down, my body felt deflated. My limbs felt heavy. After watching Rylan suffer, I felt emotionally drained. Rylan's arm wrapped around my waist, and his lips brushed against the top of my head.

"We will figure this out," Rylan assured me softly. "Come, we will meet with the others, and you can explore the house you were so excited to see."

I knew Rylan was trying to distract me, and while the idea of running through the log mansion had seemed like fun, now I was afraid that I would destroy it. I clenched my teeth together and squeezed my eyes shut as I fought down the panic that wanted to bubble up. I didn't deserve to be around anything nice, and I shouldn't be around the others. What if I did something horrible to them? I followed Rylan back to the mansion silently.

# CHAPTER THREE



I stood in the grand family room with Arthur, with only half my attention on the Guardian in front of me. I knew it was important to stay informed in all matters. The reason we were here was to assess a threat to the world. However, it was hard to focus when my mate was running around gasping in delight as she explored the house. Each sharp intake of air caused my lips to twitch upwards. Her mood had been solemn on the walk back to the house. I could see the self-disgust on her face, but nothing I could say could ease her guilt.

"—and this morning we picked up enough blood from the blood bank to keep the refrigerator stocked while we are here," Arthur said. "Last night we did not sense anything unusual in the area. When we alerted the pack that we had arrived, the Alpha, Patricia Night, asked if she could have a private meeting with us tomorrow morning."

A squeal of pleasure from somewhere in the house caused him to look in that direction. The smile that played around Arthur's lips pleased me. My mate's ability to bring emotions to the Guardians near her gave my long-time acquaintance, and now friend, the ability to enjoy life. While I was happy for him, I felt a stab of possessiveness. Mae was mine. I took a deep breath. Soon, this irrationality would pass. I just needed to finish the Joining, and Mae would be completely mine.

"Did she say what she wanted to discuss?" I asked.

Arthur dragged his gaze away from the open balcony on the second floor. "Patricia brought up concerns about a few disappearances from her pack and some missing hikers. She also mentioned several sightings of werewolves a few miles south of here. Jasmine left about three hours ago to talk to some park rangers. Hopefully, she was able to compel information from them."

My jaw tensed at the news. South was the exact location Zyroe had shown Mae where the gates would be opened.

"There is more than one werewolf?"

"She said four different ones were running around the last time she counted," Arthur confirmed.

Suddenly I was thrown back to my earlier conversation with Mae. Werewolves were quite rare. News of four in the same area was alarming. Were they forming a pack? No. That was not possible. "Why has Patricia not taken care of them yet?"

I sensed Mae approaching. I looked up and found her leaning over the balcony down into the family room where Arthur and I stood.

"Taken care of who?" she asked curiously.

"A few werewolves," Arthur told her, glancing up at her. "Find the lodging accommodations to your liking?"

"'To my liking?' I'm going to chain myself to one of the trees growing *through* the house so you can't make me leave," she said with a smile that could brighten even the darkest of rooms. "By 'taken care of' do you mean… kill them?"

"It must be done. It is a mercy for the individual. A werewolf is dangerous; they are a killing machine. They cause destruction and terror whenever they shift. The person who is cursed has no control or recollection of what they are doing," I explained.

I realized at once I had said the wrong thing. Her face fell, and her shoulders stiffened. *Mae* couldn't control her power or the damage it caused. Of course, she would compare herself to a werewolf. Before I could say anything, she turned and disappeared from view.

Frustrated with myself for causing her distress, I almost went after her. Then, I heard her descend the stairs to join us. When she approached her expression had shifted again. No longer did she appear dejected. Now she appeared indifferent. She stopped just out of my reach, determined to appear confident and unperturbed. She might be okay without contact, but I was not. I stepped closer to her and wrapped my arm around her shoulders. The contact soothed an ache deep within me.

"Patricia said whenever she and her pack go after the abominations, they disappear," Arthur continued.

*Disappear?* I confirmed with Arthur through the mental Guardian wavelength. Arthur nodded.

"What are you saying?" Mae demanded with a scowl. "They can't find the werewolves?"

Arthur stroked his goatee thoughtfully as he turned his gaze upon my mate. "Werewolves would not run away or disappear if they found themselves threatened. They are savage beasts that would turn and fight if they thought they were in danger. If the pack said they disappeared, then they are not acting normally."

"We will talk to Patricia and help her pack remove the werewolves from the area," I told Arthur who nodded.

"I also attempted to reach out to the Guardian who oversees this area and left a message when he did not answer my calls. His name is Cain Vaster. He took over not too long ago when Ekon Nwadike had to rebrand himself. I tried to reach Ekon as well but have not heard anything from him as of yet."

"Rebrand?" Mae repeated.

"After a while," I explained, "we must move on to another territory so humans do not get suspicious of us. We have the ability to look younger or older at will, so at the end of our time in our latest territory we make ourselves look older and then we pretend to pass away. Then, in our new location, we shift to appear younger so we can stay there longer. With a new appearance, new name, and money we are able to reinvent ourselves easily."

Her mouth dropped open. Both Arthur and I chuckled.

"You can change your age at will?" she gasped when she had found her voice.

"Yes, but it takes time," Arthur told her with another chuckle. "Should I wish to look twenty years older or younger, it would take about a year for the transition to occur."

Mae shook her head in amazement, her eyes slightly unfocused as the wheels in her head turned. I chuckled again.

"There is much you do not know about Guardians, but I am sure you will learn our secrets soon enough," I assured her.

"In any case, I have not heard back from Cain yet," Arthur told me. "But I will question him when I do."

"Why would you reach out to the other Guardian here? I thought we didn't want to alert anyone else yet?" Mae asked.

"It is a courtesy to let Cain know we are in the area. I will not tell him the real reason why we are here. I will bring up Patricia's concerns before steering the conversation in a direction that will allow me to gain answers without causing him to be suspicious," Arthur explained.

"Did Patricia mention the werewolves to Cain?" I asked him.

"I do not know, but that is something we can ask her tomorrow."

I felt the shift in the air as Jasmine returned. In a few minutes, she would be coming through the front door. I fought back annoyance as another unmated Guardian came near to Mae. Jasmine was more than capable of whisking Mae away or Joining with her just as much as Arthur was. It did not go unnoticed how affectionate Jasmine was with my mate.

The three of us turned as a unit as Jasmine entered. As the Guardian approached, her eyes went automatically to Mae. Her body shuddered as the curse lifted. The smile spreading across her face was almost sweet-natured, but the flash in her eyes told me what I already knew: Jasmine wanted my mate. I choked on a growl that was threatening to bubble up. It would not be long before I no longer had to stress about unmated Guardians.

"Ah, Mae, you look much better," Jasmine said as she came to stand with us. "I assume you were able to use your power?"

The shudder that ran through Mae's body was barely noticeable, but I could feel her tension. Mentally, I sighed. She was not comfortable with what ran through her veins, but eventually she needed to come to terms with it. Once she learned how to use what she had, she would feel better.

"Yeah, I figured it out."

*Her heart rate is still elevated,* Jasmine's voice whispered in my mind. *But this is a good sign that it has slowed significantly from yesterday. If she continues to expel her power daily, I think she will live comfortably for a long while. She needs to find balance, not too much power in her system but not too little either.*

"How do you feel now?" she asked my mate out loud.

Mae glared at me and then Jasmine. I almost smiled. She hated it when we spoke telepathically.

Instead of acknowledging our private conversation, Mae shrugged, "Alright, I guess."

"Do you feel well enough to go explore the area? There are ATVs in a shed out—"

"Yes! Let's go!" Mae's annoyance disappeared, and she was already heading for the front door with a grin on her face before Jasmine finished. Jasmine glanced at Arthur and me and said:

*The park rangers informed me that there have been three missing hikers in the past twenty years which isn't unusual. According to them, there hasn't been any strange activity either. The only thing mildly suspicious was on our way here last night, I could have sworn I sensed something in the air. It was so brief I could not track or define what it was. It was the same way this morning when we left to go to the blood bank. We were well out of range from the park when I felt something in the air but it was gone before I could determine what I had sensed. In any case, I will keep Mae close and safe while out.*

*I felt nothing out of sorts last night during my patrol,* Arthur told her. She nodded, turned, and left the house.

*While they are gone, let us explore the area south of here. We will not make it to where Zyroe and Autumn showed Mae where the gates will open, but we can scout for any signs of trouble that may have made its way in this direction,* I told Arthur. *The sooner we can find evidence, or lack thereof, of suspicious activity the sooner we can leave.*

Arthur shuddered as Mae's effect on him subsided. She must have moved out of range because the life in Arthur's eyes seemed to dim. A cool indifference coated his features. I suppressed my discomfort. The difference in the Guardian next to me was night and day. I never wanted to go back to that.

As Arthur and I took to the sky a few minutes later, I hung back to scan the property for my mate. I found Mae and Jasmine weaving through the trees. With my enhanced senses, I could hear Mae's laughter despite how high up I was. I smiled. It was good that she was able to find some joy in spite of the situation we had found ourselves in.

# Chapter Four



After a long day of exploring several expansive miles of the park south of the house Arthur and I finally made it home. While we had not gone as far as I would like I did learn the layout of the land. I landed just outside the front door and pulled my wings into my back. As I walked through the front door I listened for the sounds of my mate. With my enhanced hearing I could hear her stepping out of the shower while softly humming. I smiled, eager to be with her. The surprise I had waiting was not just for her to enjoy but for both of us.

Arthur clasped my shoulder and grinned. "I have a feeling I will not see you for the rest of the night so let me congratulate you now before you disappear," he said. "I am happy you found your mate. She is a good woman."

My heart swelled and I could not stop the grin spreading across my face.

"Thank you, Arthur. Without you running into her I would still be incomplete," I told him. "Let us hope the fates grant you the same blessing that I have received."

"Ah, but she is a blessing to us all," Arthur reminded me warmly. With that he slapped my back and walked away, allowing me time to finish what Mae and I had already started.

I took the steps two at a time and made my way down a hallway towards the bedroom Mae and I would be sharing during our time here. I barely noticed the house or the furnishings in it as I headed towards my mate. Just outside our bedroom doors I paused and listened. Mae was still humming softly but I could now hear her moving around the room.

I opened the door and walked in, eager to see her. Mae halted her progress towards the bed and turned to face me as I entered the room. I took in the silky pajamas she was wearing that I had included in her wardrobe order. The soft lavender against her skin was beautiful. Her cheeks looked warm after her shower and her eyes twinkled with joy as I drew closer to her. My heart pounded wildly in my chest as anticipation surged through me. Her gaze trailed slowly down my chest. I had not bothered to put on a shirt upon my return, knowing good and well I would be removing it again shortly. Her open appreciation of my body caused my blood to boil.

I stopped just in front of Mae, forcing her to look up at me as I stared down into her heart shaped face. Her tongue licked her bottom lip and I watched the motion with interest.

"You look beautiful," I told her before leaning down to kiss her. As her lips pressed against mine, I groaned. Excitement, desire, love and joy swirled around in my chest making me feel larger than life. I pulled away from her lips and asked, "I want to take you somewhere – will you come with me?"

"Do I need to get dressed?" When I shook my head, she smiled and said, "Okay, lead the way."

It humbled me that she trusted me. I pulled her towards the glass door that led out onto a small wrought iron balcony. I opened the door, and we both stepped out into the night air. I turned slightly and called out my wings. Mae's eyes widened in delight and awe. Would I ever get used to seeing her look at me in such a way? My heart soared under Mae's admiring gaze. Carefully I reached out, took her hips in my hands and drew her close to my body. Immediately she wrapped her arms around my neck. The sight of her wide grin and the sound of the acceleration of her heart in anticipation of the flight caused my own face to split into an answering grin. I leaned down and scooped her up into my arms.

As smoothly as I could manage I leapt into the sky. My wings spread out wide behind me and we caught the slight breeze. Mae's soft gasp of delight kept my grin firmly in place. She turned her head to look out around us. Her eyes were wide as she took in the dark forest that surrounded the house. Above us, the clear sky allowed us a view of millions of twinkling stars. Below us, there were small ponds far in the distance glittering in the moonlight. I could make out deer a few miles out grazing in a grassy patch. The trees swayed in the slight breeze, and somewhere, far out in the distance, I heard a wolf howl. Mae shivered and I brought her closer to my chest as we continued to soar leisurely around the property.

As she stared at the world around us, I stared at her. The faint dark circles under her eyes did nothing to mar her beauty. Her lips were slightly parted and her eyes reflected the stars in the sky. A few strands of her curly hair blew gently around her face but did not seem to bother her. Her awe gave her an angelic appearance.

"It's so beautiful out here." Her voice came out as a whisper.

I leaned forward and nuzzled my face in her damp hair.

"Is it? I have not noticed…" my voice trailed off as my lips skimmed across her cheek and found her lips.

We stopped rising, and we hung, suspended in the air. My wings barely moved as our lips connected. Mae opened her mouth, and my tongue slipped inside and danced with hers. Her hands slid up my neck and her fingers weaved their way through my hair. My arms tightened around her. I crushed her to my chest knowing that I could keep her safe and happy as long as she was here in my arms.

When I finally broke the kiss, Mae was breathless. I kissed the corners of her mouth, and she smiled. Slowly we began our descent. The flight had been short, but I was eager to get to the surprise. Instead of heading back to our room, I flew around to the other side of the house. Below us I could see lights glowing on the roof in a small, almost unnoticeable nook. As we drew closer, it was clear the light was coming from dozens of candles that I had lit before coming into the house.

I circled the area twice before I landed in the small area where a large bed with a plush comforter and a handful of pillows sat. Next to the bed was a bottle of wine and two glasses. Rose petals were scattered everywhere, and a small speaker was playing soft classical music. It was barely audible, but it added to the ambiance. I set Mae down to let her look around.

She gaped at the scene and then looked back at me, at a loss for words. What was going through her head right now? Did she understand what this was about? I smiled at her warmly. From our view, we could see out for miles. And while we could see all around us, the way the roof was pitched and with how high up we were, no one would be able to see us. We had the night to ourselves.

"Rylan, what...?" she attempted but words failed her. She tried again. "Rylan, this is beautiful. What is all of this for?"

I let go of her waist and took her hand. My wings retracted into my back as I led Mae over to the bed. When she sat down, I grabbed the bottle and both glasses and lowered myself next to her. I poured us each a glass of the red juice and when I handed it to Mae she took it warily. I chuckled as she sniffed it and smiled. Of course, I would remember she didn't drink alcohol. I took a sipped from my glass thoughtfully as I stared at her over the rim. The liquid tasted like nothing but I wanted to share this moment with her. I was surprised that my hands were not shaking with excitement and nervousness. This was it. This moment was what every Guardian dreamed of. I put down my glass and took Mae's empty hand.

"Mae Aurora White," I said her name slowly. "Tonight I want us to complete our Joining. Let me become your mate fully in heart, body, and mind. Let me love you completely, take you into my keeping, and cherish you forever. My soul aches for you."

Mae's mouth popped open in surprise. She stared at me then at the scene around us. When her eyes met mine again, understanding lit up her face. I could hear her heart beating rapidly in her chest and her breathing quickened. The smile that pulled her lips upward sent my heart soaring. She looked down and I could hear her swallow. When she looked back at me the joy had dimmed slightly. Her smile had vanished and her brows were pulled together. She placed her drink down and cupped my cheek with her hand.

Her brown eyes searched my face, looking for something. Her eyes seemed to darken and her frown deepened. She bit her lip for just a moment before she sighed and said, "By tying your life to mine, you're shortening yours significantly. My power will eventually kill me. If it doesn't, and we get lucky enough that I simply grow old and die, we won't have forever like we would if I were immortal like you. In the end, I'm the reason you'll die and knowing that kills me."

Her words shocked me, although I did not understand why. Of course; she would worry about me. I put down my glass without looking away from her.

"Immortality means nothing to me. When you leave this world, so shall I," I told her solemnly. "As it is with all mated Guardians. One cannot live without the other. Even if it was physically possible to continue, my heart would still give out knowing my other half was no longer here but waiting for me at the Golden Gates."

I leaned forward and kissed her. I could still see the worry, even sadness, in her eyes. How could she doubt me? I would do anything for her. I would follow her anywhere. Even if that meant into the next life.

"There is no me without you, Mae," I murmured against her lips. I pushed her back onto the mattress while trailing kisses along her jawline. My hands swept down her sides and stopped at her hips. "I wanted to do this back in Salisbury but I could not do that to you when you were so fragile. Let me love you for all eternity. Let me give you the world while we are here and let me hold your hand as we cross through the Golden Gates to live out our second life. Our souls need each other. I need you, Mae. Trust that this is what is meant to be."

I kissed down the side of her neck. I reached up to cup her breasts through the silky top. My right thumb teased her nipple, causing it to harden. I looked away from Mae's face to stare down at it. Her nipple strained against the fabric of her top. My mouth watered to taste it. I bunched the fabric in my hands and yanked. Mae's top tore away completely, leaving her exposed under the stars. The cool air against her skin caused goosebumps to rise. When I reached down and took that delicious looking nipple that had teased me through the fabric with my mouth, Mae cried out. My other hand reached over and played with her other one. I twisted, pulled, and suckled on her nipples until they were tight buds.

Again Mae cried out. My mouth came up and crashed down onto hers. One of my hands slid past the waistband of her pajama bottoms, and my fingers found her intimate folds. Mae arched into my touch, gasping into my mouth. She was so wet and ready for me. My body responded immediately. My thumb circled her swollen clit. As her desire pooled between the junction of her legs, I slid two fingers inside of her. Her intimate walls clenched down around me and I smiled against her lips. I stroked her unhurriedly, ensuring that her pleasure would build slowly. Mae's breathing turned to pants. Our tongues clashed. Mae groaned as she neared her climax. She moved against my hand, needing more.

I pulled away from her mouth with a grin and tilted my head, so my mouth was against her ear.

"Tell me you want to Join with me."

This time there was no hesitation. "Join with me, Rylan."

Her voice was husky and while I loved that I had caused that, it was her words that caused my erection to harden to its max.

I could not stop the pleased growl that rumbled through me. I switched up the caressing and tempo between her legs, knowing she was close. Her orgasm came hard and fast. Mae arched her back as it crashed through her. Her body shook as pleasure radiated outward, causing her legs to tremble. The way her mouth was shaped into a "O" as her eyes closed was delightful. When Mae came down from her high, I withdrew my fingers.

I removed my pants, and Mae watched as my cock sprang free. The excitement and pleasure that flickered across her face made me growl again. I knew I was larger than average. The first time we came together I was afraid I would hurt her. But somehow, we fit perfectly. Mae sat up and took me in her hand. The feel of her soft hand wrapping around me was beyond bliss. As she slid her hand up and down my shaft, my body shuddered. Her smile became wider. Her grip tightened and I shuddered again. I closed my eyes and tilted my head back.

When Mae's mouth suddenly wrapped around my erection I hissed in delight and surprise. It was followed by a long animalistic growl. I let her pleasure me with her mouth. She sucked on me, taking me deep into her mouth until I touched the back of her throat. When she pulled back, her tongue swirled around the head of my erection. She reached out and gently took my balls and fondled them. I barely heard my strangled cry as she continued this slow, glorious torture. She let go of my balls and reached between her legs. God, she was getting turned on all over again just pleasing me. She was perfect. Absolutely perfect.

But there was no way in hell I was going to allow her to pleasure herself when that was what I wanted to do for her.

I reached forward and hooked my arms under her shoulders. She gasped, letting go of me. I took the opportunity to toss her further back onto the bed. I reached forward, tore her pajama bottoms off, and then crawled on top of her. As she parted her legs, I leaned down to press my erection against her entrance. I paused, and Mae groaned in frustration.

Mae's brown eyes, now speckled with violet, stared up at me with a wild desire that I knew mirrored my own. Her face was flushed, her lips swollen from our kisses, and her curly hair had spilled over her shoulders. She was stunning. My heart stuttered at the enormity of finding her. Fate had blessed me with this incredible woman, and I was going to do everything in my power to cherish her for the rest of our lives. She was all I wanted.

Mae was *mine.*

The searing heat that greeted me as I pushed against her opening was heavenly. As I sunk slowly into her, she arched her hips upwards and spread her legs wider. I gritted my teeth as I forced myself to continue my slow push. She was so tight. The soft sigh of pleasure that escaped her echoed in my head, and I growled in response.

*Mine.*

The moment I was completely surrounded by Mae, I closed my eyes and savored the feeling. There was nothing more perfect than her. I started moving, needing the friction between us. Mae met every thrust, every demand I made of her body. Her nails raked down my back as her legs wrapped around my waist to pull me closer.

I felt her body tighten and heard her breath quicken. I pulled my lips from her mouth and inhaled the smell of her arousal. Then I bent down at the base of her neck and inhaled the smell of her blood pumping through her veins. My mouth watered, my soul cheered me on, and my cock hardened further. This was it. I was about to seal our fate and our lives together.

My fangs lengthened, and without warning, I sunk them deep into Mae's neck. Her orgasm was swift and demanding. Her body gripped me and milked me so strongly that my release followed suit. Her blood raced across my tongue and down my throat. Mae's blood tasted of the sweetest of wines. It rejuvenated my body like the rumored sacred waters of the River of Jordan and brought me closer to the salvation that came with finding a mate. Mixed within her delicious blood, I felt her connection to the gods.

While blood revived a Guardian's body and brought it back to full strength, Mae's blood took it a step further. The power in her blood, an ancient power that belonged to a god, not only brought me to full strength, but everything within me intensified tenfold. I would forever be faster and stronger than my brethren thanks to Mae.

I received another dose of this power as her orgasm heightened. The heat of her magic was overwhelming. As it soaked into my every pore, I felt it settle in the middle of my chest, where it would sit for hours until it fizzled away.

It took me longer than it should have to pull away from her. Tasting her power and sensing how it strengthened me always triggered a sort of frenzy in my mind… I had to fight it each time my fangs sank into Mae. It was seductive, to have all that power within my reach. But my love for Mae and the fear of hurting or killing her made it easier to deny the siren's call to take more blood.

I pulled away when I was full and sealed the marks on her neck with my saliva. When I looked down into her eyes, despite being slightly dazed they were glowing a bright violet. I took advantage of the light trance that befell my mate. I lengthened my nails and tore the skin just above my heart. Blood began to trickle down my chest.

Her gaze strayed to the cut, but then she looked back up to me.

"I love you."

Her declaration was soft but confident. Even in a trance, she had the mind to let me know how she felt. My heart swelled, and I gently kissed her lips.

"I love you, Mae White."

Her sweet smile dimpled her cheeks. At the sight of it, I let out a shaky breath. Without any direction, she leaned forward. The moment her tongue lapped at the cut my whole body tensed. My desire flared back up again, but I fought it back as my mate solidified our connection. I cradled her head against me as she drank my blood for the third and final time.

I felt the moment she had taken enough blood for the Joining. My soul rose and reached for hers and the other half of mine she held. We both felt it: Our souls collided, twisted, and welded together. I heard her gasp. The half of my soul that I had been missing my entire life forged itself with the half I held on to. A vast hole had been filled within me. But that wasn't the only thing I received. I felt Mae's soul, merged with mine, filling my body to the brim. I felt her love, her life, her very essence searing me, branding me with everything that made Mae who she was. Bliss stole over me. The problems and troubles of the world fell away. The threat of the gods' return faded until it was nonexistent. The only thing that mattered was Mae.

I breathed in her sweet scent and stole a kiss as her face turned up to look at me with wonder. The moment Mae pulled her head away from my chest, my wound began to heal. She lifted her hand and cupped my cheek. Her touch sent a shiver of pleasure down my spine. Something warm bubbled up in my chest. It took me a minute to realize I was already beginning to sense Mae's emotions, one of the pleasant side effects of Joining. Her happiness was my own. The joy she was feeling simmered under my skin, tasted sweet on my tongue, and elevated my own happiness. Her joy was more addictive than the power that ran through her blood. I would forever crave this feeling of her happiness.

Still hard despite my release, I began to move in Mae again. In and out, slowly, savoring our new connection. Her body clenched down on me, heightening the bliss I was feeling. I groaned and shifted our position. I sat up and pulled Mae onto my lap so she straddled me. I braced one hand behind me to keep us both upright while the other snaked around her waist. Mae's eyes widened at the new position just before a mischievous smile spread across her face. Now on top, Mae moved with surprising vigor. Her lips came down on mine hard and another groan escaped me when she bit my bottom lip. Her fingers raked through my hair.

She ground her hips against me, her body gripping me so tightly it was hard to breathe. I could feel her pleasure building. Her cheeks were flushed, her nipples beaded. She was gorgeous. I watched through hooded eyes as she threw her head back and cried out my name as her orgasm swelled through her. Her entire body lit up like a lightning storm, and I was hit with another charge of power. Feeling her undoing fed into my pleasure, and I chased her orgasm with my own.

Mae sagged against me, and I held her against my chest. Our heavy breathing sounded loud in the silence of the night. I smiled into Mae's neck as her body shuddered with aftershocks.

"I once traveled to Iceland, long ago, well before the Dutch and the Vikings," I whispered in her ear. "One night I stood among the glaciers and snow capped mountains, far from civilization. I can remember breathing in the clean air and bathing in the deafening silence. Above me were the green hues of the northern lights, cutting across the sky. While I was unable to find joy or contentment, that was the closest I had ever come to feeling at peace. It is such a simple and short moment in my long existence, but I will never forget it."

I took Mae's chin in my hand and looked her in the eyes. Her gaze settled on mine, and my heart swelled under her attention.

"Until recently, I used to think back to that moment quite often, hoping that it would bring me some type of solace. Now, that memory seems laughable. The only moments worth remembering are the ones I have with you, Mae."

She smiled warmly at me. After planting a light kiss on my cheek she said softly, "There are no words for how I'm feeling right now, but I promise to show you how much you mean to me every day."

I lifted her off me and gently laid her down on the mattress. I stared down at her body, memorizing every inch of it as if I had not done so every night since we had been together. When I moved, I twisted to lie on my stomach next to her. I called my wings out and stretched them above me. Though they had always been a part of me, they felt new as I experienced them as a whole person. Mae's eyes lifted to stare at my wings, and again I found myself warmed under the admiration in her gaze.

"Can I touch them?"

"Of course, just be careful. They have sharp edges. We can use our wings offensively and defensively. Our feathers are razor sharp and can cut our opponents if need be."

Mae nodded in understanding as she turned onto her side and propped her elbow up to place her head in her hand. Curiosity lit up her face. I watched as she lifted her hand slowly and reached out to touch me. Her pretty lips popped open slightly as her fingers ran over my wings. She sat up so she could use both hands to stroke my feathers. I watched her face, feeling her wonder and awe wash through me. I closed my eyes and bathed in this new sensation.

I had come to know Mae well within this past week. I could read her body language, and I could see the flash of emotions in her eyes before she hid it behind a mask of composure. But this… This was new and different. Now I could sense what she was feeling. I would be able to anticipate her needs and wants much easier now. I knew from stories that this new connection between us would only strengthen over time.

Mae's gasp caused me to tense. I opened my eyes to find Mae cradling her hand against her chest. I could smell blood.

Immediately, I sat up and took her injured hand in mine. Down the middle of her palm was a thin bloody line.

"Oops," she whispered in embarrassment.

I brought her hand up and trailed my tongue over her wound. The skin began to repair itself. After a moment, the cut was gone. Mae shook her head with a small half-smile.

"There, all better," I muttered and kissed the middle of her freshly healed palm.

"What can't you do?" she mused out loud.

I chuckled. "A lot."

Mae rolled her eyes playfully before giggling. Her happiness wrapped around my insides and doubled my own joy. I grabbed a strand of her hair and twirled it around my finger.

"I love you," I told her.

# Chapter Five

*Mae*

After waking up in a state of complete bliss, the rest of the morning consisted of a whirlwind of changes. First there was the ability to hear Jasmine's and Arthur's conversation taking place on the other side of the house. It sounded like they were standing on either side of me, shouting in my ears. Anything they moved or touched seemed to reverberate throughout the silent mansion. The sound of the water from Rylan's shower was deafening, and even the birds chirping outside had been overwhelming. As if sensing my rising panic, Rylan had suddenly appeared beside me, soaking wet. Patiently, he taught me how to adjust my new ability to hear from great distances.

When I had dressed for the morning, Rylan taken me outside right away to help me expel the power that had built up overnight. I had looked like a walking glow stick as we left the house. Thankfully we were far away enough that we would never run into anyone. Looking like this would certainly raise a lot of questions. When we were a safe distance away from the house, I let my body find some reprieve from the energy coursing in my veins. While this time I found it easier than yesterday to call upon it, we both found out the hard way that I had acquired a new ability. The energy blast that shot out from my palms had thrown us both backward while in front of us trees snapped in half.

Once we returned to the house, I showered. As I pulled on some clean clothes, I began feeling something in my gut. I mulled over this new sensation swirling around inside me as I headed downstairs. By the time I walked into the kitchen, I realized I was feeling joy. It was an unabashed, pure joy that did not belong to me. When I found Rylan in the family room talking with Jasmine, I realized the emotion was coming from *him*. The grin on his face, the light in his eyes… The physical evidence echoed the ghost emotion I was feeling. Had Rylan told me this was going to happen, or was this something he'd failed to warn me about? I didn't get a chance to ask him before Arthur came down and the Guardians disappeared to talk amongst themselves.

Now, as I worked on making breakfast for our guests this morning, I started to take note of other changes that had appeared overnight. Not only was my sense of hearing better, but so was my sense of smell. As I dumped a little of the bacon grease into the pan I was cooking scrambled eggs in, I almost choked on the smell. It was overwhelming. Even the cinnamon and sugar coating the French toast in the oven was too much. As I had been instructed with my new ability to hear, I focused on all the smells in the kitchen. When I was sure I could smell even the fabric of the padded stools pushed against the counter, I focused on the ability to turn it down. Immediately, it worked. My sense of smell returned to normal.

Rylan had told me that my senses would be heightened once we Joined. At the time I hadn't thought too much about it. Now the idea that I could hear the Guardians' conversation, even in another room of the house, if I wanted to was thrilling.

As I played with the new settings in my head, I found that there was a small part of my mind that seemed to be fine-tuning itself. When I focused on the sensation, it reminded me of soft static from a radio that couldn't find a signal. Luckily, when I didn't focus on it too hard, I could ignore it. After a few minutes I realized that the static I was hearing in my mind was probably my brain trying to tune itself to Rylan's. This was another thing that came along with Joining with one's mate. It was strange to know that, soon, I would be able to speak with him telepathically. The thought was exciting and scary.

I turned my attention back to breakfast. Any minute now, wolf shifters would be here. It was only nine o'clock in the morning, yet I felt like an entire day had gone by. My body certainly needed fuel, and if the shifters had risen as early as I had, I'm sure they would be hungry too.

People who shifted into wolves— like *real* wolves— were coming. As I worked on the sausage, my excitement began to grow. What would they be like? Would I be able to tell that they were shifters? Was I supposed to know about their ability to shift? Would I get to see them turn into wolves?

The Guardians must have sensed the arrival of our guests because they emerged just as the doorbell rang. Arthur went to answer the door as Rylan came to lean against the kitchen counter near me. Jasmine walked into the family room and stood near the fireplace.

I could hear Arthur open the door and greet our visitors. A moment later, he and three strangers came into view. The first shifter to come into view was obviously the Alpha. Even if I hadn't known the Alpha was a woman, the confidence she radiated would have clued me in. The woman was tall and muscular. Her blonde hair was shaved on either side of her head while the rest of it was pulled up into a bun. Her gaze swept through the first floor, and her nostrils flared.

Behind her was a tall, lean man. He had shaggy mouse-brown hair and a long nose that had obviously been broken several times. The final man who appeared was shorter than both of his companions, but the thick muscles in his arms and the mean look on his face spoke volumes of the danger he could be.

As Arthur led them into the family room where Jasmine was waiting, something shifted between all of us. The three shifters immediately whipped their heads around to look at me. Both men came to stand in front of their Alpha. The shorter one even growled at me. Next to me, Rylan shifted his stance to stand fully erect. Jasmine bared her teeth and took a step forward. Arthur turned and stiffened as he realized his visitors had turned their attention to me.

Confused about the sudden tension in the room and unwilling to feed into it, I grinned at the three shifters.

"Good morning! I hope you're hungry. I made breakfast," I said.

Two shifters lifted their upper lips to show their teeth, but their Alpha pushed passed them, her eyes trained on my face. They swept over me suspiciously.

"Breakfast sounds wonderful after the long night we have had, thank you," the Alpha said. She studied me a moment longer before the tension in her body deflated. She turned her attention to Rylan and bowed her head respectfully. "Hello, Rylan Wellington, thank you for granting us a meeting, and congratulations on finding your mate. Your mating bond smells new. May I assume you are on your honeymoon?"

My cheeks warmed in embarrassment. How could someone smell a bond? I tried to discreetly turn my head to sniff my shirt. Next to me, Rylan bowed his head in return.

"Patricia Night, welcome and thank you. This is Mae White. We are simply here to enjoy the area for a little while. My mate seems to be opposed to a true wedding ceremony, so I will hold out on giving her a honeymoon until she says yes."

I could actually feel Rylan's amusement and hurt in my gut. The hurt confused me. Why would he need a wedding when we were Joined? I was already his. He had brought up getting married before, but I just didn't see the point. Before me, Rylan had hundreds, maybe even thousands of wives. Why would I want to be another name on that list?

Patricia chuckled, making her look ten years younger.

"Good for you, Mae. Hold out on saying yes until he gives you the biggest rock he can find." Patricia turned to Jasmine as

Rylan chuckled next to me. Patricia bowed her head to the last Guardian in the room. "Hello, Jasmine Sing, I appreciate your hospitality."

Jasmine seemed the least inclined to relax. Her sharp gaze did not leave Patricia's face, and her nod was stiff.

"This is my mate, Johnathan Night," Patricia continued as she introduced the men with her. The man with shaggy hair nodded at his name. "And this here is my beta Marcus Shepherd." The shorter man did not make a move to bow, but his body did visibly relax. She turned to look at both men and said, "Get something to eat while I discuss our problem."

Without a word, both of them moved towards me, eyeing me curiously. Before I could move, Rylan was there, handing them plates and silverware. Then, he positioned himself so he was always between me and the shifters as they grabbed breakfast. In the other room, Patricia stood between Arthur and Jasmine, utterly at ease.

"There is much I wish to share with you, but I know how it will come off," Patricia said slowly, making eye contact with all three Guardians before glancing at me. She turned her attention back to Arthur and said, "It will sound like I have lost my mind, but my men are here to assure you that I have not."

"We have no reason not to trust your word," Arthur assured her.

Patricia traded glances with her men who had walked over with their plates full. They sat down on the couch behind their Alpha and began eating quietly. I made a plate as Rylan moved towards the other two Guardians, apparently no longer worried about the shifters.

# Chapter Six



"I took over as pack Alpha about six years ago when our previous Alpha, William Stone, could no longer run our pack," Patricia started. "That was when I realized that our Alpha had been keeping many secrets from us. One day, not long before I took over, William had moved our pack further north without warning. We had to leave almost everything behind and start over without any explanation. According to William's notes that he left behind after he passed away, he believed the land had become cursed.

"William thought he was going mad. He thought he had seen impossible things, like mermaids in the lake and werewolves working together like a pack. In his notes, William went on to talk about how our pack would go ballistic once a day. I hadn't noticed this, not really, but when I took over, I noticed strange occurrences within the pack."

"What do you mean?" I asked her.

"Something happens during the day... My pack becomes unsettled. Fights between two friends start. Mothers attack their children. I have had a few members of the pack try to set fire to their own homes. It's irrational behavior. It doesn't seem to affect me, and I don't know why. Even my beta and mate are affected by whatever is happening."

"That sounds like chaos," Jasmine said grimly.

Patricia let out a frustrated laugh. "It was... It still is. At first, I thought they just needed discipline, so I cracked down on the rules. But then I began to sense this… this *wave* of depravity that washes over the land. It's like a strange pulse in the air. It took a while to sense it, but when I did that's when I realized that whenever I felt it, my pack could too, and that's when they would act out. When I realized some outside force was attacking my pack, I started really digging into the notes that were left behind.

"I also started realizing there was strange behavior happening within these woods. The wildlife is all but nonexistent. What lingers behind are sickly or too old to migrate with the rest of the herd or pack. Deer attack humans without provocation. Plants that are usually harmless have become poisonous. The list goes on."

A knot began to form in my stomach. Shifters were one with nature. They would know if something was off.

"Have you spoken to Cain about these issues?" I asked her. "This is his territory."

"I have tried many times over the past few years to reach out to Cain, but I have not been able to get into contact with him. I even tried visiting his estate several times throughout the year, but he is never home. He does not have anyone working under him, so I cannot pass on my grievances. William had tried to contact Cain and even Ekon, but neither responded to his calls," Patricia explained. She looked each Guardian in the eye.

"What I need is help. Something is not right here, and I am afraid for my pack. Recently on a run, I discovered the four member werewolf pack William had talked about. Instead of engaging with us, they ran. I took a group with me to hunt them on two different occasions. We were able to corner one, but it was smart and cunning. It got away from us after nearly killing me and my pack members."

*Have you heard from Cain yet?* I asked Arthur but made sure Jasmine was included in the conversation.

*No,* Arthur responded grimly. *I cannot remember the last time I spoke to either of them before this, and the lack of response to my calls is definitely a concern.*

*Are we dealing with two missing Guardians now?* Jasmine asked. Her brows rose in surprise.

*That is what it appears to be happening,* I answered grimly. *Which is worrisome since Montana is Zein's territory, and it butts up to this one.*

*You think Zein's murder and Cain's and Ekon's disappearances could be related?* Arthur asked with alarm.

*There is no evidence of a correlation between them. It just seems like a strange coincidence,* I said thoughtfully.

Patricia spoke again: "I have decided that I will be moving the pack from this region altogether by the end of the month. With the constant wave of depravity that tears my pack to pieces, the lack of wildlife in the area, and the werewolves that roam these woods, it is what is best for my people."

"Tell us more about this wave you sense that sends your pack members into chaos," I pressed. This seemed like the most important take-away from this conversation.

"It is one single force of energy that radiates in every direction throughout the park. I'm sure you will feel it while you're here. It happens every day at random times. I tried tracking it, but there were no noticeable patterns. The effects of it only last about five minutes, but that's five minutes of hell. I did learn that whatever this is does not reach outside the park... yet."

My teeth clenched as I thought about the implications of that depravity should it touch the four of us. If the three of us lost our minds for a short period of time, we would all be in trouble. If Mae were affected, the destruction she could cause in that amount of time could be cataclysmic.

*What I felt yesterday may have been this wave of depravity that Patricia is talking about,* Jasmine said to me and Arthur.

*Did you lose a sense of time or feel unstable?* Arthur asked.

*No, but as I said, it was so brief and hardly noticeable, I may not have been in range for the full effect. Both times, we were not actually in the park but rather arriving or leaving it.*

A sense of dread settled over me as I thought about the danger Mae could be in now.

"Your concerns have been heard, Patricia Night," Jasmine said slowly. Since the arrival of our guests, she had been tense, but now she appeared the epitome of serenity. "While we are in the area, we will investigate what is going on, and we will rid the woods of the werewolves for you."

The Alpha turned her attention to Jasmine and bowed her head.

"Thank you, Jasmine, and to the rest of you for believing me. I know how strange all of this sounds. I have been trying to keep my pack together, but it is hard when so many things seem out of whack lately."

"Understandable," Jasmine said with a nod. "Please, enjoy the breakfast Mae has slaved over. While you eat do you mind if I take your men to our office? I have a map where they can point out where your pack was originally located and where you are now. I would like to know where you have spotted these werewolves as well, so we have a place to start hunting."

Patricia waved her hands to her two pack mates and both stood immediately.

"They are at your disposal," she said with a smile. "Boys, behave."

Patricia's mate grinned and winked at her. I could not help but smile at the loving look they shared. I looked over at Mae, who I found staring at the two shifters with a small smile tugging up the corners of her mouth. She was leaning on her elbows at the counter, absorbed in our conversation. I could almost hear the wheels turning in her head. Knowing how large her heart was, I was sure that she was thinking of ways to help them in their struggles.

*A wave of depravity that creates chaos, creatures that are not behaving normally, the lack of wildlife... This all sounds like the effects of dark magic,* Jasmine said to both me and Arthur.

The knot in my stomach tightened harder. If Patricia's claims were true, this would be the first proof that something wrong was happening in these parts. I clenched my jaw. If the three of us found any proof of dark magic, Mae and I would leave immediately. Bringing her to the location where Autumn and Zyroe wanted her had never felt right. After what she had gone through, I had conceded to her plea to come, but I had warned her that at the first sign of trouble, she would be removed from the situation.

Patricia walked over to Mae while Jasmine and Arthur disappeared with the other two shifters. I hesitated. Instead of following them right away, I turned and watched the Alpha approach my mate, suspicion coating her features. Patricia may not know what Mae was, but Patricia's abilities as a shifter would alert her to Mae's unique aura. I watched as Mae happily handed Patricia a plate and walked her through the items on the counter. Patricia paid more attention to my mate than the food, but she graciously took what Mae offered.

Before our Joining, I would have stayed with Mae. Jealousy and possessiveness would have prevented me from leaving the room. But now I felt whole. There was no chance that someone could steal Mae away from me. Smiling to myself, I left Mae with Patricia and followed my companions.

***

By the time I had walked the three shifters out of the house, Patricia and Mae were talking like close friends. The suspicion in Patricia's face had vanished, and in its place was a warmth not usually found in an Alpha around new people. I promised Patricia that we would follow up with her once we had some information to share. I walked back into the kitchen to find Mae cleaning up.

She looked up as I entered. She reached over and turned off the faucet. As she turned to lean her hip against the counter and crossed her arms over her chest, Arthur and Jasmine walked into the room.

"So? What's the verdict? Is this just typical stuff Guardians deal with or should we be concerned?"

"We must investigate and see for ourselves what is happening before we can determine the severity of the situation here," Jasmine answered as she walked over to Mae.

"Okay, where do we start?" Mae asked.

"While there is plenty of daylight, we should explore where the pack was previously settled. We can look for any abnormalities surrounding their old den, and we will be able to sense if magic has been used recently," Arthur suggested.

"Great. When do you want to leave? Do I have a chance to change into something more hiking appropriate?" Mae asked.

Her excitement felt like bubbles of champagne in my chest. Despite enjoying the sensation, every instinct in my body rebelled at the thought of Mae being in a place where there could be potential danger. My jaw clenched as my stomach twisted.

"While I appreciate the enthusiasm and the eagerness to help, you need to stay here. This is our line of work. The three of us will be exploring the abandoned den," I told her gently.

"What? No way, I'm coming with you guys!" Mae objected.

"It could be dangerous," I told her with a frown. "We do not know what we are going to find or what will be waiting for us once we get there. If we get to the den and nothing is amiss, then if we need to go back for any reason I will bring you."

"Would it not be beneficial for Mae to learn about the world of shifters? If we are going with the expectation of just studying the area, Mae should be safe to look around," Jasmine suggested thoughtfully.

I turned my attention to the female Guardian and said, "We are here looking for evidence of dark magic and evil. If what

Patricia says is true, then something is awry. I will not take Mae to a place where we suspect dark magic has affected the area."

Jasmine nodded in understanding.

"What the hell am I supposed to do while you're all off gallivanting through the park?" Mae demanded as she pushed away from the counter. Her hands dropped from her chest and perched themselves on her hips. Her glare was trained on me. "I should be with you guys. Let me be the fourth pair of eyes for you."

"Not this time," I said more firmly. I hated telling her no. I hated even the thought of leaving my mate for one moment. I wanted to spend every waking hour with her. But her safety was my utmost concern. Staying behind would keep her relatively safe. "If we cross paths with werewolves or if we all experience this outside force that causes an entire pack of shifters to become unhinged you will be in too much danger. Can you imagine what would happen if all four of us turned on each other? It would be a bloodbath. No, Mae, please just wait here."

Her scowl deepened.

She took a deep breath and said, "Look we're a team, the four of us. Let me come with you. I would probably be safer with you guys than left here at the house by myself, right?"

"There is no *team* Mae. This is not a game. This is a job for Guardians. You will stay here until we get back," I growled at her. I softened my voice and tried to relax my stance. "Mae, I just found you. I will not risk losing you because I was too anxious to have you with me all the time. My first priority is your safety and you will be safer here in this house than with us. I will not budge on this matter."

The echo of her anger flared hot in my gut. The surprise on her face at my declaration shifted to indifference. She, too, relaxed her stance.

"Fine."

Her sudden acceptance sent red flags up in my head. I took a step towards her. She was up to something.

"Mae…" I growled in warning.

"I said *fine*. Leave me here to twiddle my thumbs," she responded contemptuously.

Jasmine moved away from Mae. The smile she was trying to hide slipped out despite her best efforts to conceal it. Arthur coughed and stepped further away from us but not before I heard his chuckle. Before I could respond, Mae turned on her heels and disappeared into the house. Her anger burned even hotter now.

"I can stay behind, Rylan," Jasmine offered. "I will make sure she stays out of trouble."

"And here I was sure that Mae would become much more obedient once you two Joined," Arthur said from the front door.

The sarcasm in his tone grated my nerves. I was not enjoying his amusement at my expense.

"No, Jasmine. We will all go. Mae understands how important she is to me and will do as I asked," I said loudly, knowing my mate would hear me. Worry twisted in my gut. She would be alright here… right?

As if he was able to read my thoughts Arthur said, "If the pulse that was affecting Patricia's pack occurred while we are gone, the barrier spells on the house should keep her safe as long as she was inside."

I nodded my head in appreciation. I glanced in the direction that Mae had taken off in and sighed. We would not be gone long. When I got back I would make her dinner and we could spend some quality time together.

# Chapter Seven



I waited an hour to leave the house once the Guardians had left. I was so angry and upset with Rylan that all I wanted to do was storm out after them. But knowing Rylan, he would have stayed close until he was sure I was staying put. So I decided to bide my time. I was shocked, and if I was being honest, hurt, at his declaration. If he doesn't want to be a team, fine. I'll go solo.

While I waited, I headed up to the bathroom Rylan and I shared. I attempted to summon the spellbook that was hidden within the mirror to find a spell that would help protect the pack. I tried three times before I realized that I could no longer summon the book I hated so much. Jasmine had told me back in Salisbury that she couldn't sense any traces of witch in me… Was that why the pentagram on my hand hadn't shown up when I used my power? Could that be the reason I couldn't summon my book anymore? Frowning, I gave up trying to retrieve it. Even if there had been a spell in it, it didn't mean I could cast it. The only spell that had ever worked for me was when I had cursed bracelets to bind my power.

If I could find a witch who wouldn't balk at the sight of me for being a mutt, I could ask them about the pentagram and the book I couldn't retrieve. But I had no one. The only people I could talk to had up and left.

My anger flared as I headed to the workout room. How could I be useful to the Guardians if they didn't include me?

What information had they gathered from the two male shifters? They hadn't bothered to share that with me. Where were they headed? Was it far? What exactly were they looking for? What did dark magic feel like? Would I be able to feel it, or was it a thing only Guardians could sense?

Autumn and Zyroe thought it was important for *me* to be here. How was I supposed to stop anyone or learn who wanted to open the gates if I got sidelined? Instead of learning, I was stuck sitting here and doing nothing.

I worked off most of my anger working on my MMA moves. Since I had woken up this morning, I felt stronger than I had in a long time. Was this a side effect of the Joining? Or was it because I had expelled enough power that my body could now function properly? Wherever this strength came from, I bathed in it. I had lost most of the muscle mass I had gained from years of training. But if I trained like I was now, I could be back to my peak physical state in no time.

When I was done, I changed without showering, and I left the house. Rylan could go screw himself if he thought I would just sit here. Outside, the sun was shining, the skies were blue, and the wildlife was out in full force. A rabbit darted away at the sight of me. Nearby squirrels chased each other on the ground before scurrying up into a tree. Above me, the cry of an eagle caught my attention, and I looked up to catch sight of the majestic creature.

What had Patricia been talking about? Life seemed to be thriving here, at least in this part of the park. I felt like I was back on the Appalachian Trail. Being surrounded by nature was soothing. As I headed into the woods to do some exploring, I could feel my anger ebb away.

As I walked, I made sure to keep a conscious effort to be aware of my surroundings. I wasn't stupid; I knew danger could be lurking in even the prettiest of places. I also knew the Guardians wouldn't have left me here alone without checking the area.

I walked for two hours, keeping my eyes peeled for anything out of the ordinary. Unfortunately, nothing was amiss. While I could appreciate my surroundings, the mission to find something useful was a bust. The frustration I was feeling was now more towards myself than towards the Guardians. I turned to head back feeling defeated.

As I took a step towards the house, unease twisted my gut. I stopped, trying to gauge the sudden feeling. After a moment, I realized that *I* wasn't feeling uneasy; the ghostly sensation was coming from Rylan. Just as it clicked that it wasn't *me,* the feeling vanished and was replaced with alarm. Wherever Rylan and the others were, something had caused Rylan to worry.

Oh crap, had he come back and found me missing? I had forgotten my cell phone. Maybe he had tried to call when he couldn't find me and worried when I didn't pick up. Feeling a little guilty that he might be worrying about where I was, I took another step towards the house. As I started back, the oddest sensation of sand trickling down my neck and arms started up. I stopped and shuddered. Of its own accord, the power under my skin surged forward. I stared down at my hands and arms as small sparks twinkled around my skin. I stared astonished at the little light show. What was happening?

As I stared at my hands, a feeling of dread boiled up inside of me. An oily, dark impression of evil settled over my skin. Before I could react, my power erupted from my pores in a fiery blast. My scream of agony echoed in the woods around me. Fiery pain overwhelmed me as my power blasted outwards. My vision turned violet, a roaring in my ears started, and my heart raced.

Then I blinked.

When I opened my eyes, I found myself on the floor of the woods. Fifty feet in every direction the ground was blackened. There were piles of ashes where trees once stood and the soil around me was charred. The world was silent. The sun was still shining, but it was further west than I remembered. I attempted to push myself up, but the weakness in my limbs caused me to momentarily give up. I tried to drag in a deep breath, but my lungs felt deflated. My thoughts felt sluggish, and my body felt like it had taken a beating. My heartbeat felt strangely slow in my chest.

What the hell had happened?

I tried to gain my bearings. I could remember my power reacting to a weird sensation then... nothing. Fear twisted in my stomach. The last time I had lost consciousness while my power reacted was when Jasmine had tried to examine me with her mind. Oh god, what had I done while I was unconscious? My heart squeezed painfully in my chest.

I hadn't felt this horrible when it happened with Jasmine. Somehow, this experience was different.

I attempted to get up, and this time I was able to make it to my knees. I dragged in another shaky breath, but it was just as hard as it had been before. My body was shaking from fatigue. As much as I wanted to, I couldn't stay here. I allotted myself a few minutes to collect my bearings before getting to my feet and forcing myself to move. I stumbled multiple times and even blacked out once on my trek to the house.

My heartbeat never regulated itself. Breathing felt like a monumental task. My vision blurred and cleared constantly. I tried not to panic. Panicking wouldn't do me any good. The short gasps of air that I was able to draw in weren't enough, and it scared me. My heart felt out of sync with the rest of my internal workings.

I cursed myself for walking so far into unfamiliar territory. It took forever to get home, but eventually, the house came into view. After I pushed the front door open and shut it, I stumbled and collapsed at the foot of the stairs. There was no way I could climb them in my state. The fact that I had even made it back to the house had been extraordinary. So, I sat there drawing in shallow breaths.

The house was silent. If the Guardians had been home, they would have heard me enter and come to investigate. Something was wrong. Where were the Guardians? Why had I felt Rylan's uneasiness? What had they experienced? Were they hurt? A hundred different scenarios, all horrible, flipped through my head.

Just as fear for my Guardians boosted my energy enough for me to get to my feet, wheels driving on the gravel broke the silence. I heard a car stop, a door open, and then shut. My heart, already beating oddly, skipped a beat. The Guardians hadn't taken a car on their journey. Who was outside?

A knock on the door caused me to jump. I stared at the door wondering if I should open it. Before I got the chance to decide I heard a familiar voice. I sighed in relief as Rylan's voice drifted through the door. I couldn't tell who he was talking to but the conversation was brief. After a few minutes, I heard someone climb back into their car and pull away.

Rylan opened the door and began to walked in but paused as our eyes met. If I had any breath to lose, I would have lost it over the sight of his chiseled abs. Of course flying to and from the shifter's den would have required taking his shirt off so his wings wouldn't destroy the material but he could have easily put it back on before entering the house. I was glad he hadn't. I was momentarily stunned by his perfection. His gaze traveled over me, and he sucked in a sharp breath while his brows came crashing together. I looked down, confused at the alarm on his face. My clothes were shredded and had burn marks on what was left. I had been in such a hurry to get home that I hadn't thought about my appearance.

Rylan was suddenly standing right in front of me as I looked back up at him, "What happened? Are you hurt? Mae, your lips are blue."

He took my face in his hands. We both gasped at the contact. The veins in Rylan's hands began to glow violet. Whatever power he had absorbed during our time together this morning cycled back into me. As my body pulled power from Rylan, I found it easier to draw in a deep breath. The fatigue clinging to my body evaporated. My heart fluttered painfully once, and suddenly, it was back to its normal rhythm. I braced my hands against his bare chest in relief.

That was when I noticed the dried blood.

"Rylan, who hurt you?" I gasped.

The initial wound had healed thanks to his quick healing Guardian abilities, but who had gotten close enough to wound him?

"Mae, tell me what happened to you," Rylan demanded, ignoring my question.

I stared at the blood on his arm for a moment longer before I dragged my gaze up to his face.

"I went exploring after you guys left—" I paused to wince at the deep scowl he gave me. "I was on my way back when… Well, I felt *you* in discomfort." I paused again, wondering how much more weirdness would come with this Joining process. "Then, I felt something in the air, and my power reacted to it."

Rylan looked away from me. His jaw clenched and unclenched as he worked through whatever he was thinking. I could feel warmth in the pit of my stomach. The feeling was ghostly, which told me that I was sensing Rylan's anger. When he looked back down at me, his expression was tense, but there was no anger there.

Before he could say anything, a door somewhere in the house shut. I jumped at the sound. Rylan's hands fell from my face onto my shoulders to steady me.

"It is Jasmine and Arthur," Rylan assured me grimly. "There was an… incident. Jasmine thought it was best to not draw attention to the park ranger who had come to check on us, so she and Arthur came around back."

"An incident? What happened?"

"That depravity that Patricia warned us about affected Jasmine and Arthur. Luckily, it did not affect me, and I was able to step between them before someone was killed," he answered.

I stared at him, stunned. I tried to picture all three Guardians attacking each other. The images in my head were sickening. All of us, except for Rylan, had been affected by the depravity that Patricia had warned us about. He had been right earlier. If I had gone with them I would have been in the middle of that brawl.

"Is everyone alright?" My voice sounded breathless. "What did the park ranger want?"

"Everyone will be fine. The ranger wanted to check in to make sure we were okay after the strange fire that broke out in the woods a few miles from here." Rylan growled as he stared pointedly at me. "He must have been talking about your incident, Mae. What part of 'stay here' do you not understand?"

His tone should have grated on my nerves. Instead of annoyed, I found myself embarrassed. He was right; I should have stayed in the house. Then maybe I wouldn't have blown up a section of the park. I sighed while my shoulders sagged.

"I'm not a fan of being told what to do. I'm sorry." At Rylan's exasperated sigh, I couldn't help but give him a rueful smile. "Would it make you feel better if I admitted that you were right?"

Rylan scowled. "Right about what? That there is danger out there? Yes, I usually know what I am talking about," he said as he ran his fingers through his hair in agitation. "It is foolish to think it was wise to wander these woods alone. Look at what happened when you left the house. You could have died because you are too stubborn to listen to me!"

"You know, I was surviving before I met you, Rylan," I told him. "I don't—"

"You were *barely* surviving," he interrupted angrily. "Or do you not recall all the bruising and damage you were inflicting upon yourself just to maintain a semblance of control in your miserable life? Just now, Mae, I could feel your body was starving for power. Thank goodness your body took what it needed from me! What would have happened if I…" Rylan's voice trailed off as he looked away from me.

Suddenly, his body relaxed, and he unclenched his fists. When he turned back to me, his expression was a mix between concerned and thoughtful.

"Jasmine was right. When you have too much power in your system or when you are depleted of it, your body cannot function properly. We need to make sure you always balance the amount of power within you." He paused. He reached up, and with the back of his hand, he let his knuckles trail down my cheek.

"It wasn't like this before Autumn took me," I said with a frown.

"You took the bracelets off to let it out when it got too bad," Rylan reminded me. "I am sure it was the fear of letting too much out that kept you from draining yourself. We will have to look into this more. In the meantime, we need to pack. We are leaving."

"Leaving?" I repeated. "Why?"

"Because it has become clear something is wrong here. Whatever is causing this mayhem in people is also affecting you. With how unpredictable your power is you could hurt yourself or someone else if you are hell bent on it. It is too dangerous for you to be in this area at all. Jasmine and Arthur will stay behind to do some more investigating."

"But… But you just said *you* weren't affected. If we leave, what happens if Arthur and Jasmine kill themselves? We have to stay together to figure this out."

"Mae—,"

"*No*, Rylan. We aren't leaving the others to fend for themselves. We are sticking together."

"What happens tomorrow if we are all together and they attack you? I would kill them both if they tried. Is that what you want?" Rylan snapped. When I remained silent, Rylan continued, "This is not up for debate, Mae."

I opened my mouth to protest but shut it. We couldn't leave Arthur and Jasmine behind to figure out what was happening here by themselves. Who would protect them next time? My stomach sank. Something was going on in this park, which meant I needed to be here more than ever. Autumn and Zyroe were counting on me. But how could I make Rylan change his mind? At the moment, I couldn't think of a strong enough argument that Rylan would listen to.

For the rest of the day, I didn't see Jasmine or Arthur. While Rylan had been sure they were going to be alright, I wasn't happy not being able to check on them myself. When I had gone looking for them, they were nowhere to be found.

Rylan had started making the necessary travel arrangements. I left him to it. If I stuck around, we would just fight. Everything in me screamed that leaving was a bad idea. We needed to stay to figure this out *together*. But how could I convince Rylan of that? If we left Jasmine and Arthur behind, they could kill each other. Then we would be no closer to having any answers, and we would have two dead friends. There had to be another way.

It was dark outside by the time I wandered out onto one of the three back decks. I had tried to come up with some sort of plan to stop Rylan, but I came up empty-handed. Feeling discouraged about the entire trip, I leaned against the railing and stared out at the woods.

"Good evening, Mae."

I jumped at Arthur's voice. I turned to find him sitting on a yoga mat in the shadows. He was dressed simply in a tee-shirt and sweatpants. It was the most casual I had ever seen him.

"I did not mean to startle you," he said with a chuckle.

I sighed as my heartbeat slowed down. "It's alright, I was lost in my thoughts and didn't realize anyone else was out here. Do you want me to leave you alone?"

"No, please stay. I would appreciate the company."

I recalled the last time Arthur and I had been alone together and internally winced. Rylan had thrown Arthur through a wall due to the wild possessiveness and self-preservation streak in a Guardian who had not Joined with their mate. I wondered how Rylan would react now and if I should still leave before something could happen.

As the thought crossed my mind, I dismissed the idea. If Rylan wanted to leave tomorrow, then this would be my last night with Arthur for a while.

"What are you doing out here?" I asked curiously as I walked over to him.

"I was attempting to meditate," Arthur said with a sigh, "but my mind will not stop racing."

"Oh, does it usually work for you? I tried once, and I just fell asleep."

Arthur chuckled. "Yes, usually it does help, but that was before I met you."

"What?"

"It was easier to still my wayward thoughts when I did not have emotions to stir up new ones and agitate the old ones," Arthur explained. "But working through this new phenomenon is beneficial for my mind."

"Hopefully you can find a way to work through it by tomorrow since Rylan said we have to leave," I said grimly.

Arthur sighed. "It is for the best that you are not here, Mae. What happened today... What *I* did today. It was shameful to behave in such a manner. I am a disciplined warrior and to be that out of control was... It was not honorable. If you had been there, you could have been hurt."

"What happened?"

I sat down a few feet in front of him and crossed my legs. I watched Arthur's mouth turn downwards. He reached up and grabbed his goatee thoughtfully before he answered, "I do not understand it. One moment we were searching the grounds of the pack's old den and the next all I could think about was how dangerous Rylan and Jasmine were to me. I had to remove the threat to myself at all costs."

I shivered at the thought of Arthur coming after me to kill me. Pushing away the thought, I asked, "Did you find anything before that?"

"No," The disappointment that colored his voice was not about the lack of finding anything. I knew it was directed at himself and what he had done.

"I wonder why Rylan wasn't affected but you two were?"

Arthur shrugged but said nothing. He looked up at the night sky.

"It affected me, too," I told him, hoping he would forgive himself. Arthur turned his attention back to me. His expression told me he wasn't surprised. Rylan must have said something to him. "I felt it coming, but I didn't know what *it* was. Then I blacked out, just like when Jasmine had tried to do her examination on me. I woke up surrounded by disaster. Maybe it's a good thing I'm leaving. I could hurt you."

Arthur's eyebrows rose, and he played with his goatee. He said nothing, and the silence stretched between us. I leaned back on my hands and looked up.

"I wonder if you were affected by whatever negative energy was sent out over the park, or if your body reacted defensively the same way it did with Jasmine? What if your body was not allowing the energy to affect you, and its response was to reject it from your system?" Arthur said after a long silence.

I looked at him curiously. "I don't follow."

"When Jasmine tripped the internal switch inside you that caused your power to react, it threw us backward, and we were warned that only the worthy could wield the weapon, or rather, you. You blacked out for that. Whatever affected Jasmine and me, it got into our minds and manipulated us. That same energy tried to enter you, so it is possible that your body was trying to reject it."

Arthur frowned and looked away again. We fell into a companionable silence while we got lost in our thoughts.

"Arthur," I said when my thoughts became too dark to further dive into. I looked at my friend and asked, "Can you teach me how to meditate?"

Arthur smiled.

"Of course, but if you fall asleep, I will leave you out here for the mosquitoes."

I laughed softly and promised not to sleep through his lesson.

"Alright then. Sit straight up, and close your eyes."

I did as I was told.

"Now focus on your breathing. Think about how your chest and lungs expand and contract with every deep breath you take in. Good. Now, I want you to imagine you are in a dark room with no sounds and no smells. Picture that dark room and focus on it. You are there in that room simply to find solace. Keep taking deep breaths and slowly let them out as you focus on being in the moment in that dark room. Now, that dark room is your mind. Not a thought can enter that room. Here you will find solace, the inner workings that make you Mae. Remember to keep breathing…"

Initially, I thought nothing would come from this, but I had needed a distraction. But as I followed his instructions, I found myself sinking into darkness. Everything seemed to slowly fall away as I focused on that dark room that was my mind. Arthur's voice faded away and time meant nothing.

Here in this dark room, there was nothing to worry about. There was no fear of the impending doom that Zyroe and Autumn had threatened. There was no pain in my life, and the life I was going to live would not be cut short. I wasn't an orphan or a college school dropout. My power was an extension of me, not this abstract weapon I had to learn to wield. In this dark room, I was no longer the monster I had named myself. I was just me.

"Mae."

The sound of my name pulled me from the darkness. I blinked my eyes open and found Arthur staring at me wide-eyed. Behind him stood Rylan and far behind him, I could make out Jasmine's shadow leaning against the house. Everyone was watching me.

"What? Did I fall asleep?" I frowned. "I thought I was doing it."

I felt strange. Last night, after Joining with Rylan, my whole world seemed to make sense. This morning I had woken up feeling buoyant and loved. Right now, it was like the final piece of the puzzle had clicked into place.

"You were meditating," Arthur was quick to assure me. He tilted his head to the side as if to see me from another angle. "It is what happened next…"

"What do you mean? What happened?"

"You were lighting up like a sparkler," Rylan answered as he came over to me. He crouched down in front of me with a frown. "Are you alright?"

"Like a sparkler?" I repeated, confused. "I didn't feel my power reacting at all."

"You were pretty deep into your meditation," Rylan answered. He gave me his hand, and I took it. Rylan lifted me to my feet as he rose from his crouch and said, "You have been out here for hours."

"Hours?" I stared at him stunned then looked at Arthur for confirmation. Arthur nodded, his eyes still wide. "Geez… Sorry, I didn't notice time flying. Thanks for not leaving me out here, Arthur."

Arthur laughed as he rose from his mat. He clamped a hand down on my shoulder. "Any longer and I would have."

I gave him a rueful smile as Rylan led me inside.

# Chapter Eight



Mae insisted on fighting me at every turn. While I understood her reluctance to leave the others, her safety was more important to me than anything else. I attempted to reassure her that once she was out of here, Jasmine and Arthur could call others in for back up. But Mae was quick to remind me that the others could be affected by whatever had triggered the mania the day before. When I told her that *I* would come back once I knew she was somewhere safe that sent her into a whole new rage. If her power had been as reactive to her emotions as they had been before her trip to the Pocket, the house would have crumbled under her fury.

In her attempt to protect everyone she suggested to Arthur and Jasmine that they should come with us.

"We have an idea of what we're dealing with now," she had started, speaking quickly. I could feel her fear for them through our bond. "How about we all leave and make a plan on how to tackle the issues here. Then once we have a real plan we can come back with reinforcements…"

Immediately both Arthur and Jasmine had objected. The three of us Guardians had promised to handle this for Patricia and her pack. All of us leaving was not an option. Mae had become even more upset after that. Her frustrated tears were unshed as she stormed away from us.

She refused to eat breakfast and refused to pack. Her power was glowing bright this morning under her skin. Through our new connection I could feel her discomfort, teetering on the verge of pain. But she refused to go outside and expel any of it. I tried being reasonable, and I tried being firm, but when she would not budge from the couch in the family room after I had finished rounding up our stuff, I was fed up.

At any moment, whatever energy influenced the behavior of others could happen, and she would be in jeopardy. I could not allow anything to happen to her. I had to get her out of here. But when I demanded that she get up Mae simply crossed her arms over her chest, raised an eyebrow, and clenched her jaw in a show of defiance. I almost stormed over to her and threw her over my shoulder. The idea was certainly appealing. But the last time I had done that she had been royally angry and I did not want to fight any more than we already were. This should be our honeymoon stage. We should be tangled up in each other's limbs, tasting each other's skin and drowning in ecstasy. I stomped down the idea and decided to shift tactics. If demanding her compliance was not going to work I knew what would.

"Mae, the longer we stay the more likely we will run into problems. If the three of you lose it while we are here on this property you could end up unintentionally killing them. Or what happens if they end up hurting you? Can you imagine how they would feel if they did anything to harm you?" I asked her as she sat, unmoving on the couch.

Immediately the anger and fear that I felt through our bond shifted to guilt. It was a low blow, but I had not lied. They would feel just as terrible about hurting her as she would feel about hurting them. Her stiff shoulders sagged, and she looked down into her lap.

"We will figure out how to help Arthur and Jasmine from a distance," I told her gently. "We will not leave them to the wolves."

Mae scoffed at my poor attempt at a joke to lighten the mood.

"Alright… let's go," she conceded with a deep frown. I helped her off the couch and we headed towards the front door.

*Stay safe*, I said to both Guardians as we walked outside. *The moment Mae is safe I will be back.*

Both Guardians had disappeared after saying their goodbyes in the hopes that it would help sway Mae to leave. Guilt caused a knot to form in my stomach. I had tried to sleep last night to no avail. While I knew it was best for Mae to be as far away from here as possible, I was putting the other two in danger.

Her anxiousness and worry grew as we walked towards the SUV. It was so strong it no longer felt like an echo. I could sense the connection between our minds strengthening. I would not be surprised if I would be able to hear her thoughts within a few hours. I cringed as I thought about what she was thinking of me now. While I was eager to know the inner workings of my mate, I could probably wait until she cooled down to peek into her mind.

I opened the passenger door for her to get in but Mae paused. She looked up at the house, her eyes searching the windows for something… or someone. Was she watching for Arthur and Jasmine? As she stared up at the house I was sure her mind was frantically racing for ways to save the others. My stomach twisted in guilt again.

"We will figure out something," I told her again.

She pulled her gaze away from the house and turned to look at me. She lifted her hand to place it on my chest. But just before her hand made contact I was suddenly knocked off my feet and thrown backward. Years of training kicked in. I twisted in the air and landed in a crouch, twenty yards away from the SUV and Mae.

Mae's eyes were wide with surprise. We stared at one another, stunned by what was clearly an accident. A curious expression crossed her face, and she turned from me to face the SUV. For a moment, I was sure she was going to climb in. Instead, she raised her hands, and a violet wave of energy flew from her palms. I stared, shocked, as the SUV was thrown across the front yard and slammed into a tree, totaling it. Mae turned slowly towards me; her mouth hung open in surprise.

"Did you see that?"

Her whispered question was rhetorical. Of course, I had seen her fling a vehicle a hundred yards away. The grin that spread across her face was full of satisfaction and excitement.

"I did that *on purpose*. I controlled it! *I did it*!" Her squeal of delight was paired with a spin of elation as she turned to study her handiwork.

My shock was overshadowed by my pride. Her excitement and joy fizzled through my body and I grinned with her. After two years of being unable to control that chaos within her, the simple act of throwing the SUV was monumental for her. Hopefully this meant that with a little time and patience she would have that control she so clearly wanted. As she did another spin with excitement I began to walk towards her.

I was an arm's length away from Mae when I sensed the intruder. How was that possible? No one could cross through a Guardian's territory without a Guardian knowing. My eyes swept the woods, my senses expanding outwards looking for the danger. The hair on the back of my neck rose as I felt eyes watching me.

"Mae, go into the house."

"Really? Are we stay—," Her question was cut off by a loud, distorted howl just beyond the tree line nearby. Another howl answered the first on the other side of the house. The call was wheezy. It was not the howl of shifters. Mae's soft gasp of alarm caused my body to tense up tighter.

"Get in the house, Mae, *now*!" I ordered without looking at her.

A snap of a twig was the only warning I had. The thick, hairy, muscular body of a werewolf leapt towards us with a speed unmatched by most creatures. Mae's scream faded to the background of my mind as I threw myself at the abomination. I slammed into the werewolf's chest, throwing it backwards where it skidded across the ground. The creature jumped back onto its feet and snarled. Saliva dripped from its mouth. Its hairy body trembled with rage. My wings ripped my shirt to shreds. Freed from the confines of the material, I reached down to pull my sword from the mark on my abdomen.

The werewolf took a step forward while it bared its rotting teeth at me. I didn't wait for the next attack. I lunged for the creature, sweeping my blade low, knowing what it would instinctively do next. The werewolf jumped back but immediately shot forward. I twisted my blade in my hand, and with a grace that came from centuries of practice, I effectively skewered it. Its claws raked across my torso. Pain flared through my chest, but I pushed it down as I shoved the creature away with my free hand. The werewolf stumbled several feet away from me as the wound I had inflicted bled profusely.

Another snarl from behind me warned me of our second trespasser. I knew, without looking, Mae was still outside with me despite my command. Anger and fear collided. Werewolves, while bulky monstrosities, had a speed that most underestimated. The fact that they could clear the distance of a football field in a single bound was enough to strike fear into even the bravest warriors.

The sound of multiple bolts of lightning exploding up from the ground was enough to pull my attention off the wounded werewolf in search of Mae. She was right where I had left her, except now her legs were spread apart and her hands were curled into fists. Her brows were drawn together, and her concentration was focused on something in front of her. Around her were blackened spots where her power had erupted. I followed her gaze to find a werewolf watching her from the woods by the side of the house.

A third howl alerted me to another member of this unusual pack. The sound was cut off abruptly. The werewolf watching Mae turned its attention towards the third party, and I moved. I flew across the space between us. I wrapped my arm around her waist, twirled her around, and put her behind me as the wounded werewolf I had left behind staggered to its feet. Dark, black blood dripped from its chest. Its breathing came out as rough pants. It snarled and took a step towards us. The second werewolf in the woods cautiously stepped from the tree line, baring its teeth in an evil grin.

I took a step back, which forced Mae to retreat so she was flat against the house. The second werewolf lunged at us. I brought my sword up and braced myself. Before it crossed half the distance between us, it was hit from the side and thrown off course. Jasmine landed in front of us, her sica drawn and bloody. The werewolf I had wounded stumbled towards me, and I lunged at it, knowing Jasmine would keep the second one at bay. My sword sliced through its flesh and cut through bone. I ignored the shriek of rage as I pulled my sword out of its pelvis, ducked as its large claws swiped out to wound me, and slammed my blade straight into its chest where the heart was located.

The moment my blade cut through the organ, the werewolf stopped moving. Its yellow eyes grew large before the life snuffed out of them. I pulled the blade from its chest and kicked the beast backward. It stumbled and collapsed. The body began to contort. I turned quickly and headed back to Mae, whose eyes were pinned to the creature spasming on the ground. I grabbed her by the arm and pulled her to the front door.

"Do not watch," I commanded.

"What's happening to it?" Her horrified whisper tugged at my heart.

Instead of answering her, I opened the front door and shoved her inside. I shut the door behind her and turned to Jasmine, but found she and the werewolf had disappeared into the woods. The mutilated body that had reverted to its human form lay naked and lifeless. As I walked over to it, Arthur landed next to me.

"How did they get past our markers without us knowing?" he asked me as he pulled a lighter from his pocket. He lit it and tossed it on to the body. Instantly, the lifeless human turned to ash. Jasmine stepped out from the woods, her face grim.

"The creature escaped. He vanished right from under my nose." Her grim expression turned confused. "I have no idea how that is possible."

"A werewolf ran *and* disappeared," Arthur muttered to himself in disbelief. "That is not in their nature."

"They were working together…" Jasmine said with a shake of her head. "Werewolves do not run in packs. This is too unusual to be ignored."

"The most concerning part," I looked at them both, "is that they were able to sneak up on us without detection. *That* should be impossible."

Jasmine sighed. "How did Patricia track these werewolves? They hardly have any scent to follow."

"Speaking of Patricia—," Arthur started but the front door burst open. Mae ran out, eyes wide. Her whole body was glowing, and her panic became mine as it swirled in my gut.

I was halfway to her when she screamed, "Run!"

Suddenly her whole body stiffened, and she came to an abrupt stop. I watched her face go blank. Fear quickened my pace as I closed the distance between us. I grabbed her wrist and yanked her away from the house knowing what was about to happen. I had seen her like this only once before, but once was enough to know things were about to get ugly. I pulled her into my chest, ready to scoop her up and take her into the air to put distance between her and the house. Before I could get airborne, Arthur slammed into me, knocking Mae out of my arms.

An animalistic snarl bellowed up through my chest and out of my mouth as rage consumed me and I got to my feet. I slammed my fist into Arthur's face. As his head whipped to the side, I saw the wild, unbridled insanity shining in his red eyes. It was the same look he and Jasmine had shared when they had attacked each other the day before. I punched him again before I jumped back to give myself some space from Arthur. I put myself between Mae, who lay unmoving on the ground, and the others.

Jasmine attempted to fly past us, towards Mae. With my lightning fast reflexes, I grabbed the female warrior by the arm, ripped her out of the air and threw her across the front yard. She landed in a crouch before leaping back into the sky. In front of me, Arthur pulled his flail from the tattoo on his shoulder blade. As he brought his weapon up to strike me, I slammed my fist into his gut and then elbowed him in the jaw. He swung his flail, and I had to step out of the way to avoid being hit, which left Mae unprotected. A flash of movement overhead caught my attention. Jasmine was now speeding down towards Mae, her sica in her hand.

Abruptly, the world around us became blanketed in a violet hue. The ground beneath Arthur's feet exploded and a thick rope of violet lightning struck him. I watched in awe as Mae's power snaked through him. His body twitched and spasmed; his eyes bulged from their sockets. The veins under his skin began to protrude. Another bolt of lightning flashed up from the ground just inches from me, striking Jasmine in her descent.

Jasmine tumbled from the sky and hit the ground hard, her body writhing in pain. Under the three of us, dirt and stones began to levitate, the ground trembled, and the trees closest to us began to catch on fire. I spun to find Mae standing there staring in our direction with unseeing eyes. Her arms were outstretched before her, directed at the two Guardians who had attacked us.

I yanked at the power that consumed her. Her power rushed into my body with a staggering force and caused me to stumble backward. The roaring of it in my mind was deafening. It blazed a trail through my body, the burn just barely tolerable. Gritting my teeth, I found my balance and concentrated on pulling enough power from Mae to break her from this trance. The ground stilled, and the violet flames went out. Mae's head turned towards me. For a moment, I wondered if she would attack me. I braced myself.

Instead, her posture relaxed, and her arms dropped to her sides. The violet hue that surrounded us disappeared. Both Arthur and Jasmine stopped thrashing. Mae's eyes rolled into the back of her head, and her legs gave out from beneath her. I was there to catch her before her head hit the ground. At once, I noticed the blue around her lips and the coldness of her skin. Luckily, the moment I cradled her to my chest, her body responded by pulling the energy I had collected back into her.

"Is Mae alright?" Arthur's appearance at my side caused me to tense.

I snarled as I stood up with Mae in my arms. I turned to face Arthur. The horror and worry on his face assured me that he had snapped out of his sudden bout of violence. I paused as I noticed that his eyes were speckled with violet flecks.

"She will be," I snapped. "Now do you understand why I needed Mae to leave?"

Arthur reached out to touch Mae's dangling hand, "Rylan, I—,".

"I swear that I will rip out your heart and let the vultures feast upon it if you touch Mae," I warned. I was too far gone to allow anyone near Mae right now. "Now step away."

Arthur stepped back with his hands raised in surrender. Guilt and shame colored his features. The logical part of me understood that what had happened was not his fault. But right now I was in no mood to console the Guardian. I glanced at Jasmine who was struggling to get to her feet. Confident that she was no longer a threat, I walked over to the front door and pushed it open.

Briefly I wondered how they'd survived Mae's attack. So far Mae's lightning had destroyed everything in its wake. Not a tree, rock, bush, or creature had made it. Not that I would tell Mae that she had killed a few birds and squirrels.

I carried Mae across the foyer towards the stairs. My fear over what had just occurred within the span of fifteen minutes turned to anger. Mae could have been killed by one of the werewolves. An image of a werewolf clamping down its large jaws onto Mae's neck sent chills down my spine and caused my heart to flutter painfully in my chest. Then she had rushed outside to warn us of the danger only to put herself in harm's way again. How could she not see the risk here? All I wanted was to keep her safe. She was my world, and I needed to protect her.

I took her to our room and placed her on the bed. Despite reabsorbing her magic, she still looked pale and her skin was cool to the touch. In the silence of our bedroom, I could hear the sound of her irregular heartbeat. Why had it not returned to normal? I grabbed her hand and held it, hoping her body would take the energy it needed.

Nothing happened this time.

I pushed away the worry. She would be alright. I pulled the covers over her body to keep her warm. For now, rest would be the best thing for her. Once she awoke, hopefully her body would have righted itself. Forcing myself to leave her side, I quickly showered and changed into clean clothes. After checking on her again, I left the house to grab our belongings from the totaled SUV and brought them back upstairs. I would have to reschedule all of the travel arrangements.

Once everything was inside, I grabbed my laptop and lay down in the bed next to Mae. She had not moved. I tucked the comforter closer to her body and watched as her chest rose and fell slowly. Back in Georgia, she'd snapped out of her trance state. She hadn't fallen unconscious like this. Anger surged through me. This would not have happened if we had left when we were supposed to. But she had fought me on leaving. Then she had the audacity to try to fight off one of the werewolves instead of running inside as I commanded her to do. She had put herself in danger without thinking of the consequences. I shuddered violently as I thought about all the different ways a werewolf could hurt her. If they had gotten their claws on her it would have ended her life. Just like that it would have been over and we would never have had our time together.

Had she been a soldier under my command or a servant in my employment she would have been severely punished. No, that was not right. She was my mate. Not someone in my employment. So how was I to deal with someone I cared about when they were not doing what they were told? I had never been in this type of predicament before, and it left me feeling off kilter.

Resolved to remain by her side while she recovered, I opened my laptop and began working on travel arrangements and business dealings. Occasionally, I found myself distracted. I would catch myself staring at my mate for long lengths of time. My knuckles would caress her cheeks, and sometimes I would find my fingers winding through hers.

***

*Rylan,* Jasmine's voice called to me.

I blinked before glancing down at Mae and frowned. It had been hours and still, she had not moved. Her heartbeat was just getting back to normal, and the color was rising in her cheeks, but there was no sign of her waking anytime soon.

I debated not answering. The Guardian was getting on my nerves. Jasmine had disappeared the other day once we had returned from our trip to the abandoned den. I was sure it was to avoid Mae so she could elude the shame that she would inevitably have to feel from the disgrace of attacking fellow Guardians. Coward. Further, Jasmine's brief and distant goodbye this morning had hurt Mae, although Mae would never admit it. Then, she went after my mate. As much as I wished to ignore her, I knew she would not interrupt me if it were not important.

*What is it?*

*Patricia's pack called a little while ago. Patricia did not return home yesterday. Arthur went to investigate. While he has been gone, I have been studying some of the plants that we collected yesterday and have found something.*

*It will have to wait.*

*Mae is not awake yet?* The concern in Jasmine's voice did nothing to ease my anxiety. When I did not answer Jasmine continued. *I suppose I should not be surprised. She used a great deal of energy. While she rests, I need to show you my findings.*

Instead of answering I turned my attention back to my laptop. I signed the document one of my lawyers had sent over and sent an email out to the real estate agent I had used before to begin searching for a house similar to this in Georgia or in the Carolinas. My territory swept all the way down to Florida but I found the stifling heat, random rainfall, and humidity too miserable to consider actually living there. If the agent could not find anything to my liking I would simply build one for Mae. I smiled as I pictured her face when she saw the house of her dreams in front of her. I was sure it would be similar to her expression when we had pulled up to this house.

I glanced down at Mae. Despite my worry for her health and anger at her disobedience, my heart swelled. My gaze trailed over her beautiful face then across the room to my jacket. Once we went back to Salisbury, we would figure out the rest of our lives. Maybe in the near future I would be able to walk her down the aisle. I smiled as I pictured her walking towards me in a white dress. My heart rate accelerated. My smile expanded into a grin as I thought about how exciting it would be to hear Mae, my last and most important bride, speaking her vows out loud for all to hear. While the Joining was permanent and sealed our lives together, I wanted to seal our fates together in even the most basic human way to show the world Mae was mine.

My happiness faded as I thought about what had transpired today. Anger resurfaced and my grin disappeared. A happy future with a wife, a house, and maybe even kids… all those dreams meant nothing if Mae took herself out of my world because she was too stubborn to listen to directions.

I slammed my laptop closed as fear began to creep through my veins. A world without Mae would be meaningless. My heart clenched painfully in my chest as I leaned over to check Mae's pulse. I could hear it but I needed to *feel* it. I pushed down the panic at the thought of Mae ever dying. If I could just get her to listen to me… but how? I slid out of bed and forced myself to leave her side to see what Jasmine had found.

I found Jasmine in the makeshift study on the first floor. She had her back to me as she stared down into a microscope. Although she did not look up when I entered, I knew she was aware of my arrival. I shut the door but did not venture further into the room.

With a sigh, Jasmine straightened and turned to face me. I noted at once that her eyes were neither brown nor red; they were violet. Strange. The contrite expression on her face did nothing to lessen my anger towards the female warrior. Jasmine and Arthur had gone after my mate. It was forbidden, and Guardian law ensured that I had every right to eliminate them both. Thankfully, I had the sanity to remind myself that Jasmine and Arthur were both here to help Mae, and what had happened had occurred due to outside forces.

"Rylan, I know nothing I can say will change how you feel, but please know I am truly sorry," Jasmine said, her voice soft. She bowed her head submissively. When our gazes met again, she continued, "I will apologize to Mae as well once she awakens. Until then, let me go over my findings with you."

I stalked over to her side of the room. The blood in my mouth from fighting my canines only fueled my anger towards the female Guardian. This better be quick. I was not sure how long I could control my fury. When I stopped next to her, Jasmine turned towards her work. She used tweezers to push a small slide under the microscope.

"During our exploration yesterday, I gathered some wormwood, white sagebrush, and musk thistle," she started. "They are the most common type of plant life in the area. I also took samples from a few oaks, pines, and some grass samples. I wanted to see if I could find any evidence of Patricia's claims that nature is changing around here."

"I am assuming you did, or you would not have called me down here." My patience was worn so thin that my fingers twitched to strangle her. I was sure the small movement did not go amiss.

"At first, no," Jasmine admitted. She motioned for me to look at her sample under the glass. "Tell me what you see."

Begrudgingly, I looked through the microscope and studied the green cell structure. I looked up.

"There is nothing unusual about this."

Jasmine nodded and used tweezers to remove the slide from under the microscope. She replaced it with another.

"This is from the same exact leaf. Tell me what you see now."

I glanced down into the microscope. I had to do a double-take to make sure that what I was seeing was true. The cells in the leaf had mutated and were coated by a thin layer of what look to be infinitesimal pieces of dark dust particles.

"I double-checked every sample from yesterday and compared them to today's samples. They are all like that," Jasmine said softly. I looked up at her, and she gave me a pointed look. "The first sample you looked at was from last night. I created another one this morning to run another test on it. I created a third about two hours ago and the third sample is what you looked at the second time."

"What is happening to the cell?" I asked as I took another look at the sample.

"That is what happens when dark magic lingers on anything living for too long. The dark magic is mutating the cell. It will eventually kill the plant or change its properties."

I straightened up and looked at her.

She nodded as if I had asked for confirmation and continued, "The dark magic is still on the first two samples. We just do not see it nor, it appears, can we sense it."

"Impossible." If dark magic lingered in these woods, we would know.

Jasmine shrugged and said, "Maybe once it was, but that is not the case now."

"Impossible," I repeated. "How do we not sense it? What did you do to this last sample for you to be able to detect dark magic?"

Jasmine rubbed her eyes before she answered, "I do not know why we cannot sense it. Maybe someone altered the magic so it has become undetectable. If someone could do that, then they would have to be quite powerful and know what they are doing. Dark magic is not stable and quite dangerous to handle."

"It should be impossible to hide magic from us, especially magic as twisted as this."

Again, Jasmine shrugged.

"It is just a theory." She leaned up against the table and crossed her arms over her chest. "As to how I figured out that dark magic is all around us... you can thank Mae for that."

Just the sound of my mate's name on her lips caused my anger to flare up. I clenched my jaw to keep from snapping at the Guardian. When I knew I could speak without anger, I took a deep breath and pressed, "Explain."

"Her power still lingered in my body when I set up the last slide. I felt it reaching out and doing *something*. At the time, though, I did not know what." Jasmine gave me a half-smile. "Then, when I placed the slide under the microscope, I saw Mae's power not only revealing the dark magic but fighting it. Her power eventually stopped it from spreading and neutralized it."

Jasmine straightened, her eyes changing from violet to red as she stared at me. "I think this depravity that triggers violence is a form of dark magic that is floating around in the air. It's an attack on every creature within these woods. That dark magic has been triggering Mae's defense system. Her power attacks the force trying to enter her body as it did to me back in Georgia. Similarly, her power reacted by attacking and neutralizing the dark magic in the sample I showed you."

Jasmine took a step forward, her eyes bright with excitement.

"Rylan, Mae struck both me and Arthur because her power was reacting to the dark magic within *us*. She was unknowingly fighting *for* us not against us. I snapped out of it almost instantly when she struck me. Her power is humming within me now. It is in my mind like a protective barrier. I am sure that whenever this dark magic makes its way through these woods tomorrow, it will not affect myself or Arthur."

"There is no way to prove that theory without someone getting hurt. And that does not explain why I am not affected." The excitement in Jasmine's eyes worried me.

"Do you not see it? Her power hums under your skin. As your mate, you take part of her within you every time you feed, and you are a conduit for her power. Mae's power will always linger within you, and it will keep you safe. And there is a way to prove all of this." Jasmine smirked. "Mae can sense when this wave of dark magic is coming. She can alert us and Arthur and I will wait to be—"

"And put Mae in danger? This is all at Mae's expense," I told her contemptuously. "She has collapsed both times, Jasmine. I am scared she will kill herself if she goes through that again. Twice now, her body has pulled what it has needed to survive from me after both instances. I cannot and will not allow her to continue to be in a position where her life is in jeopardy. I do not want her anywhere near this place. Tomorrow we are leaving."

"Rylan, Zyroe and Autumn said that Mae needed to be here to stop the gates from opening. If Mae's power can sense the dark magic, we can use her to either track the source of it or at the very least protect any innocent lives here while we continue to investigate. With dark magic clinging to everything around us, werewolves that disappear, and a force that triggers madness... something is amiss here, and Mae might be able to help us figure it out."

"No," I snapped, taking a step towards Jasmine. I towered over the other warrior. "She will not be involved with the scheming of a god and his whore witch. Now that we know there is something to address, Mae can stay out of it and let other Guardians take over."

The fact the Jasmine was so inclined to allow Mae to stay in such a dangerous situation when she had vowed to keep her safe only days before made it even harder for me to not murder the Guardian. Jasmine sighed in frustration.

"What if Ekon's and Cain's disappearance has something to do with the dark magic here? We have to find them. Guardians do not just up and disappear. Mae could be a key in finding them. They must have found out what was going on here and that got them into trouble. What if Zein—,"

"What if Zein found out about the trouble happening here, too? Is that what you are about to say?" I interrupted. "If that is the case, and *three* Guardians have been eliminated due to the suspicious activity here, then Mae most certainly does not belong here. Thank you for proving my point."

Jasmine gave me a look of exasperation.

Before she could continue to fight me on this, I said, "Look, Jasmine. I know it is not ideal to leave you and Arthur here, but once I have Mae somewhere out of harm's way, I will come back and help. I am not shunning my duties. I am making sure that my mate is safe before I dive head first into danger. I cannot risk anything happening to her. I just found her, Jasmine."

"But—"

*Rylan.*

I jerked in surprise at the sound of Mae's voice in my head. Whatever Jasmine's rebuttal had been was long forgotten as my heart soared. My mate was reaching out to me, needed me, and she was using our own private channel of communication for the first time. Without another word to Jasmine, I left the room and went to Mae. I felt her confusion and fear.

*I am here, and I am coming to you.*

I felt her shock at my response. I could not stop the smile that tugged at my lips. Her mind had unconsciously reached out to mine the moment she awoke. With our bond solidified through our Joining, our souls would always reach out for each other when we were apart.

It took me mere seconds to make it upstairs and walk down the hall to our bedroom. I threw the door open and strolled in. Mae was sitting up on the side of her bed. As I stepped further into the room, I noted the way her shoulders sagged. Her head was hung low, and her hands, which were gripping the comforter, were white-knuckled. Mae lifted her head slowly and looked up at me. My steps faltered as I stared into my mate's tear-stained face. The dread and angst etched into her face caused my heart to skip a beat.

Worried, I crouched down in front of her. "Mae, what is it? Tell me." The pain and despair on her face were unbearable.

"Did I kill them? Did I kill Arthur and Jasmine?"

# CHAPTER NINE



*MAE*

Two weeks ago, if someone had told me I would turn down breakfast despite being fully able to keep it down, I would have laughed at them. But the next morning there I was, skipping out on breakfast to meditate on the back porch. Waking up thinking I had killed two people seemed to squash any hunger I would have normally felt.

I squeezed my eyes shut and tried to focus on my breathing. I attempted to picture that dark room I had created for myself. I didn't want to feel or think about anything. If I allowed myself a moment to do either, I'd drown in fear and heartbreak. The first time I had almost killed someone was within the first week of finding out I had power. The poor guy had just tapped me on my shoulder one night at a gas station to tell me a headlight was out before I caused the gas pump to explode. I had to wait a week to see in the newspaper that the man survived.

The guilt had been immeasurable.

At least this time, I had been able to wrap my arms around Jasmine's waist and apologize profusely. Her soft laughter at my tears did not quell my guilt. Then, against Rylan's advice, I stayed up all night waiting for Arthur to return. When he got back just before dawn, I had thrown myself into his arms and bawled all over again.

Rylan had not been able to talk me into going to sleep after that. I knew I would see both Guardians thrashing about in agony in my dreams. There was no need to replay the moment in my nightmares when I saw it so clearly while I was awake. Instead, I silently made sure all my belongings that Rylan had brought in from the car were neatly folded and reorganized in my suitcase. This time I was ready to leave.

I expected Rylan's wrath. If I had just gone with him yesterday, we wouldn't have been attacked by werewolves, and I wouldn't have attacked my friends. But instead of yelling, Rylan had remained silent. His emotions that echoed through me were so jumbled that I couldn't pin down exactly what he was feeling.

What was wrong with me? I had been so sure that staying here was the best course of action. It didn't help that the thought of leaving Arthur or Jasmine behind in a dangerous situation had felt so wrong. Turns out, I was the danger all along.

I groaned out loud and covered my face with my hands. Exhaustion was weighing heavy on me. If I stopped concentrating on meditation, I was sure I was going to pass out here on the deck. Behind me, I heard the patio door slide open. Without looking, I knew it was Rylan.

A new wave of guilt crashed over me. Yesterday, I had somehow maintained a semblance of consciousness while my body acted of its own accord. I could remember attacking Jasmine and Arthur. I remembered the moment when my body turned to face Rylan. I hadn't known what was going to happen, but I knew I had to stop myself. I had fought with every molecule in my body until finally, I was able to regain control before blacking out. What if I had killed him? The thought was so awful I visibly shook with pain.

Rylan came to stand in front of me and then crouched down so we were eye level. I couldn't stare into those handsome teal eyes, so I averted my gaze. I wanted to go home, wherever that was, and just curl up in a dark room and pretend I hadn't hurt the people I loved.

*Look at me*, he commanded.

The strangeness of his voice floating through my head had been overshadowed by the shame I felt. But that didn't make it any less weird. This way of communication was fiercely intimate. His words seemed to wrap themselves around my heart. Reluctantly, I did as he asked and met his steady gaze.

*Come, I have made you something to eat,* he said softly.

The thought of eating made my stomach clench tightly, but I didn't want to fight with him. I took the hand he offered me, and I rose to my feet. I followed him inside and into the kitchen. At the counter was a plate with a breakfast sandwich placed neatly in the middle of it. He had even thought to pour me a glass of orange juice. The thoughtfulness of such a light breakfast only added to how horrible I felt. I didn't deserve this.

*Thank you.*

My attempt to contact Rylan with my mind was shaky. I wasn't sure if I was really reaching out to him or if I was just talking to myself.

*You never have to thank me for taking care of you.*

I sat down, and to my surprise, my stomach growled. Rylan came over and sat down next to me. I wondered if he knew how regal he looked as he took his seat. Our eyes met, and I felt the beginnings of desire pool between my legs. Inwardly, I groaned. How could I possibly be thinking of sex right now?

Pushing the unwanted feeling away, I picked up my breakfast sandwich and ate it. When was the last time I had eaten? After I had woken in a panic the previous afternoon, having lunch and then dinner sounded like the furthest thing I wanted to do. Yesterday morning, I had been so adamant about not leaving that I had skipped breakfast. Had it been over twenty-four hours? Good grief, no wonder my stomach was enjoying every bite. When I finished, I pushed the plate away from me with a sigh.

Rylan reached out to touch a curl that had worked its way loose from my bun and twirled it around his finger.

*Yesterday, you defied me*, his voice was a whisper in my mind. *Over and over you continued to defy me. Long ago when wars were raged, I used to command armies. If a soldier ever defied me, they were disciplined in front of the others. Were you disciplined growing up?* The oh, so calm tone made me shiver. I turned to look at him. His attention was fixed on the lock of hair he was playing with.

*I thought you didn't get involved with human wars?*

*Who said anything about humans?* Rylan stopped playing with my curl to look me in the eyes. *Were you ever disciplined?*

*I was grounded a few times*, I said thoughtfully.

Rylan's chuckle did not hold any amusement. *What were you grounded for?*

*Sneaking out of the house.* I could still see my parents waiting for me as I snuck back into my bedroom through the window. Oh, I had been in so much trouble.

*And where would you go when you escaped?* Rylan asked, mildly interested. This time it was my turn to chuckle.

*Trust me you don't want to know*, I said, feeling a little relieved he couldn't read every thought running through my mind. *If you knew, you'd probably be more upset than you are now.*

*Upset?* He repeated thoughtfully. His tone confused me.

Before I could respond Rylan reached up and pulled my hair out of the bun. My mass of curls toppled past my shoulders and down my back. Rylan slowly snaked his hand through my hair. His fingers massaged my scalp, and I closed my eyes, enjoying the feeling. That little burn between my legs began to grow steadily warmer.

Suddenly he fisted my hair close to the roots and yanked my head back.

I cried out in surprise. I trusted Rylan not to hurt me but this had taken me off guard. I stared up into Rylan's face and found his eyes had sunken in and were now blazing red. His rage through our bond was intensified through his glare. I had to admit to myself that he had his scary moments. Rylan stood while his hand gripped my hair tight enough that I couldn't move.

"What the hell, Rylan?" I yelped, reaching up with my hands in an attempt to pull my hair free.

"*Upset* is not the word I would use to describe how I feel, Mae," Rylan snapped. "Or how I felt yesterday when you defied every single command I gave." He leaned close. His fangs lengthened and peeked through his lips. "When I say you are not safe, you will heed my every word until you are. If I tell you we are leaving, we are leaving. If I tell you to run, you run. When I tell you to stay in the damn house, you stay in this house! Not at any time did I tell you to attack the werewolf yesterday. When you defy me, you put us both at risk. When I am too concerned about you, I cannot properly eliminate a threat. You will listen to me when it comes to your safety, Mae. Do I make myself clear?"

I did not answer right away. I struggled in his grip, which only tightened the more I tried to fight it. He tugged on my hair just enough to force me to stand. Then, he pulled it again, forcing me to turn my whole body to face him. While I certainly couldn't get out of his grip he was being careful not to actually hurt me. I was outraged that he was touching me in this manner but shock and my already fragile emotional state made it hard to maintain it. It was also overshadowed by Rylan's anger. His rage was burning a hole through my chest. It was suffocating and frightening. He was truly upset about me not listening to him. I frowned. How could he think that I was defying him? I wasn't purposely disobeying his orders just to defy him. I could make my own decisions about my safety.

"I asked you a question: Did I make myself clear on what I expect?"

He tugged at my hair, forcing my head backward. Again, it wasn't painful, but certainly demanding. Rylan leaned forward, his fangs lengthening all the way. Just the sight of them suddenly distracted my outrage and shock, concern and confusion. Desire blossomed and suddenly a rush of blood rose to my cheeks, warming them. How could I feel this way so suddenly? Confusion swamped me. My emotions were all over the place. Why couldn't I settle with one and stick to it? I shuddered both from arousal and apprehension.

Slowly, Rylan bent down, keeping my gaze until he tilted his head forward to kiss my exposed throat. The heat between my legs flared hotter, and my breathing turned to soft gasps of desire. He pressed his lips just under my jaw and slowly trailed kisses downwards.

When he got to the base of my throat he paused. "Answer me, Mae."

His voice was just a growl, more animalistic than man.

God, I wanted those fangs buried in me just as much as I ached to feel his erection between my legs. I bit my bottom lip to keep from moaning.

*Bite me*, I begged him. The junction between my legs grew damp, and my nipples tightened, straining against the fabric of my shirt.

*Answer me*, he snarled. A low rumble in his chest caused my heart to flutter wildly. The tip of Rylan's tongue left a cool trail of saliva that made me shiver as he teased me.

*I'll listen to you next time*, I promised.

*Good girl.* The satisfied growl made me shudder. *If you disobey me, you will learn there are much harsher punishments besides being grounded.*

His fangs sank into my skin without warning and I cried out in shock. My arousal vanished as I quickly realized that this was far from the pleasurable bite that I was used to feeling. While this wasn't a painful bite, it was a reminder that Rylan was a predator. He was an alpha male in a world full of terrifying monsters that he oversaw. He was used to dominating others and right now, he was showing me he was in charge. I threw my hands up against his chest. I wasn't sure if it was to brace myself as my legs wobbled or to push him away. Before my hands made contact, Rylan pulled his fangs from my neck, sealed the wound, and stepped back.

"What the hell, Rylan?" I demanded, my voice breathless.

"Feeling off balance?" he asked coolly. "I am giving you a taste of what it feels like to me when you defy me. If you do not like it, listen to me in future." With that he turned and walked off before I could say anything else. I stared after him, stunned and overwhelmed.

I wrapped my arms around myself and fought back tears that threatened to fall. My emotions were all over the place. Fear and shame over almost killing my friends returned. They mixed with the feeling of being loved, frightened, and aroused.

Despite my best efforts to keep them at bay tears fell anyway. I hated all these wild feelings. I hated that I had no control over anything. Of course, I hadn't wanted to leave yesterday. Jasmine and Arthur would have been in danger from themselves. And I had stayed put when Rylan told me to run to see if I could help. I had tried to use my power to stop the werewolf he had been fighting, not to attack the one nearest me. I hadn't even noticed the second werewolf until I caught the movement out of the corner of my eye. I wasn't trying to piss him off; I just had other plans that conflicted with his.

"Mae," Jasmine's voice drifted through the wild haze of emotions. Add embarrassment to my ever-growing list of emotions I was feeling. I wiped the tears from my cheeks as I turned to face the Guardian. "How about we go for a walk to get some fresh air?" she suggested as she studied my face.

I shook my head slowly. "What if I attack you again, Jazz? I shouldn't—"

Jasmine gave me a knowing smile. "I have a feeling it will not happen again." Her brown eyes twinkled.

"I should tell Rylan that we're heading out." The moment I said it out loud, I bristled at the idea of asking for permission. I must not have hidden my expression very well because Jasmine's smile widened.

"Do not bother. We will stick close to the house," Jasmine said as she waved her hand dismissively. "He is still upset about yesterday and is being a bit… bullheaded."

I rolled my eyes at her understatement.

"Fine, let's go."

I followed Jasmine to the front door and slid on my shoes, and we walked out into the cool sunny day. We were silent as we strolled around the perimeter of the house. Jazz had been right; fresh air was exactly what I needed. I enjoyed the warmth from the sunlight that beat down on us. I slowly began to relax as the crisp air cleared my mind. As my mood improved, I began to think about things in a better light. Both Jasmine and Arthur were alright, and neither appeared upset with me. That eased my guilt and fear.

Finding that Rylan had gone out of his way to make sure I ate despite being mad at me made me smile. He really did love me. But what he had done afterwards… It was completely unacceptable. While my body had felt conflicted, now that my head was clear, my mind revolted against being bullied and utterly under his control while he dominated me. Up until that point, I had been convinced that Rylan would never hurt me. Now, I felt violated by the man I had trusted wholeheartedly. He had bullied me into submitting to him.

I could understand why he was angry. I knew he was making a point, but he could have done it another way. There was no way I was allowing him to do that again. Next time we had a moment alone, I was going to put things straight. There was no dominant one between the two of us. He had said it himself back in the house in Georgia: mates were equals. I would certainly remind him of that later.

After some time had passed, I found my attention being drawn to the lovely Guardian who walked silently beside me. At first, I thought she seemed utterly at ease and lost in her thoughts. Her graceful steps were unhurried. Her breathing appeared steady and controlled. But the more I stared at her, the more I noticed the way her eyes swept the area around us. Jasmine wasn't as deep in thought as I had first thought. She was very much aware of what was going on around us. Finally, I got tired of the silence.

"What are you looking for? Werewolves?"

Something caught Jasmine's attention, and she turned her head in the direction of the house. Her scoff made me frown. She looked down at me.

"Your mate just checked to make sure I had not kidnapped you."

"Go ahead." I told her with a roll of my eyes. "Both he and Arthur have already done it twice. You can kidnap me too, just to make it even."

Jasmine's laugh echoed in the woods around us.

"You do not need to tempt me, Mae. I am on the cusp of doing so as it is," she teased as she turned her body towards the woods. "And to answer your first question, I was searching for signs of dark magic."

Dark magic? I looked around us curiously.

"Wouldn't you have already known it was around the house if it was here?"

"Normally, yes, but something has come to light recently that makes me believe that may no longer be the case."

"What are you talking about?" I asked, wondering what I was missing. Jasmine bit her lip thoughtfully.

"It will be easier to show you," she said, her words deliberately slow. We walked around the house until we stood in front of it. She pointed in what I thought was a random direction towards the woods. "Is that the direction you walked when you decided to go exploring on your own?"

I nodded.

"I assume you touched things along the route?"

Again, I nodded.

"Good, then let us retrace your steps."

"Wait, what does this have to do with dark magic?"

Jasmine didn't answer. Instead, she headed off in the direction I had taken two days ago, and I was forced to follow behind her. Part of me worried that we would run into the werewolves again, but Jasmine seemed unperturbed. We walked several yards into the woods when Jasmine came to an abrupt stop. She was staring at something, but when I tried to focus on what had captured her attention, I didn't see anything.

"You touched the trunk of that tree right there," Jasmine told me. She walked over to a tree and pointed to part of the trunk covered in what appeared to be ash. The spot was about as wide as my hand. I didn't recall placing my hand on that tree, but maybe Jasmine could smell my scent.

"Um… I can't be certain but maybe."

"I am sure of it," Jasmine assured me.

She started walking again, and I followed. For a while, we walked, each step taking us further away from the house. I kept looking over my shoulder, uneasy with being out of sight of the house after what happened the other day. Jasmine stopped again and crouched down to touch some large ferns.

"You also skimmed your fingers along these leaves," she muttered, staring at the plant.

"Jasmine, what does this have to do with dark magic?"

"It proves my theory," Jasmine said, rising to her feet. She turned to look at me and said, "Mae, your power has made the dark magic that coats this forest detectable. The dark spot on the tip of the ferns here, where your fingers touched, is dark magic. The spot on the tree back where I pointed out, was also dark magic."

"I'm not following."

"For some reason, the three of us cannot sense dark magic here, but it is all around us Mae. We are surrounded by it. It coats everything in these woods. I studied some samples of plant life from these woods before and after you struck me with your power. Your power jumped from me to one of the samples yesterday, and it not only made the dark magic on the sample visible, it destroyed it." Jasmine turned to me and demanded, "Touch that sapling behind you, and I'll prove it to you."

Skeptical about her theory, I turned and reached out to touch the small sapling. I pulled my hand away. Nothing happened.

I turned back to Jasmine and sighed. "I don't get it. Do you want me to use my—"

"Look," Jasmine interrupted, still staring at the plant she had ordered me to touch. I turned and sure enough, dark ash coated the spot where my palm had made contact. I stared at it in surprise. How was that possible? When I turned to Jasmine, she had a grim smile on her face.

"I want to see where you had your episode the other day, just before you blacked out," she said.

I started to shake my head. Rylan would kill me if he found out that I had gone that far. Just as the thought popped into my head a steely rod of defiance caused me to straighten my spine. I wasn't going to start asking for permission to do anything, nor was I going to cower from Rylan. He needed to understand that I would be making choices for myself.

But I did have to ask, "What if whatever caused both of us to lose control yesterday happens while we are out here?"

Jasmine's brown eyes shifted slowly to red and then, to my surprise, changed to violet. She stepped closer to me and reached out to caress my cheek.

"Mae, you no longer have any threat of me turning on you. Whatever you did yesterday not only stopped the violent frenzy in my mind but also erected a barrier to prevent it from happening again. I believe whatever makes creatures turn on one another is an effect of dark magic in these woods, and I think your body knows that. When you had your episode yesterday and the day before, your power was protecting you from the dark magic. I also think your power was protecting the people you love and trust, which is why both Arthur and I are still alive," Jasmine proclaimed. Her grim smile shifted to a genuine one. She cupped my cheek in her hand and continued, "If your power reacts to danger, I will be right here to help you through it. Whatever is happening here, Zyroe and Autumn were right, you may be the only one to stop it. There has to be a reason only you can sense this dark magic."

I stared at her in surprise. I knew from the moment Autumn and Zyroe had brought me back from the Pocket that it was important for me to be here, that I might be able to stop whatever was happening. I never once doubted that their intention to get me here was for an ulterior motive. But my Guardians had been wary from the beginning.

Now, hearing that one of them not only believed the threat *and* thought I may somehow be able to stop it was a relief. But it was also terrifying. If Jasmine was worried, then something must be wrong. If studying the site where I had lost control would help her in her research to figure out what was going on, then I would take her there.

"Alright, Jasmine, we'll go, but let's be quick."

# Chapter Ten

*Mae*

To speed up our journey, Jasmine flew us directly to the spot where I had blacked out. When we landed, I handed Jasmine her shirt when her wings retracted into her back, and she slipped it on. The area around us was completely blackened. The minute we landed, Jasmine pulled out bags and began collecting samples all around the site. She took her time as she inspected the land and what was left of the plant life.

"It is interesting that the park rangers thought this was a fire when, quite clearly, it was not. I wonder if they were just fishing for information…" Jasmine mumbled to herself.

How she could differentiate between a blazing inferno and my power was a puzzle to me. Could she tell this was the ash from black magic rather than from a normal fire? That had to be it. Or maybe I was just missing something. When she was through collecting samples, Jasmine stood in the middle of the destruction, lost in thought.

Suddenly, she took off in one direction without a word to me. I had to jog to keep up with her quick pace. A few minutes later the woods ended, and we found ourselves on the shoreline of a spectacular clear blue lake. Behind the lake was a stunning view of snow capped mountains that glittered in the sunlight. I gasped in surprise at such a pretty sight.

"Patricia mentioned mermaids during our meeting the other day. I wonder if this was the lake William saw them in," she mused out loud.

I wandered over to the edge of the lake and bent down to test the temperature of the water. It was chilly. As I stood up, the feeling of sand trickling down my arms caught my attention. I stiffened and turned around.

"Jazz…"

Jasmine turned to face me. The alarm on my face must have alerted her to my distress because she leapt the distance between us in one bound.

"What is it, Mae?"

"It's going to happen—"

My power surged forward. The pain of it blazing its way through my veins caused me to scream. Blackness threatened to consume my consciousness. As it descended upon me, I took a deep breath and attempted to fight it off. I couldn't hurt Jasmine again, and that was what would happen if I slipped under. My power erupted from my pores and outward. I cried out again in agony. My vision shifted until everything had a violet hue around me. Instead of panicking, I focused on the power pouring out of me. Cautiously, I attempted to pull it back. I tried to step away from Jasmine hoping that distance would keep her safe, but she grabbed my arm, holding me still.

"Breathe through it, Mae. You are doing great." Her voice was calm.

My body shook as more power fought to pour out. I did as instructed and inhaled a shaky breath. I closed my eyes and focused on the power brimming outwards. To my surprise, I felt myself connect with it. I let go of the worry and fear of hurting Jasmine or destroying everything around us to focus solely on my power. With each deep breath, I was able to rein it in until suddenly my power stopped rushing outwards.

My eyes flew open in surprise. My head ached, and my power was now throbbing under my skin, but I had remained conscious and stopped it! My power was giving off weird violet sparks that danced over my skin, but that was something I could handle. My heart leapt for joy, and I grinned. I looked over at Jasmine to share the moment with her, but Jasmine's concentration was focused on the woods we had just emerged from.

Jasmine's head whipped side to side as she watched something that I couldn't see dart through the woods. Her body stiffened, and her wings grew from between her shoulder blades, ripping the blouse she wore. The beautiful black wings stretched out on either side of her and then swept upwards. Without looking at me, Jasmine grabbed my wrists and yanked me close to her.

"What is it?" I asked, my voice barely above a whisper. My excitement vanished as I realized something was very wrong.

"Werewolves," she muttered. "But I cannot catch their scent. It is as if they do not have one… They are hunting us. I need to get you out of here, and I will come back to take care of—,"

A wall of cold lake water suddenly slammed into us from behind, throwing us both forward. I rolled several feet away from Jasmine as she was tossed in another direction. I coughed and sputtered. What the hell was that? Since when did calm lakes have sudden tsunamis? I scrambled to my feet just as a dark shadow fell over us. I whirled around and froze, a gasp stuck in my throat. Barreling towards us from above was an enormous, grayish-blue tentacle that had emerged from the middle of the lake and somehow managed to reach us over here on the shoreline.

My heart skipped a beat as I stared at the incoming nautical limb. My mind was almost unable to process what I was seeing. As it came closer and closer with a speed I would have thought impossible from something so large, I snapped out of my terror.

"Jasmine!" I screamed as I pointed towards our new threat.

As the tentacle slammed onto shore, the ground rumbled. I stumbled but managed to stay upright. I turned and watched as the tentacle slid across the rocky shore back into the water. My heart stopped when I saw it had wrapped itself around Jasmine. Her arms were pinned at her side, but her wings were free and she was trying to fly to safety.

I screamed her name. I watched as she struggled frantically to break free, calling her name and praying that she would escape. Before I could think of something to do to help her, she was yanked under the surface of the water. I let out a scream of despair that echoed around me.

*Mae.* Rylan's voice snapped me out of my shock. *What is happening? I feel your fear.*

Behind me, a howl echoed in the forest. The sound was too close to ignore. I whirled around to face, for the second time in a few short days, a werewolf. The ugly creature was nothing like I'd imagined. Its elongated snout and yellow, gnarly teeth were obviously the main threat, but I noted the oddly long arms and the sharp-looking claws. I watched as it lifted its nose and took a long, deep breath. Yellow eyes pinned me with a look that spelled trouble. My heart thundered in my chest, my hands shook, and a sweat broke out on my forehead. My muscles tensed as I brace myself to run. Wait, no, I couldn't run. Jasmine needed me! Shit, what was I going to do?

*Rylan! Jasmine's been taken, and I'm surrounded by werewolves. What do I do?*

Rylan's answer was quick, confident, and authoritative: *Hold as still as you can. Running will cause the werewolves to chase you, and you will not win. They are stalking you now, waiting for you to drop your guard. I am sure they sense you are different and assessing how dangerous you are. Where are you?*

*Just past the site where I blacked out. I'm standing next to a lake.*

*I am coming.* It was Rylan's only response.

Despite how we'd left things earlier, I was relieved to know he was on his way. I prayed that he would get here soon.

I tried to keep my breathing steady, but as another howl picked up where the last one left off, closer this time, my deep breathing turned to gasps. I caught movement off to my right. I turned my gaze in that direction, and my breathing stopped as the second werewolf crept towards me. It had been hiding in the darker shadows.

*Oh. My. God*, I gasped in alarm in my head.

*Keep calm. Remember, do not run.* Rylan's voice was calm. I hadn't realized that I had connected with him in my moment of panic.

The second werewolf took a step towards me while the first one remained still. It took all my willpower not to retreat. The creature took another step towards me. It assessed my reaction and then advanced again. Each time it took a step, it growled. Was it grinning or was that just a permanent snarl on its face? My body shook hard. I was about to get mauled by a monster.

As my terror mounted, a familiar pulse reminded me that I had a weapon not being utilized. My power hummed under my skin— I was more than a mere human. The other day I had missed my mark when I tried to hit the werewolf when it had emerged; what if I missed again? Would it get angry and attack? I pushed the panicked thought away and braced myself. It didn't matter that I couldn't hit my mark. They didn't know I couldn't hit them, and that was all the advantage I needed. I called up my power, and it answered at once. The tree closest to me exploded into violet flames. The werewolf paused and tilted its head to one side.

I pushed power from my fingertips and more trees began to catch fire. Violet lightning bolts shot up from the rocky shore, and the ground began to shift. Somewhere nearby, out of sight, a third wolf howled. Another from farther away took up the howl, and it was followed by a fifth. The werewolf I stared down snarled at me but took a step back.

"Get out of here asshole, or I'll set you on fire, too!" I yelled at it with a false bravado.

Hopefully, it wouldn't try to call my bluff. There was no way I had enough control to hit a specific target. The werewolf snarled again before it turned tail and sprinted into the woods. The second one glared at me for a moment longer before turning and taking off. I let out a sigh of relief and then whirled around to face the water. I forced my power to settle under my skin as I tried to figure out what to do next. Behind me, the trees crackled as they burned.

*The werewolves are gone,* I updated Rylan.

*Good,* Rylan's voice was subdued, but I could feel the ghostly tension that was eating at him.

I continued to scan the water. Maybe if I could somehow get the creature's attention and draw it towards me, I could figure out a way to reach Jasmine. I searched for some sign of the creature, but the water was calm and clear. There wasn't a single ripple. But I knew Jasmine was down there and needed my help. With a deep breath, I took a step into the water.

*Do not engage with whatever has taken Jasmine,* Rylan warned as if he could read the plan in my head. I winced at his tone, but I couldn't let Jasmine die.

"Hey, Lake-o-puss, come get me!" I yelled as I strolled deeper into the cold water. I slapped and kicked at the lake water as I waded into the lake. I prayed that the sound would attract the monster. I waited a moment but nothing happened. I tried not to panic as I thought about how long Jasmine had been underwater. I splashed around harder.

"I *said,* HEY LAKE-O-PUSS, COME GET ME! Afraid I'll turn you into sushi? Once I get my hands on you, that's exactly what I'm going to do, so get ready to be wrapped up in some rice and seaweed! I bet you'll be fucking delicious you oversized, slimy, piece of shit!"

I splashed and splashed. Furious that nothing was happening and terrified that Jasmine could already be dead, I slammed my hands against the water and allowed my power to surge outward. The moment my hands connected with the lake water this time a violet electrical pulse shook the entire body of water.

"Give me back my fri—,"

Suddenly, there was a ripple. The water in the middle of the lake began to bubble rapidly. I stumbled backward out of the water and stared, wide-eyed, as seven large tentacles shot out of the water straight up into the sky. They kept climbing upwards and onwards. Even from here, I could see the suction cups on each tentacle twitching open and closed. I stared, shocked at the sight before me. My heartbeat was loud in my ears.

The tentacles paused their climb upward. They twisted and curled, reaching or searching for something. Then the eighth tentacle emerged, bloodied and flailing around weakly. There, in the grasp of that eighth limb was Jasmine who hung limp. I screamed her name, but she didn't move. No, no, no, she couldn't be dead. I refused to believe it. I screamed her name again.

The moment my scream passed my lips, the seven large tentacles jerked towards me. My mouth dropped, and I stumbled backward, closer to the forest. The suction cups on each tentacle opened and closed in unison as they came closer. I was about to be octopus food. I had seconds to decide what to do.

A dark shadow closed over me as the tentacles reached the shoreline, stretching over me, hovering just above where I stood. Any minute they would come crashing down to crush me or to grab me to pull me under. Running was not an option, standing here waiting for these things to get me wasn't an option. So, I did the only thing I could do: I decided to fight back.

Already pulsing beneath my skin, my power was there and waiting for me. I looked towards Jasmine who was still hanging limp in the middle of the lake and prayed that I could save her. I rushed towards the water and with a deep breath, I forced everything I had outwards towards the creature hiding in the depths of the lake. My power bled from me, dispersing into the water. I braced myself as the first tentacle crashed down.

The ground vibrated with the impact of the tentacle, which missed me by mere inches. Water splashed up over me, and I inhaled a mouthful of lake water. I didn't have time to catch my breath. A second tentacle slammed down on the other side of me. As the first two tentacles slid back into the water, they began to curl around me. The others fell all around me, causing water and dirt to fly in every direction. Even as chaos reigned down around me, I refused to break my focus as I continued to push my power outward. I directed it towards the middle of the lake as best as I could.

I shrieked as it burned through my veins. Every inch of me protested the violent outburst. My skull felt like it was cracking under the pressure. My heart squeezed painfully in my chest. Just as a tentacle wrapped itself around my body, I felt it flinch violently. The slimy limb let go of me, and all eight tentacles retracted back into the lake.

I screamed in denial as the tentacles began to submerge themselves under the water. Jasmine disappeared. I forced more power into the crystal clear water. Around me, the water was glowing violet and it began to bubble and boil. The water around my ankles grew hot. But I couldn't stop. I wouldn't fail Jasmine.

In the middle of the lake water exploded upwards, and a guttural, animalistic screech of pain reverberated through the air. Violet flames chased the water upwards and turned it to steam. A large bulbous, slimy head rose from the lake. Two huge black eyes appeared to melt out of their sockets. The mouth was beak-like and when the creature opened it, I could see terrifyingly sharp teeth. Violet flames shot outwards from that beak as it cried out again. Eight tentacles rose from the water and thrashed around uncontrollably. The tentacle that held Jasmine threw her across the lake in my direction. Unfortunately, she landed in the deeper water and began to sink almost immediately.

The creature began shaking violently. The tentacles curled in on themselves. It let out a final cry before its entire body erupted into flames. I would forever hear the agonizing wails the creature made just before it exploded into a fine ash. Abruptly my power came to a halt. It felt like I had hit a wall while running at full speed. I couldn't breathe. A flash of pain in my chest caused me to stumble backward. The pain intensified. I gripped my chest. My veins felt sandblasted. The pain was mind-blowing.

I glanced at where Jasmine had sunk. I had to save her before she drowned. I squeezed my eyes shut as the pain in my chest began to make me dizzy. My legs gave out from under me, and I collapsed onto my back. Something was wrong. My heart felt hot, too hot. I tried gasping for air, but I couldn't seem to get enough to draw into my lungs.

# Chapter Eleven



If I had not seen the beast with my own eyes, I would have never believed it was possible that not only did a Kraken still exist, but that it lived in a freshwater lake in Canada. The questions of how it got there and what it was eating to survive would come later. My priority was Mae. The trees near the bank of the lake where Mae had collapsed were ablaze with violet flames. The flames blazed so hot that even the rocks on the shore were scorched

*Rylan, Jasmine is unconscious in the water*, Mae's voice whispered in my head.

The fiery pain she was enduring did not stop her from trying to save the Guardian who had put her at risk in the first place. I could feel her pain as if it were my own. My anger from earlier dissolved as terror began to mount. I passed Mae's information along to Arthur, who was following behind me. He could deal with Jasmine. Mae was my first priority.

I landed next to Mae, who was eerily still. Her face was pale and pulled taut with pain. My heartbeat quickened as I crouched down next to her. The sound of her heart struggling was a thing of horror. Her shallow breathing terrified me. Her body was going to shut down if I did not do something quickly. I picked her up and held her against my chest hoping the contact would help. The previous two times Mae had lost control her body was able to use the power that she stored within me. But this time nothing happened. My soul panicked while my mind raced with different solutions.

I looked up towards the violet blaze that was destroying the woods around us and immediately found my answer. I focused on the blaze and called it to me. The blaze died down and retreated as I drew her power from the woods and into me. Before it had a chance to settle within me, I redirected it back into Mae's body. Almost instantly, I could feel the pain lessen. When the flames had all but gone out, I turned my attention to the lake and pulled what power was left in the water. I cycled it through me and back into Mae. She drew in a deep breath. By the time I had absorbed all of Mae's power in the vicinity, she was breathing steadily, and her pain was all but gone. I heaved a sigh of relief.

Behind me, Arthur dropped from the sky, diving into the lake and disappearing under the surface. After what we had just witnessed, I hesitated to leave him here to possibly face another Kraken, so I waited. A minute went by before I felt Arthur reach out.

*Rylan, mermaids have feasted on Jasmine, and the left half of her body is crushed. I need to get her back to the house,* he said.

*Mermaids?* I repeated, shocked at his revelation.

Arthur resurfaced and shot up into the sky. He landed just a few feet away from me with Jasmine hanging limp in his arms. I could see chunks of muscle missing from her arms and legs.

"Mermaids," Arthur confirmed out loud, his expression grim.

"Jasmine?" Mae groaned.

Her eyelids fluttered open, but her gaze was unfocused. My heart clenched painfully in my chest. Her body could not continue with this cycle of near depletion. She was weak and scarily pale.

"She will live," I answered grimly, knowing that if I did not Mae would panic and it would slow down her recovery. A quick glance at Jasmine had me second guessing her condition. The blood pooling at Arthur's feet was alarming and who knows how long she had been under water. There was no time to waste. We needed to get the women home.

I took to the sky and headed back to the house. During the jounery, Mae went limp in my arms. I looked down to see she had fainted. I held her tighter to my chest as sped across the sky.

***

Jasmine's recovery was not an easy one. After I had wrapped bandages over the wounds that were too deep to heal instantly, Arthur had to rebreak bones that had already begun to heal to set them properly. I wanted to hate her. She had put my mate in danger *again*. But seeing a fellow warrior in this much pain mellowed my dark mood significantly. So instead of hating Jasmine, I put space between us.

I checked on Mae regularly. She lay unmoving in our bed. Her breathing and heart rate were normal, but her body remained cold and still. The day turned to night. When the next morning came and went and Mae had still not moved, panic began to set in. I warred with myself, wondering if I should wake her to make sure she was well. Her body needed to recover, but how long should I let her rest until I conceded that something was very wrong? The anxiety and fear in my chest turned to anger towards both women.

Jasmine knew I had not wanted them to go far. She knew the dangers that were present in the area and yet she'd still taken Mae deep into the woods. It did not matter if Jasmine's theory had been proven correct. What was the cost of that information now? My mate lay unresponsive in bed while Jasmine's injuries were so severe that it would take days for her to recover properly.

And Mae… She *knew* how I would feel about her leaving and yet she had gone off with Jasmine without a second thought. Once again, she had defied me despite our talk. Mae's mounting terror had alerted me to the danger they were in. When I had left the house to find them both long gone, my heart had stopped. What if I had been too late?

Things were horribly wrong in Jasper National Park. There was no doubting that now. What made the situation worse was that my mate was somehow an important piece to correcting the wrong in the area. Mae was stuck right in the center of all of this mystery. She was in danger, and she failed to see it.

I paced through the house, too worked up to stay still. I could have lost Mae. The thought caused my heart to squeeze in agony. I could have lost her, and the last time we had spoken I had threatened and terrorized her. I had felt her shame, confusion, and anger, and still, I had walked away, leaving her there to teach her a lesson. The horrible, gut-churning guilt I felt slowly began to outweigh the anger that burned in me.

These emotions: anger, guilt, love, fear, they were too much. All of this was too new, too raw, too all-consuming. Separately, they were each hard to control, but the combination of all of them was suffocating. How did the other Guardians who had mates handle this? How did they manage to keep sane? Every decision before Mae had once seemed so cut and dry. Now, it was a struggle to think straight without always second-guessing myself.

I was on the other side of the house when I heard movement upstairs. The relief that rushed through me eased the tension in my body. I was up the stairs and in our bedroom in no time. I heard the shower running, and I walked automatically towards the sound. I reached for the doorknob to the bathroom only to find it locked. I paused, surprised by the small boundary she had placed between us. Even back in Salisbury, when we'd hardly known each other, she had never locked her doors.

*Please, just leave me alone.* The bleakness in her voice and the ghostly splash of fear doused the flames of my anger immediately. Was she… was she scared of *me?* The thought was sickening, and I recoiled from the door. No, that could not be right. Maybe she was feeling scared after the ordeal she'd gone through. Mae knew she could trust me to take care of her... Right?

I took a step back, away from the bathroom door trying to figure out what to do or what to say to ease the discomfort radiating from Mae. After a minute, I decided the best course of action was to wait until she got out of the shower. I could give her a moment to find her bearings. With a shaky sigh, I forced myself to leave the bedroom.

In the kitchen, I placed a salmon fillet in the oven and diced up some vegetables. Fifteen minutes passed before I heard Mae's soft footsteps pad down the stairs. I found myself anxious to see her. Her health and well-being were more important than a lecture. I could scold her later. Right now, all I wanted was to wrap my arms around her and hold her to me.

A moment later, Mae rounded the corner and came to a stop just before entering the kitchen. She had donned a beautiful, loose white knitted sweater and leggings. She had kept her hair down to dry naturally, and her dark locks cascaded over her shoulder. Her face was pale which made the red in her eyes stand out. Had she been crying? Her expression was utterly neutral. I tried to figure out her emotions as they whirled around inside of me, but they were all muddled together and undistinguishable.

Instead of trying to figure it out on my own, I walked over to her with the intent of asking her how she felt. But as I reached out to touch her face, her whole body recoiled from me. The flash of fear in my gut that mirrored the expression on her face caused me to freeze. My hand hovered between us as surprise paralyzed me. Mae's posture relaxed, but her beautiful, large brown eyes were cloaked with suspicion. My hand dropped to my side. My heart ached to connect with her.

"What is this Mae?" I had to figure this out. I could not allow whatever barrier Mae was building to solidify between us.

"The last time you touched me I was left feeling like shit." Her tone held no infliction.

Anger I could handle. A passionate, heated discussion that would eventually lead to making up was something I looked forward to. That way we could both blow off steam. But this… this distance was not something I expected or knew how to handle. I floundered, trying to make her understand,

"I was disciplining you, Mae. Now you know—,"

"Now I know we are not equals," she interrupted with a contemptuous wave of her hand. "Will you be dishing out my punishment before or after lunch today? I'd like to know so I can prepare myself."

"Of course, we are equals," I corrected immediately. "But your safety is the most important thing to me. You needed to learn that in order for me to keep you safe you must listen to me."

Everything Mae was feeling intensified in my gut. Her brown eyes flashed with indignation, but her expression remained impassive. This coolness from Mae was alarming. I hated the thought that our last moment together could have been filled with strife, but I didn't regret punishing her. It was for her own good.

"You know, my parents used to ground me for the same reason: to keep me safe and to teach me a lesson. I was not their equal, which is how they had the power over me to punish me. But you know what? I kept doing it. Yesterday, you asked me where I would escape to when I snuck out of the house, and I didn't tell you." Her eyes narrowed on me. "I've changed my mind. I'll let you in on a little secret. In high school, a group of us from my MMA gym would sneak out to go help people who were in trouble that lived in the city. I didn't care how beat up or bloodied I got. I was helping people, and that's all that mattered."

She paused, allowing what she had told me to process. Horror gripped my heart as her words seeped into my soul. I opened then shut my mouth.

Finally, when I found my voice, I asked in a strained whisper, "Are you telling me you went around trying to be some sort of vigilante?"

I recalled our conversation before boarding the plane to Salisbury about how she would lay hands on us if we tried to drink her blood. Then, on the plane she had shared with us her love of MMA and how she had trained throughout high school and college. There had also been that morning I had found her in my gym fighting the punching bag like an expert. It was all clicking into place.

"Call it whatever you want," she replied with a shrug.

"You never told me about this before," I accused.

I did not doubt that Mae had gone gallivanting around at night in a city full of crime to help others. She had spellbound herself to keep the general population around her safe. The agony she had endured and extreme lengths to which she had gone to make sure no one was harmed was beyond reasonable. I had seen her sacrifice herself to protect one of my employees back in Salisbury from being mauled to death by spider demons. I had watched in horror as she rushed to save Darla when Autumn had broken through the witch's summoning circle. Mae was utterly selfless. The fact that she ran around with others to make sure where she lived was safe was not even in question, but how long had it gone on for?

"Of course, I haven't told you yet! There's probably a lot you don't know about me. We've only known each other for what? Two and a half weeks now?" Mae exclaimed with exasperation. "I would still probably be doing it if my powers hadn't emerged."

A dark shadow passed over her face, and suddenly, a cool chill ran through our bond. She shook her head, and her expression shifted back to contempt. Something told me there was more to her story than she was willing to share.

I opened my mouth to say something but shut it. Once again, I was at a loss for words. Mae was right. We had only known each other a few weeks. We were both learning how to navigate this relationship. I had my frustrations with my mate, and I had been daft to think my frustration was one-sided. Not only was Mae learning the workings of the supernatural world, but she was also learning how to be Mae again. Only a few weeks ago, this young woman used to hang her head in despair. She was used to a life of isolation and pain. But now I could see her gaining her confidence back. In our brief time together, she had gone from leaning on me for support to suddenly finding that she could stand on her own. As Mae's confidence returned, as she learned how to harness her powers, I was beginning to see the real Mae.

"In any case," Mae continued, "my parents thought they were keeping me safe by forcing me to stay home. But I kept going out because I did what I thought was right. The other day, I didn't run and hide inside the house because there was no way I was going to let you face that thing by yourself. Even though I wasn't much help, at least I never have to look back and wonder what would have been different if I hadn't stepped in. Did I defy your command? Yeah, but I don't regret trying to help you.

"Then yesterday I left with Jasmine knowing that it could be potentially dangerous and knowing that it would piss you off. But I went anyway because Jasmine had a theory about what's going on in this park. This was the whole reason we came here, right? To see if there was any real threat? Well, there is and it goes beyond weirdly-behaving werewolves running around. I left to do some digging with Jasmine because I thought it was the right thing to do.

"So discipline me if you think that will help me listen to you, but I can assure you, it won't. And know that each time you decide I need to be punished, I will despise you for it. I cannot and will not love someone who thinks I should be an obedient pet. If you want me to be your equal, to be your partner in all things, we can talk through our issues like a normal couple. You will not force me to bend to your will. In the meantime, while you decide what you want from me as your mate, we have something else we need to discuss. Not only am I *staying* here to help figure out what is going on, I also think it's time we alert the other Guardians to what is going on here."

I stared at my mate, stunned. My thoughts were jumbled. How did I explain to Mae that it was never my intention to ever make her feel unequal? Suddenly I realized how wrong I had been. Again, she was right. I had thought I had the power to control her. There was an imbalance in our relationship that could not continue.

I was accustomed to being listened to because I normally did have all the power. Each role I had to assume in my lifetime required me to be dominant. A general, a king, a nobleman, a mayor… The list went on. But that was how I gained the wealth and status needed to persevere. Being superior to others gave me power over them. When no one could question or doubt me, it helped me keep my identity secret. Was I so used to being dominant, commanding, and in charge that I had thought that was how I needed to be with my mate?

Before I could find the right words to clear the air between us, Arthur strolled into the room. He walked over to us and to my surprise, and displeasure, he placed a hand on Mae's shoulder.

"Mae's right, we need to call the others," Arthur said firmly. "Things have gotten out of hand, and we need to bring in reinforcements."

A snarl began to build in my chest. We were not having this argument again. There were multiple reasons we could not allow others to know of Mae. I struggled to keep my temper in check.

"Before you object to this, Rylan, I want you to know you are outnumbered in this vote," Arthur continued. "Jasmine thinks it is time, too. That makes it three against one. And yes, Mae's vote counts because she is *my* equal."

I met Arthur's gaze and bared my teeth as my snarl escaped. How dare he wade into our conversation and voice his opinion on something he knew nothing about?

Mae smiled up at Arthur who gave her a wink.

"There is too much going on here that doesn't make sense. There are creatures that do not belong here. The shifters are now missing their Alpha. There is something in the air that is causing chaos. And most importantly, it's alarming that not only are Ekon and Cain missing, but Zein's territory butts up this one, and he was found murdered. I have a rising suspicion that he figured out what was going on here and was killed for it. I suggest we contact only a few warriors at first. Only the Guardians we trust the most," Arthur said solemnly. "Once we get them used to Mae we can extend our call for help further."

"It is too dangerous," I snapped. "We can call the others, but let me take Mae somewhere safe—"

"I'm not going anywhere," Mae interrupted firmly. "We need to make sure we figure out who is casting dark magic and stop them before this gets any crazier. No one wants a war with the gods."

I glared at her, and she glared back, testing me. For a moment I said nothing, too angry to form a coherent sentence. Mae's expression softened.

She stepped forward and said, "I know you are worried; I am, too. I don't necessarily want to be surrounded by Guardians who will see me as a threat, but this is more than the four of us can handle. I will have you, Arthur, and Jasmine to watch out for me, and I'll work hard to try to win everyone over."

*I will make sure no one messes with Mae,* Arthur added. *Even you.*

I looked at Arthur, and this time when I stared him down his eyes changed to violet.

*Back off, Arthur,* I warned him.

*Then stop fucking up. None of this is Mae's fault. Whatever is happening here, we all need to be on the same page. Let us figure out what is going on and take care of it quickly.*

"Stop talking to each other and include me," Mae said, her brows coming together. Arthur and I glared at each other for a moment longer before I sighed.

"Only the most *trusted* Guardians," I warned him.

The war between my soul and my mind raged on. I had conceded to them because, deep down, I knew they were right. It was time to call reinforcements.

# Chapter Twelve



*Mae*

After Rylan stormed off, I slipped the lunch he had started into the refrigerator. I was far from hungry. Arthur had disappeared after coming to my aid, and I was left alone with my thoughts. Part of me wanted to go check on Jasmine, but another part of me just wanted to be alone.

Quietly, I wandered the house. I had peaked into every room the first day we arrived, but I hadn't been looking for anything in particular. Now, I looked for space I could call my own. Not necessarily to hide, but somewhere I could think without distraction. I found my spot on the third floor in a smaller corner of the second loft in the house.

I sat down on the overstuffed chair near the wall of books and sighed. Despite having slept for hours, my body still felt exhausted. Across the loft, through the large three-story glass window that looked out to the front of the house, the woods looked just as stunning and tranquil as the first day we had arrived. There was nothing sinister or ominous about the thick green foliage or the gorgeous snow-capped mountains in the distance.

How many people visited this park daily? How many people walked the trails, oblivious to the danger they were in? Every single thing in that woods was covered in dark magic. How long did dark magic have to linger on something before you saw an adverse effect from it? Was it affecting the four of us? Or did it need more time to get under our skin? The thought of something sinister sitting on my skin sent chills through my body.

I dragged my legs up to my chest, wrapped my arms around them, and rested my forehead on my knees. Behind my lids, I could see tentacles with suction cups coming for me. There were the yellow eyes of a werewolf pinning me with a hungry stare, and I could hear the haunting sound of howls. I squeezed my eyes shut tighter as I tried to push the experience to the back of my mind. I hadn't saved Jasmine, and I'd ended up killing a living creature with my power.

My worst nightmare had come to life. If it hadn't been for Rylan and Arthur, both Jasmine and I would be dead. Rylan had every right to be upset with me this time. Instead, he had made me lunch. Why couldn't I just have been grateful instead of defensive? Trying to ease my guilt, I reminded myself that the last time he had made me food I had been left shaky and upset.

"Mae?" Arthur's voice pulled me out of my despair.

I looked up and found him standing a few feet away.

"Hey. Is everything alright?" I let go of my legs and crossed them underneath me.

"For now, everything is calm," Arthur assured me. "May I sit with you?"

Surprised by his request, I simply nodded. The Guardian walked over and took the seat next to mine. With a sigh, he sunk into the cushion and leaned his head back. He closed his eyes and did not say anything right away. I had thought I wanted to be alone but having him there felt right somehow. While I didn't know much about the Guardian next to me, somehow during our brief time together we had grown close. Who knew that the man who had kidnapped me would end up being one of my best friends?

I lay back in my seat and stared up at the vaulted ceiling. Hanging in the loft was a chandelier made of deer antlers. Were they real antlers or fake? Who had thought a chandelier needed antlers? It was tacky décor, but it went with the rest of the lavish mansion, and secretly, I enjoyed looking at it. I stared up the light fixture for a while, lost in my wayward thoughts.

"May I share something with you?" Arthur asked, breaking the silence.

I turned to look at him and found him staring at me. His eyes were violet. I suppressed the shudder that wanted to race down my spine. I had done that to him.

"Of course, Arthur."

Arthur looked away from me and stared into space, a frown tugged at the sides of his mouth. He reached up and stroked his goatee. When he turned back to me, his eyes had changed back to brown.

"Many centuries ago, I oversaw the territory that is now Nepal. I had a wife then, and her name was Fuli. She was loved in the community. Her family came from a wealthy class, but she was humble and worked hard to earn respect from everyone. It was an easy decision to ask her father for her hand in marriage. She was a solid choice as a wife. The marriage, like all marriages before this, was simply a business arrangement that I profited greatly from."

I nodded in understanding. Rylan had said his marriages were arranged in the same manner.

"One winter a sickness spread through our city. Hundreds of people in all different societal classes died. The young and old, men and women. The sickness took everyone it could infect. I was busy dealing with other matters elsewhere in my territory, so Fuli busied herself by helping the people within the community.

"I was gone for two years before I returned home. The city was nearly wiped out, and those left were half-starved and working hard to keep their families alive. Curious to see what my wife had been up to the past two years, I found her one night in a house made of mud and sticks. The roof was half caved in, and the residents were too sick to move from their beds. Fuli was there, not only tending to their every need but working to fix the roof. Instead of helping her, I simply watched her work. When she was done with that family, she left to tend to another one. She worked nonstop for days until she collapsed from exhaustion at one of the houses she had visited. Here, she had come to help a father feed his dying daughter.

"The man of that residence put her to bed and attempted to find food for my wife. I watched as he gave up his own meal, which he needed desperately, to Fuli. The next morning Fuli got up and kept working. People greeted her as if she were family. Fuli used what resources her family had to repair homes, feed families, care for the ill, and help cover the cost of funeral arrangements. She ran herself to the ground, trying to be there for her community. Her kindness and selflessness had not gone unnoticed by the people. In return, the community did what it could for her. They gave her the clothes off their backs when hers got too filthy or worn. They fed her, let her sleep in their beds… They supported her in any way that they could."

Arthur paused and looked away from me again. He ran both hands over his face, and he sighed.

"Oh, Mae… That woman deserved a husband that loved her. One who would give her the children she so very much wanted. Looking back on her now… I think that if I could have, I would have loved her. I am telling you about Fuli, Mae, because I think your life is about to become more difficult, like hers did once the sickness arrived. If Zyroe and Autumn believe that only you can stop whoever is behind the casting of dark magic and bringing creatures here that do not belong… I think you will find that you may have to make hard decisions. At times, you may feel like you are alone in this, and I am sure, when the others arrive, you will find yourself surrounded by some hostility."

I stared at him with a sinking suspicion that I already knew the answer to the question I was going to ask. "Do you really think it's going to be bad with the others here?"

Arthur nodded. "Yes, the others will most likely hate you from the beginning. But, I want to let you know that you have Rylan, Jasmine, and myself as a community that will support you in whatever you need to do to stop this. You have a good heart and a good head on your shoulders. Whatever you decide to do, whatever action you need to take, the three of us will always have your back."

I gave him a grateful smile as my heart swelled at his kindness.

"I know you feel guilty for attacking both Jasmine and myself the other day, Mae. But I want you to know that even if you had killed us, you did the right thing. You were defending yourself, and if destroying us was the only way to stop us, then so be it. But instead of killing us, you protected both of us. I can feel your power in me, protecting me. While you were at the lake with Jasmine, back here I could feel the fingers of the depravity wanting to poison my mind. It tried to breach the wall your power erected in my mind, but it could not affect me, Mae. You saved me from doing things I would regret."

Arthur stood and came to stand right in front of me. His expression was solemn, and his eyes were bright with fervor. He crouched down so we were eye to eye. He reached out and took my hands, which I had folded in my lap.

"Mae, whatever happens here, I promise to always stand beside you as your friend and as your soldier, should it come to that."

I stared at Arthur, stunned by his passion. This was probably the most Arthur had ever spoken to me, and it was certainly the most personal thing he had ever shared. The serious vigor in his expression spoke volumes of the truth behind every word he spoke. This was a man who had lived hundreds, maybe thousands of years, who had probably seen countless battles and met millions of people who had long since passed. I was sure that he rarely ever got to this level to talk to them with such respect or sincerity.

I shifted onto my knees, and before he could react, I threw my arms around Arthur House. He did not hesitate to reciprocate. His arms came around me and pressed me to his chest.

"Thank you, Arthur." *For being here for me*, I added.

Across the small loft, someone cleared their throat. I flinched and withdrew my arms from around Arthur's neck. Arthur stood slowly, his face hardening as he turned to Rylan who stood in the shadows watching us.

"Rylan, Arthur and I were just—,"

"Talking. I know, I heard," he interrupted. "Arthur, if you do not mind, I would like to have a moment with Mae."

For a moment, Arthur didn't move. Both males eyed each other. To my surprise, it was Rylan who caved first. He sighed and stepped to the side, allowing Arthur to move past him freely. Arthur walked past Rylan without saying a word. When Arthur was out of sight, I stood quickly, not sure what type of reaction I was going to get from Rylan. I certainly did not want to be sitting down, which left me vulnerable should he decide I needed to be punished.

Rylan walked over to me with slow, deliberate steps. He stopped right in front of me and reached out his hand for me to take. I looked down at his hand and then up into his gorgeous teal eyes. Without hesitation, I took it. My love for Rylan hadn't changed. While I was suspicious of his calm demeanor, I knew that he loved me. That had to mean something.

# Chapter Thirteen

*Rylan*

Mae was silent as I led her to our bedroom. Her trepidation swirled around in my gut, and it made my guilt, already a heavy stone sitting on my chest, even heavier. I found, however, that I could no longer feel her anger, and it gave me hope that she was willing to forgive me. I shut the door. She walked into the middle of the room before she turned to look at me. Her gorgeous, warm brown eyes searched my face suspiciously.

For the past two hours, I had alternated between agonizing on how to restore my relationship with my mate and worrying about the Guardians I had called. I found that I hardly trusted anyone in the Guardian community; certainly not with the secret my mate carried within her. I had kept my conversations brief and vague, but the urgency of the situation at hand had to be conveyed. Those coming would only know of the dark magic spreading like wildfire here and that two Guardians had gone missing. It would not be until they arrived that they would learn of Mae and her involvement.

That was when the risk to her life would multiply tenfold. No matter how much I trusted the few men and women I had called, time would soon tell how much they trusted me when I introduced them to my mate. The thought of killing my brethren sickened me, but it was more tolerable than allowing Mae to die by their hands. The thought of her death was so agonizing that I needed to touch Mae, to feel her in my arms and know that, at least for now, she was safe.

But the distance separating us felt as expansive as an ocean. It was simply unacceptable. I had caused this rift, and I intended to fix it. I had just found Mae. We should be growing closer, not further apart. There was a growing urgency to touch her, to bury myself in her, and to worship her. My fingers itched to finish what I had started the other day. But first, some things needed to be said.

"Mae, my whole life has been made up of a series of different roles that I have played. Each role I play must be mastered to a tee, or what and who I am could be exposed. Leadership roles have always been necessary to progress successfully through each phase of my life. These roles allowed me to control those around me and prevented anyone from questioning me. They were necessary in order to keep my secret. But in these roles, I was required at times to prove my authority. If someone stepped out of line or tried to undermine my authority, I found that punishments almost always worked to get others to comply.

"All I want is to keep you safe. It is my duty, not just as a Guardian but as your mate, to look out for you, and when you decide to not listen to my commands, it drives me insane. Losing you is never going to be an option for me. I fell into old habits, Mae, and that was wrong of me. Being your mate is not a role. I am not your dictator. I did not intend for your punishment to be construed as you not being my equal. As you said, we should be able to discuss our issues with one another. I am sorry for what I did and how I made you feel. I swear I will never punish you again. If I am ever upset or angry with you, I will talk to you about it instead of lashing out. You are the one person in my life that matters to me, and I feel horrible about what I have done. I am sorry, Mae."

I took a deep breath and let it out slowly as I finished my apology. I felt vulnerable and exposed as I laid out my flaws for

Mae to see. She studied my face. What was she thinking? The silence stretched, and my impatience grew, but I knew I needed to wait. I had broken the trust between us, and it would take time to fix this.

One corner of her mouth twitched upwards, and the suspicion on her face disappeared. She raised her hand and stretched it out towards me. It was all the invitation I needed. I crossed the space between us in no time, taking her hand in mine. The contact was profound. The tension lessened in my chest, and some of my worries eased. I had not realized how cold I had been feeling until warmth spread through my chest.

"I forgive you," she said as she pulled me closer to her. "And I'll be more careful when it comes to my safety, ok? We're both bound to make mistakes sometimes, I guess. We're only human."

I chuckled as I wrapped my arms around her petite frame and breathed in her sweet scent. Mae placed her head in the middle of my chest, and I tightened my hold on her.

"Both of us are far from human," I reminded her. "But yes, we will make mistakes."

"Hm... I'm going to stick to pretending I'm human. The reality is too hard to wrap my head around."

I felt her fear in my gut before the sensation abruptly vanished. I let go of her waist and took her face in my hands. I did not have to hear her thoughts to know they had turned to Zyroe.

"You can just be my Mae White," I assured her.

I leaned down and kissed her softly. Her moan and the way she relaxed into me caused my body to react. My cock began to stiffen as desire unfolded between us. I broke the kiss, knowing I had one more thing that had to be done before this conversation was over. I stepped away from her but kept my eyes firmly locked onto her face. I reached into my jacket pocket and walked back over to her. Then slowly I bent down on one knee. Mae's brown eyes widened in surprise and grew even wider as I showed her the small box in my hand.

I had proposed to hundreds of women. I had always known what to say in the moment. There were times I had been poetic while there had been moments when seduction was necessary. My proposals had ranged from simple to grand gestures. Each courtship had always been strategic. I learned as much as I could about my intended brides; they were, afterall, business ventures. I learned their likes and dislikes, and by the time it came to our courtship, they were putty in my hand.

It never occurred to me that one day I would be kneeling in front of my mate so choked full of emotion that I would never be able to get out the adequate words to profess how I felt about her. I knew almost every language. I knew poetry, ballads, and stories all about love. But at this moment, none of that mattered. None of it would be enough to express my love for the woman in front of me.

My heart was beating wildly in my chest. My tongue felt stuck to the roof of my mouth. To my surprise, my hand trembled as I held the small box out in front of me. There was never a moment in my long life that I had felt this exposed, vulnerable, and nervous.

"And you can forever be Mae White if that is what you wish," I told her. "Or… you can be Mae Aurora Wellington. I know I am far from perfect, but I will strive every day to be the man that you deserve. I will make mistakes, but I will learn and grow from them. Be my mate *and* my wife. I love you, Mae. Please do me the honor, and marry me."

I opened the box and showed her the priceless stone inside. My heart was beating so loudly that I was afraid I would not hear her response. I held my breath and waited. Mae's eyes were large and round, her heart was racing just as quickly as mine. Her mouth had popped open, but she raised a hand to cover it. I could feel her excitement and joy, but I would be amiss to ignore the cold sensation of sadness mixed in with them. She dropped her hand from her mouth, and the corners of her mouth pulled upwards.

*You're nervous*, she noted with amusement.

*You have objected to marrying me before*, I reminded her. Her smile fell some.

*Isn't a mate more permanent and everlasting than a wife? What's the point of marriage when our souls are already sealed together?* She asked me softly. *I do not want to be just one more wife to you.*

*I want to make you mine in every way possible. The others were just practice*, I tried to tease her, but the tension rolling around in my gut made it hard to be lighthearted. *Marry me, Mae.*

Mae reached out and took my face in her hands. Her eyes watered and a grin spread across her face.

"Yes, I will marry you."

The elation that rushed through me caused me to feel dizzy. I took the ring out of the box and slipped it onto her finger. A perfect fit. I swept her up into my arms and spun her around. Her laughter was music to my ears. I placed Mae on her feet, took her face in my hands, and kissed her hard. I needed to touch her; I needed to bury myself in her. I needed to become one with my mate. After all the stress, fear, and anger all I wanted was to show her how much I loved her.

Our lips collided, and my desire became all-consuming. Mae opened her mouth, and I took advantage. Our tongues danced together. I trailed my hands down her sides and pulled her closer to me. One of Mae's hands gripped my arm while the other reached down to stroke my erection. I groaned and pulled my mouth away from her. I picked her up by the waist, and I tossed her across the room onto the bed.

Mae's squeal of surprise was muffled when I crawled over her and kissed her once more. I pulled away only so I could pull the sweater off her. I ripped away her bra, leggings, and panties. Instead of tossing her panties to the side as I had done with her other garments, I paused and inhaled the evidence of her arousal on them. Her gasp of surprise and the hint of pink that rose in her cheeks was delightful. I glanced down between her legs to find her glistening and ready. I groaned again, and I fought back the lengthening of my fangs.

"You are the most gorgeous woman to ever walk this earth," I said, feeling breathless as I stared down at her. Mae giggled as she rolled her eyes. She self-consciously began to sit up and draw her legs to her chest. I scowled. "What do you think you are doing?" I grabbed her ankles and yanked her legs back down.

I pulled off my shirt and crawled over her. She reached out, and when her hands touched my chest, my whole body tensed. My cock throbbed, demanding attention, but I ignored it as I leaned down and took one of her nipples into my mouth. Her sharp intake of breath made me smile as I teased her nipple taut with my tongue. Her hands went to my hair and tugged at it. My hands trailed over her body, loving every inch of her.

I let go of her nipple and sat up. I gripped her hip with one hand while my other moved between her legs. My fingers slipped past her folds into her core. She was so wet. I growled, pleased with her body's response. I caressed her inner walls, and I felt them clench in response. My thumb teased her clit, and her body jerked in response. Mae arched her chest upwards, giving me a lovely view of her breasts.

I moved down the bed, just enough so I could lean down between her legs and kiss her inner thigh, close to the junction between her legs. She jerked again in surprise. My lips skimmed across her skin, and I breathed in her heady scent. My fingers never stopped stroking her, and my thumb continued its circular motion over her swollen clit. As I kissed her inner thighs, I gently nipped at her skin causing it to turn pink. At the sight of her blood so close to the surface, I could no longer fight my fangs from lengthening. Mae began writhing around, and her moans got louder. Her body bared down on my fingers that were buried inside of her.

"Rylan," she groaned, her body tensing as her orgasm grew closer.

I looked up at her from between her legs. When our eyes met I saw hers widen at the sight of my fangs. I felt a cold chill of her fear echo through me. Guilt and shame weighed heavy on me. One's mate should *never* be afraid of them. I had been rough with Mae when I had bitten her the last time. While it had not been enough to injure her permanently, my bite had been hard enough to be punishing.

"Wait, Rylan…" Mae started, her brows coming together in concern.

She began to pull away from me, her fear mounting. But I refused to let her escape. I gripped her hips harder to hold her still while I continued to pleasure her with my other hand. I added a third finger into her.

"No Mae, do not fear me. I will never bite you like that again," I swore, meeting her gaze.

Making sure I moved slowly so she could see what I was doing, I leaned in to kiss her inner thighs again. I sucked and nipped at her skin once again. I refused to sink my teeth into her while she was still nervous. Thankfully, it did not take long for Mae's fear began to recede. She was willing to trust me again.

Her body tightened around my fingers. Just as her orgasm took over, I took advantage of her distraction. As gently as I could, I sank my fangs into her inner thigh. Her body bowed, and she cried out my name. I reveled in pleasure as I drank in her very essence. Whilst Mae's blood was delicious and her power flooded my system, I blocked all that out to simply enjoy her. Her life force flowed through me, and I savored the sensation. Knowing she was alive and well, that she had forgiven me, and had said yes to being my wife made everything else feel inconsequential in that moment.

I did not take much blood from her. I knew her body was still recovering from her ordeal yesterday, and I did not want to weaken her further. I pulled my fangs from her thigh and licked the wound to heal it. Slowly, I withdrew my hand from between her legs. Mae panted; her body quivered from the aftershocks. I wasn't done with her yet. I sat up, took her hand, and pulled her up into a sitting position. As I pressed my lips against hers, her satisfied sigh into my mouth was a siren's call to me. My body shuddered with need.

I pulled away from her mouth and said, "I need you Mae Flower. I need to be buried inside you."

Mae's sexy smile made my blood boil. She moved to the side of the bed and said, "Lie down."

My dick grew harder at her command. I did as I was told and moved to the middle of the bed where I lay down on my back. Mae moved to climb on top me, her legs straddling either side of me. Without any preamble, she took my dick in her hand and impaled herself. We both cried out as she slid down onto me until I was buried completely inside of her. I choked on a strangled cry of delight. Her answering chuckle was deep and sensual.

She looked at me with another megawatt smile before moving. She moved up and down on me slowly at first. She threw her head back and closed her eyes as she took me at her own speed. I grabbed her hips and watched her work. My release was going to happen soon. I felt it ready to erupt, but I fought it back as I took this moment to enjoy Mae's control. Her breasts jiggled up and down, her intimate walls clenched around me, and her soft sighs were all divine.

Mae leaned forward until her chest was pressed against mine and kissed me. Her tongue slipped into my mouth as she deepened the kiss. Then, her hips really began to move. She placed her hands on either side of my head and began to thrust wildly. My hands slid down her waist, and I grabbed her ass cheeks to help her move faster. Everything about Mae was glorious and perfect. We fit together so well that there could be no question we belonged together. Sheer bliss radiated from my heart, saturating my soul.

Neither of us lasted long. Mae's body squeezed me so tight that as she came, she forced out my own orgasm. As her power hit me again, the intensity of my orgasm doubled. Together we cried out in ecstasy. Mae's body continued to pulse around me, milking me dry. When our orgasms finally subsided, Mae rolled off of me to lay on the bed.

"That was…" Mae said slowly, her voice husky, "intense."

I laughed. I could feel her happiness and the contentment through our connection. All traces of fear and trepidation were gone.

"What we have together is intense," I took her hand and kissed the back of it. "And I would not have it any other way, Mrs. Wellington."

Mae's chuckle was lovely, and while I felt her excitement, I also felt a flash of sadness again. Before I could ask her about it, there was a knock at our door. Mae stiffened and grabbed the covers to throw them over herself.

*What do you want?* I snapped, annoyed that our momentary bubble of happiness was about to pop.

*The first group of Guardians will be arriving tomorrow morning. We need to discuss details about how this is going to work,* Jasmine replied, her tone subdued.

*We will be down shortly.*

"Who is it?" Mae whispered.

"Jasmine knows we are both in here. There is no need to whisper. I am sure she is aware of what we have been up to," I growled in annoyance. "She is requesting our presence to discuss the arrival of our guests."

Mae sighed and threw off the covers.

"Will we ever have time for just us?" she complained. I stared down at her body, wondering the same thing. I placed my hand on her stomach.

"I hope so. I would rather not have an audience when we try for a family," I told her solemnly. The alarm on her face made me laugh again.

"That's not funny!" Mae snapped as she pushed my hand off her stomach and rolled out of bed. "We aren't having kids."

"You said no to marrying me but now you wear my ring. Things change." I grinned at her glare.

She picked up her clothes and headed to the closet grumbling about my sanity. An image of Mae with a swollen belly appeared in my mind's eye. My cock immediately came back to life, ready to make the daydream a reality.

Twenty minutes later we made our way downstairs. Mae immediately went into the kitchen while I strolled into the family room where the others were waiting. Arthur stood by the window, watching the woods as night descended and Jasmine sat stiffly in one of the chairs. Both turned their attention to me as I entered the room.

"Tomorrow, mid-morning the first group of Guardians is set to arrive," Arthur started, his expression grim. "We need a plan. I am assuming that none of us mentioned Mae in our conversations, correct?"

Jasmine and I nodded. Mae walked over with a plate of the food I had started to make for her earlier and a fork. She plopped down on the couch and started to eat. Her first meal in a day and half. My stomach twisted uncomfortably. I needed to take better care of her.

"Good, so how do we go about introducing her to everyone without all of us coming to blows?" Arthur asked.

"Coming to blows will be inevitable. Who knows when that wave of depravity will come tomorrow?" Jasmine said grimly.

"We cannot let that happen," I growled. "Whatever Mae has done to protect you both, she will do it to the others."

Mae choked on the bite of food she had put in her mouth.

"*Excuse me?*" she squeaked in alarm. Her eyes were wide and full of horror.

"Do not fret. If it worked on Arthur and Jasmine, it will work on the others," I assured her.

"Let me get this straight. You want to introduce me to warriors, who, mind you, will almost instantly hate me on the spot when they see me – and then as you try to convince them that I'm not a threat you want me to strike them with my power that I cannot control or guarantee won't kill them? Is that right?"

"It should work, Mae," Jasmine said, though her tone was far from confident.

"Are you willing to risk the lives of these Guardians? Usually, when my power hits something it destroys it, or do you not recall what happened to that thing in the lake? I think you and Arthur just got extremely lucky."

"A Kraken," Arthur whispered in awe as he stroked his goatee. Mae glared at him.

"Whatever that thing was, it's now very dead," she turned to me. "Rylan, you have seen what my power can do. You know this idea is dangerous. You all are assuming that if I can hit my target, AKA your *friends*, and I don't kill them, that they will be protected from whatever this force is. What if they need to be affected by this depravity beforehand for it to work? What if it does work, but then they're super pissed and try to kill me?" She sighed as she put down her empty plate. "It's too bad that they can't just hang on to a piece of my power to use in the case of an emergency."

Three of us Guardians exchanged surprised glances. Of course! Why had none of us thought of this before?

"Is there a coven nearby?" I asked Arthur.

"There is one about a hundred miles east of here. I will call the Supreme," he said with a grin.

"Make sure she brings enough gems for all of our guests," Jasmine told him with a grin. Although it was obvious that she was still in pain from her ordeal with the Kraken, this idea seemed to give her life.

"How many Guardians in total will be arriving in the next two days?" I asked.

"Eight," Arthur said.

Eight Guardians? Unease twisted my gut. It was going to be hard to convince them all that Mae was not the problem here. Jasmine and Arthur exchanged glances that told me they were thinking the same thing.

"Wait, what's going on? Why are you going to contact a witch?" Mae asked, confused by the sudden excitement in the room.

"We can trap your power in gems," I explained. "Witches do it all the time. We will have the Supreme bring stones that will be able to contain your magic, and we will give them to the Guardians as they arrive. Hopefully, that should be enough to protect them. It will be their talisman while they are here."

Arthur nodded. "I will ask her to come as soon as possible. Now, back to my original question: how do we introduce Mae to everyone?"

"We let our guests meet Mae right when they get here so it does not appear like we are trying to hide her," Jasmine said with a grimace. "The best we can do is tell them the truth about what she is and hope they will see reason. Everyone will be trickling in slowly over the next few days. If we can get our first few guests comfortable in her presence, maybe the others will not be so threatened."

Tension tightened in my gut. I did not want any of this. If there was another way to handle this situation, I would have fought the decision to bring in more Guardians, but the truth of the matter was that this was too great of a threat to ignore. We needed more feet on the ground if we were going to figure out what was going on and who was behind all of this. I clenched my jaw, fighting back the feeling of dread settling in my stomach.

# Chapter Fourteen



*Mae*

We were all up before the crack of dawn the next morning. We stood together in the woods just out of sight of the house. There was frost on the ground. You could see the mist from our breaths as we stood around and watched the Supreme, Katie Gagnon, pull a handful of clear quartz stones from a small velvet bag. Each stone was attached to a leather rope that acted as a lanyard.

The last time I had been around a witch, it had been when seven Supremes from neighboring covens had come together to tell the three Guardians surrounding me that something was afoot. They had been less than pleasant to me due to my questionable bloodline. I had expected no different from Katie. Instead, she was sweet and polite. It did not seem to bother her that I was what full-blooded witches called a "mutt."

Arthur had called Katie last night and explained what we needed from her without telling her why. The Supreme had jumped at the opportunity to work with us. She had driven most of the night to get here as soon as she could. When she arrived, she did not hide her curiosity when we were introduced, but she did not ask any questions.

"You will need to direct your power into these gems. The quartz will collect your power, and it will be sealed inside. Whoever has one of these will have a piece of you with them," she told me.

I nodded to show I understood, but I knew this was going to be hard. I had no idea how to channel my power in one direction. When I had attacked the Kraken, it had been luck that it had gone up in flames. Rylan put his hand on my shoulder.

*I will help you*, he assured me as if he could hear my thoughts.

Katie set the stones down on the ground before Arthur guided her some distance away. Jasmine followed the two, but the three of them didn't go far. I squared my shoulders and took a deep breath. My power surged forward right away. It seemed to be getting easier to call for it the more I used it. A small victory, but a victory nonetheless. With a slow exhale, I allowed my power to seep from my hands. The dirt shifted beneath our feet. I allowed a little more out. The tree close to my right side erupted into flames. Behind me, I heard a gasp, and I tensed.

*It is just you and me,* Rylan assured me.

His hand squeezed my shoulder. I nodded and continued to allow my power to trickle out of me. A crack of lightning erupted from the ground several yards away from us. Two more followed it. I tried to focus on the gems, but another two trees caught on fire. The violet blaze was hot, and the frost on the ground began to melt.

Then, Rylan was there. I felt him redirect the next bolt of lightning as it came charging up from underneath us. His grip on my shoulder tightened as he focused. I watched in amazement as the violet bolt of energy hit the gems. Instantly, they turned purple. Rylan and I shared a grin before he turned his attention to the fire that was beginning to spread. Immediately, the blazes went out. Curiously, my body reached for the power running through his veins, and I felt it return to me.

*You did it!*

I reached out and picked up the gems that were glowing brightly with my magic.

*We did it*, he corrected.

"They are ready to be used," Katie said, coming to stand next to us, staring at the stones. She looked up, and our eyes met. "I don't mean to be rude but… what are you?"

I felt the heat in my cheeks rise. At my side, Rylan stiffened. Before he could say anything, I quickly answered, "I'm an American. I know, we're a strange lot."

Katie chuckled. "Alright, keep your secret. It is probably for the best I do not know." She turned to Arthur and said, "You mentioned you would like for me to scry for someone. I can do that now if you would like."

"Yes, the shifter's pack leader, her mate, and her beta have gone missing. I have searched for her to no avail, and her pack has become anxious."

"Of course. Let me get the supplies from my car, and I will do so immediately."

Arthur followed her back to her car while Jasmine, Rylan, and I lingered behind.

Rylan turned to Jasmine. "Gabriel and Ashe will be here in two hours. Do you wish to go feed before they arrive?"

Jasmine frowned and said, "I need to talk to you about something." She glanced at me before continuing. "The park rangers work in the park all year long. What if they are tainted in some way? Our first day here, I went to ask them about any unusual activity in the park, but after what we have dealt with since we have arrived, I do not trust their responses. What if whoever is behind casting the dark magic here has managed to get the park rangers involved?"

Rylan frowned as he thought about what she said.

"I suppose it is possible. Since we cannot sense the dark magic all around us, it is possible you did not sense it affecting them. That could be something we look into. Once our guests have arrived and things get settled here, Mae and I will go speak with the park rangers again."

Jasmine nodded.

"Good idea. In the meantime, while we wait for our guests, I am going to grab something to eat." She pulled off her blouse, and I stepped forward to take it from her. On her arms were thick pink scars that had not quite healed yet. Jasmine noticed me staring and said, "Do not fret, Mae. It could have been much worse. I could have been Kraken food."

The blood drained from my face. She was right. Jasmine's wings grew out from between her shoulder blades and stretched out behind her. I stepped back to give her room, and Rylan wrapped his arm around my waist. Jasmine took off into the sunrise, and I watched until she was out of view.

The two of us headed back to the house. I made myself a small breakfast, too anxious for the arrival of our guest to eat much. Rylan hung close by. Just as I finished eating, Arthur and Katie walked into the kitchen.

"The Alpha shifter and her men are dead," Arthur told us, his expression grim. "Katie could not pinpoint the exact location of their bodies, but I have a general idea of where they might be. I will call the pack to notify them."

The silence that followed his statement hung heavy in the room. Who had killed the shifter and why? Had the werewolves gotten to them? Or was there something more sinister happening? My stomach twisted painfully. I had liked Patricia a lot. Who would take over her pack now?

"Before I leave, may I speak with you for a moment?" Katie asked me. Beside me, Rylan growled. Katie's cheeks turned pink. "I promise I have no intentions of harming your mate. I simply would like to talk."

"Of course, we can talk. How about I walk you out, and we can talk on the way?" I offered before Rylan could object. While I understood he was worried about me, his protectiveness could certainly be stifling.

As we walked out of the kitchen together, Katie surprised me by hooking her arm through mine. When I looked at her curiously, she smiled sweetly.

"I just wanted a moment alone with you. I noticed that you do not have much training with your power and how nervous you were to use it earlier," she started.

I sighed. "Yeah, I came into my power relatively recently. I'm sorry if I scared you."

"Do not be sorry," Katie said with a shake of her head. "I wanted to tell you that when I was younger, I did not know I was a witch. I did not grow up in a typical coven, but on an indigenous reservation far from here. Magic has always been prevalent in tribes like ours, but mine was incredibly strong. As I grew and matured so did my powers. Without the proper guidance of a Supreme, I messed up a lot. To help me, my people found that if I centered myself and focused on calming my inner turmoil that I was able to cast spells much easier. When I was accepted into the coven that I oversee now, I had teachers who helped me solidify my strengths and helped me understand my weaknesses."

We stopped in front of the door, and she turned to face me.

"I am not sure what you are, so I do not know who could teach you about your power or help you build a solid foundation for your power, but you should try meditation. It will help ground you, and you will learn much about yourself."

I was surprised and touched by her concern. I smiled.

"Actually, since we arrived here, I have attempted to meditate a couple of times," I told her.

"Usually, it takes time to come to know yourself and your mind, but I am curious. Did it help you at all?"

The knee jerk response was to tell her no. My power was still wild and dangerous. As she could see earlier, I had needed Rylan there to get the job done. But as I thought about it, I realized maybe it had helped a little. After my first time meditating, the following day I had been able to deliberately throw a car across the yard. The last time my power had been triggered, I had been able to fight the defense mechanism and stay in control of my body. I had even been able to keep my power from reacting at all. And despite not successfully saving Jasmine, I had been able to direct my power towards the lake creature and kill it. That may not seem like much, but… it was *something*.

"I think it may have… a little," I admitted.

"Good! You must continue to practice. Once you can center your mind, learning control won't be far behind. It will not happen overnight, but it will come," Katie assured me. "If you need my help with anything else here, please do not hesitate to call."

I thanked her and walked her out to her car.

The next two hours were tense. When Jasmine returned from feeding, the Guardians busied themselves by making sure the territory they'd marked was clear of any danger. I didn't know how far around the house they had marked to claim as their own, but I knew one was never far from me. For a while, I stood on the highest deck of the house and watched them fly around.

When I grew too anxious to stand around, I changed and worked out. By the time I was finished, I was more anxious than I was before. I showered and changed. Just as I came down the steps to the first floor, Rylan reached out to me.

*Gabriel and Ashe are coming down the road now.*

I jumped when the front door opened, and Jasmine strolled in.

"Arthur and Rylan will greet our first guests. They will let us know when we should make our appearance," she told me. She glanced at my bare feet and said, "I would put some shoes on just in case things go awry…"

"I thought Guardians were a civilized bunch of warriors. Do you really think they would attack me right away?"

"If they believe there is danger, yes," she admitted.

Outside, I heard tires on the gravel as a car pulled up. I quickly slipped on my shoes and waited with Jasmine by the front door. A door opened and shut, followed by another one. Voices mingled together, I couldn't tell who was talking or what was being said. I twirled the large engagement ring on my finger nervously. After what felt like an eternity, Jasmine looked down at me.

"It is time. Let us go meet our guests."

Jasmine opened the front door and stepped out first.

"Is that Jasmine Sing?" an incredulous voice asked. "You are a legend in the East."

I stepped out of the house and shut the door behind us. The two men standing by a large SUV looked to be in their fifties though I knew they were *much* older than that. The man closest to us was taller than both Rylan and Arthur. He was all muscle. He had tan skin, sharp facial features, and dark hair that was gelled back. The second man was shorter than Rylan, but about the same height as Arthur. His complexion was pale, highlighted by a five o'clock shadow and thick brows, but streaks of white shot through his brown hair.

"It means a lot to hear you say that when you are a legendary warrior yourself, Ashe," Jasmine purred. Was she flirting right now? I stared at her back in disbelief.

"When did you arrive? I figured we would be the—," the voice cut off. Jasmine tensed as she approached the new Guardians.

"Who is that behind you, Jasmine?" another voice asked. This voice was deep and rich. Squaring my shoulders, I stepped from behind Jasmine as we continued to walk forward.

The moment both men caught sight of me their eyes turned blood red. Their bodies tensed, and the taller one even flexed the muscles in his arms. Rylan and Arthur shifted ever so slightly, placing themselves between the new Guardians and Jasmine and me. They could still see me, but now the two Guardians had three obstacles to go through if they wanted to attack me.

I walked past Jasmine. As I drew closer, I watched the familiar shudder run through both men as my presence lifted their curse. The fangs on the taller one descended, and his nostrils flared. I stopped next to Rylan and waited for the introductions to be made.

"Gabriel, Ashe, I am pleased to introduce to you my mate, Mae Wellington," Rylan said.

The silence that followed was tense. The muscles on both men began to flex. Their jaws clenched and relaxed as their eyes trailed over me to assess the danger I presented. When the silence continued to stretch, my patience wore thin. I took another step towards the new Guardians and then smiled and extended my hand.

"Until I sign the marriage paperwork, I'm still Mae White. In any case, this is the twenty-first century, maybe I'll talk him into taking my last name," I joked.

I waited, refusing to back down. After another long silence, the taller Guardian took a step towards me. His blazing red eyes watched my face as he closed the distance between us. Next to me, Rylan stiffened.

"Gabriel Knight." The Guardian's hand engulfed mine, his grip tight and far from friendly. "Mae White, you are quite a specimen."

Gabriel Knight... I knew that name. It took me a moment to realize this was the Guardian who had sent Arthur the pictures of Zein's murder scene. While I felt awful that he had stumbled upon such a horrible scene, irritation ruffled my nerves. The grip he had me in was almost bone crushing.

"A specimen?" I asked with a raised brow. "I'm just a young woman with some crazy abilities… which you will be able to see firsthand if you grip my hand any tighter."

Rylan growled next to me, and Gabriel dropped my hand.

"Rylan, what is this? Who is this woman, truly?" the shorter man (Ashe, I presumed) snapped. "She cannot be your mate when

I so clearly have regained my emotions back. She is most certainly mine, but she is…." His upper lip curled in disgust. "—tainted. I do not think I could accept such *filth* as my other half. I would rather cease to exist."

Rylan snarled so fiercely that I looked up at him in surprise. He leaned forward in a crouch as his expression twisted in anger. His fangs lengthened, and he hissed. He took a menacing step forward, but I grabbed his wrist to prevent him from going any further.

"She is not tainted," he snapped at the Guardian. "And she is *my* mate. She bears my mark upon her neck, and we have completed our Joining. If she were yours, you would never say something so despicable."

*Do not listen to the trash he spouts,* Rylan told me.

*I'm not offended. I'm here to help save the world, not impress this asshat,* I assured him.

Ashe bared his teeth. He took an aggressive step towards me, but Rylan was there before he was able to move any closer. He pulled himself up to his full height and snarled down at Ashe, who snapped his teeth at him.

"If you cannot control yourself, you are welcome to leave," Rylan growled.

"She has seduced you, Rylan. She has blinded you three with that pretty face, but I cannot be fooled. Her power radiates like a god's," Gabriel said as he stood next to Ashe. His expression darkened as he glared at me.

"That is because she is a progeny of one," Arthur explained calmly. Both Gabriel and Ashe gasped in surprise, and possibly horror. Arthur came to stand next to me. "Mae is quite an extraordinary woman. It is because of her that we have become aware of the issues in this area. We will explain everything to you, but I need you to trust us when we say that Mae is not the threat here."

Gabriel and Ashe exchanged looks with one another. The soft buzzing in my head was loud as they communicated. Time stilled as we waited to see how the two Guardians would proceed. I stole a glance at Rylan who, without looking at me, took my hand and brought it to his lips. Ashe's eyes narrowed at the contact. After an agonizing silence, both men appeared to come to a decision. Gabriel looked at Rylan.

"I have known you for a long time. Every battle that you have led, I have followed you, and we have been victorious," he said. He turned to Arthur and continued, "The same goes for you, Arthur. Your concern over the well-being of our people is known throughout the community. I trust you both. If you say Mae is not a threat, then she is not a threat."

The way Gabriel's gaze swept over me assured me that even though he trusted the Guardians, he certainly did not trust me. Ashe glared at Gabriel, then at the two Guardians at my side, before he turned his attention back to me. His eyes narrowed in suspicion.

"You called us here for help, and it is my duty as a Guardian to make sure the safety of creatures from all walks of life are protected. I will help you with whatever is going on here… and any other threats we will face after this," Ashe promised, his voice a barely contained growl. He was talking to Rylan and Arthur, possibly even Jasmine, but his focus was solely on me. While his promise to help us was appreciated, the underlying threat sent chills down my spine.

I was sure Ashe expected me to cower at his unspoken threat. He was certainly an intimidating person and knowing that he could potentially kill me with a flick of his wrist was definitely a reason to fear him. But standing here knowing my potential and having my mate and my friends stand with me, I was far from scared. Instead of cowering, I smiled at him.

"Alright. Now that pleasantries are out of the way, can we get to the point about why we asked you here?" Jasmine drawled.

Both Ashe and Gabriel turned their attention to her.

"Let us get down to business," Ashe snapped and brushed past Rylan towards the house.

"There is one more thing…" Arthur hedged and pulled two quartz necklaces from his pocket. Both Gabriel and Ashe eyed the jewelry suspiciously. There was no doubt they could feel my power radiating off them. "Every day something happens in this park that makes people go insane. The Alpha of the pack station nearby described it as a wave of depravity. We believe it may have something to do with dark magic. When it touches you, you will feel the need to kill or destroy whatever or whoever is around you. By wearing these, we are hoping it will prevent you from being affected."

"Hoping?" Ashe repeated incredulously. He bared his teeth at Arthur and then turned to look at me again. "You want us to wear something *she* has manipulated?"

"I do not see *you* wearing these necklaces," Gabriel pointed out as he gazed at all three Guardians surrounding me.

"Because it no longer affects us," Arthur assured him.

"And why is that?" Ashe demanded.

I sighed and answered for Arthur, knowing Ashe had already guessed it. "Because they absorbed some of my power the other day, and since then they have been okay."

"So you *have* corrupted their minds," Ashe shouted and took a step towards me.

"I didn't corrupt anyone," I told him calmly. I surprised Ashe by taking a step towards him. Rylan pulled me back immediately. "Chill the fuck out, and either take the necklaces or I'll zap you later when you try to kill each other. The choice is yours." I threw up my hands in aggravation.

Without wasting any more breath, I turned around and headed back towards the house. The others could deal with this. If this was how the rest of the Guardians were going to react, then I needed to steal away for a while so I could regain my patience.

"I will take the necklace," I heard Gabriel say behind me.

I opened the front door and walked into the house. Why did I have a feeling this was going to be a long day?

# Chapter Fifteen

*Rylan*

Inside, Gabriel and Ashe listened as we told them the story of Mae. It was interesting to watch a myriad of emotions cross their faces. I watched as they tried to recompose themselves each time they felt a new emotion and struggled to remain indifferent. During their time around Mae, they would have to learn how to manage their feelings. Watching their struggle was strange. I knew exactly how they felt. Walking in to find Mae and Arthur in Arthur's VIP lounge in Chicago, I had been bombarded with emotions that Mae had invoked. It had been nearly impossible to remain calm and apathetic as I listened to Arthur explain the situation.

The difference between me and the two Guardians was that Mae was mine. I would now live curse-free while they would eventually have to endure living life without emotions once more. To get used to emotions that would not last… It sounded like a form of torture. Guilt swirled around in my gut. It was the same for Arthur and Jasmine. Their support and their help figuring out how to help Mae would mean they would be around for longer, but eventually, our time with them would end, and we would go our own way. Arthur had high hopes that Mae would be able to break the curse over all of us permanently. That was a heavy load to place on Mae's shoulders. While it would be wonderful if she could, I did not expect Mae to be the answer to lifting the curse.

As I shared our predicament, I understood how insane this all must sound. The gods were supposed to be long gone. To hear that Mae had not only had some sort of communication with one but had also had been in the presence of one was beyond worrisome. I shared all of our findings with them. When I got to the part of the story where Mae defeated a Kraken Gabriel stopped me. "How could Mae defeat a Kraken without any control of her power?" Gabriel asked skeptically.

"She is figuring it out," Jasmine said softly. "Before the Kraken grabbed me, the werewolves were hunting us, and my attention was on them. This dark energy that washes over the park hit us, and Mae was able to contain her power without blacking out and letting it control her."

I looked at Jasmine in surprise. Mae had failed to mention any of this.

"It took an immense amount of concentration," Jasmine continued, "but she did it. She used that same focus to save me."

"A Kraken, here, in the middle of nowhere..." Gabriel repeated. Barely contained astonishment coated his tone.

I turned my attention to Mae. Her constant self-doubt was her worst enemy. To know she was able to overcome whatever internal defense mechanism she had, and then defeat a creature that made Guardians quake, filled me with so much pride I thought I might burst from it. Reaching out with my senses, I found her up in one of the lofts, attempting to meditate. I had heard what the witch had suggested, and I appreciated the kindness from the Supreme. Instead of twiddling her thumbs, Mae was working hard to find control over her power. My heart swelled. My mate was doing everything she could.

"How did mermaids and a Kraken end up in a freshwater lake in Canada?" Ashe asked.

I eyed the Guardian. I had known Ashe for years, and while his reaction was what I had expected from the others, I had not expected it from him. He was usually much more progressive than most of us. While he had promised to help, he had certainly made his stance towards my mate clear. I would have to be extra wary over Ashe's every move.

"That is one of the questions we need to figure out," Arthur said. "Earlier, I found out that the shifter's pack leader, her mate, and her beta are dead. They were last seen leaving this house, and they had to travel near the lake to get back to their pack. The werewolves were also seen in that area. I am guessing that Patricia and her men were attacked and killed there. I would like to explore the lake and the surrounding woods to see if there is something drawing these creatures there."

"It is probably the dark magic in the air. But according to you, without Mae present, we will not be able to sense it," Ashe pointed out. "What are you looking to accomplish without her there?"

"We may not be able to sense dark magic, but we can track the werewolves the old fashioned way. We can look for their travel patterns and see where they have been hiding out. If we find them, we eliminate them," Arthur responded.

"Have you contacted Cain? He should have been looking into this," Gabriel asked with a frown.

"Patricia, the shifter Alpha, told us she never met Cain during her time as Alpha," Arthur said, "and he never responded to any of the previous Alpha's requests for a meeting. He has gone missing, as far as we know."

"*Missing?*" Gabriel repeated incredulously. His brows came together in a deep scowl.

"Is Cain missing or has he been murdered?" Ashe asked. "After Gabriel sent you the picture of Zein's wings and the writing on the wall, we explored the rest of his home. His territory borders Cain's, and he had notes about strange activity happening in his area as well."

"Strange how?" I asked.

"The bear shifters in Montana have found more and more members disappearing or being murdered. If murdered, their insides have been removed, which indicates someone is trying to perform ritualistic acts. He noted that vampires have been acting drunk and seem to have a lapse in their memories. He even mentions something about acid rain destroying a part of the Kootenai National Forest. Zein mentions that he, too, reached out to Cain, but there is nothing that indicates he was able to get a hold of him," Gabriel shared.

I traded looks with Arthur and Jasmine. While none of those issues seemed to apply to this area, the fact that both territories touched and both were experiencing unusual activities only solidified that something was going on.

"How do the last two Guardians that have lived here go missing and another Guardian who lives in the same vicinity get murdered without any of us realizing what is going on?" Jasmine asked after a moment of silence.

"There has been a rise in suicides within our community, Jasmine," Arthur said with a sigh. "This curse will be the end to our species at the rate things are going now. Those of us who usually keep track of everyone have been so busy trying to fill the many empty territories left behind that I am sure this is just one of the many things that has slipped through the cracks."

The solemn silence that followed Arthur's statement was filled with sorrow for our fallen brethren. While it hurt to think of how many had been lost, it also felt like a small gift to be able to finally grieve properly for them. I glanced around the room at the others and realized they were probably thinking the same thing.

"Zein's death was made to look like a suicide," Gabriel said thoughtfully. He turned to look at Arthur. "Do you think that the uptick in suicides have really been murders that have been covered up?"

Arthur looked at Gabriel with alarm. "Lately, those who have left us simply leave a note and disappear. There is no body to dispose of. So there is no way of knowing for sure… But let us hope that is not the case. It is possible that whoever killed Zein knew that Guardians have a tendency to take their own lives when they cannot handle the weight of our curse any longer. This could just be a singular instance within our community."

"If Zein had suspicions about something, why would he not have mentioned it to you when you saw him in Chicago?" I asked Arthur.

Arthur shrugged, but it was Ashe who answered, "Maybe he did not know the extent of what he was dealing with. Maybe he thought he could take care of it on his own. We all have a tendency to do things on our own rather than ask for help."

"I think it is safe to assume that Zein figured out what was going on here and was murdered for it," I told the others. "If we find out who is behind this, we find his murderer."

"Then let us do whatever possible to find this bastard," Gabriel said with a sharp nod. "Who else did you contact about the happenings here?"

"Nikolas Richter, Camille Savage, and Devon Salah who will arrive today," Jasmine said. "And three others will be joining us tomorrow.."

"If you show us where to go, Ashe and I will get a head start on checking out the lake. It will allow us to explore the area, and as the others trickle in, you will have the ability to talk to them as you have with us," Gabriel offered.

Arthur, Jasmine, and I hesitated. Gabriel was wearing the necklace, but Ashe was not. Ashe's eyes narrowed.

"Worried something will happen to us?" he asked. "Let me ask you this: Was your mate around when you all became violent? Maybe she is the reason behind it."

The snarl that passed my lips was echoed by Arthur and Jasmine. I tried to choke down my animalistic response to his accusation, but I was too pissed off to speak. I wanted to close the distance between us and throttle the Guardian.

"This was happening long before any of us arrived, Ashe," Arthur growled as he spoke for me. "It was Patricia who warned us about this unseen attack against our minds. It is not Mae."

"The only time the four of us were together when this happened was when Mae saved us from ourselves," Jasmine added as her brows pulled together in a deep scowl.

"It has nothing to do with me, asshole." Mae's disgruntled voice floated down from the third floor loft.

There was a pause before Arthur and Jasmine chuckled. I smiled. I was sure Mae had not intended for any of us to hear her. The tension within the three of us lessened. Even the corner of Gabriel's mouth tugged upwards. Ashe glared in Mae's direction but did not respond.

"I will show you where to search but stay aware," Arthur warned them as we guided them into the office.

"*Everything* here is coated in dark magic," Jasmine said.

We headed to the office, showed the two Guardians where on the map the lake was, and then Jasmine walked them out to show them the direction she and Mae had taken to the lake. Arthur and I watched the two Guardians take off before we both exchanged worried looks with one another.

***

Four hours later, just shortly after noon, our next wave of guests arrived. All four of us filed outside to greet them in the driveway. Mae fell behind on her own, letting me and the others handle the greeting. I could feel the tension rolling in her gut, but her expression was neutral, giving nothing away. I looked to the sky, and a moment later two Guardians with satchels over their shoulders came into view. They landed with a grace that came with years of practice.

The reaction to Mae was almost instantaneous. The surprise, confusion, and shock that rippled across each Guardian's expression would never grow old. Devon strolled forward towards us, but his focus was solely pinned to my mate in wonder. I stepped in front of him, and he pulled his gaze away from Mae to look at me.

"Rylan, it is good to see you," he said with a charismatic smile.

Devon's good-natured smile was renowned for getting him what he wanted. The ease with which he could charm a woman was an ongoing joke amongst other supernatural creatures. He looked older since the last time I had seen him. Thin gray strands of hair could be seen racing through his jet black hair that was slicked back out of his face. There were lines around his eyes and his skin was not tan as it usually was. It must be close to his time to change territories. "Please excuse me for a moment. It seems that I have found my missing half." The possessive look in Devon's eyes as he stared at Mae caused knots to form in my stomach. Devon tried to walk past me, but I placed a hand in the middle of his chest. I felt the tension coil in his body. He looked at me again. His pupils narrowed, and his smile slipped.

"Devon Salah," I said and then turned to the female warrior, "Camille Savage, it is my pleasure to introduce to you my mate Mae White."

*Thanks for changing my last name back*, Mae's said with amusement.

"Your mate? Impossible, my emotions have returned. What I am experiencing is the curse lifting and my soul shining back at me through this lovely woman," Devon said flippantly and tried to walk past me again.

Arthur stepped closer to me, effectively blocking Devon's view of Mae. Devon bared his teeth, his fangs lengthened, and his posture became defensive.

"She is my mate, Devon," I assured him, trying to remain calm.

I wanted to react, to rip out the throat of the Guardian in front of me for even presuming that Mae was his. It was an animalistic instinct that would forever linger in my veins. It had eased up with Arthur and Jasmine the moment Mae and I had Joined, but it was still there, just as strong as ever, around the newcomers.

"What you are feeling is Mae's ability to temporarily lift the curse over us," Arthur explained to Devon calmly.

"Impossible," Camille said a few feet behind Devon. She was a muscular woman with golden locks and piercing green eyes. The suspicious glare she pointed at my mate caused me to shift my stance ever so slightly to keep a better eye on her.

"It is very possible," Arthur assured her.

"I do not understand. She can lift our curse? Does that have anything to do with her strange aura?" Camille asked.

"This is absurd, one woman cannot break a curse a god has created. Let me speak with Mae," Devon snapped and tried to push past me.

"This is some sort of trick. She is an abomination!" Camille cried out. "Why do you protect this *thing*, Arthur? There is something amiss about her."

Understanding crossed Devon's face. His expression turned from annoyed to disgusted. His fangs lengthened as he turned his attention to Mae. His dark brows came together and his face became hollowed. He asked to no one in particular,

"Who is this woman you three protect so vehemently? Can you not sense the power in her? It is warped and wild and—,"

"Mae is a child of a god. That is what you all are sensing," Arthur interrupted him calmly. "And we are protecting her because she is innocent of any wrongdoing. It is because of her we have learned of the workings of dark magic here and how it is corrupting the very woods we are standing in. Something is afoot, and we need your help to figure out what it is before it is too late."

"Mae is a child of a god?" Camille whispered as her and Devon's eyes bulged from their sockets.

"Yes, and we will explain it all when we head inside, but first, for your safety we need you to wear these," Jasmine said as she pulled out two quartz necklaces from her pocket.

"Who are you to tell us what to do? What are those for?" Camille demanded.

"Camille," Arthur called sharply. Camille pulled her steely gaze from Jasmine to pin Arthur down.

"Arthur, you better explain why that woman's head is not on a stake and her body is not burning," she growled.

"Camille, Devon," Arthur sighed with exasperation, "I told you over the phone that there is dark magic lurking in these woods. Without Mae, we would not know the extent of how bad things are here. I need you to trust me. I trust Mae with my life, and you know I do not say that lightly. Jasmine is another individual whom I have high regard for and trust with my life."

"We called you because we need your help," I addressed them both. I glared at Devon who was watching Mae with a murderous gaze. "Someone is trying to bring the gods back to this realm. We are here to figure out who it is, where they are, and how to stop them. We have less than two months before the world could end."

"If it is this serious, why not call all Guardians to the area?" Devon demanded.

"Clearly, because of how you have reacted at the sight of Mae," Jasmine answered for me. "Convincing just two of you that she is to be trusted is a chore. Trying to convince an army of Guardians would be impossible. "

"Give them the necklaces, Jazz," Mae interrupted sharply.

I glanced over my shoulder, and my heart sank. Mae's veins were glowing, and her body began to shake. She stumbled backward towards the door as her whole body jerked. She grabbed her midsection and doubled over in pain.

"Mae!" I cried out her name in alarm.

"Take the necklaces! We are about to experience an attack on our minds," Jasmine yelled and tossed the talismans to the newcomers. Her wings ripped through her blouse, tearing it to pieces. I called upon my wings and braced myself. Both Devon and Camille watched as their necklaces fell to the ground. It was clear neither of them were going to wear it.

"An attack?" Camille repeated and turned her attention to Mae, expecting it to come from her. "What—,"

Since our arrival, I had been unable to sense the depravity that affected the others. Whether it was because of my involvement with Mae or just a genetic quirk, I could not be sure. But whatever the reason was, I was thankful that I was not affected as I watched as Devon and Camille suddenly went eerily still.

"Camille…" Arthur started cautiously, bringing up his hands in the age-old 'I surrender' motion.

For a single heartbeat, it was silent and still. Then, chaos erupted. Devon moved first, pulling his mace from the tattoo on his ankle. He spun on his heels and tried to attack me with it. I dipped out of the way and tackled him to the ground. Screeches rang out and the clanging of metal pierced the cool afternoon air. I gripped the wrist of the hand that held Devon's mace while I used my body weight to pin him down. Devon's mouth foamed. His red eyes were wild and unseeing.

Angry roars, snarls, and screams littered the air. Devon tried to kick me off him. Instead, we ended up scuffling there on the ground. He attempted to take to the air, but I grabbed his ankle and slammed his body against the ground. The spike of his mace cracked against my ribs, and I roared in pain.

*I'm going to let go*, Mae's voice was calm, but I could hear the underlying strain. There was no time to object. Devon yanked the mace out of my side to strike again. As he raised his weapon and I tensed, ready to attack, the ground erupted.

It was like Mae's power sensed those affected and targeted them. Devon's eyes widened in pain, and that was my only warning. I leapt away just as a violet lightning bolt shot up through his chest. He screamed in agony and crumpled to the ground where he spasmed as Mae's power rushed through him.

Behind me, another scream echoed around us. I turned to find Camille stumbling backwards before collapsing. Her sword fell to the ground as she thrashed about. I glanced towards my mate and found her with her legs spread wide, her arms outstretched, and her teeth bared. The veins in her head were popping out and sweat beaded her brow, but she was conscious and focused on the scene before her.

*Mae, enough*, I called out to her and was by her side in an instant. Her jaw clenched, and she closed her eyes as she tried to pull it back.

"Rylan!" Jasmine shrieked and pointed to the sky.

I threw my arms around Mae, crushing her into my chest while my wings came around us in a shield. I hissed as three blades slammed into my back in simultaneous succession. I heard Mae's scream of denial. Somewhere above us, a roar rang out. Sounds of blades clashing together told me whoever had thrown the blades was now busy with another opponent. I pulled my wings back and attempted to turn around but staggered. Mae caught me with a gasp and helped lower me to my knees.

"Mae, let me help," Jasmine's voice said from somewhere behind me. Before I could tell her I was fine, the first blade was yanked out of my back. I flinched but bit my tongue. The second blade was removed quickly, and just as efficiently as the first, followed by the third one. "The wounds are not too deep, Rylan, but you will be sore for the rest of the day."

I stood with Mae's help and turned to Jasmine. Jasmine turned and took to the sky. Above us Arthur was in the midst of battle with another warrior. Their movements were so fast that I was sure Mae could not follow the movement. Jasmine joined the fight and three of them engaged in a high stakes battle. Behind me, Mae sucked in a sharp breath and watched them. I could feel her fear through our bond but I could almost feel her trembling as she scooted closer to me.

Her small hand slipped into mine. I did not look back at her but I gripped her hand tighter. A quick glance at Devon and Camille told me they were incapacitated for the moment. The only threat came from the warrior in the sky. As much as I would like to join my friends, if that warrior broke through them to get to Mae, she needed a shield.

Their weapons glittered in the sunlight, the sound of metal hitting metal was sharp and loud. Even with two against one, the new arrival was holding his own fine. The strength and speed of this Guardian was a sight to be seen.

The fight was short-lived. Suddenly, all three of them broke apart. They hovered over us for another moment before coming down to land in the driveway. While I did not personally know this Guardian, Nikolas Richter was legendary among us. He was one of the oldest Guardians in the world. His fierce fighting style, the confidence he wore, and the battle scars he refused to hide only added to his personification of being one of the most dangerous Guardians in all existence.

"Nikolas," Arthur said in greeting as he pushed his flail into his back where it became a tattoo. "Welcome and thank you for coming on such short notice. I am sorry you had to experience a brush with the depravity that terrorizes the creatures within this area."

Nikolas ignored Arthur and looked around the front yard at all of us. I followed his gaze and found Devon on his feet, his face ashen and twisted in horror. Camille was staring down at her bloodied sword in utter disbelief. She looked up, and I caught her gaze before it slid over to Mae.

Nikolas followed Camille's gaze where it lingered on my mate. I opened my wings wide to shield her from his cold stare.

Nikolas's time with the gods was spoken of only in whispers. He had been the deadliest opponent to face when his god sent him into war. This was not the Guardian I would have called into this situation knowing his position on the gods. The new arrival turned back to Arthur.

"It appears that you left out a few details when you called me, Arthur," Nikolas accused in an eerily soft voice. "The dark magic hanging in the air is blackening my lungs. Were you looking to poison me? There also better be a good reason *that*—" He nodded in the direction of Mae. "—young god has not been properly executed and made an example of."

I bared my teeth at the old Guardian. Nikolas stared at me with hate-filled eyes. A cold, slow smile pulled his thin lips wide across his face.

"Ah, she is your mate. Does she make your heart sing? Does she complete you?" the Guardian sneered. "Whatever magic she has cast over you, over all of you, to sway you to believe every word she speaks, do not fret. *I* will be your voice of reason. She is a monster that must be destroyed. If you are all incapable of terminating her, then I will gladly do it for you."

"You will do no such thing," Arthur snapped firmly. "I called you here because of your experience with the gods. Your position here is not to cast judgment or become an executioner of an innocent woman. Now." Arthur turned around to face everyone, his expression murderous. "Everyone get inside and clean up. You have just had a taste of what we have been dealing with, and it only gets worse from here."

# Chapter Sixteen

*Mae*

"What we experienced was not dark magic or depravity as you call it," Nikolas interrupted Arthur, who was in the middle of explaining the situation to everyone. "It is the plant life trying to survive in an environment that is being constantly affected by dark magic. The plants are struggling to soak in the dark magic like they do carbon dioxide and trying to recycle it back out like oxygen. Except dark magic cannot be processed like carbon dioxide. When the plant life expels the dark magic, it comes out like a toxin. It depends on the day how much toxin is released into the air, which is why you cannot track a pattern."

The room was silent as we processed Nikolas's explanation. It was dark out now. Hours had gone by since this afternoon's chaos. After we had shown everyone to their rooms, our guests cleaned themselves up and took time to heal from their injuries. We had all reconvened in the family room. I stood by the massive window that looked out to the front yard and stared at the woods. Absentmindedly, I played with my engagement ring.

Jasmine hung close to me but was turned to face everyone else. In the reflection of the glass, I could see Arthur standing next to Camille, who sat in the leather chairs furthest from me. Devon sat stiffly on the couch. Rylan stood near Nikolas by the fireplace, his arms crossed over his chest.

While everyone went to clean up, Rylan and I had stolen away to our bedroom. I had wiped away the dried blood from where Nikolas's three daggers had lodged into Rylan's back and where Devon's mace had hit him on his side. As Jasmine had predicted, the skin was still pink and tender where Nikolas's blades had lodged themselves. Seeing the evidence of his devotion to keep me safe made me sick. If he hadn't moved so quickly, I would have been dead.

Turning my attention away from my depressing thoughts, I forced myself to concentrate on the topic at hand. Everyone was watching Nikolas. Their expressions ranged from unease to suspicion. It was clear the other Guardians in the room trusted him as little as I did.

Nikolas Richter terrified me.

He was the most frightening person I had ever encountered. He was abnormally tall, and he was easily more muscular than all the Guardians in the room. His skin was kissed by the sun which accented his long, stark white hair that he had pulled back. There were thick scars along his jawline that trailed down his neck. I didn't even know Guardians *could* scar. What had this Guardian gone through to get those?

What truly frightened me, though, were his piercing gray eyes. Outside, they had been full of a fiery rage. Now they were as cold as the arctic. The hatred in that icy gaze was a special, soul-searing type of hate directed specifically at me. He reminded me of a jungle cat. He seemed utterly at ease, calm, and at times almost bored. But the intensity in his gaze assured me that the languid way he stood was just a guise. He could attack without warning, and we wouldn't know it until it was too late. I was surprised when he took a necklace from Arthur and slipped it over his neck. I would have sworn he would forgo wearing it simply because I had something invested in it.

"You have seen this before?" Camille asked. "I have been around dark magic many times before, especially down in the rainforest where witch doctors come down with *vício escuro*. But I have always been able to sense where they have used their powers. I never thought there would be a day when I could not."

*Vício escuro?* I repeated to Rylan.

*It is Portuguese for 'dark addiction',* Rylan translated for me. *It happens when someone tries using natural magic mixed with dark magic. They get a taste for the darker stuff and get sucked into needing more.*

"Yes, long ago, where Madhya Pradesh is located today, something similar occurred," Nikolas confirmed.

"How were you able to resolve the issue there?" Jasmine asked.

"We burned most of the forest down," Nikolas stated. "It all came back after a couple hundred years."

"That would be hard to cover up nowadays," Devon said with a dismissive wave of his hand. In the reflection of the glass, I saw him glance towards me before turning his attention back to the others. "Whatever Mae did outside, could she do it to the rest of the park?"

The room grew silent, and I felt all eyes on me. With a sigh, I turned to face everyone.

"I can't do that."

"Why not? Just wave your hand and remove the threat," Devon said simply. While he seemed more civil than the other two it was clear he did not trust me. His wary expression as he studied me made that clear.

It took everything I had not to sneer at him. Oh, was it that easy? How had I not thought of something so simple as waving my hands to remove all evil magic in the woods?

"I'm not strong enough for such a monumental task. Besides, I have a very slippery control over my ability. You're lucky I didn't set your insides on fire by mistake." Everyone except for Nikolas, who simply gazed at me, cringed at the visual. "I'm new to my power, and for the past two years, I have been trying my best to ignore it. It's only been these past two weeks that I have tried to purposely use and control it."

"What a dangerous decision to try to *ignore* your power," Camille said coolly. "How did that go for you?"

"Well, I've ended up in a room full of Guardians who want to see me dead. If we're going off that, I'd say it's going pretty well," I answered just as coolly.

Jasmine started to chuckle but cut herself off, covering her slip with a delicate cough.

"In any case, even if Mae could do it, the dark magic would just recoat everything soon afterward. What we need to do is discover who is casting it and destroy them," Rylan said, pulling the attention away from me. "Zyroe and Autumn showed Mae a location about three hundred miles south of here where they believe the gates between the realms will open. We have not been able to get to that location yet, but I have a feeling that is where we should start looking for our target."

"For whatever reason, I cannot sense this dark magic you claim is here," Devon said. "If it's like that there, it will be like looking for a needle in a haystack."

Before anyone responded, everyone turned their attention towards the foyer. I was the last one to turn around. A moment later Gabriel and Ashe walked in through the front door with bleak expressions. Both Guardians had lost their shirts, probably when taking flight, and we were privy to see dried blood coating their bodies. Ashe's gaze swept over the newcomers briefly as he and Gabriel walked past everyone, making a beeline straight for me. I braced myself.

Rylan moved from Nikolas's side to step in front of the two Guardians, and Jasmine shifted into a fighting stance.

"I need to speak to your mate," Ashe demanded of Rylan.

"Whatever you have to say, you can do it from here," Rylan told him before growling menacingly.

"All is well, Rylan," Gabriel stated calmly as he stepped between both Guardians. "Ashe just wants to talk."

The room was silent as everyone watched Rylan and Ashe. Both men glared at each other, neither one of them budging. I rolled my eyes and stepped past Jasmine.

"This is absurd," I said as I came to stand next to Rylan. I eyed Ashe suspiciously but continued, "We are all adults here. Conversation can be had without all this posturing. What is it, Ashe? Are you both alright?" My gaze swept over both Ashe and Gabriel for any sign of an injury that hadn't yet healed.

"We are both in one piece because of you," Ashe stated firmly. "You warned us of the danger of taking off on our own without the necklace. Because Gabriel was so gracious to look past your heritage and took the necklace, we both made it back tonight." He took a step closer to me, but Rylan moved to block him so Ashe couldn't get any closer. Without acknowledging Rylan's movement, Ashe continued, "I tried to kill a fellow Guardian today. It was an unprovoked, malicious attack that would have ended in murder if we had both engaged in battle. But because Gabriel wore your necklace, his mind was not compromised. He was able to fend me off until the effects wore off, and I was in my right mind again. I refused to believe that there was something capable of messing with my mind. I was sure it was some type of ploy on your part. Mae, my hatred for you clouded my judgment, which put a fellow warrior in jeopardy. Shame is not a strong enough word for how I am feeling. I am sorry for doubting you."

I wasn't necessarily touched by his apology. What happened had been his fault. I stared at the harsh features of the man in front of me. After a moment I nodded, accepting his apology. If this was a trick to cause me to let my guard down, it would not work but for now I could be courteous.

"Jasmine, you mentioned you *hoped* the necklaces would protect us," Ashe said. "Your theory has been proven correct. From the blood outside, I assume the rest of you learned the hard way to trust Mae and our fellow Guardians. I hope no one was seriously injured. We went to explore the lake where Mae and Jasmine had found the Kraken. When we got there we found the water had turned jet black. The corpses of ten mermaids floated on the surface along with hundreds of fish. The mermaids were mutated and sickly. The fish were unidentifiable. We removed their bodies and burned them. Jasmine, you said the park rangers have not noticed anything unusual?"

"That is correct," she confirmed with a nod.

"Strange; you would think visitors in the area who went fishing in that lake would report to them that their fish looked like something from a science lab. When we were done at the lake, we traveled northwest towards the shifter pack. Along the way, we found the skins of your missing Alpha and her two men."

"The skins?" Camille repeated.

"Yes, only their flesh remained. They were gutted, and their insides were removed. Just as they were in Zein's territory before he was murdered," Gabriel told her. There was a collective gasp from the newcomers. The only one who didn't react was Nikolas.

"Zein was murdered?" Devon asked, coming to his feet. He and Nikolas both shot me a suspicious look before returning their attention to Gabriel.

"Yes, about two weeks ago. Shortly after his trip to Chicago," Gabriel verified.

"It is interesting that he died shortly after meeting you, Mae," Nikolas taunted. If he expected me to react, he was in for a disappointment. I wouldn't rise to the bait.

"We need to alert the shifter pack. They need to be relocated far from here until we can resolve this mystery," Arthur said with a sigh. "Did you bring their skins back so we can return them to the pack?"

Gabriel and Ashe nodded.

"If the gates are supposed to open several hundred miles away, why are there unusual occurrences here?" Camille wanted to know.

"The magic required to break open the gates would have to be immense," Rylan mused out loud. "Mix that magic with dark spells, and it most likely became unstable and has been festering outward through the park."

"I do not understand something," Devon started, his handsome face tilting to one side thoughtfully. "Why was the lake black? What killed the mermaids?"

"When Mae killed the Kraken, her power radiated across the lake," Jasmine answered. "I'm sure that if they were affected by the dark magic, Mae's power killed them. And since Mae touched the water during her attack, it turned black."

Camille stood up and glared at me. "I am confused. Mae turned the water black? Why?"

"When she makes physical contact with an object or if her power touches anything that has dark magic on it, the object turns black," Rylan replied.

"So she can reveal where dark magic is hidden?" Devon asked.

"It is not hidden; it is everywhere," Nikolas corrected.

"How do you know dark magic was everywhere? How can *you* sense it?" I asked the scary Guardian suspiciously. "No one else here can feel it."

Nikolas's pupils narrowed. Those cold gray eyes skimmed over my face; his expression full of contempt.

"Because the god I served dabbled in it often enough that I can sense it in any form it takes. Whoever is casting this dark magic is trying to conceal evidence of it, which is why none of you can feel it. But I can still sense its presence," he informed me before turning to the others. "Rylan is right. We should head south tomorrow and fan out. When we get closer to the source of all this trouble, we should be able to find who is casting it."

"Fine. Now that we know what is going on and have a plan, I am going out to explore the area nearby. Give me that necklace, Jasmine," Camille said. It was obvious she was done with the conversation.

"You do not need it anymore," Jasmine assured her.

The room stilled. Camille's eyes narrowed on her. "Why not?"

"Because with Mae's power in you, you have protection against—" Jasmine glanced at Nikolas. "—the *toxins* that trigger the madness."

"She planted something in my *mind?*" Camille's sharp shriek sent chills down my spine. "That child is an abomination we should not allow to exist. She has violated me by tampering with my mind. This must be some sort of trap. Are you looking to control me, young god? Do you not see how she has manipulated you, Arthur?" Camille demanded, turning to Arthur. "You have been around her too long. She has pulled the wool over your eyes!"

"How did Mae tamper with your mind?" Gabriel asked curiously as he turned to Camille.

She placed her hands on her hips and said, "She *attacked* us with her power when we all lost our minds. She was able to snap us out of our killing spree." She turned back to me. "What else can you do, Mae? Will we fall under the spell that you have cast over these three?" She waved her hands towards Rylan, Arthur, and Jasmine. "Will you ask us to jump, and will we be forced to ask you how high?"

"Her very existence is dangerous to everyone in this world," Nikolas added. "We are all insane to be sitting here with her talking about our plans as if she is someone to be trusted or an ally."

Devon and Camille nodded in agreement.

"Nikolas, until there is proof that Mae is a threat, we will focus on the problem at hand," Ashe responded with a scowl towards the ancient Guardian.

"Tomorrow, we should split up," Rylan snapped with annoyance as he changed the direction of the conversation.

From his expression, it was quite clear he was fed up with everyone's prejudice against me. Listening to everyone talk about me as if I was the evil one unnerved me. This was the danger Rylan, Arthur, and Jasmine had been worried about. If they all turned on me, my three Guardians wouldn't stand a chance. While I didn't disagree with them that I was dangerous, I wasn't sure if I would classify myself as evil.

"Now that you all either have the necklaces or have been touched by Mae's power," Rylan continued, "you are protected from the toxin in the air. It will be safer to travel in groups, which will allow us to cover more ground. A few of us should travel south. The rest of us need to spread out and remove the threats within these woods. There is a pack of werewolves that roam these woods during the day that need to be eliminated. After seeing the Kraken and mermaids, I am sure there are other things in these woods that should not be here."

"I will lead a group of us south," Jasmine offered.

"I will take a few Guardians, and we will check for threats in the woods," Arthur offered.

The Guardians began splitting up into groups, talking amongst themselves as they made plans for the next day. I stood there and watched them, feeling like the odd one out. I was sure that if I stepped forward to join one of the groups, I would be greeted with hostility. So, instead of interrupting progress, I left the room. As I crossed the family room, I looked over my shoulder to make sure I wasn't needed. No one seemed to notice my departure except for Nikolas, who was watching me intently.

I made my way outside to the second level deck. There I walked over to the railing and stared out into the woods. The tension coiled in my gut made my stomach hurt. My head was beginning to throb with the makings of a headache, and my power pulsed under my skin, causing it to feel too tight.

Out in the distance, the mountains were silhouetted in the dim moonlight. The sound of leaves rustling in the slight breeze was soothing. The air was crisp and much cooler than it had been. Fall was coming, and soon the leaves would be changing colors. Fall was my favorite time of year. In the last few years, my enjoyment of anything had diminished greatly, but my love of autumn had lingered.

I closed my eyes and tilted my face up to the breeze, letting it wash over me. I hoped it would wash away the anxiety and dejection that soiled my mood. This was going to be difficult living with people who hated me. It wasn't like I couldn't empathize with them. The gods had created and used the Guardians for all their dirty deeds. To have your creators curse you … that would leave me bitter, too.

It wasn't just their hatred and mistrust that got to me. It was the fact that I knew their fears were justified. I didn't know what I was capable of, and that made me dangerous. My power was strong, and it was growing stronger. Even if I was able to gain control now, who knew how long that control would last as I grew stronger?

Camille had every right to be alarmed that my power lingered in her body. While Arthur and Jasmine were excited and pleased that I had erected some type of shield in their mind, who knew what else my power had done to them? Were there going to be any negative effects? Rylan ingested my blood regularly. What was going to happen to him? Were we being too lax about the effects my power could have?

"Mae."

I turned at the sound of my name and found Devon standing by the door. I had been so lost in my thoughts I hadn't heard the glass door sliding open. I made a mental note not to be so oblivious about my surroundings. Especially when there were people here who would kill me without a second thought.

"Hey, Devon, is everything okay?"

It was a struggle to keep my voice light. I wanted to be alone. The cautious way he approached me made my back stiffen. Would he try to kill me when Rylan was just inside? Behind him I saw movement. Jasmine crossed by the sliding glass door. For just a moment we made eye contact. She glanced at Devon then back at me. Her nod let me know she was nearby before she disappeared out of sight. I relaxed.

"Okay? I suppose for now you could say things have died down," he said after a moment. He studied my face with an amused expression. "You know, it is a great feat that you are able to cause Guardians to get riled up. Anger and disgust are not traits of an unmated Guardian."

I sighed and looked away from the warrior as I said, "If I could turn it off so you all wouldn't be affected, I would. I know it must be disconcerting."

"I am not sure if any of us would appreciate knowing you could do both; turn off and on our emotions at will," Devon said with a sour expression.

I didn't know what to say to that, so I remained silent. For a while, neither one of us said anything. I was sure Devon's presence was not a coincidence, so I waited for him to say what he needed to say. Another few minutes passed before finally, Devon spoke.

"I apologize for assuming you were my other half earlier. It was such a shock to *feel*. I had been so certain…"

I could hear the longing in his voice. When I looked at him his expression was blank. I turned my whole body to face him. Where was this conversation going?

When I didn't say anything, Devon continued, "Rylan and I have quite a long history together. Our friendship… or what Guardians consider a friendship under our circumstances, has gone back for many centuries. We do business together, we have ruled over small kingdoms together and we have fought alongside each other in many battles. I know Rylan's mind almost as well as I know mine. He is a good man, Mae."

He was watching my face closely.

"You should know that Rylan deserves better than *you*. I suppose if this union is a blessing for anyone, it would be a blessing for you. Rylan takes his duties very seriously. I am sure he will tend to whatever malicious and evil whim you can dream of. Poor soul... You know, everything he does, there is a purpose to it. He has always been a Guardian that is willing to make hard decisions based on what is good for our people, not just himself. To know that fate has dealt him this hand, to give him an abomination as a mate, is appalling.

"Now that I see you are not mine, I am thankful. Whatever mind tricks you can cast, whatever curse you have placed upon his heart know that I will always despise you for it. A Guardian cannot resist his mate but to believe he actually *loves* you is beyond me. Knowing what you are, I do not understand how he cannot loathe the very ground you walk on. If it would not kill him, I would take you out of his life. It pains me to see him tethered to such a revolting creature as yourself."

Devon shook his head, obviously perplexed. I stared at him incredulously before laughing out loud. He scowled at me.

"I am failing to see the amusement here."

I wiped the tears from my eyes and stifled the laughter that wanted to continue. When I had found my breath, I looked him straight in the eye and said, "For you to think I would care how you felt about my relationship with Rylan is absolutely hilarious. I question a friendship where one friend would go behind the other's back to insult their mate. I'm not sure how good of a friend that makes you so please forgive me if I disregard anything you say."

Devon scowled.

"I came out to warn you that I will be watching you, Mae," he growled. "Nothing you do will go unnoticed. Rylan deserves to have someone watching his back while he dances with a snake."

"Do whatever you want," I said with a shrug. "Just as long as you help us stop whatever is going on here I really don't care what you do. Now, if you'll excuse me I'm exhausted. Good night."

Devon's scowl deepened as I gave him the sweetest smile that I could muster. I turned and headed back inside.

Inside, I could hear voices coming from somewhere in the house, but I didn't follow the noise. Instead, I was able to sneak up to my bedroom without running into anyone. I shut the door with a sigh and trudged over to the bed. At this point, all I wanted to do was collapse and let sleep sweep away the stress of the day.

Before I made it halfway to the bed, the bedroom door opened and I turned to find Rylan stepping into the room. My heart swelled at the sight of him. Though his expression gave nothing away, through our connection I could feel his anxiety swirling around in me. I guess sleep wasn't on the cards for me right now.

I walked the rest of the distance over to the bed, turned to face Rylan, and sat down. With a rueful smile, I patted the space next to me. He crossed the distance between us with long strides. As he sat down, he let out a long sigh that mirrored the one I had let out a few moments ago.

"You smell of Devon," Rylan stated, a frown tugging down the corner of his lips.

"Yeah, your friend decided to come out and tell me how terrible of a mate I am for existing. He wanted to tell me how much he respects you and that you deserved better," I said rolling my eyes. "Great guy, I can't wait to get to know him better."

Rylan's eyebrows rose in surprise, and his handsome teal eyes widened. God, how I loved those eyes. His brows came crashing together in anger once he got over his initial shock. Before he could say anything I continued,

"As if I needed to be told how great you are," I continued with a roll of my eyes. "You took three daggers in the back today to save my life. Thank you for that but don't do it again. You scared the crap out of me."

Rylan took my hand and brought it to his lips. The contact with my other half was soothing after a long day. I had a feeling until this was all over, every day was going to feel longer and longer.

"I will step in front of anything that would harm you Mae. You do not need to thank me. I will do anything to keep you safe. When will you learn that you are the most important thing in the world to me?" He sighed and asked, "Are you ok otherwise? I cannot imagine how you must feel after dealing with the others. Guardians can be… intimidating."

I chuckled.

"Yeah, having people hate me as much as they do is a little disconcerting but I'm ok. I can handle it. Is everyone else who's coming going to be like that?"

Rylan shook his head.

"No."

I sighed in relief and leaned my head on his shoulder. He took my left hand and stared down at the ring. I could feel a wave of happiness through our bond as he stared down at it. I smiled knowing how much it made him happy to see it there.

"I do have something I should share with you so you are not taken off guard…" Rylan hedged. I sat straight up and looked at him curiously. "The group coming tomorrow… it consists of my parents."

My whole body went stiff. Rylan's parents were coming tomorrow? My stomach dropped. What were they going to think of me? They had been around during the time of the gods, so I was sure they were going to have some strong opinions of my lineage. Would they hate me like the others? Would they demand that Rylan leave me or would they stop talking to Rylan because of me?

Rylan bit my index finger on the hand that he held, and I yelped in surprise as I was pulled from my panicky thoughts.

"Relax, they will love you."

"You don't know that. You have said you hadn't told them about what I am and what I can do. Once they see me in action, they'll freak out just like everyone else. They'll probably hate me more than Nikolas does."

At the sound of Nikolas's name, Rylan's face darkened. His brows crashed together, he clenched his jaw, and his whole body tensed. His hold on my hand became almost painful.

"You will keep away from Nikolas," he told me severely. "Arthur was wrong to ask him to come. He may have the experience and know-how to stop someone powerful enough to bring the gods back, but he will kill you in a heartbeat the moment he gets a chance. His attempt on your life today will not be forgotten. When this is over, I will kill him."

I bit my bottom lip, not sure what to say. Nikolas was a stone-cold killer. I was sure there was nothing that would stop that Guardian from doing whatever he wanted. Death clung to him like a second layer of skin. While I was sure Rylan could hold his own just fine, I knew my mate had a heart and conscience. Nikolas did not and that might spell disaster for Rylan. Instead of responding, I only nodded, hoping that once this was over we would forget about Nikolas. Deep down, though, I had a feeling Nikolas would never forget about me.

# Chapter Seventeen

*RYLAN*

The next morning I awoke to Mae's lips brushing up against my skin. She trailed sweet, soft kisses down my neck while her hand slid down my chest. The scent of her arousal hung in the air, pulling me from the last little bit of sleep that clung to me. A growl built in my chest, and I heard her soft giggle as she moved beside me. At the same time I opened my eyes, Mae removed the sheets that lay across me. Her eyes met mine and sparkled with mischief. She reached down and slipped my morning erection through the slit in the pajama bottoms I wore. With a coy smile, she moved between my legs and wrapped her lips around me.

The way she slowly took me all the way into her mouth drew a moan from my lips. When she came back up, just as slowly as she descended, her tongue swirled around the tip of my erection before she drew me further into her mouth. I could feel myself hitting the back of her throat. The warmth from her mouth and her tongue dancing up and down my shaft triggered a burst of colors to erupt from behind my eyelids. My hips jerked as she sucked hard.

I looked down to find Mae almost giddy with excitement as she took me down her throat. Naked, she crouched on her hands and knees in between my legs. Her eyes twinkled up at me as she continued to gratify me. My fingers dug into her curly mass of hair, burying themselves in the silky strands.

She reached up and cupped my balls, massaging them gently. She tugged and caressed. That, along with the way her mouth and tongue worked in unison to stroke and suck me, had me teetering on the verge of ecstasy. Through hooded eyes, I noticed her other hand was in between her legs. Her movements were frantic.

Was there anything hotter than watching your mate get off by pleasuring you? I was sure there was not.

Watching Mae pleasuring herself sent me over the edge. Just as I came, I watched as Mae's eyes closed, and her body tensed before it shuddered as her orgasm chased mine. Her power rushed through me, sending my mind and body reeling. She held me in her mouth while her body convulsed, drinking me in and leaving nothing behind. Watching her in the throes of her orgasm prolonged mine. The pleasure she invoked was indescribable.

Before her orgasm subsided I yanked her upwards onto the bed. I twisted around until I was crouched between her legs while she lay on her back, staring up at me in surprise. She was slightly breathless. Her body quivered with aftershocks. I looked down between her legs to find her arousal dripping from between her folds. She was so wet, so aroused… all from pleasuring me. My eyes rose to meet hers. A small smug smile played around the corner of her lips.

Keeping my eyes on her, I reached down and with two fingers I reached past her wet folds into her quivering core. Her body clenched around me. She closed her eyes as she groaned. I grinned and withdrew my fingers. Grabbing both of her legs I hiked them up over my shoulders and without any other preamble, I thrust into her with my still very hard cock.

She cried out and arched her chest upwards, showing off her wonderful breasts. Mae tried to move but in this position, I had all the power. I looked down at her to find her looking back up at me, her mouth slightly opened as she panted.

*Take me hard and fast.* Her voice was husky in my head.

The command caused me to grow harder. Whatever she wanted, she could have. I pulled back out, the tip of my dick just barely sitting within her entrance. Then I slammed hard back into her. She hissed between clenched teeth. I began to move with fast, deep thrusts that pulled out nearly completely before sliding all the way back in. The feeling was magical. All the pent-up energy from yesterday came leaking out with each thrust. All the worry, anger, and fear slipped away.

Mae reached behind her and grabbed the headboard. Her body jerked, her breasts jiggled, and her breathing was ragged. I felt her body clamp down on me. Her legs tensed, and just as she threw her head back as her second orgasm tore through her, I turned my hand and sank my fangs into her ankle. She screamed, and I felt her body convulse wildly. Her power once again rushed over me, which threw me over the edge with her. I came even harder than before.

When my orgasm subsided, I pulled my teeth from her skin and sealed the mark with my saliva. We were both panting hard, our bodies glistening with sweat. I could feel her satisfaction and happiness through our bond, and my soul rejoiced at my mate's contentment. I withdrew from Mae slowly, noting how she winced. She would be sore for a while after that rough session. I wanted to feel bad, but she had wanted it, and it was hard to be anything but smug knowing she would remember me between her legs all day.

"I do not know why we do not start our days like this more often," I commented as I removed her legs from my shoulders and brought them down to rest on the mattress.

"I don't know why either," Mae said with a giggle. "Let's make it part of our morning routine."

I leaned down over her, bracing myself on my hands at either side of her face, and kissed her. I could taste myself on her tongue. "Agreed."

I pushed myself off her and collapsed onto the mattress beside her. Before I could drag her close to me, she was already rolling out of bed. I turned on my side and propped my head up with my elbow.

"Where are you off to so early?" My senses told me it was barely five in the morning. Many years on this planet had taught me much about the workings of the world. I knew, without looking, the dark skies were only now softening from black to navy blue.

"I want to go work out and then meditate before we leave," she said as she scooped her clothes off the floor.

"Leave where?" Where did Mae think she was going?

"To go with the others to find whoever is casting dark magic," she said, as if it were obvious. She even rolled her eyes.

"You are not going with them to explore an unsafe area," I told her.

She paused; a frown tugged down the corners of her pretty pink lips. "Oh, are we going to go look for werewolves and other things that go bump in the night with the other group?"

"Absolutely not."

Her frown deepened, and a little scowl pulled her brows together in annoyance. "Then, we're going to bring back the shifter bodies to their pack?"

"Arthur, Ashe, and Nikolas went to do that last night," I assured her. I watched in amusement as she began to get frustrated. She placed her hands on her hips and glared at me.

"Then what the hell am I supposed to do all day?" she demanded.

I chuckled at her frustration. "*We* are going to go visit the park rangers. I would like to interview a few of them to see if we can get different answers than those Jasmine received when she spoke with them. We will go question them and then grab lunch while we are out. It will get us away from here for a bit and give us time to be alone."

Mae's smile brightened the room. "Alright, sounds good."

Mae changed into her workout clothes and left the bedroom. I got out of bed as I alerted Arthur that Mae was headed to his wing of the house.

Once he was alerted, I dressed quickly and left the bedroom. When Mae was done with her workout I was going to make sure breakfast would be waiting for her. As I thought about what was in the refrigerator that I could make her, I scoffed. Before Mae, cooking and eating were hardly something I would consider fun. It was far from necessary since I only drank blood. But now the prospect of making something for my mate delighted me.

"Rylan!" Camille's voice called out to me softly as I started to head down the stairs.

I stopped at the top of the stairs and watched as she walked down the hall towards me. Her blond brows were pulled together in concern. She came to a stop in front of me and crossed her arms over her chest.

"How are you holding up?" she asked with a frown. Her ploy of being a concerned Guardian would have been complete if it were not for the sharp flash of suspicion that momentarily brightened her eyes.

"Holding up?" I repeated with a raised brow.

"You know, with being stuck with… *her*."

Immediately my good mood vanished as I came to understand the reason for this conversation. I did not know Camille very well. She was Jasmine's acquaintance. As I studied the female warrior's face I decided I did not need to know her any more than I already did. There was something in the way that she held herself that irked me.

"Mae and I are just fine," I assured her.

"You know, Devon and I were talking last night," she started. "Mae is an extremely dangerous young woman. Her presence here in this realm could spell disaster for everyone. She needs to be contained and monitored. She cannot be allowed to walk free, Rylan. We came up with a plan that could help you."

A thick, rolling boil of anger began in my stomach as I stared at Camille. Keep Mae contained? Monitored? The thought was revolting.

Before I could say anything Camille continued, "After we take care of what is going on here we need to safely deal with Mae. If we contain her and keep her underground, away from humans and the other species, we can not only study her but we can see if she has any information about the other gods. By keeping her alive we can still make sure you get the sustenance you need to survive. You can go about your life with your emotions intact and live free from the monster fate has tied you with."

Camille smiled then. It was clear that she believed that this plan that she and Devon had concocted was ideal for everyone. Before I knew what I was doing my arm shot out and my fingers wrapped around Camille's throat. Her eyes turned red and her face hollowed as she struggled in my grip. I yanked her close to me until our noses almost touch.

"You *dare* speak of Mae as if she is a monster? The only monsters under this roof are the ones that think caging an innocent person is ok. Watch yourself, Camille. Mae has a bigger heart than all of us combined and the least of your troubles. Now, I will not tolerate another word of disrespect when it comes to my mate. Do you understand me?" I snarled.

Camille's angry hiss was cut off as my grip tightened around her neck.

*Fine*, she snarled in my head.

I let her go and she stumbled backwards. Her fangs lengthened as she bared her teeth at me.

"We are just trying to look out for you, Rylan but I see she has her claws too deep in you for you to see reason," Camille snapped.

She stepped back and stormed back down the hallway she had come. I stared after her. It was not until she was out of sight that I realized my chest was heaving up and down. With a great deal of effort I forced myself to calm down. If Devon had come up with this plan with her I knew I could not trust either Guardian. Nikolas even less so. I would have to be extra vigilant to make sure Mae stayed safe. I headed down the stairs. I walked passed the kitchen, no longer thinking of breakfast for Mae. Instead my mind was already thinking about the day ahead. I wanted to know what the other Guardians had planned before leaving with Mae.

Inside the small office that Jasmine used to study her samples I found Arthur talking with Devon. When I walked in, their conversation came to a halt. I shut the door behind me and walked over to both men. I glared at Devon who looked wary as I approached.

Devon bowed his head as I approached. "Rylan, have you spoken with—"

I cut him off, "Yes, I spoke with Camille. I am curious to hear why you would think I would find it acceptable for you to cage and study my mate like a goddamn science experiment?"

Arthur turned to glare at Devon who had the grace to look ashamed. Devon clenched his jaw and said, "She is not a good mate for you, Rylan. Or for anyone. The fates have gotten it wrong somehow. She is part god. That makes her the enemy. You cannot see this because she is your mate—"

"She is not my mate and I can see quite clearly that Mae is not the danger you think she is," Arthur growled, his hands curling into fists at his side. "If it is going to be a problem to be around Mae, you are more than welcome to leave."

"Watch what you say and do when it comes to my mate," I snapped at the Guardian I had known for ages. Devon had been one of the few Guardians I had considered trustworthy which is why I had called him. Apparently, I had been wrong to think he could handle Mae's secret.

Devon sighed dramatically. After a moment he nodded slowly. Arthur and I glared at Devon a moment longer before letting the conversation drop. Arthur looked back at me and said, "Myself, Gabriel and Devon will be flying in a grid pattern throughout the park today in search of the werewolves. We need to eliminate that threat as soon as possible. Nikolas, Camille, Ashe and Jasmine will be leaving shortly to explore the area Zyroe has shown Mae where the gates will open. A quick warning, Rylan: with his emotions back Nikolas seems... borderline paranoid. He has been watching your room from the trees all night and when I spoke to him about it this morning he vowed to keep his enemies in sight at all times. I would keep Mae as far from him as possible."

Devon shook his head as he scoffed.

"You will have your hands full watching over Mae," he told me with a shake of his head.

"Rylan is not the only one watching over Mae," Arthur told the other Guardian darkly. "Get ready. We are out of here in twenty."

Devon bowed his head and left the room, leaving Arthur and me alone. Arthur crossed his arms over his chest and said, "The others are arriving this evening; I will be back before then."

"Thank you, Arthur." I was eternally grateful for Arthur's friendship. His concern for Mae was genuine, and now that Mae and I had Joined, I could see clearly how Arthur's friendship benefitted both of us. "For everything."

Arthur chuckled and dropped his arms from his chest. He walked past me, across the room and opened the door. He paused and looked back at me over his shoulder.

"Do not thank me, Rylan. Because of your mate, I can enjoy life again. I can appreciate our friendship for what it is. It is odd. The people I have called were the ones I trusted the most. But because of Mae, I can see them with all too clear eyes, and now I see that my circle of friends is much smaller than I had thought."

Arthur looked away thoughtfully. When he turned to me his smile fell, his gaze serious.

"Whatever is happening here, Rylan, whatever danger we have found ourselves in… I think we have found ourselves in an equally dangerous playing field with the others here. Keep that in mind as we move forward."

With that Arthur left the office, leaving me alone as dread sunk like a heavy stone in my gut. I had a feeling he was right.

***

Two hours later, Mae sat in the passenger seat of the pickup truck Arthur and Jasmine had rented when we had arrived in Alberta. Her window was down, and one of her hands hung out the window, allowing it to dip and twist in the wind. The sunlight filtered through the trees that lined the road and cast a beautiful glow on her face. Her absentminded smile was angelic. I could not help but steal glances her way as I drove.

Halfway through the drive I reached over and grabbed her hand. I could see her, I could smell her, I could hear her, but I needed to *feel* her. How could such a lovely woman be real? I wondered how many times I would ask myself how I got so lucky before I came up with an answer. Her grip tightened in mine. She looked at me with a twinkle in her eyes that warmed my heart and lulled my soul into a peaceful stupor.

"Tell me what you are thinking," I asked after a while.

Mae sighed. "I'm thinking about everything other than having to meet your parents today."

I chuckled. "You have nothing to worry about," I assured her.

Mae rolled her eyes and gave an un-ladylike snort. "They're going to talk you out of loving me."

Just the thought of being able to be persuaded to unlove my mate was utterly ridiculous. The bond did not work like that. I glanced over at Mae whose face had fallen. *I* knew that the mating bond did not work like that, but *she* did not. I gripped her hand more tightly.

"If you think words could sway how I feel about you, then I have not done my job to assure you how irreversible, unbreakable, and everlasting my love is for you. I would die a thousand times over for you and would kill all who would stand between us."

The worry on Mae's face softened and the corners of her mouth turned upwards again in a small smile. "I know. I just know some people hold their parent's opinions of their significant other in high regard."

That may be true for humans, but it was not like that between fated mates. The way she spoke about this piqued my curiosity. I glanced over at her.

"Are you speaking from experience?"

Mae did not answer. Instead, she turned her attention to look out her window.

"How many times have you met someone else's parents?" I tried again.

"Just once."

She did not elaborate. Her disinclination to speak on the matter only caused my curiosity to grow. The background check I had conducted on Mae had not revealed any previous engagements, but her reluctance to get married could also have something to do with a past one that I was unaware of.

"Who was the man who introduced you to his parents?" I pressed.

"No one of any importance," she assured me with exasperation.

I pulled my gaze away from the road again to study Mae. Her mouth was pressed together in a tight line.

"Tell me," I demanded.

Mae's face softened and she chuckled. "Are we really going to bring up past relationships? If you're looking to compare lists, you will find mine significantly shorter."

"I could tell you about my last wife, Connie," I offered.

Her scowl returned and she yanked her hand out of mine. The loss of contact hurt more than I thought it would.

"No, thank you. I'd rather not hear about your previous wives."

"I think it is fair; your story for one of mine," I pressed with a half-smile in her direction.

Mae sighed and looked over at me, "Fine. You first. Tell me about… what was her name? Connie?"

Pleased she was willing to share this information with me, I gladly gave her the story about my last wife before Mae entered my world.

"Connie and I married so I could take over her father's business in the oil industry. He was getting older and wanted to retire but wanted to keep the company in the family. Connie, being the only living heir, wanted nothing to do with running the business, nor did she wish to get married to someone who would want to run it. What her father did not know was that Connie was in love with another woman. Back then, it was unacceptable to be gay, so Connie could not be with the woman she loved.

"When I learned of Connie's partner, I approached her and gave her a proposition: She could be with the woman she loved in secret while in public I would be her husband. It would make her father happy and give her the life she wanted. All she had to do was sign over her share of the company to me. She agreed immediately.

"While I went about my life handling business in the human and supernatural world, I made sure Connie was comfortable. She and her partner lived together in one of the homes I had purchased over the years and were quite happy together. As she and her partner grew older I put them in an elegant nursing home just outside of Atlanta. When Connie's partner died about ten years ago, she followed shortly after."

Mae turned in her seat and gaped at me. Her eyes were wide and her mouth hung slightly ajar. I chuckled and turned my attention back to the road. That should give her something to think about. The silence in the truck didn't last long.

Mae sighed and said, "Derek Houston was his name. When his parents found out we were dating, they suggested that he get his fun out with me, but that he should marry a white girl so he wouldn't produce any nig-lets."

My whole body tensed in surprise. Mae's mother, Autumn Chester, was a blonde witch with blue eyes. Zyroe, a god once worshipped in Africa and parts of the Middle East would have taken on the skin color of those who worshipped him to appear more connected to his people. Mae's skin color was the color of caramel, a beautiful blend of both dark and light. She was stunning. To hear that others found her less than perfect was mind-boggling.

"Did you love him?"

"No." Her answer was too quick. I glanced at her again, and she rolled her eyes. "No, I didn't love Derek. We were just… good together, you know? When I first joined the Mixed Martial Arts gym, Derek had already been training there for years. His uncle owned the place and was one of the trainers there. He assigned Derek to train me. At first, we both hated each other. I was a waste of his time, and he was ruthless during our sessions together. He never went easy on me. Derek left the meanest bruises all over me, and he broke my fingers on more than one occasion.

"I hated him so much. So much so that I practiced every day, whenever I could. I got good quickly, and one day I bested him during practice. After that, our sparring became less like two people who hated each other and more like two lovers dancing. He was the one who introduced me to the group that would go into the city and fight crime. We had a blast fighting bad guys, and I think that's why we stayed together as long as we did."

*Our sparring became less like two people who hated each other and more like two lovers dancing.* Her words swirled around in my head, and my chest tightened in jealousy. It made no sense. Of course, my lovely Mae had been with someone else. Hearing it out loud, though, made me want to find the man and kill him. Not only had he been able to hold Mae in an intimate embrace, but he also continuously put her in danger. The bastard. Mae's hand slipped back into mine, and the red in my vision began to disappear.

"Deep breaths, Rylan," she chuckled softly. I was sure she could feel the intensity of my jealousy through our bond. I did as she instructed.

"You wanted to know why I worried about how your parents will react to me. I didn't care about what Derek's parents had to say about me, but I do care about what yours will think and say. I'm a child of a… *god*," she almost choked on the word, her face scrunched up in disgust. "If they were slaves to one, then they know how horrible the gods truly were. I'm sure they will be concerned for your safety around me. In which case, they will be right to be worried. Who knows what my power does to you whenever you drink my blood or involuntarily absorb it when we have sex?"

"I promise you that they will love you instantly," I assured her.

My parents were some of the few truly decent people left in this world. I looked forward to greeting them with the ability to love them as I once had when I was a child.

I pulled into the gravel parking lot of the Nature Center and parked the truck. I turned to look at Mae who was watching me with skepticism. I sighed.

"If by some terrible turn of events they do not approve of you, there is nothing that can be said that would make me see you in any other way than the woman that I love. When we have children, it will not matter to me that they have the blood of a god running through them either. But like I said, you are worried about nothing."

She jerked her hand away from mine with a look of horror on her face.

"Stop bringing up kids! You're freaking me out," she snapped as she threw open the truck door and hopped out. Laughing, I got out of the truck.

As I shut the truck door, the scent hit me. I came around the truck and grabbed Mae's arm to jerk her back towards the vehicle. Before she could say anything I reached out to her:

*There is a vampire inside posing as a park ranger. There are four humans in total inside, two downstairs and two in a small office on the second floor. I will deal with the vampire. You can talk to the humans.*

The surprise on her face turned into excitement.

*A real vampire? Are we talking about sophisticated ones like in the movie* Interview With a Vampire *or are we talking about deranged crazy, blood-sucking assholes? No, wait, this one has to be intelligent; he's mingling with humans. Do they sparkle?*

*This is not a game, Mae. If you cannot get your excitement under control, then wait out here,* I snapped at her.

*I know it's not a game. You're here. I am sure I will be fine. It's just a lot to take in, you know? It's both scary and exciting. I can't help it, but I'll behave.*

I let go of her arm to take her hand. We headed towards the nature center, my body on high alert for any signs of trouble.

*I'm assuming that not all vampires are bad, right?* Mae asked. I could feel her excitement humming inside of me. Her faith in my ability to protect her to the point that she was more eager than scared about meeting a vampire was humbling.

*No, but they are always hungry, and that should always put you on guard,* I warned. *Their motives for providing information in any given situation may be because they believe it will not leave the two of you if they want you as a meal.*

*Do they drink a person dry or are they like a Guardian and can leave their victims alive?* she asked. She reached for the door to the Nature Center, but I was already there. I opened it and walked inside first to assess the situation. The two human park rangers looked up and greeted us warmly. The vampire, on the far side of the room, visibly cringed when our eyes met.

*The vampire is on the far left of the room. Go talk to the humans and gather what information you can from them,* I shared with her as I stepped aside for her to enter the building. The vampire's eyes fixed onto Mae at once.

*That's the vampire?* Mae asked incredulously. *I'm more afraid of his cholesterol than anything that he could do to me.*

I choked back a laugh as she wandered past glass cases filled with informational plaques and items from around the park. While she was right that the vampire looked far from intimidating, I knew that made him even more dangerous. Mae had been expecting Hollywood's version of a vampire: beautiful, elegant, and mysterious. The vampire I strolled up to appeared to be a balding middle-aged man, with large bifocal glasses, and weighed nearly triple what a man his height should.

He stood up from the stool he was sitting on and took a step backward as if to bolt.

"Good morning," I started and flashed him a grin. The vampire looked towards the other park rangers for help, but when he realized their attention was on my mate, the vampire dragged his gaze back to me.

"Hello, Guardian, what an honor it is to be graced with your presence," he said softly and bowed his head. "What can I do for you today?"

"Take me upstairs, and order the humans to leave the office so we can have some privacy. We have much to discuss."

# Chapter Eighteen

*Mae*

I didn't watch as Rylan ascended the stairs with the vampire. I needed to focus on my part. I wasn't sure what information I could gather from these two park rangers that Jasmine hadn't been able to compel out of them, but I would try. I clasped my hands behind my back and continued to study the small skeletal system of a mouse in the case before me. I moved on to the next item, a picture of an owl, a predator of the mouse.

"Good morning, miss. My name is Thomas Marque, a park ranger here at Jasper National Park. I know everything about the park so if you have any questions don't hesitate to ask me," a ranger said with a warm smile as he walked over to me. He had to be in his early thirties. He had mousy brown hair, a pale complexion, and a hook nose. "Here to enjoy a day of hiking?"

"Yes," I said with a smile. "My husband loves reading up about a place before we hike it, so here we are in here rather than out on the trails. I'm so frustrated. I'd rather be out there now when all the animals are out and about."

"Oh, you'll see plenty of animals here," Thomas assured me.

Two rangers descended the stairs that Rylan had just taken. Both men walked over to a door, which I assumed led into a back room, and disappeared from view. When they were gone, I turned back to Thomas.

"My friend was here last week and said she saw wolves," I said leaning in towards Thomas with a conspirator's smile. "I told her that wolves don't get anywhere near people, but she insisted it was a wolf. Have you seen any nearby?"

"They definitely live in the park, but they aren't usually seen around here. You are plenty safe," Thomas assured me. "Wolves aren't known for coming where humans are unless they are starving. We're too loud and annoying to be around." He chuckled. "I don't know how far you're looking to hike today, but if you take the red trail, that's a good fifteen miles. You may see a glimpse of an elk, mountain goats, a few foxes, and the American Dipper should be out."

"Oh, that sounds lovely. I'll have to let Rylan know," I said. "Do you happen to have a map with the trails marked? Maybe you could show me a few places to stop where we could get a great view of the area?"

"I have one right here, ma'am!" the second park ranger said, coming over with a pamphlet in his hands. He had bright red hair with a matching beard. He was barrel-chested, taller than his co-worker, and about ten years older. "If you would like, I can walk with you and your husband for a bit to give you a little bit of history about the park and about the wildlife."

I reached out to grab the pamphlet.

"That's so generous of you," I told him with a smile. As I grabbed the pamphlet from his hands my fingers skimmed over his. The moment we made contact the park ranger stiffened. His eyes went wide, and the veins in his face began to pop out.

"Jeff, you alright buddy?" Thomas asked with concern as the second ranger stumbled backward.

"When they come, those that are deemed unworthy will perish. We will be slaves to the whim of the Gods and love them as we were always supposed to," Jeff muttered. My heart dropped at his words. Oh shit, what was happening? His eyes were pinned to me, so I noticed when they glazed over. "We will serve them again!" he screamed suddenly.

"Woah, Jeff, what are you saying right now? Is this some weird joke?" Thomas asked as he reached out to touch his arm, but Jeff jerked away from him, reached down, and grabbed his gun off his belt. I grabbed Thomas's wrist and yanked him away from the deranged redhead.

Jeff's face started to turn purple, and his body began to tremble.

"You are unworthy," Jeff whispered to the younger ranger and pointed the gun at him.

I moved quickly. I stepped forward and slapped the gun out of my face as Jeff turned it towards me. I slammed my knee into his gut, grabbed his wrist to keep the gun from being pointed at me, and punched his throat with my other hand. Jeff coughed and sputtered, but he didn't loosen his hold on his gun. I applied pressure to his wrist and suddenly his fingers went slack. I grabbed the gun and slammed my elbow into his nose, causing him to stumble back.

"Glory to the Gods!" a voice cried out from behind me.

I turned around to see Thomas pull his gun and place it against his temple.

"No!" I screamed.

I left Jeff to tackle Thomas to the ground. As we went down, we knocked over a glass display case, and the glass shattered. I threw the first gun away from us and wrestled Thomas for his. The two park rangers who had walked into the back room came rushing out.

"What the hell is going on?" one of them shouted out as they hurried over to us.

He was older, maybe in his sixties, with tufts of white hair jetting out from under his hat. Jeff lunged at his fellow ranger with a deranged cry. With a grunt, I punched Thomas in the face three times before he went slack. I grabbed his gun and shoved it into my waistband before rushing over to pull Jeff off the elderly ranger who struggled against the attack.

"Jeff, what the hell? It's me, Winston!" the man screamed.

My fist connected with Jeff's spleen, and he cried out in pain. He spun around to attack me. Winston grabbed my elbow to pull me away, but the moment he touched me his face tensed. His grip became tighter as he leaned over me with a manic look in his eyes.

"We will serve our gods again! We must prepare for their arrival and cleanse these woods of the unworthy!" Winston dramatically declared. The fourth ranger, who was about Thomas's age, looked stunned at the chaos that was erupting between his co-workers.

My foot connected with the older man's junk, and he keeled over. I punched his face and whirled around to meet Jeff halfway as he lunged for me. I ducked, spun, and kicked his legs out from under him. As he stumbled past me, I jumped up and brought my elbow into his neck. He cried out in pain. Before I could finish Jeff off, someone grabbed me from behind. I elbowed my attacker in the side, and when he loosened his grip, I turned to find Thomas had gotten to his feet. I slammed my palm into his nose, effectively breaking it. I didn't stop there. I punched Thomas in the throat, his gut, and finished him with another fist to the face. His unconscious body fell to the ground.

As the older gentleman, Winston, reached for me, I jumped over a display case. I grabbed the gun in my waist belt, and as the older man made his way around the glass case I used the butt of the handle to hit the man in the forehead. He collapsed on the ground, unconscious. A noise from behind me alerted me to more danger.

I whirled around to find Jeff on top of the fourth ranger, strangling him. I ran over to the both of them and punched him in the face. Jeff let go of the fourth ranger to come after me again. I jumped on his back, wrapped my arm around his neck, and applied pressure. He struggled against me but, already injured and unable to get me off his back, he collapsed as he fell unconscious.

The fourth ranger jumped to his feet and backed away from his colleagues, his eyes wide with horror. He looked from me to the other rangers, then back at me as I got to my feet.

"What's happening to their faces?" the ranger asked in a hushed whisper.

I turned and looked down at the three men. Black veins were stretching from the creases of their eyes and creeping down their faces. Their skin shriveled and wrinkled. Their bodies began to twitch violently, and involuntary groans escaped past their suddenly dried, cracked lips. I cringed away from their flailing bodies. Both the ranger and I gasped when blood began to pour from their ears.

What was happening? I put my hand over my mouth to cover up a horrified shriek. Okay, I didn't have time to freak out. I had to help them. With a deep, steadying breath, I stepped towards the bodies. The fourth ranger tried to stop me, but I jerked away from his hand. This had all happened when they had touched me. I was the cause of this. My stomach twisted in fear.

I dropped to my knees next to Jeff and leaned over him to study his face. The black veins were spreading, covering his entire face. This had to be dark magic. My power must have triggered a response in their bodies. Now they were suffering. I had to do something to stop it. I reached out with shaking hands and placed them on his face.

"You shouldn't touch them!" the ranger behind me shouted out in alarm.

I ignored him, focused on the man I held and took a deep breath. If my power could protect Arthur, Jasmine, and Rylan from the dark toxin in the air, maybe it could save and protect this innocent man. My power surged forward almost immediately and, to my surprise, easily. It slipped from my palms, coating Jeff's body with a violet hue, and then it soaked into Jeff's face and disappeared into his body. His body began to seize up, his limbs flailing everywhere. I bit my lip and cringed as he hit me, but I did not let go of his face. Gritting my teeth, I forced a little more power to seep into Jeff.

Suddenly, his flailing stopped, and his body went limp. I let my hands drop, and I watched his face. Nothing happened. Had I made it worse? Had he died? I swore under my breath as I leaned over to check his pulse. Just then, a long groan bubbled up past his lips. The black veins began to recede, and his wrinkled face began to smooth back out.

"What did you do? You fixed him!" the ranger said behind me in a strangled cry of excitement and fear.

I didn't wait. Whatever I'd just done, the others needed, too. I reached for the older man next and shoved my power into his body. I waited to make sure that the dark magic receded before moving on to Thomas. As I worked on Thomas, upstairs I heard a muted shriek and glass shattering. Refusing to lose focus, I closed my eyes and pumped more of my power into Thomas. When I was done, I leaned back on the balls of my feet and watched as his face smoothed out.

I turned to the fourth ranger, who was staring at his comrades in shock. His face was ashen, and from the way he was breathing I could tell he was on the verge of fainting. I hesitated to reach out to comfort him. If my touch caused the dark magic to somehow react within these rangers, what would stop it from happening to him ?

But if he had dark magic in him, it would be the responsible thing to remove it if I could, right? Could I somehow bypass the violence to remove the dark magic in this ranger's body? The man ran both hands through his hair and tugged at it as he stared down at the other rangers.

"I gotta— I gotta call the cops or something. I'm not equipped to deal with this," he stammered and took a step back.

I called up my power again, reached out, and grabbed his arm gently. The ranger froze and his eyes glazed over. I pushed my power into him. I needed to trigger the response and then remove the dark magic without having to fight him off. His body seized. I had to let go of his arm to catch his body as he fell forward.

Gently, I placed him on the ground. Anxious to make sure he would be alright, I crouched down next to him and waited for his body to go limp. When it did, I checked his pulse and sighed with relief when I found one. Now what? I looked at all four unconscious men and felt panicked. What if someone walked in and found them like this? Did they need medical assistance? Should I call for an ambulance?

As I stood up, the ceiling came crashing down several feet away from me. I yelped in surprise and watched wide-eyed as Rylan landed gracefully on his feet while battling four creatures that I could only assume were vampires. They were thin, pale monsters that moved with an amazing amount of speed. They had slits where a nose would be, no eyebrows or hair, and pointed ears. The vampires had long jagged nails that they were using to slash and tear Rylan's bare skin. One was perched on his back between Rylan's wings, two were trying to attack him on either side, and the fourth was tearing at his chest.

Rylan's wings flapped once, hard, which bucked the vampire off his back. He roared while he grabbed the vampire on his left and ripped off one of its arms. The creature screamed as Rylan continued his assault and grabbed the vampire by its esophagus. Rylan's grip tightened, crushing its throat, and then he yanked out the trachea. The vampire collapsed in a heap on the ground before the body exploded into ash. Rylan backhanded the vampire trying to claw a hole through his chest, and the vampire flew across the room with an angry shriek.

Without any plan, I leapt forward and threw my hands up. A wave of energy from my power erupted, and the vampire on Rylan's right was hit and knocked off my mate. The creature landed on its feet and turned his attention to me with an evil hiss. I didn't give it a chance to attack. I allowed more power to come forth. The vampire screamed as his clothes caught on fire. Rylan pulled his sword from his tattoo on his lower abdomen and cut the creature's head off. The body and the head exploded into ash.

Rylan continued to move. He slammed his fist through the chest of one of the vampires and ripped a large black thing from its chest. I gasped in horror as I realized it was a blackened but still-beating heart. Rylan crushed it in his grasp, and the vampire exploded. Rylan whirled around and did the same to the vampire who tried to reattach itself to his back. The creature let out a blood curdling scream as it died.

Rylan spun and grabbed the fourth vampire attempting to escape. It hissed at us. He grabbed the vampire by the bottom jaw, sinking his elongated nails into the creature's skin. Then, he grabbed the top of the vampire's bald head and twisted his hands in opposite directions. The bottom jaw popped off like a lid on a jar. A moment later, the vampire burst into ash.

Rylan turned and ran his blazing red eyes over me. The wounds the vampires had inflicted on him were already healing. The grizzly sight of his blood mixed with the black vampire blood splattered all over him made me sick. As the tension in the room deflated, Rylan's wings retracted into his back, and he walked over to me.

"I heard a commotion down here," his voice was deep and gravelly. He shot a look at the four unconscious men on the ground.

"Yeah, shit hit the fan fast down here, but I'm alright. Are you?" I asked as I scanned his body for anything that wasn't healing.

"I will be fine," Rylan assured me, his voice gruff. "This was a setup. The vampires were lying in wait within the woods behind the facility. The one I took upstairs beckoned them when he did not appreciate my interrogation methods. They are all pawns for their master."

"A setup? No one knew we were coming here except the other Guardians."

"The master vampire behind this must have learned Guardians were in the area. I am sure he knew we would come here to investigate once we realized something was going on in the park, and he devised this trap to kill us. A vampire cannot be behind the unusual activity here. He must be under someone else's control. I need to find the master vampire before he alerts whoever is controlling him."

"Right now?" I asked with alarm. I looked at the four men on the ground. "What am I supposed to do with them? What if visitors come in?"

"Move them to the break room behind that door. Lock the front door, and flip the open sign over to show it's closed. I will not be long," Rylan ordered. With that, he exited the Nature Center and took to the sky.

I did as I was told. Trying to drag each guy into the back room took much longer than I'd anticipated. By the time I had dragged the fourth body into the back, I was sweating. How was this more work than kicking their asses?

Once they were all out of sight, I locked the front door, flipped the open sign to closed and pulled the shades down in the windows. That's when I realized I had blood from the fight on my hands. I looked around the room. Everything I had touched had blood smeared across it. With a groan of annoyance, I grabbed paper towels from the bathroom, wetted them, and went about cleaning up any evidence of a fight. I swept up the glass from the broken display case. Then, I tried to clean up the mess from the ceiling.

Finally, I gave up cleaning. It was going to take more than a broom and a dustpan to remove the debris from the damage. So instead of cleaning, I decided to do some investigating. If the park rangers had been affected by the dark magic here, then maybe they had been unconsciously, or consciously, covering up events in the park that would otherwise bring a lot of attention from the police.

First, I checked the back room. I looked through the old filing cabinets, checked employee files, and then the logbook. Nothing there stood out to me that would indicate a cover-up. Next, I made my way upstairs to where Rylan had encountered the other vampires. The room was trashed. There was barely any drywall left hanging; thick black liquid coated the edges of the jagged glass of the broken window, and was splattered over the two desks. One computer was smashed beyond repair, but the other one looked like it was in working condition. I skirted around the massive hole in the floor to get to the computer.

I sat down in front of the old monitor and wiggled the mouse. Someone had already logged on, no password needed. I began sifting through the files saved on the desktop. At first, there was nothing. There were some reports of injured hikers, a few sick animals that had to be put down, but nothing out of the ordinary. Just as I was about to give up and go back downstairs to wait for Rylan I noticed a file marked "Them."

Curious, I clicked on it then gasped.

There were hundreds of pictures in the file. Many were of the same thing. A group of hikers lined up on the ground next to each other, their hands tied in front of them, and a bullet hole in the middle of their foreheads. Their clothes had been ripped down the front and a large 'X' had been cut through the flesh on their chests.

Other pictures showed deer, foxes, rabbits, elk, and bears hanging from their hind legs from tree branches. They were completely gutted, with no intestines, bones, or blood. It was just their flesh dangling from low hanging branches. Then, there were the pictures of the birds with no eyes. Their wings had been removed, leaving behind just bloody stubs.

One picture stood out from the rest. In this one, a group of people were lying on the ground with their stomachs cut open and their intestines pooled around them. A small symbol was drawn on their foreheads in their blood. In the middle of the bonfire was a large wooden stake, burning. On the top of the stake was a man's head, his mouth hanging open at a strange angle. Posing in the picture were three park rangers standing beside the mass of dead bodies looking at the camera with vacant stares.

I leapt to my feet and made it to the trash bin just in time as my breakfast came back up. I placed my hands against the wall and gasped for air. My stomach rolled, and I heaved again. I didn't hear Rylan walk up the stairs or enter the room, but suddenly he was by my side, rubbing my back. Absentmindedly, I noted that sometime between his departure and now he had found a shirt.

"Did you catch the vampire?" I asked weakly.

"He has been taken care of," Rylan assured me. "What has caused you to be so upset?"

I pointed to the computer but didn't make a move towards it. I had seen enough. Rylan walked over to the old piece of technology and glanced at the picture. With a sigh, I turned and leaned my back against the wall. I watched Rylan click through each picture, his expression grim.

"What do the symbols on their bodies mean?" I asked. I wasn't sure I really wanted to know the answer, but I asked anyway.

"I am not well versed in the tongue of the gods. I will have to ask the others," Rylan said without looking at me. "But it is clear that these are sacrifices to them. It appears Jasmine's theory was correct; her ability to compel the rangers had been thwarted somehow. It is clear the rangers have been covering up their involvement with missing hikers and visitors to the park. Whoever has tampered with black magic so we cannot sense it must have also done something to protect the minds of those that serve them."

"Have you ever come across someone you couldn't compel?" I asked curiously.

Rylan looked up at me with a bleak expression. "No."

Oh okay, so another reason to be concerned about what was happening. I took a deep breath and let it out slowly. Rylan deleted the file with the pictures and pulled up the security program. Quickly, he removed the footage of when we'd arrived and the brief fight off the hard drive. When he was done, I followed him down the stairs and watched as he checked over the four park rangers I had brought into the back room. When he confirmed that they would be alright, it felt like a weight had lifted off my shoulders.

"We can't just leave them here," I protested when Rylan suggested we leave. "What if vampires come back and see them as a snack?"

"We cannot be here when they wake up. I was able to remove the evidence of us being here on the security camera, but if I cannot compel them to forget they saw us, they will panic and call the police," Rylan said with a frown. "The vampires have been taken care of. These men are safe."

He took my hand and pulled me towards the front door. We left the Nature Center and peeled out of the parking lot. Instead of heading back to the house, we headed towards the nearest city. Our drive was quiet. All I could think about were those pictures. I squeezed my eyes shut, trying to unsee everything. Unfortunately, closing my eyes only made it worse. I could see their faces clearly. The bloody writing on the naked bodies. That head with the jagged flesh dangling from where the neck had once been…

I opened my eyes, reached over, and placed my hand on Rylan's leg. I needed the contact. Rylan reached down immediately and grabbed my hand. I looked over at him, and he pulled his eyes away from the road to look at me.

*All those people in those pictures…* I started but trailed off.

*We will stop this*, Rylan assured me. The confidence in his voice was absolute.

*How?* I demanded. *This whole situation seems to be spiraling out of control.*

*With the others here, we will have more eyes and ears to find whoever is behind this,* Rylan said. *Hopefully, the others find something on their search that will help us.*

"Could you decipher any geological features in the pictures that would help us locate where they were doing… whatever they were doing?" I asked out loud, breaking the silence in the truck. I was getting frustrated that we were nowhere closer to finding answers than we had been when we arrived.

"The hikers were all being sacrificed. The group of people dancing around the fire were paying homage to someone, or something, and sacrificed themselves," Rylan said with a sigh. "I will have to check the map and explore the area more to have any idea where in this park it all took place."

The sacrifices could have happened anywhere in the park. There was no way we would be able to find the place these bodies had been, even with the help of extra Guardians. The park was simply too big to find a singular, unknown location. With a sigh, I turned my attention out the window and stared at the trees flying by.

"Mae," Rylan's voice pulled me from my thoughts twenty minutes later.

We were passing a small abandoned town. It was eerie to see all the boarded-up homes and businesses. Trash littered the streets, and plant life had begun growing through the cracks in the street. Most of the buildings were built into the side of a rocky hill. The abandoned structures blended in with the stone colors of the hill, giving the whole town a feeling of caveman times. As we passed a gas station that looked like it was from the fifties, I noted that it was still in use. It was probably one of the only businesses still running in this ghost town.

Scattered along the rocky hillside, I noted that there were odd statues of creatures crouching above the town. They had strange demonic looking faces and large bat-like wings that stretched out behind them. They looked oddly out of place here. I rolled down my window and twisted in my seat to keep an eye on the strange stone statues. A cold chill ran down my spine as I stared up at them. I counted four but who knows how many we had passed before I had noticed them. They didn't look all that old. In fact as I stared at them they looked like they had just been freshly chiseled from the stone they were made out of. But the town was practically abandoned. Who put those statues up there?

Afraid I wouldn't be able to find it again if I took my eyes off the statue, I reached down to grab my purse and tried to find my phone so I could take a picture of it. Did Rylan know what those statues were for? I opened my mouth to ask when I realized he was already speaking.

"I'm sorry. I was distracted. What did you say?" I asked, turning to face him.

"It appears you are getting a handle on using your power. How are you feeling?" The pride in his voice caused me to pull my attention away from the statues. I looked at him and smiled.

"It was easy to call on. I was able to burn just that vampire and not the entire building. I guess I do have at least a slight grip on my power. I think meditation is actually helping. But…" I paused, frowning as I pictured the creature going up in flames.

"But what?" Rylan pushed gently.

"Rylan, what if I had killed that vampire? It would have been the second time I've used my power to intentionally kill something. Both the Kraken and the vampire were attacking us. Both were monsters. I felt terrible killing a living thing, but I would do it again if I had to. But what if the next thing to attack me is a human? I don't think I could live with myself if I killed someone. I think living with the guilt would be worse than suffering in hell," I said.

I reached up and ran a shaky hand over my mouth.

"Trust me, you are not going to hell," Rylan said and to my surprise, he chuckled. When he caught me giving him a look he chuckled again. "I would never allow your soul anywhere near such a place. If a life needs to be taken, I will do it. Let us just hope you are never in that position."

His grip tightened on my hand, and he sent me a sunny smile. I wasn't sure why he was suddenly in a good mood, but I appreciated the effort he made to bring me over to the bright side, even if it was just for a while.

❦

# CHAPTER NINETEEN



By the time we got to an actual city, it was well past noon. Lunch was quick. I hadn't gained much of an appetite since we'd left the Nature Center, but it was nice being away from everyone else to spend time with Rylan. It was strange sitting at a table surrounded by normal people. Just a few weeks ago I would have been terrified that I would have caused the building to crumble over our heads. Now I sat here like one of them, with the most handsome man that walked this Earth.

When we left, I caught women and men staring at Rylan. They sent him seductive smiles and suggestive winks. Rylan didn't seem to notice the attention he was drawing, but I certainly did. But instead of being jealous I just grinned. He was a hundred percent mine. Let people admire him; he truly was a treat for sore eyes.

Before we headed back to the house, we stopped at a hospital. I waited in the truck while Rylan walked in through the front door. Ten minutes later, he walked out carrying a massive cooler. He put it in the back of the pickup and climbed back into the cab.

"What's in the cooler?" I asked curiously.

Rylan turned to me with a smirk. "Dinner for the others for the next few days."

Oh. I leaned back in my seat and tried to hide the disgust on my face. The ride home was relatively silent. I mulled over what had happened that morning. The more I thought about the events, the more I focused on the positives rather than the negatives. I'd just kicked three grown men's asses. It never occurred to me that one day I'd be using my MMA training again. Yeah, my moves had been a little rusty, but I had done it.

"What are you grinning about?" Rylan asked curiously, pulling me from my thoughts.

I chuckled and told him, "It felt good to use my fists again. I used to train so much back in high school and my early years of college that it came back naturally. Once this is over, I want to join a gym and get back into it."

Rylan smiled and nodded. "When this is over, I will find you a good trainer."

"You know…" I said, "the only reason you and Arthur were able to kidnap me both times was because I was wearing those stupid bracelets. Any bout of adrenaline would have sent me into convulsions and without them I would have accidentally brought the city of Chicago down or destroyed that brick house in an attempt to escape."

"You may have been able to stop a normal man," Rylan conceded with amusement. "But you would not have gotten away from a Guardian."

That was probably true. I smirked, already knowing the answer to my next comment. "Maybe you and I can become vigilantes together."

Rylan's deep scowl made me laugh.

"No," he snapped.

"Oh, come on. How cool would it be if you and I went after the bad guys? Everywhere we went we could eliminate crime and the world would be a safer place. We'd be unstoppable! We could be like the *Avengers* or the *Justice League* minus the costumes… Unless you want to dress up?" I teased.

"Absolutely not," Rylan growled. "Supernatural beings do not interfere with human issues unless it affects the supernatural world. Even if we did, I would not want you in harm's way."

"I'm human," I said with a frown.

"As human as I am," Rylan muttered.

"So is that a no on the costumes?" I asked sweetly, ignoring his comment.

Rylan sighed and rolled his eyes. One corner of his mouth pulled upwards in a half-smile.

"Fine, as long as I do not have to wear tights," he answered.

I couldn't help it. I laughed. Rylan's answering grin brightened the cab of the truck. It felt good to laugh.

"You know I wasn't really a vigilante. That's a strong word to describe what we were doing," I told him. "Really it was just a bunch of kids beating up a few people every now and then. We never killed anyone, thank goodness. I wasn't like Frank Castle or Oliver Queen."

"Who?" Rylan asked, obviously confused.

"Oh come on, you've been around for *forever* and you're telling me you don't know who either the *Punisher* or the *Green Arrow* are? They were comic book vigilantes and then they had their own TV shows for a while," I told him. "But they killed people, so they toed the line between right and wrong."

"Sometimes getting rid of the problem, rather than locking them up only for them to direct crime from inside a prison, is better," Rylan said softly.

I looked at him curiously.

"Is that what you did… or do, I guess?" I asked.

"There is no supernatural prison," Rylan told me. "If criminals do not want to die by our hands, then it is best not to be a criminal."

I stared at him in surprise. There were obviously a lot of things I still didn't know about the supernatural world.

***

Forty minutes later, we pulled up in front of the house. A flashy yellow sports car that had no business driving down the gravel drive to the house was parked out front. Leaning against the car was a tall and beautiful woman. This Guardian wore designer clothes that hugged her curves and showed off strong arms and curvy legs. She had a severe jawline, a sharp nose, and dark eyes that narrowed at us. Her dark wavy hair was pulled back into a high ponytail.

"She is early," Rylan growled with displeasure. He threw off his seatbelt and opened the door. He looked back at me and warned, "Stay in the car."

Rylan shut the door and walked over to the female Guardian, who straightened as he approached. I couldn't hear them talk, but the woman looked far from friendly. Her jaw was clenched tight as she listened to Rylan talk. I was so involved watching the two of them that I didn't notice another car pull up until I heard two car doors shut behind me. I flinched at the sound. I turned around in my seat to see two of the most gorgeous people I had ever seen walk up to the back of the truck. They split up, one going around the car passing the driver side, the other coming to walk past the passenger door of the truck.

The man who walked by first was tall, muscular, and walked like a king making his way to his throne. The strong jawline was covered with a hint of blonde stubble that was slightly darker than the golden locks on his head. His arms were thick, and his wide chest tapered down to a narrow waist.

The woman who walked by my window was tall, thin, and glamorous. Her blonde pixie cut was slightly tousled as if windblown. Her petite nose was held high with confidence. Her skin was practically glowing from being in the sun, and her pretty pink lips were turned upwards with a warm smile.

If I hadn't known who these two were at first glance, I certainly figured it out when the woman turned to look through the window at me as she passed. Her familiar teal eyes twinkled, and her warm smile grew even warmer as she winked at me. Both Guardians came up to Rylan and the female warrior. The wide smile that spread across Rylan's face spoke to the love he had for his parents. I felt his joy through our bond.

It took me a moment to realize he was feeling the love for his parents again after almost two thousand years. Rylan embraced his mother in a bear hug and spun her around. The delight on his mother's face shone bright like the sun. He kissed her cheek and set her back on the ground. She said something to him, and he threw back his head and laughed. Then, he turned and embraced his father. His father stepped back while placing his hands on his son's shoulders to study him. They laughed about something Rylan said.

They exchanged a few more words before Rylan took a step back and introduced his parents to the other Guardian who stood with him. As they spoke, Rylan pulled out the quartz necklaces and passed them out. When everyone else had adorned the simple piece of jewelry, Rylan turned towards me.

*Mae, please come out and meet everyone*, Rylan called.

With a deep breath, I braced myself to meet another group of Guardians.

I exited the truck and walked over to everyone. Both of Rylan's parents eyed me curiously, but their smiles seemed welcoming. I couldn't detect any hostility from either of them. Behind them, the female Guardian's whole body shook hard once as the curse over her lifted. I heard her swift intake of breath as shock settled over her. She stepped forward, her brows coming together, but not in suspicion. If I wasn't mistaken, she looked almost concerned.

Rylan beamed at me as I approached. This was it; I was about to meet Rylan's parents for the first time. Butterflies took flight in my stomach. Rylan's arm came around my shoulders, and a wide grin spread across his face.

"Mother, father, Zara, it is my pleasure to introduce to you my better half, Mae White. Mae, this is my mother and father: Diane and Samson Lindström, and behind them is Zara Stone."

Diane Lindström stepped forward, her eyes twinkling with mirth, and embraced me. I stiffened for just a moment, expecting to be crushed by her inhuman strength. But the moment the thought appeared, I brushed it off. She wouldn't crush me in front of Rylan. I relaxed and returned the hug.

"Welcome to the family, Mae! There is nothing I have wanted more than to see Rylan find his mate," she purred in my ear. She stepped back and placed her hands on my shoulders to study me. "You are absolutely beautiful, and the power I feel radiating off you… It is magnificent."

"Do not bogart our new daughter," Samson said as he took his wife's elbow and gently pulled her away from me. He stepped forward, grinning, and planted a kiss on my cheek. "When Rylan told us that you were special, I had no idea how special. A demi-god in the family, I would never have foreseen this."

He took a step back, beaming. Standing next to their son, there was absolutely no question both Guardians were Rylan's parents. He looked more like his father, but his lips and eyes were definitely from his mother.

Standing there under their jubilant stares, all my anxieties about meeting them vanished. Rylan had been so confident that his parents would love me, and he had been right. I should have listened to him, but how could I not have doubted him when my very existence could be seen as a threat?

"Mae, it is good to finally meet you. I have been searching for you for quite a while," Zara said, taking a step towards me.

I stared at the woman, confused. Was I supposed to know who she was? She didn't look familiar. I frowned. Next to me, Rylan stiffened. His good mood disappeared instantly. His brows came together in a scowl, and his pupils narrowed.

"You know Mae?"

The female Guardian turned to face Rylan.

"Yes," Zara answered with a frown. "She made quite a scene in a bar back in Baltimore a few years ago. After reviewing the security cameras, I became concerned for her well-being. I have been searching for Mae to help her."

My friends and I had done our share of running around the city in our attempt to keep the streets relatively safe. Occasionally, we ended up in bars, and half the time we made a scene. So which bar was she talking about?

"When word got around what this young woman had done to the Fitz gang in that bar, all the scum in that area, both of the human and supernatural variety, scattered like cockroaches and have stayed away ever since," Zara continued.

My whole body went stiff as I realized the bar Zara was talking about. I remembered the Fitz gang. They were renowned for snatching children off the street and selling them on the black market. It had been our most dangerous attempt at helping the community. The small group of us had gone back and forth about trying to do something about this gang. I had told Rylan the truth; most of what my small group of friends and I had done had been pretty mild. Taking on an honest to god gang was never something we had attempted before. But it wasn't the gang that stuck out to me that night. I pushed down the rising fear and panic that was beginning to blossom in my chest.

"After what I saw that night, I figured your mate here was in a little bit of trouble, but then she disappeared," Zara said. "I caught wind that Mae had resurfaced in Chicago just a few weeks ago. I attempted to reach out to Arthur to show him the video so I could warn him that there was a young woman in his territory who needed looking after, but he was out of town. Then, just two days ago, I got a call from him saying he needed my help with a matter up here, so I figured I would talk to him now... I see he must already know about Mae."

I tried to push down the memories of that night before terror overwhelmed me. That night had been horrible on every level imaginable.

"You have a video? Do you have it with you?" Rylan asked, his pupils narrowing.

*It's not going to be pretty*, I grumbled.

Rylan didn't acknowledge my comment. Instead, he raised a brow at Zara. A wave of nausea crashed over me.

"Yes, you can have it. I only kept it to find Mae," Zara said. She looked at me. "It is a relief to know you have someone to watch after you now."

The kindness in her voice surprised me. Knowing what she must have seen and what her duties as a Guardian were, I wondered why she wasn't trying to tear my head off. The image of the man's head on a stake from the pictures earlier popped into the forefront of my mind. My stomach churned as I pictured my head dangling from that same stake.

"Thank you for your discretion," Diane said graciously as she placed a hand on my shoulder.

Zara bowed her head respectfully. I knew I should thank her as well, but my mind was spinning. I was too busy choking down the emotions evoked by the memories of that night.

"Where are the other Guardians now?" Samson asked, drawing the attention away from me.

"A few went with Jasmine Sing south to look for any clear signs of trouble. Arthur House has a group of warriors with him to scan the area for creatures that are not native to this area," Rylan told him. "We went to talk to the park rangers to find out what they knew."

"Did you learn anything?" his father asked him.

"The rangers have been corrupted," he explained. "Whatever dark magic that has been cast over these woods has prevented us from compelling the humans. Mae was the one who learned they were tainted and was able to destroy the darkness in them.

On their computer, Mae found files of sacrifices made in these woods. There are hundreds of dead hikers buried in the park."

"Do you know where they took place?" Diane asked with a worried frown.

"No."

"Has anyone gone to visit Cain?" Samson asked.

Rylan shook his head and frowned. "It is on the list of things to do. We have not heard from him or Ekon."

"Ekon?" Samson repeated the name with surprise. "He is an ancient like us… I hope he and Cain are alright."

"We can go to Cain's residence now. With such a small window of time before the gates open, we do not have much of it to waste," Diane said, looking to Samson who nodded. "It is alarming to know that two Guardians are missing. We need to find them."

I felt the buzz of communication in my mind before Rylan said out loud, "Use that as your coordinates to find Cain's home. If he has gone missing, his place will have been abandoned for quite a while. I am sure I do not need to warn you to keep an eye out for anything that may have made his place their home."

"We will be fine," Diane said with a chuckle at her son's warning. "It was *us* that taught *you* to keep vigilant."

Both Samson and Diane turned to me.

"We will talk tonight when we return. I would love to learn all about my new daughter," Diane said with a warm smile. Despite the turmoil in my gut, I smiled back.

"I look forward to it. Please be safe," I told her.

"I will come with the both of you," Zara offered. She turned to Rylan and pulled something out of her back pocket. She handed it to him and said, "Watch it. It is quite incredible. I wiped the memories of anyone who was there that night, but rumors of a badass chick still linger on."

The three Guardians stepped away from me and Rylan. They pulled off their shirts, and I watched them as their wings began to grow from their backs. After a friendly wink from Samson, all three took to the sky and disappeared over the treetops.

Rylan looked down at the USB stick that Zara had handed him. My anxiety was beginning to skyrocket. The chill that ran down my spine was chased by another as I tried not to think about what was recorded on that small storage device. Rylan looked up at me and steadied my face.

"Let's go inside," he said softly.

Oh, shit. Rylan wanted to watch it now. As we headed towards the house, I made a face. I said nothing as my fear began to mount as we entered the house. I didn't want to relive that night. The heartbreak, the fear, the grief… The hole in my heart that had slowly healed over time threatened to crack open. I dragged my feet as I followed Rylan into the family room. He walked over to the large television hanging on the wall and slipped the USB stick into one of the HDMI slots in the back of it. A moment later, I was staring at security footage of one of the worst nights of my life.

# Chapter Twenty

*RYLAN*

Even without feeling Mae's anxiety, I would have seen and heard the signs of it. It was in the way her heart fluttered and her face paled. She had shoved her hands into the pockets of her pants, but not before I saw the way they shook. My foremost concern was that someone else had witnessed Mae's ability. I wanted to remove the video from Zara's possession at once. But now, seeing Mae's reaction, I was curious. What had happened that caused Mae to grow silent and fearful?

The video was split into four screens. The date at the bottom of the screen was dated two years ago, August 28, and it was just past midnight. One camera was pointed to the small parking lot just outside the building. Two cameras had been somehow hidden in the bar from two different angles providing us with a complete view of the small, dirty establishment. One view was facing the bar, the other facing the clientele. There were about ten men scattered about the room at different tables. They were not trying to hide their usage of drugs. The last camera screen was placed in the basement of the building. My stomach sank as I realized what I was seeing in the fourth screen. There were twenty children all chained together, gagged and blindfolded.

The video was edited to jump ahead. Suddenly, a half-hour had gone by. In the bar, the men were rowdier now, and the children were still trapped in the basement. Movement on the upper left-hand screen that pointed to the parking lot caught my attention. Five people dressed in black moved along the shadows, circling the bar before they disappeared. The video was cut again, now another fifteen minutes had gone by. Someone dressed in black walked back into the frame. The figure walked into the middle of the parking lot, heading towards the front door. The individual stopped, pulled the ski mask off their face, and there, standing just outside the door to the bar was Mae.

Her face was half turned away from the camera, making her expression unreadable. She dropped the mask to the ground and shook her hair out of its braid before walking through the front door. On the second screen, I watched Mae enter, as did everyone else in the bar. Her presence drew the attention of every single man, even the bartender, who had been pretending to clean a glass behind the bar.

Without looking around, she headed over to the bar and sat down. The third camera view allowed me to see her face. I noted the dark circles under her eyes, the hard set of her mouth, and the suspicious gaze she let linger on the bartender. They spoke to each other. The bartender reached down and pulled out several shot glasses. As he began to pour liquor into each glass, Mae ran a hand down her face, but not before I saw a flash of agony she was trying to hide. She turned in her seat to survey the room.

The bartender said something to Mae, and she turned back to face him. In front of her sat five shots. She looked down at them, then back up to the bartender. She gave him a half-smile before downing all five shots back to back. The two of them exchanged words again, and this time Mae chuckled. She stood up, reached over, and grabbed the bartender by the front of the shirt.

Mae pulled the bartender towards her, smiled at him, and then kissed him. There was no fight from the man as Mae ran her fingers through his hair. She broke the kiss and shoved him away. Mae grabbed an empty shot glass sitting in front of her, turned around, and chucked it across the room at the nearest gangster. She hit her mark in the forehead. The man leapt to his feet while the rest of the room went still. Mae said something to the man before throwing her head back to laugh. The man charged over to her. Mae stopped laughing. The amusement on her face vanished as she got up and met the man halfway across the bar.

When he grabbed for her, all hell broke loose.

The man went down fast. Mae's strike to his throat and fist to the temple toppled him to the floor. At once, the rest of the gang members were on their feet and charging towards her. My heart nearly stopped as I watched my mate take on men more than double her size. I would not have believed she was capable of taking down so many men at one time. The way she moved; it was almost like a dance. She never stopped to catch her breath. She hardly flinched when a fist connected with her. If someone grabbed her, Mae slipped out of their grasp with ease.

As the chaos ensued, I watched as Mae's movements grew faster. Almost inhumanly fast. As she turned and landed a punch on a nearby gang member, he literally flew across the room. As she turned to her next opponent, I caught just a glimpse of her eyes. They were glowing violet. The room shook, and the walls began to crack.

In the frenzy of violence, none of Mae's opponents seemed to notice the wall of the bar begin to crumble. Chairs and tables moved on their own accord. The shot glasses that lingered on the bar counter exploded one by one. Mae's opponents likewise began to fall. Without even making contact, her hand shot out and a man was thrown into the two men behind him.

Movement in the fourth screen drew my attention away to the chaos in the bar. As Mae continued to take down every man in the bar, the children began to move around. Four individuals in black masks came into view of the camera. They worked quickly to free the children. It took a few minutes, but then the four masked individuals herded them out of view.

Upstairs, Mae suddenly stopped moving. She fell to her knees and grabbed her head. Four men took advantage of her sudden distraction and jumped forward to grab her. Mae threw back her head and screamed in obvious agony. I could see the veins in her face glowing. The four men were thrown back in different directions. The tables and chairs lifted off the floor and exploded into large pieces. The windows shattered, and every liquor bottle behind the counter broke. The lighting in the bar flickered on and off. In the camera view overlooking the parking lot, eight cars exploded and burst into flames.

The few men still standing backed away from Mae. Slowly, Mae rose to her feet and faced them. One pulled a gun out and pointed it at her. Mae raised her hand, and the gun exploded. He screamed, and the lingering gang members tried to turn and run. Mae was there before they could get far. It took only a moment before all three were lying with their friends on the ground, out cold.

Mae stood in the middle of the mess, her shoulders heaving up and down. In the far corner of the room, something moved. The Mae in the video did not appear to notice but next to me Mae gasped. As the lights continued to flicker on and off, a woman appeared out of thin air in the corner of the room. Her blonde hair was pulled up out of her face into a bun to reveal sharp features. The cloak she wore was dark green and covered the rest of her body. She stood there watching Mae with a smile. As Mae in the video turned in her direction, the woman vanished.

Next to me Mae gasped in surprise.

In the video, Mae grabbed her head and sank to her knees. From this angle, I could see my mark on the back of her neck as her hair tumbled to one side. She didn't sit there long. Mae jerked her head towards the door as if someone had called her name. She got to her feet slowly and stumbled towards the exit. A masked individual rushed to her side as she appeared out in the parking lot. The unknown person scooped Mae up in their arms and darted out of view.

The video ended.

"It wasn't in the plan to go in and take out the Fitz gang," Mae said softly next to me.

I turned to face her, unsure how to deal with the raging emotions I felt. She would not look at me. Instead, she stared at the floor.

"I told you. We weren't really vigilantes, and this was *way* out of our league. But when we heard about the kids in the basement… Well, we had to do something. Cops never patrolled that area of the city. When we got there, we realized we had miscounted how many members were there, and we were wildly outnumbered. A handful of guys were blocking the back door where we needed to enter. If I hadn't gone in to distract the others, they would have heard the fighting, and they would have come out with guns drawn.

"It was dumb of me to go in alone, but I didn't care. That morning I had helped bury my parents after a week of planning their funeral. I was so grief-stricken that I wasn't thinking right. Since their death, things had started happening. Things would randomly blow up, mirrors would break, rooms would shake… It hadn't taken me long to realize I was the cause. Unable to control it, I was terrified. I needed to talk to someone. That morning, after the funeral, I told my friend Rebecca. As I was telling her about it, I accidentally blew out the windows of her car. She was so scared of me that she pissed herself before she took off. So when I walked into that bar, I was ready to…"

Mae's voice trailed off. She didn't have to tell me what she felt. I could feel her reliving every emotion through our bond. I reached out to take her hand, but she took a step back.

"After we left the bar and dropped the kids off at a nearby police station, we went back to our hideout. No one could explain what had happened… so they chalked it up to an earthquake. Oh god," she whispered and squeezed her eyes shut. "It all just flooded out of me that night. It hurt so bad. I thought I was going to split in half right there in the middle of the bar."

"I walked out of our hideout and headed home. On the way, I stopped for gas and a bottle of water. Just as I was about to climb into my car someone tapped me on the shoulder and… Well, you know what happened. I got the hell out of dodge and haven't been back home since. For a few months I tried living in different places, tried to keep a low profile, but my power got so out of hand I decided that removing myself from civilization was the best bet, so that was when I took to the Appalachian Trail," Mae scoffed. "You know, it's been exactly two years since the start of this, and my life has only gotten crazier."

When she looked at me, her expression was grim.

"How mad are you?" she asked softly.

"Mad?" I tasted the word as it rolled over my tongue.

Yes, I was angry. Her decision to take on a bar full of dangerous men had been reckless, even downright suicidal. The thought that she had given no thought to her well-being was terrifying. What if she had lost the fight? Would they have killed her outright, or would they have made her suffer? The thought shook me to my core. Through our connection, I could feel the heavy emotional turmoil she was battling. Her misery was so acute that it pulled at my heart. I could not allow her to feel this way. I put my anger at her recklessness to the side as I closed the distance between us.

"You put yourself in danger, Mae. Yes, it angers me that you would do something so foolish," I told her. "But I can feel how confused and scared you are as you relive that night. It is almost suffocating how strong your emotions are. This event caught on camera was just a single moment in your life. It is gone. Do not remember it with fear or sadness. When you look back to this night, let it be the moment that marked the beginning of your true destiny."

I paused to make sure she was hearing me. When I was sure she was paying attention, I continued.

"Mae White, I am so proud of you."

She blinked in surprise. "You put your life on the line for children who meant nothing to you. You and your friends could have decided it was too hard to get to them and left. Even in your emotional state, you knew it would be unacceptable to leave those children down there. Your heart is too big to allow fear and grief to stop you when other lives are at risk. That large heart and your stubborn refusal to walk away from danger will help us stop whoever is trying to bring back the gods."

I wrapped my arms around her body, and she leaned into me. Slowly the strength of her emotions began to recede.

"I also saw what you can do when you focus, and I am beyond impressed," I added thoughtfully. "Did you not see how those men flew without you touching them? Did you see the gun explode? That was you. You were so focused that you were able to funnel your power to do exactly what you wanted it to do without any training, and that had been back when your power was at its most volatile. It was just like when you threw the car across the driveway. Just think about what you will be able to accomplish now that your power is not nearly as unpredictable and you have some control."

I leaned down and pressed my lips against her forehead. She looked up at me, the haunted gaze in her eyes slowly disappearing.

"I love you. While all of that sucked, I'm glad that it led me to you," she told me solemnly.

"And I love you," I muttered and took her lips with mine.

She sighed and opened her mouth, allowing me to deepen the kiss. Memories of our time together this morning floated through my consciousness, and I felt my body begin to respond. With another sigh, Mae pulled away. The anguish in her expression was beginning to fade.

"I didn't even notice that my attacks never even landed on some of those guys. I am pretty sure I blacked out for some of that fight," Mae said, her tone colored in disbelief. "And who was that woman watching me? How did she appear and disappear like that?"

"It was Autumn," I answered. Mae's eyes widened in shock.

"What was she doing there?" she asked in surprise.

"Probably making sure your power had surfaced after causing the accident that killed your parents," I suggested.

Mae frowned, and I felt a flutter of hurt between our bond.

"She wasn't really there," I said. "It looked like she was projecting herself from wherever she has been hiding."

Mae frowned. "You think she caused my parent's death?"

"Either she did it herself, or she hired someone to cut the brakes on your parent's car." I nodded. "She was the only one who knew what you are truly capable of. She probably checked in on you often to see how you were progressing. When she realized you were not showing any signs of the power Zyroe passed to you, I am sure she decided to take matters into her own hands."

I felt the sharp pang of sadness between us. I opened my mouth to offer some words of comfort but Mae shook her head.

"So now what?" she asked.

I debated letting the conversation of her parents' murder drop. While Mae needed to come to terms with it, a quick assessment of her fragile emotional state told me that maybe I should let it go for a while. So instead of pressing the issue, I changed direction.

"Now, we are going to work on your focus. We have time before everyone returns, so let us use it to find some control with your power. With practice comes skill."

***

Three hours later, Mae and I were both covered in sweat and dirt. It had taken a while for Mae to find her footing. Having her concentrate was the biggest obstacle. I could feel her constantly battling fear. The fear of her power seemed to divide her attention. When I told her this, she huffed in annoyance.

"Knowing I could hurt someone by accident makes me nervous. I can't help that," she argued.

When the next hour passed with no success, we shifted gears.

Instead of focusing on an object, I began to spar with her. This was something she knew and was comfortable with. I could feel her enjoyment in hand to hand combat. Once I was sure she was warmed up, I stopped playing fair.

She noticed when I began to use my enhanced speed to duck her blows or to land some of my own. She didn't complain though. In fact, through our bond, I felt the thrill of her excitement as she was forced to think and move faster. After being knocked, pinned, and pushed down several times, Mae's enjoyment faded. Her frustration with continuously being bested suddenly became our biggest asset. Her attacks became more strategic.

As she focused on trying to best me, I felt her fears slide away. This was the Mae I had seen in the video. Her sharp gaze watched my every move. She continuously shifted her weight, ready to defend or attack when necessary. While she managed to duck and block a few of my attempts to get her, she was no match against someone with my speed. I continuously landed gentle blows on her body and pinned her down. Whether it was from frustration or an actual attack, the first time she used her power to stop me from sweeping her legs out from underneath her, I was thrown backward twenty yards.

I landed on my feet, but for the first time, the breath had been knocked out of me. Mae's expression mirrored my surprise before a large victorious smile swept across her face.

"Again," I snapped, not allowing her to get distracted.

I rushed at her before she had a chance to protest. I snarled and lunged. I was almost on top of her before she threw both hands up. This time when I was hit with her power, I was prepared. I absorbed it instead of letting it throw me. That brief second when I allowed her power to soak into my skin was all that Mae needed. She twisted, and with a high kick, she was able to make contact with my jaw. I could feel her control in the movement. I knew she had purposely held back from hitting me hard, not that a blow from her would ever physically hurt. But then, her power flared outwards from her attack. While her foot had barely touched me, her power behind the kick was another matter. I was hit hard and thrown sideways. My wings opened, and I stopped myself before falling into a nearby shrub.

"Oh my god! Rylan, are you okay?" Mae shrieked as she hurried over to me.

The moment my feet touched the ground, Mae grabbed my face and studied it, making sure there was no damage. There was none, of course, but I allowed her to do a thorough inspection so she would feel better.

"I'm so sorry. I really didn't mean to hurt you, I just… It just happened."

"You did well," I told her proudly as she dropped her hands away from my face. "We will work again on this tomorrow. How do you feel?"

Mae rolled her eyes. "How do I feel? I didn't just get hit in the face with a blast of power."

"Do I look injured?" I asked with a raised brow. Mae took a step back and crossed her arms over her chest. Her eyes swept over me. When our gazes met, a smile tugged up the corner of her lips.

"Actually, it's quite the opposite. No one should look as sexy as you are covered in sweat and dirt like this. As always, you look perfect."

Her unbidden compliment threw me off guard. Mae took the opportunity of my speechlessness and threw herself at me. Her arms came around my neck, and her legs wrapped around my waist. I caught her up and twirled her around, laughing at her playfulness. Mae's answering giggle was music to me. Her lips came crashing down against mine. The world fell away as utter delight and happiness blinded my senses. Her tongue forced itself into my mouth, and I welcomed it. I slid my hands up her thighs and cupped her buttocks.

Suddenly, Mae's body tensed. She pulled away from me as her eyes turned violet and the veins that ran up her neck into her face began to glow. Shit, the toxins must have been released into the air. Her whole body jerked, and she groaned. I could feel her body warming as her power flared to react to the toxins. Her body grew so hot I worried there would be internal damage. It grew brighter as she jerked against me and the tree.

I could feel her pain and fear, but she remained silent as she fought back the explosive response to the toxicity. I tried to breathe for both of us. My grip tightened on her legs to steady her as her body jerked again. Sweat dripped down the side of her face as she squeezed her eyes. Just as abruptly, her body relaxed and the glowing under her skin vanished. She sagged against me, breathing hard.

"You did it, Mae," I whispered in her ear as she dragged in a deep breath.

"It gets a little easier each time," she admitted breathlessly against my neck. Nothing about what I had just seen looked easy. I held back a grimace. "Let's get back to the house and clean up. The others should be home soon."

With a sigh, I let her slide down my body and placed her on her feet. She turned to leave, but I grabbed her hand and pulled her back to face me. I planted a kiss on her lips and whispered, "We will continue this later."

# Chapter Twenty-One



*MAE*

It turned out that almost everyone else had already arrived home. When we walked inside the house Arthur, Nikolas, Camille, Jasmine, Ashe, Gabriel, Jasmine and Devon were all gathered around the counter sipping on glasses full of blood. My stomach rolled at the sight and I couldn't help but make a face. Jasmine and Arthur chuckled as they looked up in time to catch my expression. The others didn't bother to waste their time looking in our direction.

I skipped up the stairs to take a shower while Rylan walked over to the other Guardians. Under the warm water I allowed myself to relax. I thought of the four park rangers that I had fought off today. They had been so corrupted with dark magic they would have killed each other. Would they remember? Would they have felt guilt? Who had done that to them? Then I thought of the pictures on the computer. All of those people… murdered. How did they cover up all of those murders? Wouldn't families be concerned about missing relatives? I tried pushing away the awful images.

I braced my hands against the shower wall and allowed the water to run down my back. My mind turned to the video I had watched with Rylan. My blood turned to ice. The absolute terror of that night still haunted me. There had been so much pain. And Autumn had been there to witness the entire event. My hands turned into fists that pushed into the wall. Instead of helping me, she had just watched the scene unfold. She was *pleased* that I was there struggling to contain the chaos that was leaking out of me. I shook my head, disgusted. I hated her. I hated that she had created me. I hated that she had killed my parents and I hated that she had some sick plan for me. How she thought I could stop the end of the world from happening was beyond me.

Angrily, I straightened up and turned off the water. I stepped from the shower, dried myself off and got dressed. I took a moment to calm myself before I left the bedroom to find the others.

Voices carried throughout the house, and I followed the sound to find everyone had convened in the second story loft. As I entered the space, the conversation died down and heads swiveled in my direction. It was clear that I was certainly not welcome. I could almost feel the temperature in the room drop.

My pride was the only thing that kept me from turning tail and running. Mentally I braced myself as I crossed the space of the loft and headed towards Rylan. I held my head up high and even forced myself to smile despite the dark glares following me. Just to rub a little salt in the wound, I made it a point to meet Nikolas's steely gaze, knowing that he hated me the most. Rylan held out his hand as I approached, and I took it, grateful for the connection. I turned and looked around at the Guardians in the room. The only three missing were Diane, Samson, and Zara.

"Is it wise to discuss strategy and findings with a god in the room?" Camille jeered as the corner of her upper lip pulled up in disgust.

"Rylan, have you confirmed that Mae has had absolutely no contact with her father or any other gods after their initial meeting? She could be a mole," Devon asked.

He clasped his hands behind his back and pulled his cool gaze from me to look at Rylan.

"She is not a mole," Rylan asserted while ignoring Camille's comment.

"Mae can be trusted," Jasmine confirmed with a nod.

"Would someone please explain why Zyroe would want to help us stop his brethren from returning to the world? Why would he produce an heir with some rogue witch? It is not his style," Gabriel asked.

When he crossed his arms over his chest, his whole body seemed to flex in response, giving him an even larger, more intimidating appearance.

"Zyroe is the god of justice," Rylan said thoughtfully. "There are stories that say he helped the Guardians and the others on Earth to push his brethren into the next realm. Maybe he sees the others' return like a jailbreak? He is one of the few gods who would see a return to Earth as a way to escape punishment and not approve."

"What do you know of Zyroe?" Nikolas asked him with derision. "You were not there, nor have you ever known the true intentions of a god's motives. It is wise not to speculate."

"You would know best, Nikolas," Jasmine pointed out. "What do you know of him?"

"Nothing," Nikolas stated coldly. "Which makes him… *and* his daughter, a true threat."

"Why would we even bother to call any of you to ask for your help if I was planning something with Zyroe?" I tried to keep my voice calm, despite my rising annoyance. I was tired of all the finger-pointing. It was getting us nowhere. "It would be counterproductive to call you all here if I was trying to open the gates discreetly."

"We would not know what would be counterproductive to any plotting you have with your father," Camille interjected, glaring at me from her seat on the other side of the room. I rolled my eyes. For the love of…

"In any case, I think the more important issue at hand is that whoever is trying to open the gates has some history with the gods," Ashe said.

"Wizards are notorious for coveting more power. Perhaps a god reached out and seduced a wayward wizard with the idea of power if he freed them?" Gabriel offered. Ashe nodded thoughtfully.

"Do we know of any missing wizards or witches that have toed the line with their magic recently?" Arthur questioned.

"It is not a wizard," Camille retorted. "We all keep a close eye on the witches and wizards in our territories. We would know and sense any wrongdoings before it got to be a problem this big."

"As more Guardians take their lives because of this blasted curse over us, we are struggling to ensure all territories have a Guardian presence," Arthur interjected. "Things could easily slip by while we shuffle Guardians to newly unmanned territories."

"Or when they go missing or are murdered..." Ashe grumbled.

The tension in the room grew thicker. Muscles were flexed, jaws clenched. I stopped a shudder from running through me. The Guardians in the room were naturally intimidating. Seeing them upset over the news of a murdered Guardian made them even more frightening.

"Who is capable of murdering Guardians?" Camille asked of the group. "This is insane that it took our arrival to learn of any of this. The shifters, they had no notion to reach out to the nearest Guardian for help?"

"It is not like there is a directory with all of our numbers or even our names," Jasmine interjected. "Those change all the time when we need to switch territories. They probably had no idea who to ask for or who to look for."

"What has been done to locate them?" Devon asked angrily.

"Diane, Samson, and Zara have gone to explore Cain's residence. Hopefully, they found clues that will help us figure out what happened to the Guardians who oversaw this area," Rylan said with a frown.

Disgruntled murmurs and low conversation broke out. I took advantage of the distraction to talk to Rylan,

*What was discussed while I was gone?*

*Arthur found a pack of werewolves,* Rylan answered slowly. The tight set of his mouth told me this was bad. *They were taken care of, but he believes there could be many more. Jasmine's group found ancient writing carved into random trees. Nikolas translated them as names of past gods. None of them could pinpoint an exact location of where the dark magic is coming from.*

I shuddered as the reality of the situation grew graver. Rylan removed his hand from mine and placed his arm around my shoulders.

*Do not be frightened. We* will *stop the gods' return,* he told me confidently.

"If we find who's behind this, we can avenge Zein, Cain, and Ekon's deaths," Arthur said loudly over the side conversations. Everyone quieted down. "So we need to figure out a motive and who, or *what*, would bring back the gods."

"Who benefits the most from murdering Guardians and bringing the gods back?" Jasmine asked out loud.

"It has to be someone with a strong motive to bring back the gods," Nikolas mused. "Somehow whoever is behind this must have some type of relationship with one or more gods, or their family used to."

"A child of a god would have the motive to want to open the gates," Camille heckled. She turned to look at me. "Did you want to meet your father, little one?"

"Camille, enough," Rylan snarled.

"It could be a Guardian," I muttered more to myself than to her.

Heads swiveled in my direction. Oops, I forgot about the heightened hearing. Had I thought the temperature in the room had dropped when I first entered the room? Well, now, it certainly dropped another ten degrees.

*Mae*, Rylan warned as he stiffened beside me.

"You would accuse a Guardian of trying to open the gates?" Nikolas's hiss of indignation cut through the silence in the room.

My comment had been more of a jab rather than a true accusation. It was stupid to provoke a group of people who already hated me, but why did I have to put up with their chauvinism? In any case, I had already put my foot in my mouth. I guess it couldn't hurt to consider the possibility that it could be a Guardian...

"From what I have learned, Guardians were the closest beings to the gods. You were *literally* created by them to serve them. Could it be possible that out of all the Guardians there are and have been, maybe someone may have *missed* serving their god?" At the swift intake of breaths from several Guardians in the room, I knew I was probably digging myself a hole, but I pushed forward. "Think about it, as insane as it might sound, there were some Guardians who probably lived better lives despite being enslaved. Maybe they were treated better by their god or whatever, but in any case, once free will was granted to you do you think that maybe some didn't see it as a bad thing to want to stay with their masters?"

"I will rip the tongue from your mouth, child," Nikolas hissed. His eyes blazed red as he took a step towards me. Rylan stepped in front of me and snarled defensively.

"What Mae says is blasphemy!" Camille cried out as her face hollowed and eyes turned red.

"Of course the young demi-god would look for the good within her own people!" Devon snapped, his dark brows coming together in a deep scowl.

Yelling broke out amongst the Guardians. Okay, so my idea wasn't so smart. Too late to take it back now.

"Actually, Mae may have a point," a soft voice drifted over the unrest in the room.

To my surprise, the conversation ceased immediately. Everyone turned to look at Jasmine. Her dark eyes swept the room as she made it a point to meet every angry gaze.

She crossed her arms over her chest and said, "To gain enough strength and power to single-handedly bring back the gods, this person must be collecting magic from somewhere. More than likely from creatures who have power. Name another species that has access to all the other supernatural creatures on this planet? We have ledgers, notes, and books on the different species and what they are capable of. With that information, it would be easy to begin picking off individuals that we have noted with extraordinary strength in their magic.

"Because the dark magic is so thick here in this area, that must mean that someone has been casting it for quite a long time. Someone would need to have not only started collecting power long ago, which would make them immortal, but also keep the missing supernaturals they are using to siphon power from a secret. A Guardian could certainly do that. And what other creature would be strong enough to even attempt to harness all of that power they collected throughout the years?"

The only sound in the room was the heavy breathing of outraged Guardians. No one seemed to know what to say. Rylan and Arthur exchanged looks while Ashe frowned thoughtfully. Everyone had been quick to argue and threaten me when I had suggested that a Guardian could be behind this. With Jasmine, no one seemed to know how to react or what exactly to do with her theory. The respect the others in the room gave her was something earned, not given. I frowned as I realized I did not know much about my friend or her past. I would have to rectify that.

Abruptly, Rylan growled.

"The others have arrived. They have brought a trespasser who has been toeing the line of our territory," he told Arthur and Jasmine. He looked back at me. "Stay here."

"Um, no," I protested quickly. He was not going to leave me in a room full of hostile Guardians. It didn't matter that Jasmine and Arthur were staying behind. Rylan sighed but he didn't argue with me.

I followed him out of the loft, down the stairs, and out the front door. Outside Diane, Samson, and Zara stood in the driveway. The sun was just setting behind the trees and stars were just beginning to glitter in the night sky. The woods behind the arrival of the last Guardians silhouetted their frames, giving them a surreal appearance. Gripping the back of his neck, Zara held the young park ranger Thomas in her hand. When his eyes landed on me, he began to struggle against her hold.

"We found him lurking just beyond the premises," Zara said and tossed the man to the ground. "He was holding this." In her other hand, she held a hemp drawstring bag that was leaking some type of dark fluid.

"Yes, it is you! I have come to warn you!" Thomas proclaimed as he scrambled to his feet. Before he could get his footing, Rylan knocked him backward. Thomas landed on his butt, but he didn't appear too perturbed. His gaze stayed locked on my face.

"You came for me?" I asked, confused. Thomas bobbed his head up and down eagerly.

"How did you find us?" Rylan asked and took a step to the side to place himself between the ranger and me.

"I can *feel* her," Thomas said with awe as he pointed to me. "My heart cries out for the attention of the True One."

"The True One?" Samson repeated with a scowl. Again, Thomas nodded animatedly.

"Yes, there was a false god who blacken my soul and blinded me from the truth, but you—" he said, staring at me with a wide grin, "—You cleansed my soul. I seek only to obey and to serve the True One."

He reached out as if to touch me despite the distance between us. Rylan growled. The crazed look in Thomas's eye hadn't been there when I had first met him, and it gave me the creeps. There was something off about him. What was going on?

"Who is this false god?" Rylan growled. "What do you mean by *True One*?"

"What did you want to warn Mae about?" Diane took over the questioning. "How can you feel Mae?"

Thomas gripped his head as if in pain and squeezed his eyes shut.

"No, no, no," he muttered. "I will only speak to the True One. Only she matters, only her words are worth hearing."

The reverence in his voice and the words he spoke only caused my unease to grow. Instinctively, I took a step back towards the house. Thomas stopped shaking his head, and his eyes flew open in a panic. He reached out for me again, his face twisted in worry.

"No, True One. Do not leave me!" he cried out. "I am lost without you. Guide me, let me serve you, do what you please with me, but do not leave me!"

"Mae, question the man," Diane commanded softly, her eyes on the ranger.

I looked at her, then to Zara who was watching me with curiosity, before turning my attention back to Thomas. He was waiting with a childlike eagerness for me to say something.

Drawing in a steadying breath, I asked, "Do you know the name of the man you claim is a false god?"

Immediately, Thomas shook his head, his expression becoming forlorn.

"I would tell you, True One, if he had given me a name. He came to me, to all of us, in dreams and forced us to serve him."

I thought of the pictures I had seen earlier that day, and my stomach rolled.

"Did he make you kill people?" My voice came out as a whisper. Thomas nodded eagerly, pleased to provide me with the information I requested. "Why did you listen to him?"

"He twisted our minds, made us think we were doing it for the greater good," Thomas told me.

What person believed killing others was for the greater good? How sick was this false god to force these people to do such terrible things?

"Are all the park rangers involved with the killings?" I asked, not wanting to know the answer. Thomas nodded again. "How long has this been going on for?"

"We have been serving him for a long time. Long before I arrived here. We all have been fooled by the false god, True One."

"Why do you keep calling me that?" I snapped, tired of the weird title.

"Because you are the True One. I can feel you coursing through my veins. Your presence in my mind is like the air in the spring, sweet and crisp." He emphasized the "p" in crisp with joy.

Rylan's parents and Zara turned their attention to me, curious about his response. I felt the soft buzz of communication as Rylan filled them in on what happened this morning. When the buzzing stopped, I looked back down at Thomas who waited patiently for my next round of questions.

"You said you came to warn me. Warn me of what?"

"The False One will come to destroy you. He felt when you severed our tie to him, and he became angry. He doesn't like to be bested. He kills anyone that stands in his way, and now you stand between him and his goal." Thomas raised a victorious fist in the air. "But I know you will be able to stop him! You just needed to be warned. That... and the sacrifices to help you gain your strength."

Sacrifices? I stood there baffled by his words. Then I noticed the way all the Guardians turned their attention to the bag in Zara's hand. It was still dripping. In the gravel drive, a dark spot had grown and was beginning to glitter in the rising moonlight. Oh no... no, no, no. The air in my lungs vanished when I realized that whatever, or whoever, he had sacrificed was in that bag.

Had I done something to cause this reaction when I had tried to remove the dark magic in Thomas? Should I have just let the dark magic kill them? Just the mere thought of allowing someone to die sickened me. But was Thomas better off now than he had been? It hadn't just been Thomas I had tried to fix. So where were the other three?

I already knew the answer before I could ask it out loud. That bag in Zara's hand, that had to be what happened to the others. Had they taken their own lives, or had Thomas murdered them in my name? People were dying because of me. For me. To help me. I took a step back again but stumbled. My stomach heaved. In front of everyone, I turned and hurled onto the drive. People were dead because of me. Dead. The word repeated itself in my mind.

The others were right. They should be worried that I was here in the midst of all of this. What good could come of a child of a god being here on earth? It didn't matter that I still felt as human as I had before learning about who my father was. I was hurting people without even trying. My heart slammed against my chest as panic began to set in.

I straightened and glanced at Thomas who was watching me patiently. He nodded to me once, as if he had conveyed something to me. Then, he reached down into his boot and pulled out a pocket knife.

"Now you know of the False One," he said proudly. "Allow me to lend you my strength."

Before I could register his intentions, he flicked it opened and shoved the knife into his throat. My hands flew to my mouth to cover my scream. His eyes fluttered shut and his body fell over.

In my head, I was screaming. Watching the life seeping out of Thomas's eyes, still fixed on me, was horrific. My body shook. I couldn't think with all the screaming in my head.

"We need to alert the others," Samson said at once. Without another word, he stepped over Thomas's body as if it was nothing and passed me to head inside.

"We need to find more park rangers, press them for more details. Someone must know what this 'false one' looks like," Diane told the rest of us.

"Compelling them to give us information will not work. Jasmine tried and failed," Rylan said as he shook his head. "Whatever we do, we must act fast. If this man is right about retaliation from our unknown foe, we should expect trouble within the coming days. Mae's presence has been detected, and whoever is behind this will see her as a threat."

Zara said something, but I was done standing beside a man who had taken his own life. Their calm discussion of what to do next felt wrong. It was as if they were unfazed by this man's hideous act. I headed back into the house.

My body felt numb as I walked through the front door. In my head I could see Thomas shoving that knife into his neck over and over again. As I approached the stairs Nikolas slid into view. He crossed his arms over his chest and planted himself directly in front of the stairs.

"What is wrong young goddess?" he sneered. "Cannot stomach a little blood?"

"Move, Nikolas," I said. My voice sounded strange to my ears. Nikolas's pupils narrowed.

"Look at the mess you caused. That is, what? Four lives lost because of you?" He taunted. "Are you sure you are not a monster? From where I am standing, it certainly appears that you are."

I could hear the cold loathing hidden beneath his mocking tone. I met his gray eyes with a frown and said, "You're right. I did cause the mess out there. And I'll regret it for the rest of my life."

My voice broke on the last word. Instead of allowing myself to break into tears in front of the terrifying Guardian, I stepped around him and took the stairs two at a time.

Once inside my room I shut the door and collapsed onto the floor. I was out of breath, and I couldn't seem to catch it. Tears blurred my vision and spilled down my cheeks. Four men were dead because of me. Four. I had taken a bad situation and made it worse. So much worse. I thought I had helped them. I was a monster, and what made this so much worse was the fact that I had begun to believe otherwise.

As I sat there crying into my hands, minutes trickled by. Eventually, the tears began to slow as fatigue overrode guilt. Just as I was about to pull myself up off the floor there was a knock on the door. The sound made me jump. If it were Rylan, he would have walked right in. Was it Arthur or Jasmine? I got to my feet and walked over to the door. Cautiously I opened the door and found Zara standing there. A frown tugged the corners of her mouth downwards.

"I am sorry to bother you, but I wanted to check to make sure you were alright," she said. I opened the door wider and stepped out into the hallway with her.

"No, I'm not alright," I told her honestly. "I swear that I did not mean for that to happen. I thought I was helping…"

Zara shook her head and said,

"You cannot blame yourself. Dark magic tampers with the mind and soul. Who knows how long they were affected by it? Your magic may have removed the bad stuff but the side effects of that darkness would have lingered. It would have eaten away at their minds, twisting it permanently. You cannot blame yourself for what that young man did out there."

I stared at her, frowning. She stared back. Her dark brown eyes searched my face for something. Maybe it was the same thing I was looking for in hers.

"Why are you checking on me?" I asked curiously. "Why don't you hate me like everyone else?"

Zara rolled her eyes before answering, "The others are being ridiculous. Until there is a reason to be suspicious, I tend to give people the benefit of the doubt. It is not your fault that one of your parents happens to be our enemy."

I gave her a rueful smile.

"Thanks, I appreciate you giving me that courtesy."

"If I am truly being honest," Zara hedged with a thoughtful frown. "After I saw you in that surveillance video, I felt this... this overwhelming need to find you. I do not fully understand why but... I think it has something to do with fate. I think I was meant to be here to help you with this. I know that probably sounds strange."

I laughed.

"Trust me, hearing that fate may have brought us together is the least strange thing I have heard since meeting Guardians."

Zara grinned and said, "Good, I am glad that did not scare you. I will let you get some sleep. We will talk tomorrow. Goodnight, Mae."

She turned and walked off. I watched her until she disappeared down the stairs. I went back inside my bedroom and collapsed onto the bed. It made me feel a little better knowing that at least Zara did not see me as a monster. But how could I not be? She may not think I killed that man outside but I had. Inadvertently, I had killed all four park rangers.

Whatever happened here within the next month and a half, hopefully, we could stop it. After that... I needed to find a way to make sure that no one else's blood would be on my hands.

# Chapter Twenty-Two

*Mae*

Five days had passed since Thomas had shown up. If I had thought tempers would cool or that the others would begin to trust me by now, I was sorely mistaken. If anything, as time passed, they hated me more. I didn't blame them. After everyone had heard about the park ranger, they believed I could manipulate their thoughts. If the situation weren't so serious, I would have laughed at them. While I didn't have that ability, Guardians certainly did. When I brought that little fact to light after a snide remark made by Camille, it only infuriated the Guardians even more.

Despite the constant jabs and snide remarks, I tried hard to find common ground with these new Guardians. I attempted to strike up conversations. I listened when they shared stories about their lives with one another. When I tried to participate in the lighter conversations, I was either ignored or harassed. Trying to befriend people who hated me felt like a losing battle, but I refused to stop trying.

During the day, everyone was gone, so having to worry about what I said or did was only limited to the mornings and at nights when everyone returned. After what I had done to the park rangers, I resigned myself to stay behind. I didn't need anyone else to get hurt because of me.

In the mornings, before he left, Rylan and I trained together. Now that I knew how hard I needed to focus, mixed with my meditation, I found it was easier to call my power to me and use it. By the fifth morning, I was able to keep Rylan an arm's distance away from me the entire training session. I was even able to control where my lightning struck.

Well, most of the time.

On that particular night I waited on the back deck for Rylan to arrive. The clouds overhead were dark, and the air was thick with the promise of rain. I stared up at them as I lounged in one of the wicker loveseats. The silence in the woods surrounding the house was eerie. The animals knew a storm was brewing, and they had taken shelter. Soon, I would have to move inside, but until I felt a cool drop of rain I would remain outside.

Nikolas and his group of "I hate Mae supporters" had arrived home first tonight. After attempting to talk with Devon and Camille about their day, I had given up and headed out here. I had been out here for an hour and hadn't been bothered by anyone. The solitude was enjoyable. It was cool enough now that the mosquitoes had died off for the season, leaving me to enjoy the fall weather in peace. Somewhere off in the distance, thunder rolled. It was a soft warning of what was to come. I smiled. I loved storms.

Something moved in the clouds, drawing my attention directly above me. I yelped in surprise and rolled off the couch just as a massive stone fell from the heavens. With a loud bang and the cracking of wicker, the massive boulder destroyed the very seat I had been lounging in. What the hell? I scrambled to my feet. Just as I turned to look upwards, something hard hit me from the side.

It was like getting hit with a body-size sledge hammer. Every bone in my body screamed in agony as I was thrown across the deck and pinned down by something heavy. My eyes flew open to see a creature so strange I could hardly process what I was seeing. It had a face like a medieval version of a demon. It's bottom canines protruded from its mouth, and it had a wide, flat nose with smoke billowing from its nostrils. Its body, which was pinning me to the deck, was strangely human; though the thick tail with a spiked ball at the end that swung around wildly behind it was certainly not. The wings that spanned from its back were large and bat-like.

The most terrifying part about this creature was that it was made from stone.

Before I could fully comprehend that what I was seeing was real, the creature raised its fist. I screamed in terror, knowing that if that thing hit me, it would be over, fast. My power surged forward. I grabbed control. Energy sizzled and from my chest a bolt of lightning shot upwards, shooting through the stone creature. It exploded into a fine dust.

I rolled onto my stomach. I tried to get to my feet, only to find that my body wouldn't cooperate. I fell to my knees, still reeling from the pain of being hit with a statue. A shriek that sounded like a drowning eagle alerted me to incoming danger. I looked up then dove out of the way as another stone monster tried to grab for me.

A burst of adrenaline helped me get to my feet. I rushed for the sliding glass door. A cold stone hand grabbed me from behind by the neck. It yanked me back and threw me across the deck. I slammed into the railing and shuddered under the impact.

I threw up my hands and blasted the creature backward with my power. It stumbled backward only to take to the sky and disappear in the dark clouds.

"Help!" *Rylan!* I screamed as I got to my feet and ran to the door.

Before I made it halfway across the deck, the floor under my feet exploded. I fell to the side as another stone creature emerged. Its large jaws opened and closed like a snapping turtle's. It lunged and grabbed me. Trying to break the hold of this mobile statue was futile. The monster flew across the deck and tossed me over. I screamed as I plummeted to the ground.

Just as I was sure I was about to splatter, a pair of strong, warm arms caught me. Instinctively, I threw my arms around Samson's neck as he took to the sky with me in his arms. Multiple screeches rang through the air as thunder rolled. I stared up at the sky and gasped as over a dozen stone monsters began to descend from their hiding place within the clouds. They flew in an oddly synchronized spiral around us, getting dangerously close as they closed in on us.

One of them broke rank and shot towards us. Samson stopped flying, bringing his wings close to his body, and we dropped from the sky. The creature missed as it flew by us. Samson's black wings opened back up, and we shot towards the house. Above us, four creatures dropped from their formation to charge after us. Just as the nearest one reached for Samson, something streaked by us and hit the creature so hard it broke into large pieces and fell from the sky.

I watched in awe as Devon twisted around to face the next descending creature opening its wide jaws. As Devon went in for his attack, Jasmine came up beside Samson and fended off an oncoming stone creature approaching us from the right. From under us, a creature grabbed Samson by the ankle and yanked him downwards. I clung to Rylan's father as he was pulled from the sky. Another creature slammed into us from above, and we toppled downwards.

Samson somehow managed to kick off the creature holding on to his ankle while he used his wings to knock off the creature from his back. When we hit the ground, he landed on his feet in a crouch.

My voice came out shaky. "Thanks."

We both looked up and stared at the stone creatures circling above us. Where had these other ones come from? There had to be over fifty of them. But we weren't alone anymore. Every Guardian had arrived and come ready for battle. What a sight to be seen. The clang of weapons, roars of anger, and shrieks of protest rang out above us as Guardians and creatures collided.

"What are—," I stopped as I watched the sudden change in the clouds above us.

Lightning lit up the dark clouds, beginning to churn wildly as they changed from gray to deep red. Next to us, Rylan landed, his face a mask of fury. Samson placed me on my feet, and I threw my arms around my mate, relieved to see him. Rylan pulled me against his chest and kissed the top of my head.

Our reunion didn't last long. Rylan whirled us both out of the way as a massive rock slammed into the ground right where we had been standing. Above us, half a dozen creatures came barreling towards us. I felt Rylan's muscle tense just before we were airborne. He raced up to meet the monsters head-on. They converged on us. When they were just about an arm's length away, Rylan veered to the left. At the same time, I threw my hands out in front of me, and my power rippled from my fingertips. The creatures were thrown backward, and lightning rippled up from the ground into the small group of monsters. Some turned to dust while others just fragmented into pieces that fell to the earth.

Thunder roared. It was so loud that the air felt like it vibrated. Nikolas and Ashe shot past as several monsters trailed behind us. Rylan weaved expertly through the danger, trying to get me away from the battle. But the creatures seemed to know Rylan's plan and intercepted every attempt to get away. I threw my hands up and protected us with blasts of power and bolts of lightning as Rylan maneuvered around the danger. No matter how hard we tried to escape, they just kept coming.

Gabriel dropped from the sky and slammed into a creature that approached us on our right. As Rylan twisted out of the way a scream of agony cut through the sounds of battle. I looked up and watched Camille as she spiraled out of control towards the ground. Diane caught the falling Guardian and whisked her away. Two more screams of pain followed Camille's, and I searched the sky to see Gabriel grab Devon as he toppled out of the air. Nikolas shot forward and caught Zara as she fell.

I looked up to see what was attacking the Guardians from above. Red snow began to fall from the dark clouds. As it landed on the stone monsters, the creatures began to sizzle and disintegrate. Ashe was in the midst of a fight with three of them and didn't see the threat coming from up above. When the red snowflakes touched the Guardian, I watched as his whole body flinched violently. Ashe didn't cry out, but his attacks faltered. The monsters around him screamed, but continued their fight despite disintegrating right before our eyes.

"It is acid snow!" Jasmine roared her warning to the others. Her voice carried through the night like a siren. "Do not let it touch you!"

Rylan headed towards the house, but as the first red flakes landed on the roof and deck, the building began to sizzle and catch fire. He changed direction only to be blocked by eight of the stone creatures. Some were already crumbling apart as the red snow landed on their bodies. Rylan gave them a warning snarl as they descended upon us. At the same time, red snowflakes began to land on us. I watched in horror as red snow melted on Rylan's bare shoulder and it began to eat away at his skin. Several snowflakes settled on my arms. I bit back a scream as my skin sizzled away.

Diane, Nikolas, and Samson flew between us and the monsters and ran defense as they attacked us. Around us, more cries of pain rang out, but the battle didn't seem to be slowing down. Rylan landed under nearby trees to protect us from the elements. Unfortunately, the snow ate through the leaves and branches. He placed me on my feet and used his wings to cover us both as the red snowflakes began to fall harder. As he shielded me, his body twitched in pain.

We were in trouble. I had to do something before someone got killed. This red snow was going to eat away at all the Guardians.

The monsters moved too fast for me to try to strike them all with lightning and blasting them backwards only slowed down their attack. I couldn't do anything about them, but maybe I could do something about the snow. With a deep breath, I drew my power inwards. If I could blast the clouds above us away, maybe I could at least remove the environmental threat.

"Rylan step back," I told him as I let my power build.

"No," he growled.

"Rylan, trust me," I growled back as the pressure under my skin intensified. "Back up and warn the others to brace themselves."

Rylan snarled his displeasure, but he let his wings drop and he took a half step back to give me some room. Not waiting another second, I lifted my hands and let my power shoot outwards. The blast of energy rocked the earth beneath me and threw everything in the air upwards. Rylan must have sent out his warning because the Guardians immediately got out of the way while the monsters and the acid snow were both hit.

The creatures scattered, but they were not my concern. I shoved my power harder upwards into the cloud. My heart was beating rapidly, my skin felt like it was on fire, and my vision blurred. I pushed until I knew that if I kept pushing, I would collapse. So instead of forcing the cloud upwards, I held up a makeshift barrier my energy had created between the clouds and the rest of us hoping that would give the Guardians some coverage. It worked. Instead of floating down to the ground, the red snow began to collect on top of my energy shield.

The stone monsters shrieked their anger. As if they knew I was the one stopping the snow from falling, they all turned their attention to me. Immediately, they swarmed downwards towards me and Rylan. I gritted my teeth and tensed as the creatures attacked. Rylan moved to stand in front of me, his sword drawn and ready.

Suddenly, a wall of Guardians blocked the incoming monsters. Every single warrior came to our rescue. The Guardians and monsters collided. The sound of battle, only a few feet above us, was deafening. Large stoney pieces of monsters crashed down around us. Rylan ran defense, deflecting anything that could hit me as I continued to hold back the acid.

I could feel the red snow burning my barrier, trying to eat its way through it. As the layer of red snow began to build, my shield grew heavier. It was taking a lot of energy to maintain the shield and to hold it in place. I wasn't sure how long either the shield or myself would last. If I didn't do something soon, my barrier would collapse and all that acid snow would fall like bricks to the ground and eat away at all of us in seconds.

I closed my eyes and let the sounds around me fall away just like I did when I meditated. I slowed my breathing and focused on the barrier above us. A faint smell of smoke wafted through the air momentarily distracting me. With a great deal of effort, I forced myself not to open my eyes to watch the flames engulfing the house.

Instead, I struggled to find my connection with my own fire within me. For the past five days, I had been able to gain a tiny amount of control over my power. I could fend off Rylan's attacks with a blast of energy, and I found that I could summon my violet lightning at will. While I still struggled to have it erupt where I wanted it to, just the fact that I could call upon it was a feat within itself. But during my training, I had yet to figure out how to summon my flames without everything going to hell in a handbasket.

But I needed it, like *now*. This wasn't a training session. This was life and death and not just my own. If this barrier fell, we'd all be in trouble. So, I focused. I listened to my internal workings, searching for some connection that would allow me to harness the flames. I could do this. I just had to figure how.

Power wove through my body. I filtered through it, searching for that connection I needed to the fire that would help us. In that moment, I wasn't afraid of what was inside of me. This power wasn't my enemy. It was a tool to help me fight against a true foe. If I could just figure this out, I knew it would bring me to a whole new level of control. I would be able to do anything.

It was then that I realized that whoever was behind this attack against us saw me as a threat. They knew what I had been uncertain about this whole time: I could stop them. All I needed was to get a grip on the power rushing through me. And I could do that. I'd stop this attack, and then I'd come after them.

The sudden boost of confidence strengthened my resolve. At the same time, I found the piece of the puzzle I had been looking for: the link to my fire. I grabbed at the sudden ability and forced it through my hands upwards. My eyes flew open. Above us I watched as violet flames burned along the surface of my energy shield. The red snow sputtered and cackled like gunpowder, creating a dangerous light show above us.

As the last of the red snow disappeared from the top of the barrier, I pushed the flames higher. The dark clouds began to evaporate. Thunder boomed and red lightning lit up the sky. I pushed my power up higher and harder until the clouds above us vanished and only the stars and waning moon were left. The moment the danger from the clouds was gone my strength vanished.

My legs gave out from under me, and I collapsed. Exhaustion clung heavily to me. My breathing came in gasps, and my body shook from fatigue. Lying on my back to stare up above me I watched as the Guardians took down the stone monsters one by one. A few that made it to the ground faced off with Rylan, who was making quick work of them. I watched as his sword cut through stone. One of the creatures met its fate as Rylan beheaded it. The head fell and rolled towards me, stopping just a foot away from my face. I turned and stared at it.

My gut twisted as I realized the creature looked familiar. I had seen this thing before. But where?

The sound of battle around me began to die down until finally, it was silent. Several Guardians landed nearby while the rest of them flew off. Voices took the place of the sound of fighting. Suddenly Rylan stood above me. Weakly, I raised a hand, and he helped me to my feet. Unfortunately, my legs weren't ready to hold me up, and immediately gave out. Rylan scooped me up in his arms.

"Are you alright?" he asked.

As he spoke, I could feel him pulling my power from all around and redirecting it back into me. Instantly, I felt less tired, though I was beginning to feel aches and pains that I hadn't felt earlier.

"I'm fine." I dismissed his question with a shake of my head. "What about you? How's everyone else?"

"We are already healing," Rylan reassured me. His brows furrowed in concern. "Mae, you used an enormous amount of power, and you are still conscious. The last time you used even a fraction of this type of magic, you were dying. How is this possible?"

"She has been practicing with it and meditating. She has built up endurance," Jasmine answered as she strolled over to us. "That was incredible, Mae."

Jasmine's tank top was torn and covered in debris. Her dark hair was windblown, her red eyes were blazing with excitement, and when she threw back her head to laugh, it was filled with euphoria. She was as stunning as she was crazy. How could someone who had just faced monsters be so relaxed? She must have seen the confusion on my face.

"I have been in many battles, Mae," she said, "but this one was, no *is* different. I enjoyed the fight, and now I can bathe in the feeling of success."

Behind her Camille, Devon and Ashe approached us. I tensed in Rylan's arms. What trouble were we about to deal with now? Behind us, commotion drew my attention away from the advancing Guardians. I watched in fascination as the Guardians who had taken off right after the fight were now handling the fire that had started in several different places over the house. They worked as a team, passing buckets of water to each other. Someone had found a garden hose and was hosing down the deck.

"Mae, what you did tonight was incredible," Devon said, bringing my attention back to the group of Guardians before me. "The second attack against us was unforeseen and quite frankly, undefeatable. Without the protection you provided for us, we would have had to flee, which is not in our nature. From what I just overheard, you risked your well-being to help us. For that, I owe you. No longer are you my enemy, but a fellow warrior who I will gladly stand next to in battle."

I didn't know what to say. I felt the heat in my cheeks rise as his glower relaxed. Next to him Camille and Ashe exchanged glances. With a deep sigh, Camille turned to look at me.

"I agree with Devon," she said. "You helped us tonight. One of us could have seriously been injured or even killed. Please accept my gratitude."

Unable to keep from pointing out the obvious, I blurted out, "You guys, you all came to rescue *me*. Whatever these things are," I said and waved my hand at the head that still lay on the ground, "came after me, and you were there to stop them so *thank you*. I know you're not a fan of me and could have easily let them kill me."

"While we may despise you, so far you are innocent of any wrongdoing. We protect the innocent people of this world," Devon responded.

The look upon his face made me think that he had sucked on a lemon. I almost laughed. Okay so a friendship between Devon and I didn't look bright, but at least he seemed to have a moral code, so maybe he wouldn't stab me in the back the moment he got the chance.

"They are called gargoyles," Rylan informed me while he pinned Devon with a glare.

I gaped at him, unable to handle what I heard. I turned and looked at the stone head. With everything else I had seen so far these past few weeks this should have been easy to accept, but for some reason, my mind wouldn't wrap around it. So, I let it drop.

"What is important now, is to prepare for the next attack," Jasmine interjected.

"Agreed," Rylan said with a nod. "We need to begin setting up night watches. Marking our territory has done nothing to help us in detecting danger. We need to be alert and ready for anything." He glanced up at the cabin, and I followed his gaze. The small fires that had been burning were now out, and the other Guardians had disappeared into the house. "We should reconvene with the others and discuss our next steps."

With that, we headed inside. Instead of gathering with the others right away, Rylan took me upstairs to our room. The moment the door shut behind us, Rylan placed me on my feet. While I was relieved that I could stand on my own, I was surprised when pain shot up my leg, and my ribs protested. I gripped my sides with a hiss. Before I had a chance to pull my shirt off, Rylan was already there doing it for me. He sucked in a sharp breath as the fabric of my shirt fell to the floor.

I looked down and found massive bruises already forming across my stomach and chest. Between both collarbones was a perfect hand shaped bruise where the gargoyle had pinned me down. I was bleeding in a few spots, and there were welts on my skin where the acid snow had settled. Rylan reached down and ripped off my jeans, and we both stared down at the dark marks that marred my skin all over my legs.

Rylan's gaze met mine. I saw his fear and concern before I felt it through our bond.

"Rylan, I'm fine," I assured him quickly.

"I am not leaving your side again. If I had been…" he whispered. His voice was twisted in agony and anger.

"The attack still would have happened," I interrupted firmly. "Let me get changed. I won't look so gruesome with clean clothes."

He may have let me walk away, but when I turned my leg buckled and a shooting pain caused me to hiss. Automatically, he scooped me up and carried me to the bathroom. He placed me on the counter and began administering first aid.

First, he placed a kiss on each wound. After a kiss, he gently lapped at each bloody spot. He did this with each cut. His lips trailed across my face as he leaned forward to place a kiss on a particularly tender spot right under my eye. His hands rubbed up and down my arms in a soothing gesture.

By the time he had finished, my body was craving his. I shuddered as he pulled away, and I saw the same raging desire there in his face. He leaned forward and touched my lips with his. I moaned against him before I wrapped my legs around his waist. His tongue slipped inside my mouth, seeking a passionate dance with mine. He pressed his hips into the junction between my hips, and I felt how hard he was for me.

As much as I wanted him, there was something I needed to do before we let everything else fall by the wayside and got lost in each other's embrace. I forced myself to pull away from Rylan. My whole body seemed to protest, and it took a great deal more self-control than I thought I had. He frowned when I put a hand on his chest to keep the distance between us.

"We need to go downstairs and speak with the others."

"The others can handle whatever needs to be taken care of," Rylan assured me.

"I'm sure they can," I said with a nod. "But I need to be down there, too. I don't want to seem like some dead weight that can't contribute to anything. We escaped for a bit so I could gather myself, but I want to show that I haven't been scared off and that my mate doesn't need to coddle me each time something bad happens."

Rylan made a face. "Fuck what they think of you. And what if I want to coddle you?"

I giggled. "Coddle me when we're done talking to everyone."

"I am going to do much more than that when we are alone again," Rylan promised with a seductive smile.

# Chapter Twenty-Three



By the time we reconvened with the others, I could tell the atmosphere in the house had changed dramatically. Most of the hostility that had been building towards my mate had been redirected to our true foe. When Mae and I walked into the small office where everyone was studying a map of the park, the room went silent. My beautiful mate, still limping, walked in with her head high and did not waver under the gaze of the warriors before her.

I took over for Arthur, who had been leading the discussion about security and how we should prepare for another attack. There was no question that our unknown foe would try to strike at us again. If our foe had any doubt before about Mae's ability to stop them, all doubts were likely vanquished now.

The group was humbled. I could sense it as we talked. Some of these Guardians had not seen battle in quite a while, and during the fight, it had shown. Last night had also put Mae in a new light for them. Seeing her in action had filled me with pride. Her bravery and determination had not only stopped our foe but gained her respect among the other warriors. Her retaliation had been powerful, and she had remained completely in control. If there had been any question about her origins before, there were none now. The ability to push back an attack of that magnitude was unheard of. But despite the certainty of her lineage and proof that she could indeed be dangerous, the intensity of hate and distrust from the Guardians had significantly decreased. Since we only had four weeks left and were no closer to finding the "false one," that was an excellent turn of events. We all needed to be on the same page, and finally, it seemed we were getting there.

By the time we had gone to bed, the air seemed to have cleared, to my considerable relief.

What I had not anticipated was the sudden interest from the Guardians in Mae. The next morning, Mae and I were followed outside by a handful of warriors who wanted to watch us train. If Mae was bothered by the small gathering, she did not mention it. She used blasts of her energy this morning more offensively than defensively. She was able to set plants on fire deliberately and even managed to hit four of the five targets I had created with her lightning. Her victorious grins and occasional quirk of her eyebrow when she bested me sent surges of desire through me.

But despite her growing control and confidence as we worked, I could see she was stiff with pain. There was nothing I could do for the bruises that had darkened overnight or the aches in her muscles. Her pain worried me. With Mae injured, it made her more vulnerable. While her injuries would eventually heal, I was concerned that if she pushed herself too hard, she would not recover as quickly. So that morning, I cut our session short despite her protests.

"Rylan, I promise I'm fine." Mae sighed dramatically as we headed back to the house.

"I intend to make sure you stay that way. We do not need to push you today after you overexerted yourself last night."

I pushed open the front door and allowed her to walk in first. She kicked off her shoes in a huff and began to walk towards the kitchen.

"But I feel fi—," she paused. "Wait a minute. I remember!"

She whirled around to face me. Her gorgeous brown eyes twinkled with excitement. Before I could ask her to elaborate,

Camille, who had followed us in while the others lingered outside, beat me to the punch,

"What are you recalling, Mae?" Her tone was genuinely curious.

A glance at her face told me that whatever prejudices she'd held against my mate had been put aside.

"The gargoyles last night. I thought they looked familiar! I remember where I've seen them before," she said with a grin. "Rylan, when we went to lunch after we stopped at the Nature Center, we passed this old abandoned town. The only place open was this really old looking gas station that looked like it was built into the rocky hillside. I noticed a few statues sitting higher up on the hill and remembered thinking how out of place they looked. The statues were identical to the gargoyles we fought last night!"

"Then, that is where we need to go look," Gabriel said, coming down the stairs. He must have overheard our conversation.

"What if they're not there anymore?" she asked.

"Gargoyles usually protect places that hold something of value. They must return to the spot their creator designated them to stay when they are not in battle. If you saw one perched somewhere, it will have to return there once it has completed its master's orders," I explained to Mae as Ashe, who had been in the family room, walked over to join us.

"So the gargoyles I saw must be guarding something," Mae said. "I wonder what it is? Hopefully it's something that will help us solve the mystery of who's trying to open the gates. It's not anywhere close to where Zyroe and Autumn had warned us to look though."

"I think it is safe to assume the gargoyles you saw and the ones that attacked us last night are working for the same person," Jasmine said as she leaned over the second story loft's balcony. "When my group scouted the southern end of the park that Zyroe showed you, we noticed subtle movement along the slopes of the mountains. When we went to check it out, there was nothing there, but it was rocky, which would make it easy for a gargoyle to blend in. Since none of us had expected a gargoyle in such a remote place, I would not have thought to look for signs of one."

"We need to go and check out both areas," I told them. "Gather the others. We need to split up and figure out what gargoyles are doing in both places."

Jasmine nodded and disappeared out of sight to find the others inside the house while Camille turned and left to grab the Guardians who were still outside.

"Hold on, Rylan. You and Mae were several hundred miles away from Jasmine and her team. That is a massive distance between the two locations," Gabriel pointed out with a frown. "Why would our foe spread themselves so thinly?"

"Who says they are spread thin?" Ashe offered thoughtfully. "Maybe he has many working under him that we do not know about. Maybe our unknown foe is hiding things all over the Alberta providence. They could be hiding weapons, housing warriors, collecting provisions…Who knows?"

Camille returned with the others. It did not take long for everyone to gather together. Someone had grabbed the map of the park and a map of the entire providence of Alberta and tacked it to the wall in the family room so everyone could see. I stood before everyone, waiting for them to settle down. Mae had grabbed an apple and situated herself next to my mother and father. She appeared completely at ease between the two warriors.

My family. My heart swelled with pride. I glanced at Mae's apple and frowned.

*You need to eat more than that,* I scolded.

Mae rolled her eyes. *Later.*

*You will forget,* I pushed.

*I'm not going to make a commotion in the kitchen while we plan for battle,* Mae retorted.

I raised a brow. *Are you expecting a fight?*

*Well, yeah.* She frowned. *We're looking for trouble, and I'm sure we'll find it.*

"This will be a covert mission," I said out loud for everyone to hear while I glared at Mae. I turned my attention to the masses. "We have two leads that will hopefully give us some direction regarding where our enemy may be hiding. We must split into three groups. This means we will be walking into possibly dangerous situations with small numbers. If you can avoid detection and engaging in battle, do so. We are looking for anything that will give us insight to our enemy's plans.

"The first sighting of a gargoyle was here," I turned and pointed to the map of Alberta, in the area where the gas station was located. "The elevation varies tremendously for miles. They will see us before we see them if we try to fly in. We will need to drive there. The second group will go here, towards the southern tip of the park around the base of the mountains. Once you get close, you will need to stay hidden in the shadows the woods provide. If there is a gargoyle on the mountain, we can assume there will be more, and they will see you all arrive unless you come around from here," I pointed.

"Where do you want the third group?" Bishop asked.

"Here," I answered. I looked at Mae, but before I could continue, she cut me off.

"Don't you dare say to stay with me, because I'm definitely coming with you guys. It's non-negotiable."

I glared at her while a handful of Guardians laughed out loud at her defiance. I turned my glare towards them, which only caused more laughter. I sighed; I had already learned my lesson by leaving Mae behind. In any case, I wanted her by my side.

"No, you will be with me," I assured her. "You have certainly proven that you can handle yourself. The reason we need a third group is because there could be another attack while we are gone. There needs to be a small group here to intercept any danger. If someone is hiding something of value where these gargoyles are located, hopefully we will find it, and it will tell us who is behind the madness in this area.

"Keep a sharp eye out for anything. We could potentially find Zein, Cain, and Ekon's murderer with the information we gather today. Stay vigilant of your surroundings. There is no telling what danger could be hiding in plain sight in each of these locations. At the first sign of trouble, fall back. Do not engage. This is simply a recon mission. We will reconvene and discuss our findings and go from there. Now, let us split into groups and head out as soon as possible. We do not have time to waste."

*** 

Three hours later, I could see the small gas station Mae had mentioned come into view. We had another ten minutes before we arrived, but the tension in the truck began to climb. Diane sat in the passenger seat, her eyes already scanning the rocky hillside for danger. Behind me, Mae sat quietly. I could feel her excitement and anxiety as surely as I could feel my own. Next to her Jasmine read aloud the text messages coming in from group two.

In the car behind us, Nikolas and Gabriel hung back. I heard Mae shift, and suddenly her hand was on my shoulder. She said nothing, but she did not need to. Her need to have a physical connection as we drew closer to possible danger was something I could understand.

A few minutes later, we pulled into the old gas station. The convenience store that was part of the hill had paint peeling off it, the windows were filthy from dirt, and the signs that hung on the other side of the glass had long since faded.

"I don't see the gargoyles." The disappointment in Mae's voice carried through the car.

"That does not mean they are not here somewhere," Diane assured her.

I pulled up to a pump and turned the car off. Without hesitation, all four of us climbed out. I walked around the car to fill up the gas tank while Jasmine came to stand next to me. My mother and Mae hooked arms and walked into the store together. To the store clerk, we would look like tourists just passing through. The other car of warriors drove by. They would be parking nearby but out of sight. We would see them soon enough.

*I am heading around the store to start the climb*, Jasmine informed me. I nodded, and the Guardian casually strolled off, appearing to be interested in the area. When the tank was full, I pulled the truck around to the side of the gas station where there were no cameras and parked.

*I'm heading up.* I reached out to Mae first then alerted Diane of my departure. Both responded with requests to stay safe. I hesitated for a moment, using my hearing to make sure everything inside was going well. Both women were to talk up the clerk for a bit to see if they could gather information from him. When it was clear Mae would be safe on her own, Diane would join the rest of us while Mae stayed near the base of the hill to keep an eye out for trouble.

I began my climb up the hill. There was an old hiking trail that I followed up. As I ascended, my senses flared out in every direction. If one of us could catch an unfamiliar scent or sense dark magic, we would catch a break. I highly doubted I would sense the latter. Since we had arrived in this godforsaken park, my ability to sense danger had been ripped away from me. It was disconcerting and left me feeling inept.

As we searched on foot, pretending to be interested in landscape and plant life, the way curious human tourists would, we began trading notes. There were fresh prints of gargoyle footsteps here and there. Certain rocks had been used as perches to watch the land below. Jasmine found a spot where a hex had been cast and left its mark on a greener area of the hillside.

Diane joined us further up the hill. I glanced below to find Mae casually strolling along the edge of a patch of trees. It was not dense, but that did not mean something could not hide there waiting for a victim.

*Stay in sight of a Guardian,* I warned her. She stopped and looked up at me. With the heightened senses of a Guardian, I could easily make out her eye roll even from the great distance between us. Her nonchalant attitude when it came to her safety caused my anger to rise.

*Relax. I'd rather not become gargoyle food. I'll keep you all in sight, I promise.*

My anger vanished the moment she promised to stay within sight. It was replaced by amusement. Gargoyles did not eat food, a thought I did not share with her just so she held onto that little fear.

*Rylan,* Jasmine's firm whisper in my head broke my concentration after an hour.

My eyes scanned the bottom of the hill for Mae. I found her scaling a smaller hill nearby. As promised, she was making an effort to stay within sight of us.

*What is it?* I responded. Her tone alerted me to danger.

*There is something——* Her voice was abruptly cut off as the ground beneath our feet began to tremble.

Jasmine was nowhere to be seen, but I knew she was close. I took to the sky. Pieces of my shirt fell away as my wings ripped through the fabric. Rocks exploded and tumbled down the hill creating a destructive avalanche. I twisted in the air searching for Mae and found her rushing to get off her hill as it rose beneath her feet. Just as I began to race across the sky to help her, Nikolas was already there. He scooped her off the side of the hill, away from danger.

*Petra thērion,* Diane's voice echoed through everyone's head as the rock beast rose from its slumber. What once was a rocky hillside was now a monstrous beast not seen in centuries. Its roar was thunderous. Another roar echoed the first. The hill that Mae had been climbing was now that of another *petra thērion.*

We dove into action. These rock monsters were on the same level of stupid as trolls, but the destruction they could cause by just walking across the terrain could be devastating. With Mae out of the way, I joined the others in the sky as we drew our weapons from our marks and went to battle.

# Chapter Twenty-Four



The term, "royally fucked" seemed to have encompassed my life for the past two years. But this was a new type of fucked I hadn't dealt with yet. Was the term "majestically fucked" a thing? Was that more fucked up than royally fucked? I really didn't have time to wonder because I was plummeting to my death thanks to a Guardian who thought that killing me while the others were busy was a good idea.

When Nikolas had swept me off my feet, the world around me appeared to be falling apart, and I was relieved to see him. But that relief was put out faster than a lit match in a category five hurricane.

"Whoever is behind opening the gates between the realms will be dealt with. We do not need the help of a god. It is my greatest regret that I must do this to an innocent child and her mate, but a god roaming this Earth will only bring devastation."

Those were the words he uttered right before dropping me from some crazy height. As I fell, I watched as two monstrosities rose from the ground. It was like watching two snowmen come to life, except these snowmen were made from hundreds of large rocks that had, just a moment ago, been lying utterly still under our feet. The Guardians were already in action. Half of them were attacking the top of half of the largest monster while the others tried to trip the second one by weaving around its feet.

I would have been impressed by the way they were able to come together so quickly and work like a unit if I weren't about to die. There was no time to scream out for help; no one would be able to get to me in time. I was on my own, and somehow, I had to save myself.

As I flailed around in the air, I forced myself to stop panicking. I closed my eyes and reached for my power. I couldn't fly, but maybe I could at least break my fall. With an ease I would have been excited about not given the circumstances, my power answered me. I twisted so I was free-falling like a professional skydiver and held out my hands in front of me. Just as I was about to hit the treetops of the nearby woods, I let my power free. Immediately, the blast of energy shoved past the trees and against the ground. The moment my power hit the ground, I began to slow down. While I couldn't stop the fall entirely, when I did hit the ground I didn't die. Instead, the breath was forcibly knocked out of me, and my bones were painfully jarred.

"You should have let the fall kill you. It would have been less painful," Nikolas's cool voice said a few feet from me. Before I could ask, "Less painful than what?" he was standing over me with one of the small daggers he'd pulled from his tattoo along his forearm. He held it high above his head.

I rolled out of the way just as he brought the dagger down. Without even realizing I had reached for it again, my power blasted out of my hands. I threw Nikolas backward as he attempted to stab me again. I got to my feet and faced the coldhearted Guardian. I watched as he pulled the two other daggers from his forearm. His gaze never left my face.

"Nikolas, stop this," I tried to stay calm. I wanted to reach out to Rylan, but he was in the middle of something. I couldn't let the others be down one person while he came to my aid. It would be devastating to learn that Diane or Jasmine got hurt or killed because Rylan had come to save me.

"You do not belong here," he told me. His expression was grim and full of determination. "Lay down your life for the good of mankind. I have seen the trepidation and fear you have of yourself. I saw how it affected you when the ranger took his life. You have goodness in you. Do not let it fade as your power continues to grow. Your presence on Earth will only cause destruction and mayhem. Do not allow any more lives to be lost on your account. Allow me to provide you with a merciful death."

"You wouldn't be just killing me. What about Rylan? If one mate dies, so does the other!" I snapped.

"It is an unfortunate loss, but it will be for the greater good," Nikolas answered calmly. Without warning, he threw all three daggers at me. His move was so swift I didn't have a chance to defend myself other than drop to my stomach. Two of the blades sailed past me, but one lodged into my shoulder, just where my heart would have been before I'd fallen to the ground. I cried out in pain and rolled onto my back. I reached for the dagger in my shoulder to pull it out, but let it go when the pain was too much.

*Mae,* Rylan's voice was suddenly there in my mind. Of course, he would know when I was in trouble. To think I could hide it was absurd.

However, I didn't have time to answer him. Movement in my peripheral vision was my only warning another attack was coming. I threw my power outwards and knocked Nikolas away from me again. He snarled his rage and lunged for me. Surprising Nikolas and myself, without hesitation I yanked the dagger embedded in my shoulder and threw it at him. He had thousands of years of experience under his belt throwing the weapons he'd been born with. I had about a second to figure out the weight of the blade before it left my fingertips. It flew past him harmlessly.

Nikolas slammed into me with all his might sending me backward. He used his knee to pin me to the ground while he reached up with both hands to grab my head and snap my neck. His eyes were glowing red now, his face had hollowed, and his fangs poked out from his lips. Death was a promise that swirled around in his eyes. This was going to be an easy win for him. Who was I to stop a warrior who had been alive for so long, with the strength of ten men, and a hatred so strong that he wasn't seeing me for me but as one of the gods he used to serve?

I wasn't the enemy here. I never had any intention of becoming a god, playing the role of a god or throwing my weight around like the gods of Nikolas's time. While I knew life wasn't fair this felt extra unfair. How dare he decide that I was someone who should die? I had done nothing but try to hide from what I was. When I ran into Arthur and Rylan, I hadn't been searching for answers, but when they offered to help me find some, I leapt at the opportunity. Not because I wanted to justify my role in this world, but so I wouldn't become the monster I knew I could be.

I had found my answers. I knew who my parents were. I knew now where my powers derived from, and I knew control was possible. I knew my purpose in life was to *save* lives, not take them. I might stumble, and I might fall a few times in the process of learning, but that didn't make me like the other demi-gods. I was not a monster. The knowledge that I was not and could not be a monster bubbled up in my chest. I was here to *save* lives... The thought swirled around in my mind as something in me clicked.

I felt a confidence in myself I hadn't felt in a long time. I wasn't a monster, I wasn't going to be killed by some bigoted Guardian, and I wasn't going to let the doubt in myself stop me from finding out who was going to open the gate between the realms.

The power under my skin seemed to feel my confidence come to life. It roared to the surface as my resolve solidified. I was going to stop a monster, not become one. So Nikolas could just fuck right on off with his lack of faith in me. I didn't need it. I had faith in myself.

My power sparkled along my skin, and my veins began to glow. I clenched my jaw as the strength of my power caused my body to jerk. Just as Nikolas attempted to snap my neck, I shoved the palm of my hand up into his face and connected with his nose. With my power behind the force of my hit, Nikolas was suddenly airborne, blood trailing after him. I got to my feet and turned to the warrior who had all three daggers in his hands. He launched them at me while shooting forward.

With my power surging through me so strongly, everything around me felt like it was moving in slow motion. Without a thought, I knocked the blades aside with a simple backhand motion. I threw my fist forward and struck Nikolas down with my power. His body slammed into a tree, but he was on his feet in an instant and moving towards me again.

But just like his last attack, he appeared to barely be moving. I put power behind a roundhouse kick and struck Nikolas square in the jaw. All without me physically touching him. He snarled and took to the air. I refused to allow that unfair advantage. I called up a lightning bolt that hit Nikolas before he made it past the treetops. He crashed back down to earth.

As he fell, he twisted and flew at me, knocking me to the ground again. I slammed a fist full of power into his jaw, and he grunted in pain. He hit me back, but I felt immune to pain now. His fist, which should have shattered my jaw, deflected off me. I kneed him in the groin, but he didn't flinch. His fist repeatedly struck my face before I could attack again.

After being hit a fifth time, I realized I wasn't immune to pain. Shock kept me from feeling his blows at the moment. I knew that if I survived this, I was going to regret every punch he dealt. I slammed my fist into his side, effectively knocking him off of me.

I climbed to my feet, but Nikolas was there, and he grabbed me by the front of my shirt and threw me a few feet away into a tree. I slammed into it, the breath leaving my lungs forcefully. I sat up while trying to drag a deep breath in. Suddenly, Nikolas was above me trying to shove one of his daggers into my gut. I grabbed his wrist with one hand and shoved at his chest with the other.

With my power actively charging through me, I was able to keep the dagger from moving any closer to me despite Nikolas's best efforts. I had to stop this fight before he killed me. But could I kill him? I recoiled from the thought. Even as he attempted to kill me, I still wasn't able to consider taking a life. My strength was waning as I tried to keep the dagger from piercing me. I stared into his red eyes and saw the victory there. He knew I wasn't a killer. All he needed was to wait for me to weaken, and he could finish what he started.

But I also saw, deep within those gray eyes, regret. He may hate *what* I was, but that didn't necessarily mean he hated *me*. He had said he saw me as an innocent victim in all of this. That I was a death that had to happen. That didn't mean he *wanted* to murder someone innocent. He just believed it was the best thing for the world.

An idea popped into my head. I knew I couldn't kill him, despite the situation, but I couldn't let him kill me either. I needed to stall for time. I would let the other Guardians dish out whatever punishment saw fit for Nikolas when they realize what he had tried to do. I wasn't a killer, and I wasn't planning on changing that today.

I summoned all my power inwards. The small violet sparkles that danced along my skin grew bright and an intense heat filled my chest. When I couldn't handle the pressure anymore, I let my power go. An explosion erupted from my chest outwards, throwing the Guardian off me. Nikolas hit a tree, and it cracked under the force. As Nikolas landed on his feet, the tree toppled over on top of him, pinning the Guardian to the ground. At least, momentarily.

Suddenly, the ground beneath us trembled. It cracked open, and I screeched as the ground under my feet suddenly disappeared. I fell into darkness, followed by dirt and debris. My head hit something hard as I fell, and I slipped into unconsciousness.

*** 

A terrible throbbing in the back of my head woke me. As I regained consciousness, I began to feel every blow Nikolas had landed and more. Everything hurt. I was sure I had a broken rib, a broken jaw, and a ton of internal bleeding. When I attempted to move, I hissed in pain. My hiss was followed by a round of coughing as I drew in the dirt that was floating around in the air. I opened my eyes and blinked as they adjusted to the darkness.

All around me pieces of earth lay crumbled and broken. Large rocks were lying dangerously close to my face. I looked up and found that a few trees had somehow smashed together to form a tent-like structure to block the ground that had fallen into the Earth after me. Sheer luck. That was all that kept me from being crushed under tons of dirt and rock. Not a single ray of sunlight peeked through the debris overhead.

So how could I still see? I turned my head, wincing as I did, and noticed I was in some sort of tunnel. At the far end of it, I could see a bluish hue. For a moment I panicked. A light at the end of a tunnel was never a good sign if you were wondering whether you were still alive. I squashed the thought of possibly being dead though. I wouldn't be in this much pain if I were.

Hadn't Rylan mentioned something about this area being a coal mining town? The fight between Nikolas and I must have made part of an old mining tunnel collapse. Now I was stuck down here. How long had I been out? I shifted, and despite the protest from my body, I sat up. My head swam, causing me to feel nauseous. I brought my knees up and hung my head between them while the world righted itself. Was the battle with those stone creatures over? Where was Rylan?

*Rylan?* I reached out tentatively. A tremendous amount of relief rushed through my connection to my other half.

*Mae, where are you?* The fear in his voice was laced with concern. *Why could I not reach you?*

*I fell in some sort of tunnel and hit my head. I just woke up,* I lifted my head and looked at the blue light. *I thought these mines were abandoned? I think someone's been down here recently. There is a light not far from me.*

*Don't move towards the light!* Rylan snapped. I snorted out loud, knowing he was thinking the same thing I had. *We are above the area where the ground caved in. How did this happen? Where is Nikolas? I thought he had you. No one can reach him.*

*The ground caved in underneath us when I used my power,* I explained to him but paused as I realized something. *Rylan, I don't know where Nikolas is. I hope he's not down here with me. He tried to kill me. I was defending myself when the tunnel collapsed. He was pinned under a tree the last I saw.*

A rage blew through me like a fireball. I shuddered under the intensity of Rylan's anger.

*Mae, there are no trees fifty yards in any direction,* Rylan told me with despair. *He must be down there with you.*

At his words, my stomach dropped. Nikolas was somewhere in the rubble with me? Guardians were nearly immortal. If I'd lived through this fall, so had he. I had to get away from him before he found me.

*Get me out of here, now!* I didn't want to die in a dark hole. Gingerly, I got to my feet. I braced myself against the wall as the world swayed. I left all pride at the door. *Please, Rylan, get me out of here.*

*I will be with you as soon as I can,* Rylan promised. He sounded calm, but I could feel his terror and anger swirling in my gut. *We need to figure out how to move the debris without causing the rest of the tunnel to collapse. Unfortunately, it will take some time.*

*Can you find another way in? There has to be an entrance somewhere,* I said, panicky.

*Jasmine is trying to pull up maps of the mines, but it will do us no good if other sections of the tunnel have collapsed,* Rylan explained. *Just hold on. Don't touch anything in case it triggers debris to fall on you.*

Okay, I wouldn't touch anything, but I wasn't going to stay here where Nikolas could be regaining consciousness at any minute. I took a step towards the blue light, but my legs trembled hard, threatening to buckle on me. The movement caused pain to ripple through me. I clenched my teeth to keep from moaning. Unfortunately, my jaw hurt the worst, and clenching my teeth only made it hurt more.

*I can feel your pain,* I heard the ache in Rylan's voice. *Where are you hurt? Are you bleeding?*

I looked down at my shoulder where Nikolas's dagger had lodged itself in my shoulder to find that it was still bleeding profusely. If I didn't get help soon, I would be in a lot of trouble.

*I'm hurt everywhere. Nikolas can pack a mean punch. One of his daggers got me in the shoulder. It's bleeding pretty bad. Don't let me die down here, Rylan,* I pleaded as I placed my hand over the wound. I sucked in a deep breath.

*I will not let you die.*

Rylan's confidence rang through his voice and our bond. I looked towards the blue light and forced my feet to head in that direction. Obviously, there was something down here. If someone still used this tunnel, then maybe there was an exit nearby. I just prayed it wasn't on the other side of the debris that had closed up the rest of the tunnel.

The closer I got to the light, the brighter it became. I could hear a faint humming and then there were random clicking noises that stopped and started back up again. I rounded the corner and stopped mid-stride. My jaw dropped open.

*Mae? What is it?* Rylan's voice drifted through my head.

Somehow, I had fallen right into a science laboratory. The tunnel had widened to the size of a warehouse. Along the wall were high tech machines that lit up and made the clicking noises. Hanging along the far wall were monitors displaying different sections of the park. In the middle of the room was a massive glass tube filled with a blue gas swirling and sparkling within. A group of ten people holding hands wouldn't be able to wrap around this ginormous glass cylinder. The sheer size of it made me wonder how in the world someone had managed to get it down here. Attached to this glass tube, which lit up the entire room on its own, was a thick clear tube that fed out from the top and split into hundreds of smaller tubes.

Those small tubes ran along the top of the ceiling all around the room before descending on to a capsule. The capsules were what took up most of the space in the lab. There had to be well over fifty of them. To me, they looked like something you would see in a science fiction movie where someone wanted to preserve their body. I could almost picture someone climbing in, closing the glass door, falling asleep, and then waking up a hundred years later looking exactly as they had when they had climbed in. These capsules were tilted upwards instead of laying flat and what was in them was the most shocking, and horrifying, thing in the room.

There was a single person inside each one. But they didn't look like people anymore. Their skin looked mummified, stretched over their bones so tightly that if they moved, if they *could* move, I was sure it would rip right off. There were IVs attached all over their bodies. Blue gas was being siphoned out from their bodies and being pulled to the large glass tube in the middle of the room. As I approached a capsule and peered in, I noted black feathers laying by the person's feet.

*Rylan…* My shock was beginning to fade as horror took over. *Talk to me, Mae!* Rylan demanded.

*There are other Guardians down here. They're trapped and sickly...* I answered as I stepped further into the room. *Something really bad is happening to them, I wish you could see this...*

*Go back to where we can find you. Get out of there, now!* Rylan's panic had finally settled in his tone. He had forgone trying to pretend to be calm for me.

Instead of listening to him, I limped further into the room. Whatever was happening here, it couldn't be good. How did these Guardians get down here? What was happening to them? My stomach rolled as my internal warning system went off. This was wrong, I had to get them out of here. I came and stood in front of another capsule and began to examine ways to open it.

When I found a latch, I tried tugging it open. Nothing happened. Upon further examination, I realized it was magnetized to stay shut. There had to be a button to release the latch somewhere in the room. I glanced around at the machines that lined the wall and growled with frustration. Where was I supposed to start? There were buttons *everywhere*! Frustrated, I grabbed the edge of the glass and tried to yank it open. Nothing happened.

I was about to start cussing out loud when a slight movement caught my attention. I spun around to find Nikolas standing at the mouth of the tunnel, staring around the room with his white brows pulled together. I took a moment to look him over while he was distracted. His pants were ripped and stained, there was dried blood covering his arm, and his white hair was in disarray. But there was no sign he was in any pain. Shit, he could still kill me if he wanted to. My mouth dried as fear trickled down my spine. I called up my power immediately and braced myself for a fight. Nikolas's gaze swept over me. He was probably assessing how easy it would be to kill me now in my condition.

To my surprise, Nikolas raised his hands in a sign of surrender. I didn't trust him. Instead of standing down, I tensed further, bringing my hands up ready to fight him if needed. It didn't matter that every inch of my body ached in some way. I wasn't going to go down without a fight.

*Mae?* Rylan's voice was a plea. He was dying knowing he could not reach me. *What is going on?*

*Nikolas,* I told him.

*I will kill him! I swear to god I will kill him!* he yelled in my head.

His fury and fear were just an echo of his emotions, but they felt as strong as my own. I pushed Rylan's bellowing to the side to focus on the danger at hand.

"There is a more pressing issue than trying to kill you," he said flatly. He walked further into the room, and the tension in my body heightened. His gaze traveled over the capsules, and I could see his jaw clench and unclench. "Many of these warriors were thought to be dead. We thought it was suicide, but it appears that is what their kidnapper wanted us to believe."

*We are breaking through the debris. I will be with you shortly,* Rylan vowed. I could almost hear him breaking through rock via our connection.

I stepped to the side as he approached. He glanced at me and frowned.

"You were trying to open one of these up," he mused.

"I was trying to get her out," I growled. The aches and pains in my body were amplified as the tension rose in my body. "They are magnetized shut. There has to be a button or something to open them, but I'll never find it in time. I'm sure whoever is overseeing this will be around sooner rather than later."

"Use your power," Nikolas told me. I wasn't sure if my eyes were bulging out of my head or not, but I stared at Nikolas.

"My power? My *godly* power? You want me to use it?" I asked incredulously. "Did you not just try to condemn me to death because of it?"

Nikolas's cold stare was more intimidating now that he had tried to kill me. It wasn't just an unspoken threat anymore. I refused to cower under it though. He could kiss my ass if he thought I was going to belly up so he could gut me like a fish.

After a long pause, he said, "Yes, I am suggesting you use it. It will cause the machines to malfunction and release everyone. The others will be here shortly, and we will be able to get them out."

I moved further away from him so there was a good distance between us. Without turning my head too far in one direction, I looked around the room again at the trapped Guardians. How long had they been down here? What was getting sucked out of them? Just as the question presented itself, I answered it: magic. This was the magic our enemy was gathering to open the gates. He had been using the power of the Guardians to gain enough energy.

The ground beneath my feet shook hard, and a light dusting of dirt fell from the ceiling. I looked at Nikolas again who had his head tilted upwards as if he was listening for something. The ground shook with a deliberate pattern. Something was going on above us.

*Rylan, what's going on?* I reached out.

*More* Petra thērion *have arrived. There are five of them, and they are trying to draw us away from where you are. Whoever is behind this knows his lair has been compromised,* I could almost hear his teeth grinding in frustration. *What is happening down there?*

*Nikolas seems to want a short truce to help get these Guardians out.* I glanced over at Nikolas who had turned his attention back to me. *Lead them away from here. I think if they all gather right above us the ceiling will cave in. Stay safe, Rylan.* I turned my attention to Nikolas and glared at him.

"I'll do it," I snapped at him. "But because I planned to free them to begin with, not because I'm taking orders from my would-be murderer."

He said nothing, but his face hardened.

I took a deep breath and centered myself. I needed utter control, or I could make this whole place collapse on us. I called upon my lightning bolt, and it answered right away. I placed my hand on the nearest capsule, and the glass broke as the electrical charge left my hands. The entire machine sparked and sputtered before turning off. The ripple effect was immediate. All the other capsules in the room shut down.

But my power didn't stop at the capsules. I watched as the violet energy coursed through all the machines along the wall, causing small fires and explosions. It reached the massive glass cylinder full of Guardian power, and the case shattered violently. Massive pieces of glass flew in every direction. I threw myself to the ground as Nikolas jumped behind a capsule.

The explosion rocked the entire laboratory. The ceiling cracked. Several large slabs of concrete fell, narrowly missing the Guardians stuck in their prisons. The large industrial lights that had been wired lazily to the ceiling flickered out. A small emergency light popped on giving the room an eerie green hue. In the corner of the room where a large boulder had crashed down, a hole about half the size of a manhole cover allowed light from above to filter down into the lab.

"Nikolas look!" I pointed.

I leapt out of the way as a small chunk of the ceiling came crashing down in front of me.

Nikolas turned to where I had pointed. His wings grew from his back. As he lifted into the air, I noted the way one wing seemed slightly bent, as if parts of it were broken and had yet to heal. He flew to the small spot and hovered there for a moment. Then, he began punching the opening, widening it. I wasn't sure how far down into the tunnels we were or how long it would take Nikolas to break through enough of the rock to get us out of here, but I didn't wait to see.

When I was sure most of the danger from the explosion was over, I rose to my feet. I got up delicately, cringing and flinching as I moved. My body was shaking from fatigue and pain. The blood on my shirt was dripping onto the ground as I moved, leaving a trail. I grabbed the nearest latch and yanked it open. Nikolas's plan had worked. My relief was short-lived as I began removing the IV's from the body in the capsule. The Guardian didn't budge as I worked to remove him. It was only when I went to grab him under the arms that a small, almost inaudible groan escaped his lips.

"Hey, you're going to be okay," I whispered. "We're here to help you."

He didn't open his eyes, nor did he make another sound as I haphazardly attempted to pull him out of the capsule. Despite his fragile state, this was still a grown man twice my size and trying to move around dead weight was not easy, especially in my condition. I laid him down on the ground and moved immediately to the next person. Behind me, Nikolas continued to punch through the rock to break through to the surface. I had gotten about twenty Guardians out when more light flooded into the warehouse.

I turned to find Nikolas landing next to the first Guardian I had freed. He scooped the man up, and I watched as he flew towards the larger opening. I was sure Nikolas wouldn't be able to fit through the hole but to my surprise, he brought his wings in as close to his body as possible and shot through the small alcove to the surface. It was tight, and I noticed debris fall back into the lab as he and the person he held skimmed the tight space to get out.

The ground still shook overhead. Dirt and small rocks continued to fall. Rylan had said they were going to try to lead the monsters away, but they weren't far enough. The ceiling was going to collapse if we didn't hurry. My heart thumped painfully in my chest as I thought about dying from a cave in. That was not how I thought I would go out.

I continued pulling the Guardians from their cases and placed them on the ground. A few groaned as the first one had. Most of them remained silent. I checked for a pulse and to my surprise, each Guardian still had one. How they had survived whatever torture they had endured was beyond me. I whispered words of encouragement and assured them their freedom was near.

I continued to do this until it became too difficult. My breath came in shallow gasps, and the room wouldn't stop spinning. Around me, Nikolas made slow progress of taking each Guardian from this horrible place and out into the fresh air. His wing still looked wrong; how long did it take for a Guardian to heal bones? I'd ask Rylan once I got out of here. I pulled out the last Guardian from his capsule and heaved a great sigh. The last five Guardians laid on the ground, unmoving. The moment I removed the last one, my legs gave out from underneath me. I braced my hands against the ground, and I stayed like that for a minute while I tried to gather enough strength to finish the job.

A loud crack warned me of the danger above me. I looked up to see a large frisson in the ceiling moving at an alarming pace. When it got to the other side of the room, the entire lab shook so hard that I was thrown face-first into the floor. I scrambled up to my feet and watched as the ceiling began to fall towards me. I screamed in terror and threw up my hands protectively.

# Chapter Twenty-Five



*MAE*

My power surged forward. As the rock and dirt fell, it slammed into a barrier only several feet above my head. The impact against my power was enough to break me. My body shook violently, and tears streamed down my face as I gritted my teeth so hard I thought they were going to crack. I held my hands up and forced myself to focus. Around me, the empty capsules were destroyed as the lab caved in. The thundering noise was deafening. Dust and dirt were thrown into the air, making it hard to breathe. All around me, massive pieces of the tunnel slammed into the ground, surrounding me and darkening the space.

*Mae!*

"Mae!"

Rylan's voice in my head echoed Nikolas's shout coming from somewhere nearby. Shit, was Nikolas stuck somewhere else in here? If he was, I couldn't save him. I knew I wouldn't be able to hold the multiple tons of rock and dirt above me for very long. Already, I could see it inching closer as my strength waned.

*I have five Guardians still trapped down here*, I told Rylan. *I am holding up the roof the best I can but I can't hold it for long.*

*I'm heading back to you now*, Rylan assured me. I could feel his panic and terror. It mirrored my own.

"Nikolas!" I shouted through gritted teeth. "Where are you?"

"I am near."

It was true. His voice was coming from just beyond a rock close to me.

"Are you trapped?" I asked him.

"I still have access to the exit I created," he assured me. It was odd how calm his voice was. "Can you lift the rocks you are holding? I can slip in and grab you."

I cursed as I pushed my power to its limits. I could feel the odd thumping in my heart and drawing in breath felt harder than holding up the entire weight of this tunnel. Ever so slowly the debris began to rise. It didn't get too far but it was enough for Nikolas to be able to slip through from wherever he was. He came and landed beside me and stared up at the ceiling that was floating above us.

"Hurry," I snapped through gritted teeth. "Get the others… Can't. Hold. On. Much. Longer."

Nikolas glanced at me with a look I did not have time or patience to interpret before he moved. He grabbed a Guardian and was gone without a word. My arms trembled, and the ache in my shoulder blended with all the other aches and pains in my body. Part of me acknowledged that Rylan had been right. I was glad we had stopped training earlier this morning. I hadn't recovered from the night before. I was certainly feeling it now. Nikolas returned and carried out another body.

"Well, well, well," a mysterious voice drifted through the darkness. Bumps raised along my arms, and the hairs on my neck that weren't plastered in dirt and sweat rose. "What do we have here?"

On my right, the debris suddenly began rolling to one side. Pieces of rock continued to move until a man stood only twenty feet from me. I could only make out his silhouette, but the movement behind him alerted me to wings. Another Guardian? Nikolas suddenly reappeared but froze as he realized we were not alone.

"Ah, Nikolas, it has been quite a while…" the man drawled.

I could almost hear the newcomer smiling.

"Cain?" Nikolas whispered, aghast at the other Guardian. "You are behind all of this?"

Apparently, Guardians could see well in the dark. Also… *Cain?* As in the missing Guardian whose territory we were in?

"I would like to say yes and take all the credit, but alas I cannot," the man replied with a sigh. "This was all Ekon's idea. He brought me into his plan many years ago, and only now has it come to fruition."

"Th-this is madness! You are kidnapping and using our own people to bring back those who enslaved us. For what purpose?" Nikolas demanded and took a step towards the man in the darkness.

"Oh, do not fret Nikolas. We are not so foolish as to single out just the Guardians to siphon power from. At first it was fairies and shifters, then witches and wizards. We pretty much wiped out the entire elven species. When we ran out of options, we turned to our own brethren to supply the power we needed," Cain boasted. "It was a waste of time to continue to try to gather magic from any other species when Guardians not only last much longer due to our immortality but also are much more powerful than the rest of the species that walk this planet."

"Nikolas just get the others and go," I snapped. *Rylan, Cain's down here with me and Nikolas. He and Ekon are behind this. Tell the others.*

*The others will handle it,* Rylan said. *I am just above you. I can see the bodies that Nikolas has laid out.*

*There's not enough room for anyone else down here.* I don't know if this came out as a whine or a statement, but with the weight of the tunnel crushing me it was hard not to feel panicked.

"We were worried that you had been murdered," Nikolas said incredulously. "Is Zein somehow a part of this too, then?"

"Zein? Oh no, quite the opposite. The poor fool accidentally stumbled upon my park rangers carrying out a sacrifice to the gods after trying to find me at my residence. Unfortunately for him, I had been there watching the sacrifice. When he killed my rangers and headed home, I followed and took care of him before he could tell the others. I knew he would be quick to alert you all. I would have brought him back here to join the others, but he was quite a fighter, so I killed him and made it look like a suicide." Cain paused and a manic giggle drifted from his direction. "Well… I tried to make it look like a suicide. I, perhaps, got a little carried away after I sent the suicide note."

Zein's wings pinned to a wall with a bloody message written between them came to mind and I shuddered. That's what his *carried away* looked like? This Guardian was insane.

The sound caused a thrill of fear down my spine. I glanced at Nikolas who took a step closer to me and Cain. Cain laughed again.

"I made it look like a suicide for each of the Guardians I managed to kidnap," he said after getting ahold of himself. "I wondered if any of you would be suspicious at the rise of the suicide rates in our species within the past century but no. Apparently you are all such a miserable lot that suicide seems more plausible than a fellow Guardian being kidnapped."

Next to me, Nikolas snarled.

"Nikolas, just go!" I cried out as the roof dropped a foot.

It couldn't have been more than a few inches above where he stood. He needed to get out of here with the others. Cain and I could share a grave if that was what it took to stop him.

*Rylan, Cain admitted to killing Zein,* I reached out to Rylan.

*Forget Zein! Tell Nikolas to get out of the way!* Rylan roared in my head.

"You must be the *True One*," Cain's tone came out mocking. "I wondered what the little bitch who bested us would look like. You are just a child. The rangers were quite quick to alert the others of the presence of a 'true god' in our midst. Once I heard of your presence, it was easy to follow the trail of magic you leave behind. When you defeated me the other night, I could have sworn I had a real adversary, but look at you."

Cain paused. I couldn't see his face but I could almost feel his eyes traveling over my body.

"You're a mess. You're dying right before my eyes." The man chuckled. The sound was dark and sinister. "But do not fret. I will save you, child. You may have taken my Guardians, but they were all but drained anyway. The power that is coursing through your veins will more than make up for their loss. In fact, I am sure with your power, Ekon and I will be able to open the gates sooner than expected."

Something moved in the darkness. I could feel the air move as whatever it was passed me and slammed into Nikolas, who was thrown backward. As I opened my mouth to scream, a thick gas suddenly clogged my throat and entered through my nostrils. I tried to cough, but my body refused to obey any command I gave it. As icy darkness coated my senses and forced me towards unconsciousness, I felt my power fade. My eyelids closed of their own accord, and I could hear the rest of the tunnel fall in on me.

*Rylan…*

***

I drifted in a strange haze as my body swayed. Odd… I shouldn't be moving. I should be crushed under tons of stone and debris. How wasn't I dead? Where was I? The feeling in my limbs slowly started to return. I hadn't even noticed that I had lost sensation in them. With the ability to feel my limbs came the pain of every ache in my body. I groaned.

A few minutes passed before I realized I was being carried. I opened my eyes, but when I did everything appeared blurry. I squeezed them shut as dizziness swamped me. I knew it wasn't Rylan who carried me. Was it Nikolas? I began to panic.

"Do not fret, child. We are almost to our destination." The mocking tone of my kidnapper sent chills down my spine.

Cain.

What was he about to do to me? What had he already done without me being aware of it? I tried to struggle in his arms, but I didn't have complete control over my body yet. I reached for my power, but the dizziness made it hard to concentrate.

*Rylan? Rylan, Cain has me,* the words felt slurred in my head, and I knew, somehow, that my message had not gone through. Was this Cain's doing?

A strong smell hit me. It was a mixture of puke, shit, and death. I tried to struggle again, wanting nothing to do with whatever had caused the smell to linger in the air. I opened my eyes, and this time I found my vision clearer. I looked up to see Cain's face staring directly ahead of us. I didn't think I had any expectations of what our foe would look like. But good looking wasn't it. He was a lean individual with a strong jawline, a thin long nose, and thick brows. He had high cheekbones, a very slight five o'clock shadow, and thin, pink lips.

"Where are we going?" I demanded.

I wanted my voice to sound strong. Unfortunately, it hardly came out as a whisper. He didn't answer me. To him, I probably wasn't worth his time. That was fine. If he wanted to pass me off as someone of no consequence, it would only benefit me. It would make it easier to thwart his plans if he didn't take me seriously. I was going to stop him. I just needed a little more time to collect myself.

Somehow, I needed to find the strength to struggle out of his arms, run away, and recover. It sounded easy enough. When I tried to struggle in Cain's arms again, I found moving my arms and legs was getting easier. Cain came to an abrupt stop. The scraping of metal captured my attention. I turned my head to see a werewolf standing before us. The creature was even more hideous up close. I expected it to snap or bite me, but instead, it held still while holding open a rusty cell door.

Cain stepped inside and unceremoniously dumped me on the stone floor. I hissed in pain as my head smacked against the hard floor. Cain stood over me, watching me with disdain. Oddly enough his gaze didn't scare me as much as Nikolas's had. Not that Cain's black eyes were not frightening. I could feel the evil in him as surely as I could feel my own unsteady heartbeat. He looked over his shoulder to the werewolf still standing at the cell door.

"Get the bindings, and find Ekon," he ordered.

The werewolf nodded before shuffling away. Cain turned his attention back to me. I struggled to sit up and felt a small victory when I made it. It was cold down here in what I assumed was a dungeon. It was poorly lit with torches burning along the wall, too far apart to see much of anything. Somewhere close I could hear a moan of distress and the scratch of chains against the ground. The sound was chilling.

*Rylan, where are you?* My voice sounded less slurred but full of fear.

I couldn't tell if this time I had managed to get a hold of him or not. I had a feeling I had been unsuccessful again. He always answered me if I called him.

"I sense how different you are," Cain said after a short silence. His tone was thoughtful. "You could almost be a god with that power running through your veins. But I have spoken to and been in the presence of true gods. Their very being causes one to quake with fear. Looking upon you, being in your presence… It only makes me laugh. But I am curious, so maybe you will fill me in with some details?"

Cain sighed and pressed his index finger against his lips as he thought over his questions. He pulled his hand away from his mouth and asked, "How did you find out what we were up to?"

I gave him a sweet smile, ignoring the pain in my jaw. "My mother had a vision that the world was going to end, so she sent me to stop it from happening."

"Did she now?" Cain mused as he stroked the stubble on his chin. "I suppose I can believe a simple witch was able to have such a profound vision of the world that she knew coming to an end. But I cannot believe she knew exactly where to look. How did you find us?"

"She had help from my father to figure it out," I baited the Guardian.

I knew my answer was vague enough to annoy him. Cain's eyes narrowed.

"Your father is where you must have gained such power since you do not smell like a witch," Cain said, more to himself than to me. "Your father, who is he?"

"He calls himself Zyroe. He figured out where you were going to try to open the gates. He and my mother created me to stop you," I told him matter-of-factly.

Instead of balking at the information as I had hoped, Cain chuckled.

"I am surprised to hear that Zyroe sired a child. He was a god that had very little interest in copulating with humans. I am sure he regrets the decision now. It seems you have failed at the only task ever required of you."

"I'm not dead yet," I stated, with a little too much confidence for someone unable to stand. "I can still stop you."

"You are not dead *yet*," Cain confirmed with a nod and a half-smile. His smile fell, though, as he stared into my face. "A daughter of a god… I wonder if your blood is as potent as your father's? It is rumored that the taste of a god's blood would give me great power."

I tried to keep my heart rate steady, which was easier than I thought given how slowly it was moving. Rylan had warned me never to let anyone else taste my blood. I wasn't about to cave and let someone try it now. I sighed and held up my wrist to him.

"Okay, give it a try," I offered with a shrug. Cain's eyes narrowed suspiciously. With a roll of my eyes, I pressed on, "Go ahead, give me a lick. The others said it was delicious. The best thing they have ever tried… Well, that was before two of the three just dropped dead suddenly. The other went bat-shit crazy. He gouged out his own eyes before the others could stop him."

I paused, then added in a whisper I hoped sounded fearful, "That was a little scary."

I was a terrible actress, but I sent up a prayer that Cain was believing it. Cain made a look of disgust and shook his head.

"The gods will grant me power of my own before long. I do not need to sample tainted goods," he told me. "In any case, you have failed at your job of stopping us. Even if you were at full strength, there would be no way the Guardians with you would trust you enough to lead them into battle. I know my brethren. They probably recoil from your very presence."

Cain squatted down to get eye level with me. His smile grew wider.

"Those poor fools. They simply do not understand. We were created to serve our gods. We were rightfully punished when we turned on them. It was Ekon's idea to set things straight, to make things right again with our masters. We will be servants to our great creators again, not babysitters to the creatures who should be worshipping our gods."

I blinked in confusion. Shaking my head, I asked, "I don't understand. Why would you want to be enslaved again? From what I've heard, it sounded awful."

"The *others* will be enslaved once more," Cain assured me with a malicious grin. "Serves them right for turning their backs on their masters. We will be rewarded. Not only will they be pleased that we were able to bring them back, but we will have an army of the undead waiting for them. The park rangers were quite useful when it came to bringing us sacrifices. You know, it took some tweaking, but we were able to alter the very makeup of dark magic. Can you believe that? We made it nearly impossible for anyone to sense it, and we could use it to control the minds of humans. Instead of compelling one human at a time, we could control the entire National Park Service here. We will show the gods how much we have evolved and what we have learned. They will be quite impressed at all we have accomplished for them."

"What guarantee is there that they will reward you? And with what? They're going to destroy the world. There won't be anything to give you."

"There is power, my dear child," a light, raspy voice answered from behind Cain. "They will reward us with our own power. People will worship *us*."

While I couldn't see the newcomer right away, hearing the voice scared the living shit out of me. A heavy sense of dread seemed to float into the cell with us, followed by a chill so cold I had to bite my bottom lip to stop from crying out in alarm. The hairs on my arm rose, and my hands trembled in fear. My power surged under my skin, lighting up my veins. Cain's eyes swept over my body, and a cruel smile twisted his features. He knew I was scared. He also knew I was too weak to do anything about it.

"It will be what some call the day of Judgement," the raspy voice continued.

I looked past Cain to see a man standing just outside the cell door. He was cloaked in a thick material that seemed to naturally billow around his form. The air went from offensive to downright dangerous. As if the very air around him was toxic. A heavy sense of foreboding warned me that this was the man I needed to concern myself with, not Cain. Cain rose from his squat and turned to look at the man behind him.

"The gods will cleanse the earth of those who will not accept them," the man said quietly. "Those left will love their gods and their worship will bring the gods back to full strength. When they see all that we have done, the gods will thank us with our own followers, our own slaves, our own land. No longer will we have to mingle with those unworthy. I have been planning this since the gods were banished. I have wanted this for so long…

stealing the magic from others has been a slow process. It was not until this modern day science came along that things really began to pick up pace. All of my hard work, all of this planning, everything is coming to fruition, and it is marvelous. I welcome the fiery wrath that will befall this world."

"Ekon, meet our little friend. She will be the last little bit of power we need to open the gates," Cain greeted the man pleasantly as if they were merely neighbors and not two people looking to bring upon the end of the world.

"So much power from someone so young... How glorious. She will help tip the scales in our favor," Ekon sounded beyond pleased.

I pulled my knees up to my chest and found the movement was no longer sluggish or difficult. Even though there was still pain, either from Nikolas or my fall into the tunnel, I knew I could get to my feet if I had to. Whatever Cain had done to me was wearing off. The moment I had an opening, I was going to fight my way out of here.

"We must be quick. She's dying on us," Cain said with a sigh. "Perhaps we will patch her up while the wolves get the machine ready."

"Make it happen. Have the others destroyed, we no longer need them now that we have her," Ekon agreed. He paused for a moment before he continued, "With her here, it will be only a few days before the gods arrive."

"We were already ahead of schedule by two weeks," Cain mused. The smile on his face was sickening. "I'll get the wolves to grab medical supplies while they put a capsule into the van. It would be ideal to have her at the base camp," Cain said, more to himself than to Ekon. He looked at me and grinned. "Maybe you will catch a glimpse of Elliot's Peak before you die. It's a lovely mountain range. A perfectly remote area with a weak clinch in the gates. The gods will be able to come through unnoticed with ease. By the time they let loose their wrath, it will be too late for anyone to stop them."

"I'll stop your plans," I told them both. "I'm not going to make any of this easy for you."

My power was there and ready for me to use. I was beyond tired, my body ached, and it was a long shot, but if I could just have a few more minutes to recover, I could get to my feet and fight these two men. I wasn't sure I would win but I'd be damned if I just rolled over.

Both men chuckled, but it was Cain who responded, "Oh, but child, you already have. You walked right into our lair and handed yourself right over to us." He paused while he ran his fingers through his hair. "And everyone who has entered here made that same statement. So far, none of them have succeeded. Even without being spell-drugged, you can hardly stand on your two feet. Now you're about as harmless as a maggot."

Movement behind Ekon drew my attention. The werewolf had returned. He handed something to Ekon, who chuckled and handed it off to Cain.

"I have things to do back at the base camp. I will see you there," Ekon said. He studied me. "Make sure we hook her up quickly. She does not look too well."

With that, he turned and walked away.

Shit, I was losing my opportunity to take him down. I tried not to panic. Did I have it in me to jump up and fight right now? My limbs were heavy but mobile. My power was still there, waiting to be used. I wasn't completely drained yet.

Cain toyed with the object Ekon had passed to him. Up close I could see it was a thick metal shackle. Cain reached down for something by his feet, and that was when I noticed the chains. They were short and attached to a welded metal hook in the wall. Realizing he was about to chain me up, I attempted to get to my feet. I had hardly gotten to my knees when Cain grabbed my wrist and dragged me closer to him. He lifted the metal shackle that the werewolf had brought.

"Do you know what spellbinding is?" he asked.

All the blood drained from my face as horror choked me. I looked at the metal shackle then back to Cain's face. Oh god no. Not that long ago, I had spellbound myself to keep my power from hurting others. Back then I had trapped my power behind a neatly built wall in my head where I managed to keep it at bay. If I accidentally let my power slip past that mental wall, I received a painful shock to my system.

Back then my power had been trapped in my mind. But now my power ran freely through my body. There was no trapping or hiding it any longer. If he put that shackle on my neck, who knew what would happen? I highly doubted it would be a simple shock to my system this time. Cain must have read the horror in my face because he laughed.

"Ah, so you *do* know. Good, no need to explain then."

Cain grabbed me before I could move and slammed the shackle shut around my neck. The cold metal pressed against my skin was enough to make my skin crawl. Then, I felt the effect of the binding, and the cold no longer mattered.

A fiery pain unlike anything that I had ever experienced caused my body to convulse involuntarily. I had been thrown into an inferno with a noose around my neck. I could feel the spell trying to bind the power within me. I could almost feel invisible red-hot cords wrapping around my limbs and sinking into my skin to hold my power at bay. But I was too powerful. My power was just as fiery as the burn that was causing my flesh and soul to sizzle. It surged hard against the spell, and the world turned white.

The ground beneath me buckled and shook hard. The ceiling began to crumble as my power fought back against the spell. I screamed as I felt the binding spell fighting back against my body's attempt to break its hold on me. My body shifted into survival mode. Somehow, I found myself on my feet. The world came back into focus with a new violet hue to it.

Cain's eyes were wide with awe and horror as he backed away from me. The burning in my veins increased as rage and anguish mixed with the binding spell. Without conscious thought, I raised my hands up and my power exploded around us. The spell placed on the shackle around my neck disintegrated, and the entire dungeon began to shake violently as energy spilled out from my body.

I felt detached from my body. It was on autopilot. Violet flames shot from my fingertips and swirled around me as my power continued to fill the space. The flames licked the walls, which were beginning to bow. The fire swirled around me in a thunderous protective dome. The iron bars of my cell began to melt. Cain attempted to grab me. His snarl was lost under the roar of my power. With a flick of my wrist, my power hit him and threw him out into the hallway. He was on his feet in an instant. His wings ripped his shirt to pieces as they grew from his back. He lunged at me again. This time I sent flames charging towards him.

His scream was lost in the roar of fire now destroying the entire dungeon. Walls, steel bars, and pieces of the ceiling were beginning to get sucked into the growing fiery vortex swirling around me. The violet haze grew heavier upon my consciousness. I knew what was about to happen. I would get lost in the power while it destroyed everything. It was my body's defense mechanism. I almost let it happen. The pressure growing in my body was threatening to rip me to pieces. If I allowed myself to be consumed by my power, my consciousness would slip away, and I wouldn't feel any of this pain.

But if I allowed myself to slip away I would lose all control. I would be just a vessel of the power my father had housed on Earth. I didn't want that. I wanted to be me: Mae. So, instead of losing myself to the fire, I took a deep breath and clung on to control. I tapped into the chaos I was creating around me and increased it. The world around me crumbled. The horror in Cain's blazing red eyes as my power blasted outwards was satisfying.

As the world crumbled around me, the debris got caught in the swirling fiery mass of power. Underneath me, the ground beneath my feet fell away. Instead of falling with it, I found myself hovering over the spot where I had been standing. I curled my open hands into fists as I tried to hold onto my control. As I fought to bring my fingers to my palms, I began to lift upwards, taking sections of the dungeon with me. As I ascended, I destroyed everything in my wake. My vortex of destruction took the brunt of the force as I smashed through the different levels of Cain and Ekon's lair.

Something temporarily blinded me. It was then that I realized it was the blaze of the sun stealing my sight. I blinked rapidly until I could see again then looked down as I continued to rise into the sky. Through the chaos that whirled around me, I could see the massive hole in the ground that I had created in my escape.

Movement caught my attention. A short distance away, I saw that Cain had risen with me. His wings were flapping hard to keep him from being sucked into the destructive bubble that surrounded me. But he was staying close, watching me with the hunger of a man starved for power. The sickening desire that pooled in his eyes sent fear snaking down my spine.

*Rylan*, I called out hoping this time he could hear me.

*I hear and I see you. I'm coming*, Rylan promised.

I didn't dare pull my eyes off Cain. Whatever he was planning was making him bold. He inched his way closer to me and my maelstrom of destruction.

I realized then how hard my body was shaking. My vision was starting to blur, and my breathing was labored. Oh shit, he was waiting for me to lose strength. His plan was so simple and so achievable I wanted to cry. I could feel my body weakening.

As my power began to wane, debris began to fall from the vortex I had created.

Unsure how far away Rylan was, I knew I couldn't count on him getting here in time. And I could not let myself get recaptured. I had to do something… I closed my eyes and drew in a deep breath to steady my nerves. I pulled my power inwards. As I did, the flames swirling around me went out and debris began to fall. I pulled all my energy inwards until the world went silent.

When the last stone fell to the ground below me, I knew Cain was coming for me. I didn't panic. I didn't even bother to open my eyes as I focused. I knew I had collected enough energy when I began to tumble from the sky. Without another moment's hesitation, I released everything that I had.

# Chapter Twenty-Six

*Rylan*

Knowing our enemy had my mate was enough to make my blood run cold. Insanity threatened to override common sense as panic suffocated me. My soul screamed for her. It had been over an hour since I heard Mae's voice calling my name. The knowledge that I could still sense her soul was what kept me from falling to pieces. Occasionally I could feel her fear and confusion flickering in and out. Another sign she was alive.

When Nikolas had emerged without Mae, it took Diane, Gabriel, and Jasmine to keep me from killing the warrior. When the others were able to subdue me, Nikolas admitted to everyone that he had tried to kill Mae while they had been distracted. Shock shook each of the warriors in the group.

"I was wrong," Nikolas told me when the others had pinned me to the ground once more. "And I deserve the ultimate punishment. I went after your mate, who is innocent of any crimes, knowing what it would do to you should she perish. I thought it was the best option for the world. But she is not the enemy here. While I tried to kill her, she simply tried to defend herself. She never had any intention of trying to kill me in return. When I found her in the laboratory, she was trying to save our people despite her grave injuries. And when the roof collapsed and she faced our enemy, she demanded that I help the others, not her. Mae is selfless and kind, unlike the demi-gods past."

When I pressed him about Mae's injuries, Nikolas explained the beating he had given her in his attempt to kill her. My rage helped me to break free of the other's hold on me. I attacked Nikolas. My sword almost pierced his heart this time. The fury that consumed me was uncontrollable. While the others managed to get me off of Nikolas, I could not be contained. I fought everyone as I tried to reach the Guardian who had gone after Mae.

Finally, Diane stood in front of me, grabbed my face in her hand, and reminded me that Mae still needed me. That's when I finally stopped trying to kill Nikolas. Yes, Mae needed me… I had to keep a level head for her. I would kill Nikolas later when she was safely in my arms.

Somehow, we had to figure out where Cain had taken Mae. Unfortunately, when Jasmine was finally able to pull up archived plans of the mining tunnels on her phone we found the labyrinth would be too tedious to tackle without knowing exactly where Cain was. That, along with the uncertainty whether the rest of the tunnels would be clear stopped us from plowing straight into the ground to create a new entrance into the mines.

"We must be relatively close to Ekon's and Cain's lair," Diane assumed. "Or he would not have appeared so suddenly after the collapse of the tunnel. He was probably checking on what the commotion was while his *petra thērion* were taking care of the intruders above ground. That means there must be an entrance nearby that is used exclusively for his and Ekon's use. I think we need to spread out and look for a well-trodden area. That is where the entrance will be."

"There are not enough of us to split up to find an entrance that would be well hidden in this rocky terrain," I said, dismissing her plan. "And someone needs to stay with the Guardians Mae rescued to make sure they are safe. I do not trust him—" I nudged my head towards Nikolas. "—to be of any help. That would leave too few of us to comb over miles of a landscape that can easily hide an entryway."

"It has to be close," Gabriel argued. "How else did he get here so quickly when the trouble started?"

"He could have already been in the vicinity," I exclaimed with frustration. "If I could just get through to Mae—,"

Without warning, a fiery pain rippled through me with an intensity that could rival a dragon's fire. An invisible force latched itself to my neck, choking me with its grip and taking me to my knees as the pain intensified. I roared as an unknown pressure fought back against the attack. It felt like two suns had collided with one another and were battling for the chance to remain in existence within my very essence.

*Rylan, what is going on?* Diane's worried tone yanked me from the clutches of the attack.

Quickly, the pain vanished as if it had never been. The moment the connection was lost I realized *I* had not been attacked. The way the pain had come and gone meant only one thing.

"Mae's in trouble," I snarled and leapt to my feet.

Just as I pulled my weapon from the mark on my torso the ground began to shake.

"Watch out!" Gabriel warned as the ground beneath us started to crack open. The five of us stumbled back as whatever was left of the tunnel Mae and Nikolas had fallen into began to cave in.

"We have to move the others further back to safety," Diane warned as the ground continued to shake.

"I have to get to Mae!" I roared, desperate to aid her.

I could not remember a time when I had experienced pain so great that I had fallen to my knees. If I could be rendered helpless through our connection, Mae's pain must have been extraordinary.

"There, look!" Jasmine exclaimed.

She pointed west, and we all turned to see a fiery purple mass lifting out of the ground several miles away. I did not hesitate. I took to the sky immediately and headed towards Mae. Even if her signature color had not indicated it was her, my soul reached out in that direction knowing its other half was trapped inside.

*Rylan*, Mae's voice rang with exhaustion and pain.

*I hear and see you. I am coming*, I assured her as I drew closer.

I flew faster than I'd ever thought possible as I closed the distance between myself and Mae. I could see her through the mass of debris that had collected within her fiery sphere. Her arms were outstretched in front of her while her entire body glowed with the intensity of a shooting star. Her hair whipped around her while her torn and bloodied clothes clung to her petite frame.

She was utterly magnificent.

Mae's attention was drawn to something off to my right. I followed her gaze and found Cain watching my mate. His glee was so profound it scared me. He was waiting for an opening, but for what? To kill her? To steal her away again? Whatever Cain planned to do, he would not get the chance. That bastard was going to die.

As I drew nearer, I could feel the heat of Mae's fiery hell at the same time my body began to consume it. My body ate up her power as if it were starved for it. It broke down the chaos easily and reinvigorated it. I held it to me, knowing I would need it once I got to her. Unfortunately, I didn't get a chance to collect much when suddenly the chaos that whirled around her came to a complete halt.

Debris crashed down around her while the fire flickered out. Mae's head bowed while she held her shaking fists out in front of her. Her shoulders sagged, and I saw her take in a shaky breath.

"Mae!" I roared a warning, hoping she would hear me.

I was so close… Cain came tearing through the sky, arms outstretched before him. A wicked grin split his face in two as his arms stretched out in front of him to grab my mate.

Suddenly, Mae's head snapped up, and she stared at Cain coming towards her. She threw her hands down by her waist, unclenched her fists, and beneath us the ground erupted, decimating whatever structure was underground. Explosions rocked just underneath the surface, spewing flames and smoke that I had to weave and dodge despite my significant distance from the ground.

While the ground either collapsed or flew upwards, Mae began to fall from the sky. Cain's progress to her had slowed as he was forced to twist and turn from the chaos. My heart raced as Mae's body disappeared into billowing black smoke.

*I got Mae. You take care of Cain*, Jasmine said.

I could feel her presence close behind me as I flew through the sky. Despite my anger towards the Guardian for most of this trip, I was relieved that I could trust her in this moment. My fury drove me to fly faster. I pulled the sword from my tattoo, and I was on Cain before he realized I was there. My sword cut through his side and blood rained down to the ground below. Cain's roar of rage and agony was drowned out by the ringing in my ears as red filled my vision. He twisted out of reach and pulled his falchion sword from the tattoo on his chest.

"She's mine," he roared. "Her power belongs to us. You have failed, warrior! The end is near, and you cannot do anything to stop us."

*I have Mae*, Jasmine assured me.

Cain raised his weapon and blocked my next attack. The clash of metal sent sparks flying. Cain blocked two of my next blows, but I caught him under the arm with the third. He used his wings to try to block me, but I twisted and dropped underneath him. My sword came up and met his falchion again, but this time I did not break away. While our blades vied for the upper hand, I brought my wings together in front of me. My feathers slid down his arms, cutting his flesh and severing tendons and muscle.

Cain roared and flung himself backwards out of reach, but I was on top of him before he could figure out his next move. My sword cut through the air. It was so sharp that its progress did not slow down even as it sliced through Cain's neck. The other Guardian's eyes widened in surprise and alarm. Then, slowly, his severed head toppled from his shoulder and fell from the skies. Cain's body hung suspended a moment longer before gravity pulled it downwards.

Without waiting to see the carcass hit the ground, I turned and flew back towards the others where I knew Jasmine had taken Mae. I dropped from the sky when I approached. My feet had hardly touched the grass before I was running towards Mae, who Jasmine had placed on the ground. Jasmine and Diane were knelt around her, both talking softly to my mate.

"Move," I said as I came to Mae's aid.

Jasmine shifted to get out of my way while Diane remained by Mae's side. I fell to my knees as a strangled sound escaped me.

Up close, I could see the horror of what Mae had endured over the past few hours. A cry I did not bother trying to hide slipped past my lips as I studied her face. She was hardly recognizable. Her right cheek was so swollen I was sure half the bones in her face were broken. The crimson trails down both of her cheeks were evidence of the bloody tears she had cried. Blood still dripped from her ears. Just under her jaw were deep scratch marks that indicated she had tried to claw off the metal shackle that was wrapped around her neck. Blood caked her clothes. Bruises marred most of her skin, and her hair was matted with dirt and grime.

A knot formed in my throat. I could not breathe. My mate… I could sense her life flickering like a flame in the wind. Gingerly, I lifted her limp body and nestled her into the crook of my arm. I reached up and tried to remove the shackle around her neck. As I unlatched it and tried to open the shackle, I found that it had melted into the flesh around her neck. The thing was welded to my mate. If I attempted to pull it off, I would kill her. Nausea swamped me. I had never once thrown up, but at that moment I felt the need to.

I forced my body to heel. This was not about me. It was about Mae. She was suffering, and she needed me. With a deep breath, I forced the power that I'd collected back into her body. Her entire body, though still unconscious, seemed to relax. Mae's breathing became less shallow and some color rose in her cheeks. It was not much, but at least she would be a tad more comfortable.

"I have contacted both groups and have told them of our findings. Zara and Samson are on their way to help us transport our new guests while the second group is on their way back to the house," Diane said softly. "Take her home and get her help, Rylan."

A knot formed in my throat making me incapable of speech. Was there any helping her now?

"Get back or lose your head, Nikolas," Gabriel warned behind me.

An involuntary hiss slipped past my lips as I turned my head slightly to look over my shoulder.

"You *dare* to come near my mate after what you have done?" A red haze clouded my vision. "You have broken one of our most sacred laws, Nikolas. If you do not listen to Gabriel, I will dispense justice right now."

Nikolas did not look away from me as he moved around Gabriel and came to stand in front of me. His expression was void of emotion, which was not unusual. What was strange was the blazing intensity in his eyes. He raised his right hand and placed it over his heart.

"Rylan, you know what I have done, and I will not ask for mercy as you deal out your punishment. Words will not carry the weight of my regret for what I have done. I misjudged your young mate. I expected treachery and lies from her. The gods I have known never knew any other way of being. When I realized what

Mae was, I assumed she was the same and that she had somehow blinded you all to her true nature. But I was wrong. I was the one blinded. There is nothing but true goodness in her heart. I am truly sorry."

"I do not need nor want your apology!" I roared.

In my arms, Mae flinched and let out an agonized groan. Immediately, I relaxed my hold on her and brought her closer to my chest.

"I understand. I would accept no apologies, either, in your position," Nikolas acknowledged. "But I want to offer something else that will be more beneficial to Mae's well-being… I can heal her."

There were three gasps of shock behind me. Diane snarled and shook her head. "What are you talking about? That's impossible," she demanded. "None of us have such abilities."

Nikolas glanced at her before turning his attention back to me. A shadow of pain and disgust rippled across his face.

"My god was Wyvonine, a god who took pleasure from those that suffered. When he created me, he gifted me with the ability to heal others, just so he could continue their suffering," Nikolas explained without any inflection. "Please, allow me to do this one thing. Allow me to save her, Rylan."

Foolishly, my heart fluttered at the hope he had ignited. He could be lying. He was half the reason that Mae was dying. His sudden change of heart was suspicious, but… Did I have a choice?

"If you can save her, do so. If this is some sort of trick, I will pull your still-beating heart from your chest before you can inflict further damage," I vowed through gritted teeth.

"I will save her," Nikolas promised quietly. The hard lines in his face softened ever so slightly. "I committed an act so foul the half of my soul I carry has been stained beyond repair, but it is worth it to try… And while my time on this earth may be over soon, it does not have to be so for Mae or you."

I nodded my head to indicate he could approach my mate. I forced myself to place Mae's body on the ground, but I kept one of her hands in mine. Diane moved so Nikolas could take her place. He sunk to his knees slowly on the other side of Mae and gazed upon my mate's face with sorrow. As he reached out to touch her with both hands, an involuntary snarl bubbled up in my chest. Nikolas paused to gauge my reaction. With a deep breath, I collected myself. I nodded when I was under control of my murderous instincts. He reached out with both hands and placed them upon her chest. He bowed his head and closed his eyes. When he looked up at me, his irises had changed to black.

"This will hurt her, but it will fix her," he told me softly.

Without waiting for me to acknowledge his words, Nikolas began the healing process. Blue light emanated from his palms. The light soaked through the bloodied and torn shirt into Mae's body. Mae twitched. The movement was so slight that I almost thought I had made it up. I heard a muffled snap, and Mae's leg twitched hard. Her lips parted just enough to groan in distress. Another snap, followed by a hard jerk of her jaw caused another, louder, moan. She cried out as a blue light began to glow just beneath the entirety of her skin. Her arms weakly began to flail. I grabbed both of her hands and held them to my chest

*It will be alright, I promise,* I whispered into her mind, praying that it was true.

*Everything hurts.* Her voice was so small and far away it scared me.

But she was talking. She was back with me. My heart somersaulted.

*I know, my Mae Flower. Bear with me just a little bit longer,* I assured her.

Mae's hands began to warm in mine. Sweat beaded her brow. To my surprise, the swelling and discoloration in her face began to decrease. The dark bruises that marred the skin began to fade before our eyes.

*So hot,* she whimpered.

*It is almost done,* I promised and kissed her knuckles.

Sweat dripped down her face, and tears slipped past her closed eyelids. It was a small relief to see that these tears were crystal clear and not blood red. Another cry, strangled and pained, echoed around us. Her body gave a dramatic jerk before going still. Nikolas removed his hands from her chest. Mae's chest rose slowly, and then she gave a long, grateful sigh. Her eyelids fluttered open, and although her gaze was unfocused, my heart cried tears of joy. Behind me, I could hear noises of surprise and gratitude. Mae's brows came together, and her free hand fluttered towards the shackle around her neck.

Without hesitation, I reached forward and unclasped the cursed metal. As I threw the shackle to the ground, a sigh escaped Mae's lips. Where the shackle had once been welded to her skin, there was now thick and angry scarring wrapped around her neck. It would be a gruesome reminder of the suffering she had endured. Of my failure to protect her...

*Mae,* I called to her as I scooped her up and pulled her into my chest.

What was she thinking? How did she feel? What could I do for her? Mae turned her head, slowly, as if testing to make sure it would not hurt, and our eyes locked. Her brown eyes were slightly glazed over, and her eyelids half drooped.

*Rylan,* the relief in her voice was profound.

More tears rolled down her cheek, and I reached up to wipe them away.

*Do not cry,* I scolded her gently.

My heart was dancing in my chest. The knot in my throat was working its way loose and the tension in my body began to recede.

*Cain tried to spellbind me,* she told me as she touched the scarring around her neck.

My whole body recoiled. *That* was what had caused her so much pain. The sick feeling returned as I realized how dangerous binding her power could have been. She could have died.

*I thought I lost you,* I whispered in her mind.

The angst I had been feeling crumbled into pure unadulterated relief now that she was safe in my arms. It did not matter that our lives were tied together. Even if they were not, the thought of living in the world without Mae was unfathomable.

"She will be tired and sore for the next few days, but you can take her back to the house without an issue," Nikolas assured me.

Mae flinched at his voice. She turned her head to look at him, and I watched the distrust coat her expression.

"Do not fret," I assured her. "You will never see him again after today. He may have saved your life, but that does not release him from his sins."

Mae's eyes turned violet as she assessed the Guardian who had tried to kill her. Nikolas sighed so deeply one would have thought he carried the weight of the world on his shoulders. He pinned her with a solemn look and opened his mouth to speak.

"Dear Mae, I was wrong about you. I have seen the purity in your soul and heart. I know what I have done is unforgivable, but I hope you will understand, at the very least, that my intentions were not malicious. In an attempt to make things right I pledge my life to you. Wherever you lead, I will follow. Forever."

"That is a very moot vow," Diane snapped from behind me. "Since your life will end the moment she gets in the car."

Mae shook her head slowly. She closed her eyes, and her body went utterly still. For a moment, I thought she had fainted. When I gripped her more tightly, her eyes fluttered back open. She looked up at me with a mixture of determination and exhaustion.

"No one is going to kill Nikolas," she declared with a raspy but determined voice. "We're going to need everyone if we're going to stop Ekon and Cain. I know exactly where their main hideout is, and I know they are two weeks ahead of schedule, giving us only two weeks before the end of the world is here."

My grip tightened on Mae again. This was it. This was why we had come here, to stop the gates from opening. The threat was real.

"Cain has been taken care of," I assured her.

"Good," she said as her eyes closed again. "One less asshole we have to deal with."

## Chapter Twenty-Seven



To say the next few days were strange would be an understatement. First, there was the fact that we now had an additional forty-two Guardians living in the house. I found myself being barraged with gratitude and constantly being touched. The contact ranged from clasping my shoulder in camaraderie to a caress on the cheek. It was uncomfortable to find myself surrounded by people who thought I was some type of savior. To go from being reviled to respected by most of the warriors in the house gave me whiplash.

When I complained to Rylan about it behind closed doors, he said, "Imagine being rescued after years of imprisonment and being able to truly appreciate it. You not only saved them from a terrible end, but your presence allows them to enjoy the fresh air, their renewed strength, and the ability to connect with people they have not seen in who knows how long. To them, and me, you are a blessing."

After that, I never complained again.

If they weren't touching me, they were stroking the purple quartz necklaces that they proudly displayed around their necks. Calling Katie had been one of the first things Arthur had done to ensure everyone's safety.

With so many Guardians in the house and the majority of them malnourished, drastic measures had to be taken to feed everyone. Every morning Zara would appear in the driveway with a tour bus full of unsuspecting, compelled humans who served as breakfast for everyone. The tourists would file out of the bus and stand there, unmoving, while Guardians came out to feed on them. When the Guardians had their fill, the tourists would climb back on the bus, and Zara would take them back to where she found them. By the fourth day of this, I made sure to avoid looking out the window. It was an eerie sight watching people stare blankly at the house while they were being fed on.

When the new Guardians had recovered enough to join the rest of us, they bombarded us with questions about what they had missed out on in the world while they had been imprisoned. In return, the newcomers informed us of what they knew of Cain and Ekon's plan. The magic Nikolas and I had found swirling around in the glass case in the laboratory was nothing compared to what was being stored at Elliot's Peak. After hundreds of years of drawing powers from Fae, Guardians, witches, and wizards, Ekon certainly had enough to open a door into any realm he wanted.

They confirmed my story that Ekon and Cain had used the park rangers to kill visitors of the park so they could be used in an undead army for the gods upon their arrival. But the army wasn't only filled with the undead. Ekon had many creatures at his disposal. Most were there willingly. Ekon even had a hand in the genetic mutation of the werewolves. He'd used humans who had volunteered to permanently become monsters. He then experimented on them until they were cunning beasts rather than the mindless killing machines a typical werewolf would have been.

While learning Ekon's plan was terrifying, it was also exciting. Ekon no longer had the element of surprise on his side. He knew we would know where to look for him now, and that we would learn about everything that he had been up to. We could prepare appropriately for whatever he threw our way.

The house was filled to the brim with Guardians. With the ability to feel emotions, the house was loud with laughter, playful debates, and passionate speeches. Then, there were the orgies. If there weren't two orgies happening somewhere in the house at any given time, it was a slow day. One night, I had slipped from my bed and had gone downstairs to get a drink of water only to find a handful of Guardians all tangled up in each other right there on the kitchen floor.

Embarrassed, I had tried to slip away unnoticed only to find Rylan had followed me down to the kitchen. I wasn't surprised. Rylan had not left my side since our return to the house after Nikolas's attack and my escape from Cain. What did surprise me was when he pressed my back up against the wall, just out of sight of the Guardians, to kiss and caress me passionately until I was delirious with lust. When I was sure he would throw me over his shoulder and carry me upstairs to ravish me, he surprised me further by pulling his erection free, slipping my panties to the side, and thrusting up into me right there with an orgy happening only a few feet away. The kinkiness of the act sent me spiraling to a whole new level of arousal, and when I came, I had to bite into Rylan's shoulder to keep from giving away our hiding spot.

But the strangest thing of all was how easy it was to control my power. It came to me with such ease, it was almost a joke to continue to practice with Rylan, which I did every morning. I could focus my power to blast a single target. I could catch whatever I wanted on fire and even put it out on my own. Even the lightning would bend, arch, and twist in whatever direction I wanted it to go in.

Even though I did not need Rylan to run interference when it came to the destruction, I did need him to help me maintain a healthy level of power within my body. Whatever power I threw out, Rylan pulled it back and recycled it back to me. While I might feel physically spent after practicing, I never felt drained as I had in the past. It was a heady feeling knowing that with Rylan's assistance, I could take on the evilest person in the world.

Which was exactly the type of confidence I needed. It was precisely what we planned to do in just two days.

The planning had started the morning after our return. The second group that had gone off the day before had spread out, veering unknowingly towards Elliot's Peak as they searched for signs of our enemies. The group stumbled across the sights of the ritual sacrifices. Luckily, even without the new Guardians' warning of a zombie army, the group had burned the piles of bodies that had been poorly covered up with dirt. They found symbols burned into the ground and mutilated wildlife that was strung up high in the treetops.

They also figured out how the werewolves were able to vanish without a trace. There were trees within the forest that, if approached by a creature cursed with dark magic, would become doors that led down into the mining tunnels. They had managed to capture several werewolves and used them to access the tunnels. While they had not caused miles of the tunnels that ran under the park to dramatically collapse, as I had, the group did manage to cause a few cave-ins to prevent the enemy from having so many access points to emerge from.

With this information, the Guardians had enough to strategize an attack. It was agreed that offense would be the best tactic. We would approach Elliot's Peak at midnight, the darkest hour. A group of Guardians would have already planted bombs earlier in the tunnels, which would detonate on the west side of Elliot's Peak. It wouldn't cause a ton of damage but enough to draw attention to the area and away from the rest of us who would be lying in wait on the east side of the mountain range.

Once enough commotion was raised, it would be my turn. Ekon's power supply was somewhere in the center of Elliot's Peak. A few Guardians suggested sneaking me into Ekon's lair to destroy everything that way. The idea was shot down by the majority, who agreed there were too many unknown factors to be a plausible plan. Rylan came up with the idea that satisfied everyone. He simplified my role to one simple task: bring down the entire mountain. Everyone else would do their part to keep Ekon's minions away from me.

I did not doubt that I could do it. With how strong I was and how destructive I could be, taking down a mountain almost seemed like a fun challenge.

While we were as ready as we ever would be the night before our attack, I felt uneasy. I walked out onto the deck, which still had holes from the gargoyle attack, and leaned against the railing trying to set aside my discomfort for a while. The trees around us were beginning to change color. There were hints of purples, yellows, and oranges beginning to flare up in the thick green foliage. The cold breeze that drifted through the night caused bumps to rise on my arms. Fall had officially arrived, and nature was preparing to give us a beautiful display of change.

"It is a beautiful night, is it not?" a soft voice said behind me.

I turned around to find Diane stepping out onto the deck with me. She moved gracefully around the large holes in the deck to come to stand beside me. She looked out at the forest around us and a smile tugged the sides of her lips. I turned to look back out at the park.

"It is," I agreed. "I hope we will get to enjoy it without this black cloud hanging over our heads soon."

"I have seen many seasons come and go. This one will be like all the other autumns that have come before it. Do you know what I hope, Mae?" she asked, turning her head to look at me. I looked at her with a frown. "It is my hope that I get the opportunity to know you better."

I smiled, "I'd like to get to know you too."

"It is hard being a mother, Mae," she said slowly. "You only want the best for your children. Rylan is my only child. I was unable to conceive again once I gave birth to him. I suppose I spoiled him a little while he was a young boy. I did whatever I could to make him smile."

I tried to picture Rylan as a young boy. Did he have long blond hair or did Diane keep it cut short? Was his laughter as infectious as it was now? Had he been a stubborn child or easy-going? I tried to imagine it but I struggled to see past the handsome man he was now.

"When he reached maturity, I watched the life drain from my son's eyes as his emotions faded. His eyes stopped twinkling with mirth and his mouth never turned upwards again." Diane said after a pause. "I lived in a constant state of fear for the last one thousand, eight hundred and forty-two years that Rylan would cave to the darkness and take himself out of my world. That fear kept me up at night. I reached out to him constantly to check in on him. When he called me a few weeks ago to tell me about you, the moment I heard his voice I already knew that fate had blessed my son."

Diane turned her body to face me and I mimicked the movement. She took my hands in hers and said, "When he spoke your name I heard the reverence behind it. He laughed with merriment. Mae… Do you know what that did for me? To hear his delight? I wept happy tears long after we had hung up. You gave me back a piece of my heart I did not realize was missing. My son walked this earth with me and yet… he had been lost to me as well. He is back and that is because of you. Thank you, Mae. I hope once all this is over we can become good friends."

My heart swelled at her words. I gave her a weak smile and said,

"You don't care that I'm not right for him? My father is a—"

"Nonsense," she said, cutting me off sharply. "You are absolutely right for my son. I do not think I have met a woman with a heart as pure as yours and a soul to match it. You will find that fate does not make mistakes when it comes to pairing mates."

My smile grew stronger at her confidence.

"Thank you. I have had my doubts," I admitted. Diane's kind smile reminded me of my own mother's. Sadness tugged at my heart as I thought of my mom.

"Of course, that is only natural. Especially in the beginning. I am sure having the others believe you a creature of evil does not help boost your confidence," Diane said with a roll of her eyes. "But trust fate and Rylan. In time you will see how perfect you two are for each other."

The sliding glass door opened behind us and we both turned at the noise. Jasmine stepped out to join us. At the same time I felt a soft buzzing in my head.

"Diane, Mae," Jasmine greeted as she came over to speak with us.

"Jasmine," Diane said, bowing her head. "If you would both excuse me, Samson is calling for me."

Jasmine bowed her head in return. Diane gave my hands a quick squeeze before letting go and heading back inside. As Rylan's mother walked into the house, Arthur stepped out and shut the door behind her. He walked over to Jasmine and I and came to stand on the other side of me.

"What are you guys up to?" I asked curiously.

"We wanted to come check on you," Jasmine said with a smile.

"Afraid my mother-in-law was scaring me away?" I joked. Both Guardians chuckled.

"No, we are not here because of her," Jasmine assured me.

"We could tell something was bothering you when you stepped out," Arthur explained. "I think we all keep forgetting this is the first battle you are about to experience. Are you nervous?"

I hesitated. How could I admit to them my deepest fear? Would I come off as a coward? I bit my bottom lip and turned to look out at the forest again. Unease twisted in my gut, back with a renewed vengeance now that I had turned my attention back to it. With a sigh I spoke without looking at either of them. "What if tomorrow… What if I end up killing Ekon?" My voice was barely a whisper.

Murder. Could I do it? Could I really watch the life drain out of someone's eyes and be ok with it? Yes he was a terrible person but could I be the one who did the dirty work? My skin crawled at the thought of looking at someone, anyone, in the eyes and deciding that their life was over.

"Then, you kill him," Jasmine said with a shrug. "You will be doing the world a favor. Though I doubt that you will get the honor. There will be many Guardians with you who would love to be the one that takes him down."

I already knew the possibility was slim that he would be able to reach me. The plan was for most of the Guardians to surround me so that nothing could prevent me from tearing the mountain down. While keeping me safe would be their major goal, I was sure if Ekon was spotted, someone would break rank to kill him. But still, my gut twisted painfully.

"It is not Ekon that she is worried about," Arthur declared softly. Out of the corner of my eye I could see him watching my face. "You do not want to kill *anyone*."

There it was, out in the open. Now that my fear had been spoken out loud, shame overshadowed everything else. We were going to war with the enemy. A situation could easily occur where I might have to kill someone to save a life. If not Ekon, then maybe one of his soldiers. The Guardians inside had talked about how much blood they wanted to shed and lives they wanted to snuff out. But that wasn't me.

I used to find trouble in the streets of Baltimore with my friends and break it up. I did things that were not necessarily legal in order to help others. But this was completely different. This was an actual *battle,* not a small brawl on the streets. I wanted nothing to do with killing people. It was an unspoken rule amongst my friends that we never crossed that line. There would be no coming back from something like that. I wasn't a religious person, but something about taking another's life felt so morally wrong that it was making me ill.

"Rylan mentioned that when a mated pair dies, they end up passing through these Golden Gates together. But what if me killing someone makes it so we *can't* go through the gates together? You guys are the world's judge, jury, and executioner. That is the role you all pledged to take when you gained your freedom from the gods. It's alright when you do it. But I never signed up for that.

"I don't have such a clear purpose that would allow me to feel anything other than guilt if I took someone else's life. It is not my place to decide who lives and dies. I don't want the reason I can't join Rylan behind those shiny gates to be because I was forced to do something terrible and avoidable in this life. Having another person's death on my hands *and* ruining Rylan's chance at happily ever after… I just…" My voice trailed off as my frustration and fear collided.

Both Jasmine and Arthur frowned.

"Mae, your purpose on this Earth is the same as ours. Do you not see it? A Guardian has vowed to keep those within the supernatural world safe, and when that world is threatened, we eliminate the danger. You have been tasked to protect the *entire* world, and now your world is threatened. It is time to eliminate the danger to it. That danger is in the form of Ekon and the gods that he wishes to bring to this realm. Your soul will not be stained because of the position you were forced into. Tomorrow night, you could be drowning in blood, but when all is said and done, your soul will still shine. Remember, at the end of the day, killing someone to protect yourself or others is not immoral; it is survival."

I frowned as I processed what Jasmine was telling me. While maybe during the first part of my life I had not realized my role in the world, the last two months had certainly changed that. She was right; I had been created to do the very thing I was dreading.

I was gifted with power, blessed with a mate and friends who would fight by my side, and lucky enough to have stumbled upon warriors who shared a common foe. I could not ask for a better hand to be dealt with. I would have to accept that in killing someone, I was fulfilling my role as protector of the world. As I realized how true her words were, relief eased the tension in my shoulders.

I threw my arms around Jasmine's waist and squeezed.

"Thanks, Jazz," I mumbled into her shirt.

She returned my hug, and I felt her lips brush the top of my head.

"The fact that killing someone, no matter the situation, seems utterly abhorrent to you strengthens your character, Mae. Keep your innocence and your moral compass locked safe within your heart, and you will be fine," Arthur said softly.

He stroked his goatee then shook his head regretfully as he sighed, then continued, "While I cannot guarantee you will not be forced to take a life, I promise that I will make sure the opportunity is as slim as possible for you. The Golden Gates will open for you and Rylan because, in the end, the only thing that matters in this lifetime is that your intentions are pure and your actions mirror the behaviors you seek from others."

I turned to him and smiled. "Thank you, for everything. You have no idea how much it means to me to hear that you both have such faith in me," I said.

Behind us the sliding glass door opened once more. I looked back to see Rylan stepping out to join us. Afraid that he would pick up what we were talking about I shot Jasmine and Arthur a warning look before walking over to him. With their words swimming around in my head I was already starting to feel better.

"Thanks, guys, I'll see you in the morning."

With that I dragged Rylan back inside the house, ready to head to bed for the night. We didn't make it far. We were stopped a handful of times to speak with groups of Guardians who wished for us to partake in their conversations. We laughed, listened, and shared stories. The simple joy of seeing everyone so lively despite the situation they had been in just days before was touching and rewarding. After Zara's story of how she had to help deliver triplets a young Fae was carrying, Rylan finally excused us, and we headed to our bedroom.

When Rylan shut the door, I headed to the bathroom to brush my teeth for the night. I was exhausted, and with the bed only a few feet away from me, I had to go through my nightly routine now, or I'd pass out before I got the chance. As I ran water over my toothbrush, Rylan came to stand in the doorway of the bathroom and leaned against the frame.

"I heard what you said to Jasmine and Arthur," he announced as I brushed my teeth.

I paused and glanced at his reflection in the mirror. He was scowling again, and his mouth was turned downward. I dragged my gaze from his and rinsed my mouth out. Finally, I turned around to lean my back against the counter and crossed my arms over my chest.

"It's rude to eavesdrop."

"It is upsetting to think that *you* would be the reason we would not walk through the gates together should something happen to us," he said, ignoring my comment.

He sauntered over to me and stopped when there was no more space between us. I dropped my arms to my side as I stared up at him. Rylan's hand came up, snaked around to the back of my neck, and wove his fingers into my hair. He gently yanked on my curls causing me to gasp as my head was tilted back. His cool teal eyes swept over my face.

"Mae, I have had almost two thousand years to tarnish the half of my soul that I possess. I have committed unspeakable crimes without a second thought. If Hell were a vacation spot, you would find me lounging on the fiery beaches most days. Just because we have taken an oath to protect the innocent and keep the supernatural world safe does not make me a good person. I have only just recently begun to rethink everything I have ever done, said, or become throughout my life, and that is because of you. I want to be better for you. So, for you to think you could do something so hideous as to overshadow anything that I have done, is laughable. If anyone in this union would prevent the other from crossing over into paradise, it would be me.

"But that is not how this works. That is not how two mates who have Joined together, as we have, will face the unknown of death. We are one unit. It is not an either-or situation. Should fate be unkind to us and the flame to our life force flicker out, as one we will pass into the unknown and through those gates where souls go to find peace. The gates will accept us, but let us hope that it will be in a long, long time from now because I have not had enough time with you here yet."

Tears pooled in my eyes as his love overwhelmed me. His confidence of how intertwined our lives were and would forever be destroyed the last little bit of my anxiety and fear for what was to come. My heart swelled to twice the size as I stared up at the sincerity shining in those mesmerizing eyes. Slowly, he lowered his mouth and pressed his lips to mine. Just the light touch caused moisture to pool between my legs. I sighed against his lips as my whole body leaned into him. He tugged at my hair harder, and I gasped. He took the opportunity to slip his tongue past my lips.

I slid my hands under his shirt and skimmed my palms up his solid frame. His body shuddered at the contact. My thumbs teased his nipples and when he trembled again, I pinched his left one. Rylan pulled away from my mouth with a warning growl. His eyes changed color to that blazing red that warned me that he was now more Guardian than man.

Rylan removed his hand from my hair and let it drop to my shoulder. Without warning, he reached up with the other hand, and with both hands, he ripped my shirt down the middle. I was mid- gasp when he yanked the rest of it off me. He threw the torn shirt over his shoulder, grabbed my arms, and turned me around so I faced the mirror. I stared at his reflection and watched as he easily tore my bra off and allowed it to fall onto the floor. HE took both of my wrists in one hand, grabbed the ripped shirt off his shoulder, and to my surprise, began to tie my wrists together behind my back.

As I realized what he was doing, I giggled and started to struggle. Physically, he could overpower me, but with my power, I could easily break free. I could feel the junction between my legs throbbing. I could use a little fun and excitement not tainted by darkness and death.

"Tighter," I whispered over my shoulder.

Rylan grinned and tugged roughly on the knots. When my wrists were secure in their makeshift binds, Rylan stared into the mirror at me. His brows were slightly pulled together, puckering the skin between them. His mouth was set in a firm line, and those red eyes brightened further as his pupils narrowed. His gaze traveled from my face down to my breasts. With my hands bound behind my back, my breasts were pushed forward for Rylan to view.

He reached around me with a hand on either side, and gently he twisted and pulled at my nipples until they were tightened buds. My gasps turned to moans as he cupped my breasts, massaged them, while his thumbs brushed against my nipples. He lowered his head and planted kisses along the arch of my neck, never stopping his kneading of my swelling breasts and teasing my aching nipples. I could feel wetness soaking my panties and threatening to soak through my pants.

Rylan let go of my breasts just long enough to turn me around. His eyes captured mine, and one corner of his mouth twitched upwards. The devilish glint in his eyes warned me that something else was coming. He reached down, unbuttoned my jeans, and pulled the zipper down. He helped out of my pants. As he straightened his hand slipped between my legs and his fingers purposefully slid across my swollen clit. I moved to spread my legs wider as my whole body shuddered at the contact. Rylan's fingers slid down my folds, causing my body to shake with pleasure again. A loud moan involuntarily slipped past my lips as his fingers sunk into my core. I closed my eyes as he stroked me with one hand and used his other to reach up to play with a nipple. He planted a swift kiss on my lips, but it didn't last. He removed his hand from between my legs, reached up, and used my arousal to coat my nipples.

Before I could say anything, he leaned down and blew cool air against my tightened buds. Coated in my own arousal, the cool air intensified the stimulation, tightening my nipples to new extremes. I cried out in surprise at the sensation, and Rylan gave me a smug grin. Rylan leaned forward again, this time to take one nipple into his mouth while one of his hands expertly teased the other. The nipple in his mouth was sucked on, lapped at, twisted, and teased. The mounting pleasure between my legs was startling. I could feel my body tensing, my breathing turning to pants, and my moans chasing one another.

Rylan switched to the other nipple while the first received a slight reprieve from the onslaught of attention. He shifted his body so his thigh pressed against the junction between my legs, applying pressure to my clit. I leaned my pelvis harder into his leg and rubbed myself against him. Just when I thought I couldn't take anymore, Rylan's fangs sank into my breast.

I screamed his name as my world shattered, and I came hard. Rylan's body lit up with my power. As I floated back down from my orgasmic high, Rylan swooped me up into his arms and carried me into the bedroom. I still had not regained my breath when he tossed me onto the bed. I landed ungracefully on my side since my hands were still tied, and I glared at him as I struggled to get to my knees.

Rylan chuckled as he disrobed in front of me. I took the moment to fully appreciate every inch of him. It was amazing to see all those muscles that roped his body flex and relax as he moved. I licked my lips as his erection sprang forward. Rylan grinned and climbed into bed with me. He gently grabbed my shoulders and planted a kiss on my lips. He pulled away for a moment to put his hands on my waist. Before I knew what he was doing, he was flipping me around so my back was facing him. I gasped as he pressed his hand to the middle of my back, which caused me to fall forward with my butt up in the air. I struggled against the restraints as I tried to right myself. I turned my head to the side so it wasn't pressed into the sheets.

Suddenly, Rylan was pulling my legs further apart, and his hand slipped between my legs. His fingers slid into me and stroked my insides slowly. Again I struggled with my restraints. Then his fingers hit the right spot. My toes curled, and I arched back so my butt rose higher for him. My eyes rolled up in my head, and I bit my bottom lip to keep it from quivering. My breathing grew heavier as my body began to coil tightly.

Rylan removed his hand away from between my legs and slammed his erection into me. His thrusts were wild, hard, and wanton as he took me. As he hit that one spot over and over just right, I felt my body detonate. As I came around Rylan, he continued his intense strokes, which only prolonged my orgasm to extreme lengths. It didn't take him long. Rylan's release triggered my third orgasm. My voice was hoarse as I cried out his name over and over as his cock jerked within me. Each twitch of his cock caused aftershocks of pleasure to ripple through me. When he finally withdrew from my body, I felt the loss.

Rylan leaned forward and untied my wrists. When I was free from my restraints, I turned and lay on my back as he came to lie down beside me. I scooted closer to his body and planted a deep kiss on his mouth. His hands settled on my hips as our tongues danced lazily together. When I pulled away, my body was starting to hum, ready for another round.

"We'll have our forever, I promise," I whispered against his lips.

"Forever," Rylan agreed. "I love you, Mae."

# Chapter Twenty-Eight

*MAE*

The following morning, I was on my way down the stairs when a commotion outside drew my attention. I looked over at the front door to find it wide open. Cautiously, I walked barefoot out into the chilly morning to see what was going on. I only made it a few steps before I came to an abrupt halt. My mouth dropped open at the sight before me. Apparently at some point last night, we had gained a few new guests who were now all standing around in the front yard. Black feathers fluttered in the breeze. Glints of steel made the front yard appear to sparkle as our guests showed off their weapons.

If I hadn't known better, I would have thought black feathered angels had descended from heaven. There had to be over a hundred new warriors standing before me.

"Impressive, isn't it?"

I jumped at the sound of Arthur's voice behind me. He chuckled at my surprise and came over to stand next to me.

"Definitely," I agreed with a nod. "Remind me again how I didn't realize Guardians existed before you?"

"We try to keep a low profile," Arthur said with a shrug. "Have I told you recently I am glad I kidnapped you? Without you, none of us would be the wiser about Ekon and Cain's plot. We would be sitting ducks if the gods managed to break through the gates."

"Comparing Guardians to ducks is like comparing an atomic bomb to a sparkler," I snorted with amusement.

Arthur laughed and placed a hand on my shoulder. "An atomic bomb, huh?"

"Is that the girl?" a voice asked loudly from somewhere within the group of new Guardians.

The large group turned in my direction all at once, and suddenly, I found myself the center of attention. I became hyper-aware that I was only wearing Rylan's white tee-shirt, pajama pants, and no shoes. I guess the goal to sneak into the kitchen, make a small breakfast, and then take it back upstairs to eat it in bed without being seen wasn't going to happen. While the new Guardians I had saved hadn't given me any flack about where I came from and what I could be, this fresh group could be an entirely different story. I braced myself for the wave of suspicion and hatred.

A massive Guardian who competed with Nikolas in sheer size was the first to break from the crowd and approach me. He had short dark blonde hair, a slightly bent nose, and fists the size of hams. He stopped a few feet in front of me.

"You are Mae White," he stated. When I nodded, he mirrored the gesture. "My name is Nathaniel Barr. We heard what you did for our people trapped in Cain's laboratory. On behalf of all of us here, I want to thank you for saving our brethren. Our numbers were dwindling, and we thought it was because of our curse and the loneliness that comes with it. It never occurred to any of us that someone could be collecting Guardians. We have become a race that believes that we are superior to all others, but this experience has humbled us greatly. We are grateful that you put your life on the line to help our comrades.

"We have gathered here this morning because we received calls from those we thought lost who told us everything. Mae, your goal to stop the end of the world has become ours as well.

We are here to fight alongside you to stop the gods' return. We are all at your service," he said, gesturing to the others behind him.

I stared up at the Guardian in surprise. I had not expected this reaction. Relieved that our new guests weren't here to kill me, I smiled at Nathaniel.

"Hi, Nathaniel, thank you so much for coming. While I wish we could have met under less dire circumstances, I'm pleased to see you and everyone else here. We need all the help we can get. Hopefully, when all this is over, we can get to know each other better. In the meantime, make yourselves at home. If you don't mind, I'm going to get dressed before I meet everyone else."

Both Arthur and Nathaniel chuckled.

"Go, young one," he said and then grinned. "We are enjoying this unique gift you have bestowed upon us."

For a moment, I was stumped as to what he was talking about. Then, it clicked. Duh, emotions! I simply smiled before scurrying back into the house and up to my bedroom. As I rushed around the bedroom getting ready, I popped my head into the bathroom.

"You could have told me we had guests!" I scolded Rylan.

"You could use that enhanced hearing you have now to check your surroundings," Rylan chuckled from the shower.

"*'You could use that enhanced hearing you have now,*'" I mimicked under my breath in annoyance as I shook out my curls to give them more life and headed to the closest to grab a change of clothes.

Back downstairs, I found Katie the Supreme waiting for me with necklaces ready to harness my power. When we went outside to fill each necklace with a little piece of me, we were followed by a large crowd. They watched with great interest as I worked. When we handed them out, the Guardians each took one without any protests. If only it had been this easy to begin with.

The rest of the day was all about the battle prep. Our new arrivals brought the total number of Guardians up to two hundred. They had traveled far and wide to get here in time. They had not only brought explosives, extra weapons, and traps but also different types of protective gear as well. I was suited up with a leather pleated armor. While it was stiff and less protective than the suits of armor some of the Guardians planned to wear, it was more flexible and lightweight.

Now that we had a new number of warriors our battle plans changed. Twenty-five Guardians would go and plant explosives and ground traps at the base of the mountain to the west early this evening and remain there, hidden until the time was right. They would be our eyes and ears on the ground. Thirty Guardians would stalk the mountain, continuously moving and watching for any signs that Ekon might make his move before we were ready.

The last one hundred and forty-five Guardians would be my army, which would move with me as I approached the mountain. The Guardians expected trouble. Ekon would search for me in the chaos, knowing that I was the one he needed to stop. Knowing he would throw everything at me, it was the smartest move to have me surrounded by warriors to make sure I was able to finish the task. The Guardians would leave here in waves so it wouldn't be obvious that an army was coming.

The first group of Guardians, the ones who would plant the explosives, left around two o'clock that afternoon. The drive would take three hours and it would be a slow, grueling process to discreetly plant the bombs. The group included Nikolas and Devon. Before they left, I made it a point to wish everyone good luck and reminded them to stay safe.

After their departure, I went back inside and found Jasmine waiting for me in the kitchen. She pushed a plate towards me that had a sandwich, chips, and a pickle on it.

"You need to eat. You'll need your strength for what's to come tonight," she said as she sat down with me at the island.

"Thanks, Jazz," I told her graciously as I bit into a chip.

"You need your sleep, too. If you can nap, I would recommend doing so," she suggested.

I rolled my eyes as I picked up my turkey sandwich. Yeah, like I could sleep knowing that I was about to stop the end of the world.

"It was just a suggestion. I know you did not get much last night," Jasmine said with a chuckle.

My cheeks warmed. She was right. I had drifted off to sleep for a short while but awoke to a passionate hunger for my mate, which Rylan happily satisfied. Repeatedly. In between our throes of passion, he had jokingly mentioned that I was going into heat. Maybe that's what it was because I was starved for Rylan. Was it because my body knew that this mission could be our one and only together? The reality was that people were going to get hurt, and it could be one of us.

"Are you nervous?" I asked.

Jasmine was heading out to scout the area, which meant she was going with the second group of Guardians that would be leaving shortly. Jasmine tilted her head to the side with a frown.

"I would be lying if I said no, but I know it is just jitters. I have fought many battles and the outcomes always varied in severity. This is just another one. We will all make it back here in one piece, and then we can relax for a while. Perhaps we can talk Rylan and Arthur into traveling to my territory in Spain. You will love the food, and there are plenty of beaches we can lie on."

"I have a curse to break after this," I reminded her.

"Trust me," Jasmine said, placing her hand on my shoulder. "After tonight, you will need to recover. You may have gained control and some stamina with your power, but you have not tested what your limits are. We will be there to support and help you, but most of this mission rests on your shoulders. That is a lot of pressure for someone who is new to her power and who has never been in a large-scale battle. You will want to relax on a beach for a few days after this."

Trying not to let Jasmine's assessment of how *not* ready I was for this battle affect me, I forced a smile.

"Alright, after this we'll go to the beach and drink mimosas every day for a week. Then, we get down to business and break the curse over the Guardians, deal?"

Jasmine chuckled.

"Deal. We will purchase a bathing suit that will attract the eye of every man for miles just to get Rylan all bent out of shape," Jasmine teased. I laughed.

"Better yet, go to a nude beach and watch Rylan go insane as everyone's head turns in your direction," Zara suggested as she joined us in the kitchen. We all laughed.

Shortly after lunch, Jasmine left with the second round of Guardians. Amongst the group were Camille and Ashe. As I had done with the first group, I made sure to talk with each member before they left. I took a mental picture of each of their faces and committed it to memory. Not caring who saw, I threw my arms around Jasmine and kissed her cheek.

"Stay safe," I commanded firmly.

After Jasmine's group left, my anxiety began to climb. I was not afraid for myself. With all the Guardians that were going to be with me, I knew I would probably be the safest person in the woods tonight. But what about Jasmine, who had quickly become family to me? What about everyone else? If they died tonight, mateless… they'd cease to exist. There would be no Golden Gates for their soul to cross. I shuddered before forcing myself to push those thoughts aside. We'd all be fine. Maybe there would be a few injuries, but Guardians healed quickly.

As the day faded away, small fractions of Guardians who were assigned to protect me left to get a head start to make sure the path I would be taking to get to the base of the mountain would be clear. Upstairs in my bedroom, I dressed in a dark long sleeve shirt, dark-colored jeans, and then the leather armor. I slipped on my engagement ring last. It probably wasn't wise to wear jewelry into battle, but this was something I needed to feel safe. In the closet, I stood in front of the full-length mirror and wondered who the woman staring back at me was. She looked confident and ready for anything. The scars around her neck and wrists were testaments of the struggles that had brought her to where she was today.

During the few years I had participated in vigilante activity, I had gone into every mission cocky, pumped full of adrenaline, dressed in all black, and ready for a fight. I had always known people had my back, and the possibility of death had never crossed my mind. Fast forward two years later, and here I was dressed like a warrior, feeling relatively calm, aware of my shortcomings, and scared for the strangers who would be standing alongside me to fight with me.

It wasn't long before it was time for the rest of us to leave for the night. While we would be walking to the mountain under the cover of night once we got close, the sun was only now just beginning to set as I slid into the backseat of the truck. Rylan climbed behind the wheel. Once he was settled, I leaned forward and placed my hands on his shoulders, needing the contact.

There was a hum of excitement in our bond, like he wanted to fight. But there was a solemn undercurrent to his mood, too. Our gazes met in the rearview mirror but neither of us said a word while the others climbed into the car. Arthur slid into the passenger seat while Diane and Samson slid into the back with me. We waited to take off until everyone else was ready. Soon, a long line of cars was southbound.

The ride wasn't necessarily quiet although there wasn't much talking. Diane and Arthur were continuously answering calls and texts as warriors updated them on what was happening as we approached our destination. I stared out the window, my stomach twisting with anxiety. While I was anxious, I wasn't overly scared. This was as prepared as we could be for such a situation. The Guardians' strategic plan to distract the enemy while another group infiltrated their territory was solid enough that I didn't feel the need to worry. I would do everything possible to make sure the gates never opened; that was all I could do. Hopefully, it would be enough.

Three hours later, Rylan turned off the headlights and pulled off on the side of the road, following the lead of the cars in front of us. One by one, headlights behind us began turning off, and the cars disappeared into the darkness. Without a word, we all climbed out of the car. Rylan took my hand and pulled me to the side as Guardians from the other cars began to disappear into the woods all around us.

Despite the gravity of the situation, I couldn't help but admire the way the leather armor Rylan wore clung to him. When he turned to face me, I felt my cheeks burn with embarrassment, knowing I had been caught ogling. Although Rylan rolled his eyes and gave me a half-smile, I could see this was not the time for flirting. He reached out and gently took my chin in his hand. His mouth pressed into a grim line while his eyes pierced me with a look of utter determination.

*Remember, do not use your power unless absolutely necessary. We cannot draw attention to your location,* he reminded me. I nodded. *You will always be surrounded by allies. Trust that we will keep you safe even when it feels like the world is closing in on you. Your job is to destroy that mountain; our job is to make sure you get there and back safely.* Again, I nodded. We'd discussed this at length the day before. *Do not try to be heroic, Mae. If someone is in trouble, one of the others will help. Do not get involved.* He knew me too well. *Remember to use your heightened abilities. Listen to the sounds around you, and keep an eye out for anything that looks suspicious.*

*Rylan, I know. I'm ready.* I sighed loudly.

I wanted to get this over with. His little pep talk was causing my nerves to get worked up. He leaned down and swiftly planted a kiss on my lips. When he pulled away, I saw a flash of pain in his eyes before it disappeared.

*I have been in many battles, Mae. This is the first one that I actually care about who lives and dies.* His voice was soft in my head. *Stay close to me. Never leave my side.*

*Hey, I promised forever with you. I won't leave you at any time during this battle, or for the rest of our lives,* I promised him. I reached out and squeezed his hand tightly. *Let's stop this asshole.*

Arthur came up beside me followed by Diane, Samson, Gabriel, and Zara. They had donned their armor, their personal weapons ready in hand. With their wings out and relaxed behind them and their red eyes sunken into their hollowed faces, they looked like true warriors. They were magnificent and terrifying.

"We will be right here with you," Arthur assured me as he placed a hand on my shoulder, "and the others are near. In an hour, you will hear explosions; that will be group one. Once we hear them, we move fast and stay low. We will not have time to doddle. Keep low, and stay quiet."

I nodded to show I understood. The six Guardians created a loose circle around me with Arthur at the lead and Rylan right beside me. My heart began to pound rapidly as we began our trek through the night. This was it; this was what all the drama in my life these past two years had boiled down to, stopping Ekon.

As we began walking, I did as Rylan requested. I played with my new heightened ability while mentally kicking myself for not practicing before tonight. It was slightly overcast, which gave us an advantage as we moved through the night almost soundlessly. If I strained my eyes hard enough, I could see Guardians traveling in the trees above us. They moved like leopards with stealth and grace, leaping from branch to branch. If they weren't in the trees, they were prowling through the night on foot close by. I could hear the soft footfalls of other members of our team while occasionally catching glimpses of them as we moved.

Just as Arthur promised, after an hour of trekking through the woods, I heard sounds of explosions. It was so far off that if I hadn't been using my heightened hearing, I probably would have missed it. Arthur signaled in front of us to halt, and immediately, I stopped. I glanced over to Rylan, whose gaze was sweeping the woods. I looked away from him and waited for Arthur to give the signal that it was time to move. My muscles flexed as I waited for the signal. It was like I was waiting for the gun to go off at a racetrack. A few minutes went by before Arthur made the call to move.

This time we took off quickly. I knew the others were moving slower than they would like in order to accommodate my human speed, but no one complained. In fact, no one made a sound. A few times I would get the familiar buzzing sensation that told me the Guardians were using telepathy to communicate, but these were few and far between. Above the trees, Elliot's Peak grew larger as we drew closer. It would be a while before we got close enough for my power to be effective, but seeing the mountain made me want to try to destroy it now.

Another hour passed before the hair on the back of my neck began to rise.

"I have been expecting you, young one," a raspy voice drifted through the woods, loud and clear. I forced myself not to gasp at the sound of Ekon's voice. My head whipped around looking for the bastard. "Did you think I would make it easy for you to stop me? Your little tantrum may have destroyed one of my labs, but it did not disrupt progress. I want you to see for yourself what you failed to accomplish."

*He is using a location spell. He is searching for us but does not know our exact location yet. If you talk back, he will know where we are,* Rylan warned. I clenched my jaw.

*How do you know that?* I asked him as I continued to search the woods around me for any signs of Ekon.

*I am a Guardian. I must understand spells, curses, and more if I am to protect those around me,* he replied.

"I hope you enjoy chaos as much as I do," Ekon continued. A sinister laugh wound its way through the night sending chills down my spine. "Let the games begin."

The feeling of sand moving across my skin warned me of the impending danger. I shuddered as my power surged forward.

*Mae*, Rylan said and reached for me.

*I don't know how Ekon is controlling it, but the toxin is being released into the air*, I warned him and braced myself as my power bucked against my willpower, trying to escape.

Of course, Ekon could manipulate the toxins in the air. Why hadn't we thought of that? Was it something only those who used dark magic could control?

I stumbled as my body lit up, but Rylan kept me upright and moving forward. I felt Rylan pass on the warning to everyone. Around me, the Guardians tensed, expecting to feel the effects. They wouldn't though, I was sure of it. Zara's, Gabriel's, Diane's, and Samson's necklaces were shining through their shirts, and the others had gotten a direct dose of my power, protecting them from the danger.

While it didn't affect us, around us the wildlife suddenly awoke. Sleeping birds took to the sky, and a herd of deer stampeded nearby. Some fought each other while others ran in confusion. They didn't seem to notice our presence, lost in the madness the toxin caused. In the distance, a wolf howled, followed by a handful of answering howls. Were those normal wolves, or were those the howls of werewolves? With my enhanced hearing, they sounded closer than they probably were. That didn't make it any less scary, knowing that monsters were lurking nearby. I clenched my jaw harder, trying not to make a sound. I could hear yelps and snarls, more howling, and then sudden silence. The other Guardians in the woods must have taken care of the threat.

Beneath our feet, the ground began to rumble. In front of us, I watched as the snow that coated the tip of Elliot's Peak began to fall away from the mountainside. Rock moved and broke away with the snow, causing mini-avalanches. A whole section along the side of the mountain began to move. Someone close to me gasped as we all watched a massive door that had been made to look like part of the mountain slide slowly open.

*We need to move faster*, Rylan snapped. I picked up the pace, and the others adjusted their speed.

Something dark, possibly smoke, began to billow out of the enormous opening on the mountain. It rose high into the night sky in an oddly cyclone-like manner before disappearing into the clouds. I couldn't make out what it was but the others could. I could feel them communicating with each other. The buzzing was loud and intense for a short burst before everyone fell silent again.

*Gargoyles are circling above. Keep moving forward, we will keep an eye out for them as they search for us,* Rylan explained before I could ask.

I watched the sky as I continued to run. Following the cyclone of gargoyles, the second group of Guardians, led by Jasmine shot upwards into the sky from the other side of the mountain to chase after the threat.

My heart pounded louder now. Somewhere gargoyles loomed over us, and the thought of not knowing exactly where they were was terrifying. Ahead of us, coming from that same opening in the mountain, a large metal contraption began to emerge. As the metal machine cleared the entryway, I realized it was a massive, metal ring. In the middle was a blue orb that looked suspiciously like the power that had been trapped in the destroyed lab.

*Shit, Rylan, he's going to try to open the gates now!* I realized as my heart sank.

*Keep moving*, he commanded.

The quick, short buzz in my head warned me something was wrong. Something whizzed above our heads and hit a nearby tree.

*Fae!* Rylan roared. Arrows were flying all over the place. In front of me, Arthur's wings lifted upwards and spread out on either side of him as he used himself as a shield to protect me. There were shouts and cries as a battle nearby broke out. Screams of agony and anger littered the night. Fires began to break out all around us as the Fae set their arrows on fire. My heart raced as smoke filled my lungs.

We were getting closer to the mountain, but we were still too far for me to do any damage. The blue orb floating in the middle of the metal ring began to grow bigger and brighter. The clouds above the mountain began to darken, and thunder rolled. I forced myself to move faster. We couldn't let Ekon start that thing up.

Above us, a shriek caught my attention. I looked up in time to see a massive boulder falling from the sky. It was Diane who yanked me out of the way just in time. The rock smashed into the earth where I had been just moments ago. She placed me on my feet, and we were running again. Guardians in the trees around us shot upwards to attack the gargoyles that had found us. There had to be hundreds of gargoyles overhead, but the Guardians who took to the sky didn't seem phased. There wasn't time to stop and watch the spectacle overhead, so I pushed on.

Flaming arrows stopped zipping past us so frequently. I sent up thanks to whoever was listening that there was a group of Guardians ahead of us taking care of the dangers, allowing us to focus on our task. Arthur lowered his wings just as he jumped over the first body. I leapt over it and tried to ignore the blank face staring up at me. The copper scent of blood lingered in the air as we ran. Bodies littered the ground, and it was hard not to notice the faces twisted in pain, the groans of the dying, and the nasty wounds the Guardians in front of us inflicted on the Fae warriors.

On the mountain, the blue orb had grown to the width of the metal ring. I watched in dismay as the ring began to tilt upwards to face the sky. The clouds began to part over the mountain. There was nothing but stars, for now. If we didn't hurry, that was where the gates would open.

The ground under us rumbled, and whitish gray things began to sprout up around our feet as we moved. Upon closer inspection, I realized the things erupting from the ground were rotting hands. Someone had mentioned that the bodies used in sacrifices could come back as an army. Well, the undead had arrived.

Images of the time I had been in the Pocket flooded my consciousness. Those rotting hands had been there too, reaching from out of the darkness to pull me in. Mentally, I screamed in fear. I couldn't let those things catch me. My body trembled, not from fatigue, but terror. I knew what those fingers would feel like if they touched me.

As the undead rose from the ground, the Guardians who had been spread out all around us in the forest began to close the distance to take care of the immediate threat. Moans and sickly gulps for air began to fill the silence around us. Another round of arrows from our right took us by surprise, and Zara and Samson moved to block the attack.

*Ekon knows where I am now, doesn't he?* I asked Rylan as he grabbed me to pull me out of the way from the pieces of gargoyle that were falling from the sky. He placed me on my feet before slicing through four undead creatures that came at us from the left.

*Yes.* It was his only response.

The undead filled up the woods quickly, moving at a speed I would have thought impossible for something that had little to no muscle or tendons. My protective circle of Guardians stayed close while the others took care of the problem. It was a relief to see that once a warrior was able to slay an undead creature, it seemed to stay down.

A loud humming noise boomed over Jasper National Park before the blue light spinning in the middle of the metal ring shot upwards into the sky. I shrieked in horror as the stars disappeared, and a colorful, iridescent light show appeared in the sky. The light faded just enough for us to see massive steel rods spaced evenly all in a row. Fingers that belonged to giants and claws and talons that belonged to animals were wrapped around the rods, yanking the metal as if to pry it open.

There it was: the gates between the realms had come to life, and the gods were trying to return. The blue light emanating from the metal ring began to pulse, and each time it did so, the steel rods seemed to shutter and bend under the pressure. The gates weren't open yet, but they were about to be if I didn't act fast. We were almost to our destination. Just another mile or so, and I was sure I could destroy the mountain and the machine. But we had to get there *now*. I was slowing everyone down.

*Rylan, fly me the rest of the way!* I demanded. *We don't have time to waste running on foot.*

*No, you would be an easier target in the sky,* Rylan objected just as another round of arrows came flying towards us. He opened his wings, and I heard arrows hit him. He didn't swear or cry out in pain as he was hit multiple times. I could feel his pain through our connection. Each time an arrow hit him, I jerked under the sudden pain. The arrows ceased as screams and the sounds of battle erupted from behind me.

"Rylan!" I screamed.

Rylan's wings came down, and he was running beside me once more. He yanked three arrows from his gut, one from his chest, and one that had nestled just above the collar bone.

*I am fine. Move,* he growled.

"Your father will be so disappointed in you, young one," Ekon's voice twisted through the woods again, sounding closer than before. "Maybe you will be lucky enough to see the disappointment in his eyes before the others turn you and your world to ash."

The gates in the sky groaned under the assault of the power that Ekon had collected over the years. I could see the gates bending under the pressure. Fear began to choke me; time was running out. Around us, trees began to bend and twist on their own. The crackling of wood and the groan of a tree trunk twisting and turning began to override the sounds of Guardians battling the continual uprising of undead warriors, Fae archers, and gargoyles. Under our feet, the ground rumbled harder as a new threat rose from beneath us.

Thick tree roots twisted upwards, trying to grab us as we ran. Branches came swooping down to pick us up. Trees were breaking apart to fall on top of us while bushes began to shoot out thorns. A vine caught my ankle, and I went down, hard. Around me, my protection detail began getting caught in the madness. Roots came up and wrapped themselves around Arthur while a tree branch yanked Rylan away from my side. Gabriel was able to cut the vine off my ankle before a handful of vines grabbed him.

"I can burn the forest down," I shouted. "If everyone—,"

"No! Conserve your energy," Diane shouted as she pushed me out of the way of an undead monster that reached for me. She sliced through it before a tree came toppling down on top of her. To my surprise, she caught it and tossed it away from her into a cluster of the undead.

Samson grabbed my hand to help steady me as I ran, but a large tree branch swung low and hit him in the ribs, knocking him away from me. Before I could make it a few more steps I was caught around the neck by a root and yanked backwards. I landed on my back with a huff. I tried to pull it away, but it only wrapped around me tighter, cutting off my air. Arthur's flail came down on the vine, and he yanked me to my feet.

"Run, Mae, we're out of time. *Run!*" he bellowed as he grabbed my hand and pulled me towards the mountain.

Rylan appeared beside me moments later. He took my other hand, and we sprinted towards the mountain. Zara's voice shouted out a warning. Rylan grabbed me, and simultaneously we did a flip backward as a huge tree root swiped at our feet. I was right side up and running again in less time than it took to gasp in surprise.

After what seemed like an eternity of running, the woods that had come alive in a murderous fashion thinned. Once we broke free from the trees altogether, we ran onto the shoreline of a small river that stood between us and Elliott's Peak. Behind us, I could still hear nature's attempts at murdering the other Guardians, the moans from the undead, and arrows being shot from Fae bows. Above us, more Guardians had joined the fight against the gargoyles, and the enemy was slowly thinning out.

In front of me, Elliot's Peak towered over us. The mountain range was stunning and would have been such a serene sight… if it weren't for the doomsday device sticking out of it.

"This is it, Mae. This is the spot. Bring down the mountain!" Rylan yelled as he and Arthur whirled around to face whatever was behind me.

A blast of energy shoved me forward. I fell to my knees. While every instinct told me to turn around and look to see who had attacked us, I pushed through it to focus on my task at hand. I got to my feet and threw my hands up while calling on my power. The sheer strength of throwing all my might into the blast almost knocked me backward. I gritted my teeth and dug my heels into the stony riverbank. The mountain shook. Large avalanches began sliding down the mountain's slopes. I did not let up on my attack. I pushed my power forward, and violet energy continued to shoot out from my hands and pummel the mountain.

Noise and lights flashed around me. Sounds of metal and battle seemed to be drawing closer. I could have sworn I was hearing chanting, but I didn't turn around to see what my Guardians were facing off with. They were counting on me to do this.

As my power began to eat away at the base of the mountain, I took a deep breath and summoned my lightning. Above us, large bolts of violet lightning began to erupt from Elliott's Peak.

They blew chunks of rock off the mountain. The snow was swept upwards and melted. Large chunks of the mountain began to crumble down. Beneath my feet, the ground began to shake as Elliott's Peak began to fall apart.

I threw more weight behind the power blasting through my hands as lightning continued to destroy the mountain from above. There had to be something else I could do to stop that blue beam from opening the gates. With all the power coursing through me, I struggled to lift my head enough to stare at the metal ring that controlled the power Ekon had stolen. With all the concentration that I could muster, without completely stopping my attack against the mountain, I stared at the machine. It was so high I wasn't sure if it was possible, but…

A thick, violet bolt erupted upwards into the sky directly from where the machine was housed. The blue light beaming up into the sky flickered out. The iron gates in the sky vanished, leaving behind only stars and clouds. What was left of the metal contraption swayed before toppling into Ekon's lair hidden within the mountain. A massive mushroom cloud of fire and smoke erupted from the opening. Another explosion from far overhead was the sound of victory.

"No!" Ekon's voice screamed into the night. "*No!*"

With all the strength I could muster, I fell to my knees and slammed my fists into the ground. The world around me flew upwards as my power rushed into the riverbank and rippled towards the mountain. Elliot's Peak gave a loud groan before it began to crumble. The top crumbled inward first. The rest of the mountain followed suit, caving in on itself and sealing whatever Ekon had inside away forever.

I pulled back on my power while I panted. My heart was racing, and my body was trembling with fatigue and adrenaline. Despite the cold night, I was sweating profusely. The sound of battle behind me forced me to my feet. I stole a quick glance at the mountain as it crumbled before I turned my attention to the chaos behind me. Arthur and Rylan were fighting off a handful of undead soldiers nearby. Samson and Diane were spread out on my other side, using their wings to block incoming burning arrows as they headed for me.

"You did amazing, Mae! Now, let me get you out of here," Jasmine said grinning, as she landed in a crouch next to me. She threw her arms around me and kissed the top of my head. "Here's to beaches and mimos—"

"Jazz!" Rylan's voice shouted from behind us.

Jasmine let go of me to whirl around to face the approaching threat. The moment she turned to meet her opponent Jasmine was struck in the chest with a red stone attached to a long stick. The surprise on her face turned to agony just before her body appeared to crack like glass. A strange glow peaked out from the lines that were forming all over her body. Before I could do anything, Jasmine's body shattered into hundreds of pieces and fell to the ground at my feet.

My scream of anguish was lost in the sound of battle around me. My heart shattered right along with Jasmine's body. Jasmine. My friend. My family… She was gone. I turned to look at the hooded figure who had killed one of the only people in this world that had cared about me. I realized that the stick in this person's hands was a staff. I had seen enough movies to understand that I was staring at a wizard. Before I could react, the hooded mage jerked forward before falling to the ground dead. Three daggers were lodged into the wizard's back. I looked up to see Nikolas just a few feet away, running towards me.

"We need to get you out of here!" he yelled over the sounds of battle around us.

I looked around and noted that there were now a handful of witches and wizards who had joined the fight. It looked like most spells were bouncing harmlessly off the Guardians when they used their wings to protect them. But Jasmine… She had turned directly into the attack. My heart twisted in agony.

"You are not going *anywhere*," Ekon's voice hissed.

I twisted around to find the Guardian standing just a few feet away from me.

The first time I had seen Ekon, it had been in the dark dungeon within his other lair. His face had been clouded in shadow. Now that I could see him, I knew I would never be able to *unsee* him. His skin was pulled so tightly across his face that it was as if I was staring at a skeleton. While the other Guardians had sunken eyes in their Guardian form, Ekon's eyes were bulging from his face. The familiar red irises were replaced by a blackness so deep that my soul quivered in alarm. He was dressed in a simple brown cloak, similar to what a monk would wear. Behind him were four sets of Guardian wings protruding from his back. They appeared bent and broken, wilted, and dull. The stench of death that wafted over me wasn't from the battle; it was from him.

"Did you think it would be that easy to stop me? I have enough stolen power running through my veins that I can still open the gates. Dabbling in the dark arts has made me stronger than all of you. All I need to do is kill you first," he hissed taking a step towards me. Rylan landed between us, his sword drawn and ready. "Ah… a mated pair. How perfect. I do not have to kill her. I can just kill *you*."

Nikolas came to stand beside Rylan while Samson, Gabriel, Devon, Ashe, and Zara came to stand beside me. From where I stood, I could see the blackness in his eyes begin to swirl. Even before my mind processed that Ekon was about to attack, my power was already reacting to the dark magic he was about to throw at us. I pushed myself between Rylan and Nikolas just as Ekon launched his attack.

# Chapter Twenty-Nine



My heart froze as Mae threw herself in front of me. She threw up her hands and deflected Ekon's spell. He hissed in anger and pulled a heavy, ancient gold sword from beneath his robe. He took a step forward. I grabbed Mae's hand and yanked her backward. A roar overhead warned me we had a new threat to worry about. I pulled Mae behind me as a dark shadow blanketed us.

"I have been bathing in the power of my victims for years. My power surpasses that of anyone on this battlefield, including you, *child*," Ekon taunted as he took a step forward. "Tell me, do you have the power to stop a dragon *and* an immortal?"

Ekon lunged towards us at the same time as another roar rippled across the battlefield. Nikolas, Zara, Devon, and I leapt forward to deflect his attack while the others fell back to protect Mae. Ekon wielded his sword like a true warrior. He blocked every blow the four of us attempted and managed to amputate Devon's hand in the process. Devon fell back as the rest of us sparred with the devil.

Above us, a steady stream of fire came roaring down over us. The heat of the fire caused the air to become stifling. I could feel my skin beginning to burn and bubble. But the flames from above never actually touched us. Just as suddenly as the attack came, it was gone. Ash fell from the sky.

*Your mate just reflected dragon's fire at an undead dragon and killed it,* my father's voice alerted me. The pride in his voice could not be mistaken.

Nikolas lunged and attacked Ekon while the deranged Guardian focused his attention on me. Ekon dipped and twirled out of the way only to meet with Zara's blade. Ekon leapt back, and I saw him draw on his dark magic. My gut told me that if we were hit with it our lives would be over.

*Move!* I yelled the warning as he threw his attack at us.

We leapt out of the way just as Mae jumped forward to meet his attack head-on. I watched as her violet power shot out from her hands and slammed into the blackish-blue ball of energy Ekon had hurled our way.

"You cannot stop me, child!" Ekon screamed as he jumped out of the way as his attack was thrown back at him. "I deserve—,"

Mae's next attack cut Ekon's speech off. Lightning bolts erupted from the ground around his feet and twisted around him, creating a makeshift cage. As she ran towards him another shadow descended over us. Ekon's gaze shifted for just a second upwards before he smiled. I looked up in time to see the skeleton of a long-dead dragon dip towards us with its jaws open, flames already erupting from its mouth.

"Mae!" I roared and ran towards her.

She skidded to a stop and twisted so she could face the danger coming from above. She threw her hands up, creating a shield over everyone nearby just in time. The moment the flames hit the shield, they bounced off and shot back towards the dragon. The flames devoured the skeleton. Bones turned it to ash. The heat blistered my skin and sucked the air from my lungs. But none of that mattered. Because while Mae sheltered us, Ekon lunged for her with his sword aimed at her heart.

I slammed into him, pushing Ekon away from my mate. I felt the cut of his blade slice into my shoulder, but the burn of the pain was pushed to the wayside as I tried to shove my own sword into his gut. I felt the gathering of power as he snickered under his breath. Someone slammed into Ekon as his dark magic blasted outwards. I moved out of the way just as his attack blasted past my face. Samson slammed his fist into Ekon's face and brought up his axe to chop the evil Guardian into two. Ekon threw his hands up and drew on his magic to stop Samson. Seeing the attack, Samson took to the sky.

Violet flames shot by me, hitting Ekon and effectively stopping his attack. Ekon screamed as flames devoured him. He twisted his hands, and the flames went out. With a loud snarl, Ekon whirled around and threw a blast of power at Mae, who was ready and deflected it easily. Her lightning blasted up through the ground by his feet. He roared his anger and threw another blast of magic at her. She ducked out of the way of the attack before sprinting at him.

What was she doing? There was no way she could go hand to hand with Ekon. I hurried to grab her. But Nikolas was already there, yanking her back as Ekon swung his sword with a speed Mae would have had no chance of outmaneuvering. A third roar bellowed over the battlefield and a stream of fire spurted towards us as a third skeletal dragon came swooping down. The stream of fire destroyed everything in its wake, and it was coming towards us, fast. Guardians dove out of the way, Fae ran, and the witches and wizards tried to shield themselves from the heat.

With danger approaching, Mae braced herself to shield us from the flames. With her attention split, Ekon moved to attack Mae. I rush forward with my sword raised. Arthur got to the Guardian first. He came up behind Ekon, his flail raised high in preparation for a fatal blow. Ekon must have sensed him because he turned around, swinging his own sword, and raising one hand to blast him with his twisted power. I heard Mae scream Arthur's name. A lightning bolt spewed up from the ground between Guardians, forcing both to fall back. Ekon turned and threw his power at Mae, who threw up a shield to deflect the attack.

The heat of the flames grew unbearable as they came closer to us. I shot towards Mae, grabbed her by the waist, and soared out of the way of the dragon's flames. Something hit me from behind. My wings absorbed a spell one of the mages below had thrown, but I was forced to land as pain made my movements stiff.

"*Watch out!*" Mae screamed in terror.

She hit me with a blast of her power, and I was thrown out of the way. Ekon's black magic slammed into Mae who was unprepared for the attack.

Pain that wasn't mine exploded within me, causing me to howl in agony. Mae's whole body tensed up just before she collapsed on the ground. Arthur and Nikolas landed on either side of her, weapons ready, as Ekon approached her unmoving body. I charged him with my sword raised. At the same time, Arthur and Nikolas lunged at Ekon. Ekon braced himself.

What none of us expected was the blast of violet fire that weaved its way past all three of us and brought Ekon to his knees. He threw his hands up as his body was engulfed in flame once again. He attacked blindly, throwing out dangerous blasts of dark magic. I was forced to retreat as deadly power shot past me. Nikolas hit the ground while Arthur took to the sky.

Mae slowly got to her feet. Her eyes were glowing, her power like static electricity skimming over her body. Her expression mixed pain with determination. Black lines crawled up her neck. Whatever Ekon's power was doing, it was making its way into her system. Before I could react, Mae threw her hands up, and the world around her and Ekon erupted in violet flames. The blaze created a towering wall all the way around them, effectively preventing anyone from joining in the fight. My heart pounded wildly in my chest. I had to get to her.

"Mae!" *Mae!* I screamed her name in terror. I could feel her pain growing. I wanted to call the flames away from her and I knew that I could, but I hesitated. I did not want Mae distracted from her attack.

*Trust me*, the strain in her voice caused my heart to twist in pain.

Mae threw her power at Ekon. He tried to deflect her attack by launching his own in response. When he did, their powers collided. The force of the impact threw everyone in the nearby vicinity off balance. I was on my feet again in seconds, and I moved close to the barrier Mae had erected. Around the other side, I could see Arthur, Nikolas, and Zara looking for their way in.

Ekon and Mae's power twisted together. Both fighters were vying for an attempt to overpower the other. A violent gust of energy and power swept around us as the world lit up. My heart was stuck in my throat as neither of them let up. Zara tried to inch closer to the wall of violet fire, but she shrieked as she was burned.

I could feel Mae's pain as she gritted her teeth and pushed herself to her limits. Her whole body was glowing as she fought back Ekon's attack. Ekon took a step towards her, trying to push his magic into her. He was taunting Mae. I could see the way his mouth moved, but I could not hear what was said over the roar of the fire. I was sure he expected her to cower from him, to crumble under the weight of his attack and his words. But he did not know my Mae. He did not know about her stubborn streak or how large her heart was. She was fighting for all of us, protecting us from this monster. She would rather die than let this Guardian do damage to the world and to the people she loved. She would back down for nothing.

The wall of flames around the two began to creep inwards, towards them. Violet bolts of lightning exploded from the ground beneath Ekon's feet causing him to stumble towards the incoming flames. I could see him beginning to tremble. His power was weakening. Mae's violet essence surrounded them, pushing harder, stronger than what Ekon could handle. Then, a lightning bolt hit Ekon square on and it didn't let up. His whole body shook under the power behind Mae's attack. His screams were heard over the roar of their power.

Then, he exploded.

His body turned to dust. The dark magic that had been housed within his body shot outwards. Mae's power continued to spill out of her. She screamed her determination as she tried to destroy the dark power that was unmanned and unhinged. I screamed with her, calling her name, aching to help her.

As she fought the chaotic dark magic looking to escape into the world, her body let off a strange flash of violet light. A flood of her power crossed over the battlefield and into the woods and over the mountain range. There were shouts of surprise, howls of denial, and gasps of alarm, but my attention remained on my mate. The dark magic she fought to destroy continued to swirl dangerously above her in a ball of wild energy. Without warning, her power cut through the dark magic and neutralized it.

Time seemed to slow as the world lit up so brightly that it turned white. I could feel pain. I wasn't sure if it was my own or Mae's. As I was encompassed by the light, I could feel the very fibers of my being becoming unraveled. The sheer magnitude of agony was mind-boggling. My mind felt like it was becoming unhinged from the agony of being pulled apart cell by cell. Just when I thought I could not take any more, the world stilled.

Abruptly, the pain subsided to a dull ache. I drew in a deep breath as I steadied myself. My very being quaked after enduring such an explosion. How I had lived through it was a miracle. My heart stopped. What about Mae? I forced my eyes open, not realizing they were shut. Dazed and confused, I found myself lying flat on my back. I rolled to my stomach, and I pushed myself onto my knees. When I knew I would be able to stand without falling, I rose and proceeded to look for my other half. After the explosion, I expected the ground to be decimated. Guardians would be getting to their feet, and our enemy's minions would be backing off when they realized it was over.

Instead, I found myself under a bright spotlight in some unknown location. I was surrounded by a darkness so black that even with my heightened senses, I could not see into it. There were no other sounds except for my own breathing. Although I knew I had never been here before, it was strangely familiar. As I slowly turned around to examine my surroundings, somewhere inside of me it clicked. While I had never been in a Pocket before, Mae had been, and I had shared her memories of this place.

I should have been alarmed or frightened. Instead, I felt nothing as I continued my slow rotation. There behind me in the small space on the ground and crumpled a few feet away lay Mae. The black streaks that had crawled up her neck had made their way up her face. Her body appeared almost deflated. Her leather armor was in tatters, and her blood was pooling under her.

My heart felt curiously hollow. Slowly, the daze and confusion I was feeling began to fade as I became aware of how alien my body felt to me. I didn't belong in this weird shell. It didn't feel right. I wanted to shed this form and free myself from my physical bonds of this world. Deep within my very essence I could feel an ache in my tattered soul as it wept. It, too, wished to be free of the body it was trapped in. It was reaching out for a piece of itself that was missing.

That missing piece was Mae.

Mae was not here. Her body was here, but Mae, my beautiful and strong Mae was gone. I was only mildly surprised not to feel much heartache. Maybe because I knew everything would be alright soon enough. I did not belong in a world that did not have her in it, and I would correct that soon.

I walked over to and knelt before Mae's lifeless body, wondering if I was in some sort of limbo between life and death instead of a Pocket. Hopefully, this part would be swift; my soul ached to be with my mate. We were too far away from each other.

I scooped up her lifeless body and held her close to my heart. Her body was cold and stiff. Lowering my head, I pressed a kiss to her forehead.

"I am sorry, Mae Flower," I whispered out loud.

My words were lost in the silence.

*Be proud, Guardian,* a voice rang out.

Suddenly, the darkness felt full. I was surrounded on every side. Eyes from an unseen force peered down at me. The hair on the back of my neck rose in warning. But that was all the effect the voice had on me. It did not matter that this could be a new threat. They could take my life, and I would thank them for it. Then Mae and I could be together again.

*My daughter has fulfilled her purpose,* the voice continued after a moment.

Zyroe.

No wonder my body reacted immediately to his presence. A Guardian in the presence of a god was like a mouse in the presence of a cat. My eyes swept around the spotlight again, and that was when I noticed Arthur, Nikolas, and Zara's bodies lying unmoving further away. How had I not noticed them before?

*But just because her mortal life on Earth is done does not mean her life is over…* Zyroe continued in a slow, thoughtful tone.

In my arms, Mae's body began to warm. Color slowly crept back into her face, and the effects of rigor mortis began to lessen as her body relaxed. Her chest rose as her body sucked in a shaky breath. The exhale was slow and long. I felt the moment her soul returned; it was at the same moment mine began to rejoice. There was an instant state of bliss that washed over me as the woman who carried my soul and heart came back to life in my arms. Tears blurred my vision.

I did not question Zyroe how this was possible. At the moment, I did not care. All that mattered was that she was here with me once more. Everything else could wait.

*She will face new obstacles in her new life as an immortal,* Zyroe mused out loud. I was not sure if it was for my benefit or not. I could almost feel his excitement in the energy around me. *But I have been anticipating her arrival ever since her conception, and I will make sure she is ready to handle the new trials life will offer her. However, I had not considered she would bring others with her. If it will help ease the transition into our world, I will allow the others to join us. But you have tethered your life to my daughter in a way I cannot undo. There is no question that you will remain by my daughter's side for all eternity. So, Rylan Wellington, welcome to the family.*

To Be Continued…

Hey Readers-

Did you enjoy Song of Resurgence? Yes? No? Either way I would love to hear your feedback! The best way to help an author know what you like and disliked is to leave a review so please make sure to go online to Amazon's Kindle store and to Goodreads to leave a review of Song of Resurgence.

Also, remember to sign up for my monthly newsletter at my website www.salemcrossauthor.com so you can be the first to hear about the release date for Song of Transcendence: the final book of the Ballads of Mae series. This novel comes out Spring of 2021.

Follow me on social media at www.Facebook.com/salemcrossauthor and on Instagram at www.instagram.com/salemcrossauthor to hear about what goes on in my daily life and how I find inspiration for my stories.

Thank you for your support!

-Salem Cross

<u>*Ballads of Mae Series*</u>
*Song of Desolation*
*Song of Resurgence*
*Song of Transcendence*

# About the Author

Salem Cross is an avid writer who finds inspiration for her stories in even the smallest details in her life. She lives on the coast of North Carolina where you will either find her lounging on the beach or curled up with her three dogs on the couch while she reads a good book. She enjoys travelling, running, and woodworking. Visit her website at www.salemcrossauthor.com to find out more about Salem Cross.